CULT ON THE HILL

D. L. WATERHOUSE

Copyright © 2022 by D. L. Waterhouse

All rights reserved. This book or any portion thereof may not be reproduced or transmitted in any form or manner, electronic or mechanical, including photocopying, recording, or by any information storage or retrieval system, without the express written permission of the copyright owner except for the use of brief quotations in a book review or other noncommercial uses permitted by copyright law.

Printed in the United States of America

ISBN:	Softcover	979-8-88622-687-4
	eBook	979-8-88622-688-1

Republished by: PageTurner Press and Media LLC
Publication Date: 09/29/2022

To order copies of this book, contact:
PageTurner Press and Media
Phone: 1-888-447-9651
info@pageturner.us
www.pageturner.us

AUTHORS NOTE

People often ask me: "What *genre* do you write in?" I ponder their question carefully, in an attempt to appear as though I know what they're talking about. Then, I reply: " I write Christian fiction." Some seem surprised. Most ponder my answer carefully in an attempt to appear as though they know what I'm talking about.

Actually, I like to call them metaphors. A metaphor could be simply a word or phrase intended to imply some other, deeper, more profound consideration or an illustraton; a parable, presented in story form as a visual aid demonstrationg the particular point the author would like his reader to consider.

There are two *genres* of people: those who like to read and those who don't. I'm sure both will enjoy this story.

PREFACE

CULT ON THE HILL is just that: an analogy, a mataphor if you will. It illustrates many of the real life issues that are involved in transitioning from an un-believer in the gospel of Jesus Christ, to, believer in the gospel of Jesus Christ.

Most people have heard of Jesus Christ, and have probably, already formed some opinion in regard to religion; from whatever sources involving religious instruction they have been exposed to in their lives. However, I would venture to suspect, that their opinion is based on religious ideology as apposed to the truth, as that truth is in Jesus.

If you would permit me, I would like to show you that truth threaded into this story that I have written. If you stop to think about it; the whole bible is like this story: parable after parable, historical event after historical event, all portraying the same gospel: the Son of God who came to this earth in the form of humanity; who lived his life in perfect conformity to the Divine law of his Father; gifting his life of righteousness over to the sea of humanity born into sin; and there in the garden of Gethsemane through to the cross where he took upon his own self the fallen sinful nature of mankind from every generation; dying the second death from which there is no resurection which only fallen mankind deserved, so that mankind might have the eternal life that only the Lord Jesus Christ deserved; then to come forth from the tomb on the third-day, (resurecting from a death from which there is no resurection) according to the prediction written in the scriptures; fulfilling every detail of the prophesies concerning him, written hundreds of years before his birth. Then, ascending back to his Father, leaving mankind with the promise of his imminent return when he would receive unto himself every man, women and child from every generation since the world began who has believed in him regardless of their sinful condition.

The story you are about to read is a dispicable story. It is difficult to imagine that humanity has, in every age, demonstrated such depths of dispicable behavior, or worse, that certain individuals in this story have demonstrated. So what is the point in writing a story of this nature? Did you know that there is no sinner, at no time that has ever out sinned the grace of God. It is important that everyone should understand this; for it is the lack of this understanding that is the reason behind every suicide, every dispicable criminal act, every school shooting or act of semetic hatred, every war, or act of revenge. Christ has taken the guilt of every sin ever comitted by fallen mankind, from every age and by virtue of the life of his Son, satisfied the righteous law of God in its regard. In view of that fact it could be said: this fiction story, is not fiction at all.

CULT ON THE HILL

by
D.L. Waterhouse

INTRODUCTION

Daylight quickly faded in southeast Alaska as night rapidly descended upon the forest. Soon, darkness would transform the gigantic, looming cedars into eerie monsters, and the old growth stumps into ominous creatures of the night; crouching in wait for their unwary prey.

The young girl quickened her pace as she made her way through the woods, occasionally casting fleeting glances over her shoulder as she grew increasingly suspicious for her safety. A strong breeze blew through the tops of the trees, while the occasional thud of a falling limb crashing to the ground sent cold chills down her slender back. Shivering from the chill, she stopped to listen.

The young girl had already walked over half of the two miles from the compound on her way to the fishing village of Kake, Alaska, located less than twenty miles east of Sitka. A sleepy little town where nothing ever happens. Yet, concerned for her best friend, she pondered: *what will Rebecca say when she realizes I have run away?*

Rebecca was the girl's confidante, the only one in the religious group she knew she could trust. *I hope she won't be too upset with me because I didn't wait for her.*

The girl's shivering grew more frequent and she zipped her thin jacket closer against her neck. *Maybe Rebecca was right. Maybe this wasn't a good idea. What if I get lost in the dark—or worse? And what if I cannot find a way off the island before the guards from the compound find me and take me back?* Her steps quickened. "I would rather die," she said aloud to the ominous audience of trees.

Far away a timber wolf howled, then another, and another, as they crooned a song of warning to their prey before beginning another night of hunting.

As the minutes passed the path became more and more difficult to see. She told herself there was nothing to fear, yet her heart pounded in her chest.

Suddenly, from behind a tree, the little girl caught a brief glimpse of movement. A large figure lunged toward her. For a moment terror paralyzed her body as huge hands grabbed at her. Sensing her imminent peril, she panicked and began struggling with all her strength, clawing furiously against the powerful arms that groped at her. But she was too small. A huge, cold, metallic hand smashed against her face, smothering her ability to breath. As she clawed at it, the sharp strands of the steel laced gloves lacerated her fingers and ripped her nails from the quick.

A million thoughts and images raced through her mind. For a moment, as though it was only yesterday, she saw her little sister, Megan, lying in a tiny casket; her three-year-old body so peaceful and still. She saw her mother crying over her as though she had had no responsibility in her death. Now, a lifetime, *her lifetime*, though but a short twelve years, passed vividly before her in the few, waning seconds that were left.

The attacker threw her to the ground and rolled on top, his crushing weight suffocating her. Her brain begged for oxygen. Brilliant flashes of light blending every color of the rainbow streaked through her brain until they melted into a brilliant universe of white. Slowly, her struggling ceased and like a general anesthetic, unconsciousness gently relieved the girl from the terrifying reality of her end.

CHAPTER 1

The salty waters of Hamilton Bay splashed against the gravel shore as two men leapt from the bow of the police boat into the surf. Sitka Police Chief, Ivan Borski, and part-time rookie Patrolman Ralph Parker approached the stranger waiting at the water's edge.

"Are you Mr. Janes? I was told I would be meeting a Mr. William Janes."

"Yes, sir, I'm William Janes. You must be Chief Borski."

Jerking his thumb over his shoulder in the direction of his junior officer, the chief replied, "That's right. This is Patrolman Parker. Where's this body you say you found?"

"Right over there." Janes indicated toward the decomposing carcass of an old growth cedar covered with several inches of moss, lying a mere twenty yards away. "She's on the far side of that deadfall."

Chief Borski climbed across the rotted log and paused before proceeding any further. Straddling the ancient blowdown, he peered at the naked body of a small, black girl lying face up; her right arm twisted grotesquely behind her back; the fingers of her right hand visible from under her left rib-cage. Her half-closed, glazed, gray eyes stared blankly into eternity.

Borski let out an oath and wagged his head. "She's so young. Too damn young to wind up like this!"

William Janes looked quizzically at the police chief and remarked, "Is there some other age that would make getting murdered any less horrific?"

Borski glanced at him, "I get your point, Mr. Janes, I was just saying…"

Rookie officer Parker stepped closer alongside the chief, his eyes taking in the sight of the young girl's naked torso.

"She might be black, but a few more years and she would have been a real looker," he said callously.

Borski glared at his junior officer, "Get over it, you perverted—"

"I don't see any sign of gunshot wounds, or knife wounds." Parker interrupted, ignoring his boss's comment.

Borski squatted beside the corpse examining as much as he could without disturbing the crime scene.

"There are other ways to die besides getting stabbed or shot," he replied. "Did you bring the camera? We need to take some pictures before we move her."

"I'll get it," Parker said as he wheeled around to go back to the boat.

Borski was obviously irritated with Parkers un-professionalism.

"You should have brought it with you. What did you think we came here for?" Parker did not answer.

"When did you say you found her?" Borski asked, looking up at Janes.

"Yesterday, about noon."

"Are you the one who called it in?"

"No, sir. I'm in charge of a crew of surveyors. We stopped work when one of my men stumbled across the girl. I sent them all back to Kake, to call it in while I waited here for the police to arrive."

"You mean you've been here all night?"

"Yes, sir."

"Have you disturbed this crime scene at all?"

"No, sir. I'm camped about two-hundred yards over that way on the beach." Janes pointed farther down the shoreline from where the boat was anchored.

"When are your men coming back?" Borski asked.

"I told them we would wait until you gave the okay. I didn't want my guys contaminating the area."

"That was darn-right savvey of you, Mr. Janes. I appreciate that. Most citizens aren't usually that aware when it comes to crime scenes."

"Crime scene!" Parker had returned. "What makes you think it's a crime scene, Chief? It looks to me like a drowning, just like the one last year and the year before."

"What do you know about it? You've only been on the force six-months."

"I heard about them. Plus, I read about it in the newspaper. It said both girls drowned, so I figure this one did too."

"That will be up to the coroner to decide," Borski said. "Besides, the body is at least twenty-yards from the shoreline. And look at her fingernails, they're all cracked and split—like she'd been clawing at something. Fighting for her life, I'd say."

"Could have fallen out of a boat and clawed at the hull, trying to get back in."

"Maybe, but I don't see a boat, or any wood or paint under her fingernails. You would think there would at least be splinters in her fingertips. Even if she did fall in the water and manage to make it out this far, how come she's naked? No, this body has been posed to look like a homicide because the killer wants us to know up front that he's way ahead of us. Give me the camera."

Parker handed the camera to Borski who began taking pictures.

"Did you bring the stretcher?"

"No."

"Then go back to the boat and get it. What do you think we were going to do, leave her here?"

Mr. Janes said to Borski, "Speaking of the coroner, don't they usually come out to the crime scene before you take the body away?"

Borski scowled slightly.

"We only have one and he's on vacation, won't be back for a few more days. We'll handle things until then."

Officer Parker returned with the stretcher and Chief Borski, impatiently, took it from him.

"Parker, put your rubber gloves on and help me roll her onto the stretcher."

"Hey, Chief, how come we're doing this? This isn't even our jurisdiction. Isn't Hamilton Island state land? Why aren't the state police down here doing this?"

Deep furrows lined Borski's forehead. Exasperation was turning his face a bright red. "Don't you think I know that? I contacted Captain Daily as soon as I got the call. He told me they would get someone down here as soon as possible. In the meantime, he wants us to record the crime scene and put the body on ice. So as soon as I finish you can pick up the other end of this litter. And don't stumble with it. You fall on this body and Harvey finds your DNA on that girl, I'll pin this murder on you."

"How long before me and my men can go back to work?" Janes asked.

"We'll tape this area off and as long as your people don't go beyond the tape you can start as soon as we're done here. How are you getting back and forth from Kake, float plane, or boat?"

"We've been using an air charter out of Sitka."

"The next time you're over there, stop by the station. I need to get a written statement from you and the man who found the body."

"I can do that for you. I'll get my men back to work and be over first thing in the morning, say about ten?"

"That will be fine. I also need the names and work history of all your employees that are working on this job."

"Certainly Chief, not a problem. Did I understand you to say that this has happened around here before?"

Borski snapped one more picture and placed the camera into its case. For a long moment, he looked at Mr. Janes, studying his demeanor.

"That will be up to the state investigators to determine."

"When will they be here?" Janes asked.

"In a day or two."

"What if, whoever did this…?" Mr. Janes paused.

"Kills again, before they get here?" Borski interjected. Janes nodded.

Borski tossed the camera onto the girl's, lifeless body and reached down to pick up the litter.

"Then, I'll go after the pervert myself. Let's just hope to God that don't happen."

Janes looked cynically at the chief. "Hope to God? I'm sure that girl was hoping to God too. A lot of good that did *her*!"

Borski, having come from a strong Russian orthodox background, picked up on the atheistic inference.

"Just because crime exists doesn't mean God doesn't" he said.

CHAPTER 2

Homicide Detective Lieutenant Mark Kerrigan thumped a pencil on the rim of his coffee mug as he sat staring across the desk at his partner of eight years, Sergeant Billy Foster.

Kerrigan, a twenty-five-year veteran of the Alaska State Police, had spent the last eighteen years in the Homicide Division Special Victims Unit, headquartered in Anchorage, Alaska.

"Hey, Foster, did I ever tell you the one about the gas station attendant that married a movie star?"

"Only about a hundred times. Listen, if you ever come back again in another lifetime, do us all a favor and bring a batch of new jokes, will ya? Twenty-five years is way too long to have to listen to your old tired, two liners, which wouldn't have been so bad except they weren't even funny the first time."

"How would you know, Foster? You ain't even been here that long. Besides, it's only been twenty-four years and eleven months. So anyway, this gas station attendant married a movie star, see, and while he was filling her—"

"KERRIGAN!"

Both men looked in the direction of the captain's office.

Billy Foster chuckled. "Daily wants you. Go tell your jokes to him."

"He's the one who told it to me in the first place."

"I know better than that. Daily's as serious as a heart attack. He don't tell jokes."

"You don't know him like I do. Me and him are best buds."

Lt. Kerrigan rose from his desk and leaned backward, arching his back. Satisfied that all the skeletal portions of his large frame were still intact, he slowly sauntered his way to the captain's office, shutting the door behind him.

"What's up, Cap? Are you going to give me my walking papers a month early?"

"Not on your life, Kerrigan. Have a seat. Actually, I intend to milk every minute out of you I can before you retire to your armchair."

"You mean you got a case for me?"

"You might say so. Have you ever heard of Mr. Lou Worley?"

"Who hasn't? Ain't he that rich guy that took down Gino Pasteli and his drug organization a few years back?"

"That's right. He also built several learning centers. One up in Bettles, another at Naknek, and the one they just opened last year, down in Sitka."

"So what does Worley have to do with my last month on the job?"

"I want you to work with him."

"Work with him? Doing what, building learning centers? I can hardly bend down to—"

"No! Work with him on a murder case. Ivan Borski, the chief of police in Sitka, has a body on ice. It was discovered on Hamilton Island two days ago at the head of the southeast cove—young girl. I want you to work this case with Worley."

"What are the people of Sitka paying Borski for? Isn't that his job?"

"Not his jurisdiction. Body was found on state land."

"You mean I'm supposed to wrap up a murder investigation in the next thirty-days, while I drag a civilian around with me everywhere I go?"

"You better have it done in thirty days. Any more than that and I'll process you out of here, send your check back to the finance department, and give your gold watch to Foster. Then again, I suppose I might be able to talk Worley into picking up the tab for your extra salary until the two of you solve the cases."

"Cases? That sounds plural. You mean there's more than one?"

"Yeah! Didn't I mention that? There are two other cold cases with the same M-O."

"What does Borski have down there, a wannabe serial killer?"

"We don't know. Maybe, or maybe one that's relocated from somewhere else. It'll be your job to figure that out."

"So, what can you tell me about the victims?"

"They're all dead."

"Very funny, and Foster said you didn't have a sense of humor."

"Foster said that?"

"Yeah. So tell me about the girls."

"The first girl was Native American. We're not sure if she was Alaska native, or lower forty-eight native, but she was definitely native. A fisherman found her naked body floating in Security Bay on Kuiu Island two years ago. The second victim appeared to have been of Latino descent. She was found one year ago in the woods by Hood Bay on Admiralty Island—also naked."

"Why are we just now getting around to investigating cases that go as far back as two years? What am I supposed to use for a fresh crime scene?"

"They were both originally ruled as drowning. Borski can fill you in on the details. Besides, they got pictures of the crime scenes."

"A lot of good that will do me, those pictures were taken of drowning victims, not murder victims."

"Well, the first one was. The coroner reported cause of death on the second girl as *death by drowning*, but they found the body a hundred yards from the water. The circumstances were suspect enough that Borski spent a little extra time documenting the scene, same with the last girl."

"Who is 'they'?"

"What do you mean?"

"You said 'they' found the body."

"Oh, yeah. Surveyors. The Forest Service was taking bids on a logging project. They had surveyors on the island marking the boundaries."

"Is there any indication the body was dragged into the woods by an animal?"

"Not according to the coroner report. Until now, there was nothing conclusive enough to file either of them as murder cases."

"How old were the girls, early teen, late teen, twenties, what?"

Daily paused. He looked pensively at Kerrigan.

"All three are estimated to be between the ages of eleven and fourteen years of age."

Kerrigan shifted in his seat and looked at the floor. Pronounced furrows appeared on the brow of his forehead.

"Sounds like a real sicko. So, why me?"

"You've been sitting around here for the last two-months on desk duty waiting for your gold watch, so I thought you might like to go out with an extra feather in your hat. You solve this one and I'll see to it you get a bonus along with that watch."

"Sure, I'll take the case, but I got one question. What do I need with Lou Worley?"

"For starters, you'll need him for transportation. He can take you wherever you need to go in his private plane, unless of course you'd rather swim. He'll also provide you room and board at the learning center in Sitka, unless of course you'd rather camp in a tent."

"Gee, Captain, you really should consider stand-up comedy. What if Lou Worley gets in the way and gets hurt, or worse?"

"Worley made it through two tours of duty in 'Nam, and survived every gunfight he was in with Pasteli's drug thugs. I don't think you'll have to worry about him getting in your way. He's also a designated state cop—even has a badge. You might want to worry more about staying ahead of him in this investigation. You'll soon figure out, he's one sharp cookie."

"I'll take your word for it. When do I meet Mr. Worley?"

Captain Daily reached into his desk and pulled out a manila file folder. "You'll find a phone number in this file along with the preliminary coroner reports on the three victims. Give him a call tonight, I want this case wrapped up in thirty days. That'll be all, Lieutenant."

"One more thing, Captain."

"What is it?"

"What was the nationality of the last girl?"

"I believe she was African American. What difference does it make?"

"It just makes it kind of personal, that's all."

"Personal how?"

"My wife and I, we couldn't have children of our own, so we adopted three girls when they were infants. Of course they're all grown now and have their own families but…"

"But what, Lieutenant?"

"It's just that…one of our girls was native Intuit, the other two were Latino and African American."

"I see. Well, that should give you plenty of incentive to get this guy before he kills again."

Kerrigan opened the door to leave, then paused and looked back at Captain Daily.

"One more thing, Captain."

"You're starting to repeat yourself, what now?"

"You wouldn't really give my watch to Foster, would you?"

CHAPTER 3

"Lou! Baby, your phone is ringing," my wife hollered above the whine of the blender.

"I'm coming." I rounded the corner separating the dining room from the kitchen where my phone sat charging on the breakfast bar.

"Hello, Lou Worley speaking."

"Worley, this is Captain Daily. Do you have a minute?"

"Sure, Captain, how can I help you?"

"I was wondering if you would help me with a murder investigation."

"I'd love to. What do you need?"

"I have three dead bodies in Sitka."

"Three! In Sitka? That's over six-hundred miles away."

"I know. One is only two or three days old, the other two are cold cases, one from last year, and one from the year before. I've assigned Lieutenant Mark Kerrigan to all three and was wondering if you would be willing to work with him?"

"Be a privilege. Where's he going to stay while this investigation is going on?"

"Are there any facilities available at your learning center in Sitka, that he could use?"

"I'm sure we can find a place for him, maybe even with an office. Do you want me to provide him transportation, too?"

"Actually, I would much rather *you* were his pilot. He may need some help with this one. However, don't misunderstand me, Mark's the best detective I got, or might ever have, for that matter. I just need you to watch his back."

"Are you thinking this perp might be a serial killer at work?"

"Could be, and if it is, it might take a man of your particular set of skills to help Mark apprehend him."

"So really what you want is a body-guard for Kerrigan, is that right?"

"You could put it that way, yes. He has one month left before he retires from a brilliant, twenty-five-year career in law enforcement, as well as a wife, kids, and grandkids. I want him to come back from this alive. He's a damn fine investigator. The best I've ever seen. But down there I won't be able to provide him with backup and neither will the Sitka police department."

"That's fine, Captain, I'll be glad to do it. Have him call me before he leaves."

"Thanks, Lou, I appreciate it. There is one more thing."

"I'm listening."

"If it takes longer than a month to wrap this case up, I'll have to process…well, it's just that we're on a tight budget around here."

"Don't worry about it, Captain. I'll take good care of your investigator and if we don't wrap this up before his retirement, I'll spring for the rest of his salary. We'll find this guy, I promise."

"Thanks, Lou, I owe you."

"You got it backward, Captain, it's the other way around."

I said that to Captain Daily for good reason. You see, Daily and I didn't always see eye-to-eye.

I first came to Alaska from the state of Washington in June of 1995. For me it was love at first sight. Within a year I had moved my entire family to Wasilla, across the Knick Arm and northeast of Anchorage, in the Matsu Valley.

In only a short time my three sons-in-law and I had acquired a great deal of gold in the mining business. However, the accumulation of wealth brought with it certain challenges I was not expecting. Fortune brought fame; fame brought evil men and their evil behavior; like Gino Pasteli's drug organization that murdered my best friend—Pastor William Shearer.

Because I had the means to do so, I felt that it fell on me as a citizen to join the fight against the evils that threatened not only Alaskans, but Alaska's natural resources—I'm speaking of the international poaching operation that at the time was headquartered in Alaska. The head game warden, my good friend Officer Calvin Trent, and I killed a few of them and jailed the rest. At least most of the rest.

At the time, the law enforcement community was not quite sure what to do with me. With the help of a few friends, I had decimated the drug organization operating in Alaska, controlled by a Chicago mobster named Gino Pasteli, and put out of business one of the largest international poaching rings in the world. For this, the head mafia boss from Chicago ordered a contract on me and my family. I'm not sure why, possibly because his son was one of the casualties in our war on drugs. In fact, it was my shotgun that killed him and my finger that pulled the trigger; other than that, I don't know anything about it.

None-the-less, when it came to me, local law enforcement had two choices: either make me one of them, or prosecute me. They chose the first option, and overnight I became a cop.

As far as Captain Daily is concerned, he and a couple FBI agents had, in my opinion, dropped the ball big time in an investigation that involved the attempted kidnapping, with intent to commit murder, of my wife. Fortunately, I happened to come along just in time to shoot one of the would-be kidnappers in his knee. My wife killed the second one, in self-defense, of course, and if the state police had not arrived when they did the third one might have gotten the same eternal reward as his buddy. One-more-thing, I can't let this go without mentioning that in the process of catching those bad guys that day, I demolished two perfectly good airplanes. One of which was mine. But that's beside the point.

Anyway, at the time I considered them all--the FBI, that is--to be totally incompetent and had taken matters into my own hands, only to learn in the end that Daily was far more on top of his game than I had originally given him credit for. It was Daily and those two FBI agents who managed to get me into the federal prison in Kansas City where I was allowed to meet personally with Mr. Gino Pasteli, the crime boss, and persuade him that it would actually be in his best interest to take down the hit he had out on me. Fortunately, and may I say miraculously, he agreed, and so far we are all still breathing.

Since then, Daily, who was a lieutenant at the time, made captain and we have become great friends. And let me just say this: I will never forget, or be able to re-pay, the Alaska State Police for the honor and support they have shown me and my entire family since inducting me into their law enforcement community. Pardon me, I have another phone call.

"Hello, Lou Worley speaking."

"Mr. Worley, this is Lieutenant Mark Kerrigan with the State Police Homicide Investigation Division/Special Victims Unit. Captain Daily asked me to call you, said you would be providing my transportation and lodging while I work a murder case down in Sitka."

"Glad to meet you, Lieutenant. I've been expecting your call. Can I call you Mark?"

"Lieutenant will be fine. When will you be ready to go?"

"I can have the plane loaded and be ready in the morning. Will that work for you?"

"That'll be great, where do we meet?"

"I'll pick you up at Merrill Field, seven AM, in front of the Aero Flight Center."

"What are you flying?"

"Look for a yellow and black Quest Kodiak. It's a single-engine turboprop. Have you ever seen one?"

"Yeah, I've seen one, it may have been yours. Looked like a bumblebee on steroids."

"That's the one. Only it'll be on amphibious floats this time. Meet me at the Aero Flight Center across from the threshold of runway three-four. Bring as much luggage as you want."

"You got a deal, see you there."

The weather was twelve-hundred-foot ceilings and five miles, visibility in light rain when I departed my home airstrip at Wasilla. Fifteen minutes later, I was turning final onto runway one-six-right at Merrill Field. Moments later the amphibious floatplane gently settled onto the wet tarmac and taxied to the fuel ramp in front of the Aero Flight Center at the south end of the runway.

I saw the lieutenant well before I pulled up to the fuel island. A tall, well-built fellow who by his facial features appeared to be in his early fifties, dressed in grey khakis and a Seattle Seahawks warm-up jacket, leaned against the wall of the FBO (fixed base operations) office. His luggage sat next to him on a portable luggage rack. A cigarette dangled from the corner of his mouth and flopped lazily up and down as he talked to Jamie, the lineman. Jamie laughed vigorously at something he had said to him. As I taxied the Kodiak toward him, the man looked up at me, his subtle grin fading to something resembling more of a sneer. Taking a long last draw on his cigarette, he flicked it toward the parking lot. *Obviously, hasn't been around airports a lot.* My first impression of Lieutenant Mark Kerrigan was less than impressive. Jamie rushed to retrieve the cigarette butt and put it in the butt-can positioned next to the wall less than six-feet away.

Kerrigan was a ruggedly handsome man, in a chiseled sort of way. In a cowboy hat, he might have looked a little like Bret Maverick, only bigger. None-the-less, like Bret Maverick, he gave off the impression that he was both un-flappable and un-impressible. I guessed him to be about six-foot-four and maybe two-hundred-twenty pounds.

I feathered the four-bladed prop and let the turbine continue to turn as I descended the ladder from the pilot's seat.

I hollered over the whine of the turbine, "Are you Kerrigan?"

He nodded and reluctantly shook my hand.

"Good to meet you" I said.

"Likewise," he said.

I'll bet. I handed Jamie a twenty and said to him, "Thanks for picking up that butt. Load his gear in the airplane for me, would you please?"

"Yes, sir, Mr. Worley, be glad to."

I tossed a webbed cargo net over the luggage and hooked the carabineers to the deck-rings in the floor. After giving Lieutenant Kerrigan a quick briefing on how to be a passenger, making particular reference to the NO SMOKING sign, I fastened him into the co-pilot seat and filed an IFR (instrument flight rules) flight plan to Sitka, Alaska.

The Kodiak climbed rapidly through the wet clouds on its way to our assigned altitude of eleven thousand feet.

We emerged into clear air at nine, and I leveled off at 11K MSL (mean-sea-level). We were above the weather and the air was smooth with un-restricted visibility. I requested a VFR-on-top clearance that would permit me to leave the confines of the Victor 319 airway and proceed direct to Sitka. Lieutenant Kerrigan was the first to speak.

"This is a nice machine. I'll bet it cost a paycheck or two."

"Thanks, I bought it a few years ago from the Quest Aircraft Corporation in Sandpoint, Idaho. Best airplane I've ever owned."

"Must be nice. How far to Sitka?"

"Just over six-hundred miles. Should take about four hours or so, depending on winds."

"How far can this thing go on a load of fuel?"

"A little over a thousand miles, again, depending on the winds."

Kerrigan relaxed back in his seat. The slight grin appearing at the corner of his mouth suggested he might be somewhat impressed with his new partner. I was hoping we would hit it off okay, but the first few minutes weren't exactly promising.

"I want you to know I appreciate you being willing to do this, you know, the transportation and lodging and so forth."

"Not a problem. I'm looking forward to helping you catch this guy. Anything I can do to help, just let me know."

Kerrigan looked at me. His grin had disappeared. A look of disapprobation replaced it. He said, "You need to know that I'm not too keen on the idea of having anyone help me with this case. This was all Daily's idea. So, I guess now would be as good a time as any to establish the ground rules for our working together."

"I know! You're the man in charge. I'm just here to help. I got it. I have no problem with that."

"It's more than that. I can't take a chance on a civilian getting hurt, so all I want from you is the transportation and living accommodations. No matter where this investigation takes us, I want you to stay in the airplane at all times. I can't be looking over my shoulder for a killer and another potential victim, meaning you, at the same time. You're not my partner and you never will be. You're just my taxi driver, do I make myself clear?"

"Clear as that air, " I said, pointing out at the incredibly beautiful, blue sky. "Only one problem."

"What's that?"

"I'm not some thirteen-year-old victim. I'm a cop too, and I intend to stick to you like iceworms on a glacier. How clear is that?"

"Whatever you say."

"Well, I guess you'll get used to it sooner or later, or go back to your desk job, because that's the way it's going to be. I figure it this way: If Daily thought for a minute I would be more of a liability to you than an asset, he wouldn't have asked me to do this in the first place. If it will ease your mind any, I'll stay out of your way as far as the investigation is concerned, but you can be sure I'll be listening and watching everything from no more than a few feet away, and with a 10-gauge shotgun slung over my shoulder. Make no mistake about it."

Kerrigan was quiet for a moment. Then he looked at me once again, a slight grin wrinkled the corner of his mouth. I looked right back at him, except I was not grinning. He began to chuckle.

"Yeah, I guess you'll do, he said, "I had to be sure I wasn't getting stuck with a lightweight, if you know what I mean."

"I know what you mean, just don't be so worried about me that you can't do your own job. And in the meantime, let me do mine. Remember, I'm the only one you got watching your back."

Kerrigan turned to consider the view through the windscreen. The grin had returned. "I'll try to remember that."

Neither of us said much for the next hour. I thought I would let him have a chance to mull over the situation that he had made perfectly clear he wasn't too *keen* on.

"I have a van at the airport. We can load our things and drive directly to the learning center if you want. I've made arrangements for you to have one of the faculty apartments complete with your own private office. It has phone, fax, and Wi-Fi if you need it. I'll also show you where the cafeteria and exercise & conditioning facilities are located. Or, if you choose, you can order room service sent in. Do you want to get settled into your room first?"

Kerrigan looked at me. The snarl had returned. "Do you think we're down here on vacation or something? I can get settled in later. I want to see Chief Borski first."

"All right, I'll give him a call, and—"

"If I wanted him to know we were coming I would have called him myself. I want it to be a surprise."

I took a deep breath and fell silent. It was apparent that it might take a while for Lieutenant Kerrigan to learn to appreciate my finer qualities.

Named after a former mayor, the Rocky Gutierrez Airport Real Estate at one time was a burial ground for deceased tuberculosis patients from the nearby Mt. Edgecombe Hospital. Many local pilots refer to the airport as the Mausoleum. I'd rather not be reminded of the fact.

Air Traffic Control (ATC) cleared us for the LDA/DME approach to runway one-one-right. Minutes later the pontoon retractable wheels came in contact with the pavement at the Sitka International Airport.

I taxied to a large hangar where several of the learning center aircraft sat parked and set the brakes.

"Do you own this, too?" Kerrigan asked, pointing to the huge hangar.

I finished conducting the shutdown procedures and as the turbine wound down, I turned to face the detective.

"All the learning centers are owned and funded by the Shearer/Worley Foundation. That includes all buildings, aircraft and real estate. I just build them."

"Yeah, but aren't you the one who funds the foundation?"

"Yes, I funded the foundation, initially. But there are a lot of people involved in running both the foundation and the learning centers. I just oversee the building projects. However, now, the flight schools and various businesse's operated by the schools are generating their own revenue. That revenue goes into the general fund to meet operational and expansion costs."

Kerrigan squinted as he looked at me suspiciously.

"Just how rich are you anyway? I heard you're a billion—"

"It's not important, let's get this stuff loaded into the van."

One of the maintenance personnel, a young fellow named Gary Wren, who worked for the foundation's maintenance department, arrived to tow the aircraft into the hangar. I pulled him aside and said to him, "Gary, I have some personal things in the baggage compartment. Keep that area locked for me, will you?"

"Sure thing, Mr. Worley. Are you staying long?"

"I'll be in and out on a regular basis for the next few weeks. My passenger and I will be staying at the center."

"Why don't you just fly into the flight school airstrip?"

"We'd like to keep our business away from the school property for now."

"What business is that?"

"We'd rather keep that under wraps as well."

"Yes, sir, Mr. Worley. Your secret's safe with me."

"I'll be back in a minute," I said. "When my passenger gets done with his smoke, tell him to wait for me in the van."

"Sure thing, Mr. Worley."

A few minutes later, I returned from the washroom and headed toward the van. I quickly noticed that Kerrigan was not in it. I went to look for him where I thought he might have gone to have a smoke. He was not there, so I returned to the shop to find Gary.

"Gary, have you seen my passenger?"

"No, sir, Mr. Worley. I haven't seen him."

"If he shows up, tell him to stay here until I get back."

"Sure thing, Mr. Worley."

I'll bet Kerrigan's gone to see Borski without me. So this is how it's going to be.

I scrolled up Kerrigan's number and mashed on the green button.

"Yeah, who's this?"

"It's Worley, who do you think? I left your stuff in front of the terminal building. There are two bed and breakfast facilities in town. They're both probably full by now, not to mention the steep prices for tourists. You're on your own from here on out. I'm going back to Wasilla. I'll call Daily and let him know you want to do this by yourself. Seeya."

"Wait a minute, Worley. I was just—"

I flipped the lid shut on my phone and waited in the van in front of the terminal. Ten-minutes later, the passenger door opened and Kerrigan climbed in.

"You sure are touchy."

"You're about to become a long distance swimmer. I have better things to do with my time than to waste it chasing you around. You need to make up your mind if you want my help or not."

"Relax, soldier, let's go see Borski."

The one thing I hate more than anything is arrogance. And it dripped off of Kerrigan like honey off of bear lips. I was already sorry I had agreed to this proposition. If it weren't for those poor little girls…

The Sitka Police Department consisted of the chief, Ivan Borski, and-three daytime patrol officers plus-three night shift officers, two homicide detectives, and one scruffy looking vice cop. During peak tourism times, additional, part-time officers would be added to the force.

We turned onto Airport Road and proceeded to the F-99, then west across the O'Connell Bridge. F-99 turns into Harbor Drive and then Lake Street.

I parked the van in the visitor parking area and shifted sideways in my seat to peer at Kerrigan.

"Where were you planning on going? Did you think you were going to walk all this way?"

"I went to the terminal to get some cigarettes. What are you, my mother?"

"Tell me next time, I don't like being alone."

"You're not my babysitter."

"Actually, that's exactly what I am. Now listen, I want to tell you something about Borski."

"I'm listening."

"He's not as dumb as he looks."

"Did I say he looks dumb?"

"No, I'm just giving you a heads-up. He and his family are Russian immigrants. He came with his parents from Russia when he was only eight years old. They came the long way through Sweden and New York. Don't get him started telling you the story or we'll be here all day."

"Suppose I want to hear it."

"Whatever! At any rate, his mother died when he was ten. His father became a New York City cop and got himself killed in the Bronx six-months before his retirement. When Ivan was old enough, he joined the force, too. However, after his father died, he moved his family to Sitka where he started out working the night shift, walking the beat."

"What makes you think I care where he came from?"

"I thought you said you wanted to hear it?"

"I said…never mind."

"I'm telling you this because I expect you to treat the man with some respect, that's why. You seem to have a problem respecting people. I know it might come as a surprise to you, but not everyone in the world is-a murderer."

"How do you know? How many homicide investigations have you solved?"

"A couple, maybe three. A few others I solved on the spot with my 10-gauge shotgun."

"Okay, so you're a regular Rambo. I probably should have *you* investigated."

"They already have."

"Do you want to know how many I've solved in the past eighteen years? Almost four-hundred."

"I don't need to know, and furthermore, I don't care. I know that Daily put you on this case because of two reasons: One, you're the best."

"You got that one right. What's the other one?"

"Well, I'm sure it was because you don't work well with others."

"That's what you think. I only had two partners in twenty-five years, what makes you think I don't work well with others?"

"Were they your partners or your bodyguards?"

"My partners!"

"Well, you said yourself I'm not your partner. And I told you I took this job as your bodyguard. So, if I were you, I wouldn't let me out of your sight from now on."

"I don't see why I need a bodyguard in the first place."

I looked at Kerrigan and grinned.

"Maybe you'll understand better after you've talked to Borski."

"How so?"

"Well, whoever is killing those little girls appears to be plenty proud of what he's doing or he wouldn't be leaving their bodies lying all over the place, like calling cards for someone to find. I think this guy wants us to chase him so he can coax us in and kill us, too. In other words, he knows who we are, but we don't know who he is. Do you see my point?"

"I already came to that conclusion. I'm actually surprised that you're that smart."

"That's why our killer has the advantage over us right now."

"Why's that?"

"Because he already knows how smart we are. It's us who are at a disadvantage because we're still trying to figure out how smart he is."

"That won't take long."

"I have a feeling it might take you a little longer than it will me. In fact, you might even have to learn the hard way."

Kerrigan looked at me for a long minute.

"If you're right, maybe he'll tip his hand, partner and if he does, I guess we'll see how good a *body-guard* you actually are."

"I thought you said I'm not your partner."

"I changed my mind."

I nodded my head and grinned. "That's the smartest thing you've done all day."

CHAPTER 4

I initially met Chief Borski during the planning and building phases of the Sitka Learning Center several years ago. He can be a hard man to get to know on a personal level and even harder to become friends with. None-the-less, I managed to do both. Largely because the Learning center had not only contributed to the economy of Sitka, but had also gone a long way in reducing the crime rate not only in Chief Borski's jurisdiction but throughout the entire state. For instance, the teen suicide rate among the natives had been at an all-time high until our school publicity campaign effectively took over 70 percent of the delinquent children and un-employed adults off the streets, placing them into school and job training programs. Since then, the suicide rate has fallen to the lowest, per capita since Alaska became a state and the crime rate has dropped to 50 percent of what it had been before the school opened.

Unfortunately, as a consequence, the Sitka Police Department's budget got slashed a bit, resulting in the layoff of almost 40 percent of the police force. Borski of course wasn't too thrilled about that at first, but soon realized it was actually working in his favor--less crime, less personnel, less headaches, more vacations, allowing for the chief to spend more time on his fishing boat. I guess you could say he holds me responsible for that, which is probably the reason he has invited me to go fishing with him over thirty times in the last three years. None of which I have ever turned down.

Lieutenant Kerrigan and I entered through the double glass doors and approached the desk sergeant's long and lofty counter, barricading the public from the inner workings of the police department. On the far side of the counter, an unfamiliar, rookie patrolman worked the phones. I had never seen him before and out of curiosity, glanced at him a second time in an attempt to read his name tag.

The desk sergeant, Sergeant Max Unger, rolled his eyes and wagged his head from side to side in a humorous simulation of exasperation as he saw me approaching his counter.

"You and the chief going fishing again?" he asked. Knowing full well we were not.

"Not this time, Maxi. But I sure wish that was the only reason I've come to Sitka today. I see you've got a new hire."

"Sure do, Lou. Trying to show this rookie the ropes so I can start thinking about retiring."

"What's his name?" I asked.

"Parker, Ralph Parker. He helps around the place a couple days a week. Helped the chief bring the girl over from Hamilton Island the other day."

Officer Ralph Parker looked up at me and I couldn't help noticing a look come over his face as Maxi introduced me. I'm not sure how to describe it, but it was definitely a look. Kind of like "What business is it of yours who I am?"

"Sergeant Unger, I'd like you to meet Lieutenant Mark Kerrigan, state police, homicide. We're here to see the chief, is he available?"

"Nice to meet you, Lieutenant. We've been expecting you. I'll let the chief know you're here."

The counter was too wide to reach across for a formal greeting, so the two men merely nodded to each other. Kerrigan blurted out, "Tell him we ain't got all day."

I cringed. A couple of the officers in the back looked up. Maxi acted like he hadn't heard Kerrigan's comment but I noticed he squinted slightly and glanced sideways in Kerrigan's direction as he picked up the phone to buzz the chief.

I said to Kerrigan, "Was that necessary?"

"Was what necessary?"

"You know what I mean."

Kerrigan grinned slightly as he peered at the wanted posters plastered over the wall.

"Just setting a precedent."

"You'll soon learn the precedent is already set around here."

Kerrigan sneered, "Really, how do you figure that?"

"You'll see."

"Mr. Worley! The chief will see you now."

Maxi buzzed open the electronically locked door that separated the offices from the public entrance. I stood and started for the door. Kerrigan followed behind.

"Hang on a minute Worley, let me go first."

"Oh, sure, by all means. I was just—"

Sergeant Unger interrupted, "The Chief only asked to see Mr. Worley, Lieutenant. He said he'll see you next."

Kerrigan grew red in the face.

"That's a crock of…does he want the state's help with this case or not?"

"You'll have to ask him that question, Lieutenant…when it's your turn. In the meantime, have a seat until the chief's ready to see you."

"I don't need this crap. Worley—"

I anticipated what was coming next so I skated through the electronic door as fast as I could and quick stepped it down the hall to Borski's office. Pausing briefly for a moment in front of the chief's door, I rapped on the glass and let myself in.

Ivan Borski was already out of his chair and coming around his desk with his hand outstretched to greet me.

"Good to see you, Lou. How's the family?"

"Everyone is fine, looking forward to the Fourth of July at the lodge. Are you and the missus coming this year?"

"Wouldn't miss it for the world. Do you think you'll have this case wrapped up by then?"

"I hope so. If not, the rest of the family can go ahead without me. Even if I can't make it, I'll see that you and Luda have transportation to and from."

"Don't underestimate yourself, Lou. Knowing you, I have no doubt you'll have this case solved in plenty of time. By the way, how'd your lieutenant like them apples?" Borski said, grinning ear to ear.

"I don't think he did. He said he meant to set a precedent."

"Oh, he did, did he? Well, he certainly managed to do that, all right. Although I'm not sure it's the one he had in mind."

"I'm sure he'll get over it."

"I don't care if he does or doesn't. I didn't want anyone but you on this case in the first place. So tell me, Lou, are you working for him, or is he working for you?"

"He's the lead investigator. I'm just here to provide transportation, lodging, and security."

"So Daily got you in on this just to be his bodyguard and benefactor, is that right?"

"That's about the size of it. But I don't have a problem with it. I owe Daily a lot from years past, and you're my good friend, so anything I can do to help either of you I'm sure willing to do it."

"Well, if it's okay with you, it's okay with me. But I'll tell you this much, I'm the head cheese inside these city limits, so if he thinks he can come waltzing in here and start dictating how things get done in Sitka, Alaska, he's got another think coming. The only precedent that's getting set today is that I do business with you and you only. Whenever he's on state land he can be in charge of whatever he wants, but on my turf, it all goes through me."

Borski reached across his desk and pressed an inter-office mike button. Maxi answered.

"Yeah, Chief."

"Send him in, Maxi."

"He's not here, Chief. He left."

"HE LEFT?" Borski's voice could be heard all the way down the hall. "Did he say where he was going? Maybe he stepped out for a smoke."

"Do you want me to check, Chief?"

"Hell no! If he comes back tell him he missed the only opening I had today. I'm a busy man, who the h—"

"He's back. Chief, he just came through the door, must have stepped out for a smoke, like you said."

Borski paused to let his cheeks change color. "All right, get him in here. Lou, reach around behind you and lock that office door for me."

I looked at Borski, a little puzzled, then turned in my chair and pushed the lock button on the door handle.

I could see what was going on. It was a power struggle. I've seen plenty of them. Even been in a few myself, sad to say. I understand it, but at the same time it all seems like such a waste of time. However, in defense of

Chief Borski, Mark Kerrigan did need a lesson in humility, and if he didn't get it from Chief Borski, I'm sure he would get it from me sooner or later. So, I decided to set back and watch the game play itself out.

Chief Borski sat back in his chair as we both listened to the sound of heavy footsteps coming down the hall. Kerrigan paused briefly in front of the door before turning the knob in an attempt to enter. Realizing the door was locked, he waited.

I half expected he would knock and Borski would say something like, "*Come-in, Lieutenant Kerrigan, so glad to meet you.*" and we all could have gotten off on a brand new foot—I should have known better.

Without knocking, Kerrigan turned and started back down the hall toward the electronic door that was also locked.

Borski got up and said to me, "Let's go, I'll take you guy's down to the morgue."

I opened the door and stepped into the hall. Kerrigan was standing in front of the electronic door, with one hand leaning against it, and the other resting on his left hip while staring at the floor.

"The morgue is this way, Lieutenant." Borski said. "Follow Mr. Worley." I couldn't help but smile a little at that one.

Kerrigan didn't move for several more seconds, then slowly sauntered his way down the hall toward the elevator. I held the door for him as he entered. Kerrigan purposely refused to look at either of us.

The ride down to the basement was rather quiet. The elevator door opened and Chief Borski hit a baseball-sized red button mounted to the concrete wall directly in front of the elevator. We all entered the morgue through a set of electronically locked, bomber hinged metal doors.

The morgue was a large, cold room with several stainless steel, waist-high portable tables. On the left wall there was an assortment of tools and surgery type instruments, some of which looked like they had come from a butcher shop. On the right, several more portable tables lined the wall awaiting more lifeless bodies. The back wall consisted of five huge reefer doors, the kind you would expect to see in a packing house.

An elderly gentleman wearing green surgery scrubs pulled a cloth mask away from his face and greeted us. Borski said to him, "Harvey Stiffler, meet Mr. Lou Worley." Turning to Kerrigan, he said, "Harvey is our chief medical examiner."

"Does that mean you have more than one?" Kerrigan asked.

Borski gave the lieutenant a hard look. "Just the one," he said.

I stepped forward to meet Harvey with a handshake, not sure just what…might be on his hands. Thankfully, he removed his glove. "Very nice to meet you, Harvey. You can call me Lou."

It was obvious to me that Borski was not going to introduce Kerrigan so I attempted to do that for him, not wanting to aggravate the lieutenant any further.

"Harvey, this is Lieutenant—"

Kerrigan not only interrupted, but didn't even gesture a greeting. He said to Harvey. "So what are you the chief of if you're the only one?"

"The department," Harvey answered.

"You don't say!"

"Harvey, we've come to see the new girl. Mr. Worley will be investigating this case for the state police," Borski said.

Kerrigan stepped forward, his face as pink as a country ham. "Worley's not the investigator on this case, I am, so you can direct your comments to me."

Harvey looked confused. He glanced first at Borski, then at me. Neither of us appeared to have any objection so he did as Kerrigan said.

"This is my report on the latest victim's cause of death," he said, handing the case file to me. Kerrigan reached out and snatched it away from my hand.

"Is this the same file I got from Captain Daily?"

Harvey looked puzzled. "I'm not sure. I haven't sent this report to anyone as yet. Maybe you have a copy of the preliminary report I made of the first two cold cases which I sent to the newspaper."

Kerrigan did not reply and Harvey continued, "This is the file on the third victim, which includes pictures of the body and crime scene." Harvey reached across the table and picked up a large manila envelope and dumped the contents out on the stainless steel counter. Five plastic sandwich-sized zip lock baggies fell onto the table, marked as evidence.

Kerrigan said to him, "You sure this was a murder?"

"It's all in my report, Lieutenant," Harvey answered.

"Harvey, until we get a chance to read the file we would like to hear it from you. Are you quite sure it was a murder?" I asked, looking Harvey straight in the eye.

"Yes, Mr. Worley. No doubt about it. Murder by asphyxiation."

"Does she have a name yet, other than Jane Doe?"

"If she does I don't know it. I made dental impressions and took a DNA sample, but haven't sent them to the lab. Thought you guys would want to do that."

"Can you walk us through the evidence bags and tell us what you have?"

"Sure thing, Mr. Worley. The first one marked Physical Evidence A is what's left of the girl's fingernails. I removed them intact, along with the broken pieces that were stuck to her skin. You will also find particles of metal that I found under her fingernails that appear to me to be fragments of steel mesh."

"Where do you suppose that come from?" Kerrigan asked.

Harvey looked at the chief and then at me. Neither of us showed any sign of objection so he directed his answer to Kerrigan.

"They could have come from any number of things, as long as it was made of steel mesh, for instance, an apron, gloves, or Sir Lancelot's necktie. I can't say for sure."

Kerrigan chuckled. "Sir Lancelot?" Harvey didn't respond.

Chief Borski said, "The fillets in the fisheries use steel mesh gloves. Sometimes you can find them working on the docks filleting fish for the tourists, fresh off the boats."

"I'm already aware of that, what else you got?" Kerrigan asked with a note of irritation.

"Teeth impressions."

"You already said that, what else?" Kerrigan pressed.

"I took pictures of any signs of a struggle, bruising, scratches, and the like especially around the mouth and throat. She was obviously suffocated and perhaps tore her fingernails up clawing at whatever was suffocating her."

Kerrigan asked, "What about sexual assault?"

"You mean rape?" Harvey asked.

"What else would I mean?"

"No, sir, no evidence of that. However--"

"However what?" Kerrigan looked at Harvey anxiously waiting for what he considered might be the key piece of evidence that would make this humiliating interview worthwhile.

"She had been sexually active with someone on an ongoing basis, I just don't believe it was her attacker," Harvey said.

"Why don't you think it was her attacker?" Kerrigan queried.

"Because there is little evidence of trauma in, or around, the vaginal area. Therefore, I believe it had to be consensual."

Kerrigan replied, "What do you mean by 'little'? Was there trauma, or wasn't there?"

"There was some. The evidence actually suggests that the girl had been sexually active with someone and whoever that someone is, or was, he was an adult and he was not exactly gentle with her. However, I believe that if it had been an attacker, raping her, there would have been much more bruising and damage to the tissue."

I said to Harvey, "Can you tell how old she was?"

Harvey thought a moment and said, "Probably eleven, maybe early twelve at the most."

I felt a bit of nausea come over me and my knees felt weak. For a moment I had to lean against the table to hold myself up.

"Well, consensual or not, it's still statutory rape. Was there any semen available that could be used to identify him?" I said.

"Yes, I found semen. The samples are included in the evidence file."

"How long do you think it was from the time of her last sexual encounter to the time of death?" I asked.

"I can't say for sure, but in my opinion, it would have been within six to eight hours at the most."

I said to Ivan, "Chief, can we keep this evidence for a while?"

"Of course you can Lou, it's your case, not mine."

"You mean it's my case," Kerrigan reminded us. 'Which reminds me, I want the files on the other two cold cases too."

"I have them here, Lieutenant," Harvey said, handing two more file folders to Kerrigan.

"So, Mr. Stiffler, I understand that your conclusion of cause of death for the first girl two years ago was death by drowning, is that right?"

"Yes, sir, it's all in the report."

"Why is it you now suddenly believe that girl to be a homicide victim?"

"Well, the physical evidence all points to drowning, but in the light of the last two victims, we, or that is, I, have come to the conclusion the first one may have also been a homicide. After you read the report if you have any questions, feel free to give me a call."

"Harvey, what about the second victim from last year, I thought you came to the same conclusion about her? When did you decide that one was a homicide?" I asked.

"I figured it was a homicide from the very beginning, but again, the physical evidence was inconclusive, but to be on the safe side, we treated it like a crime scene."

"What physical evidence? Do you mean you found water in the lungs?" I asked.

"No, there was no water in the lungs like the first victim, but like the third victim there were signs of a struggle and sexual activity. It was primarily the fact that they were all found either in the water, or near the water, that we assumed at first they were drowned."

Kerrigan looked at Borski.

"I want to see the scene myself, and talk to the guy who found the body. Can you take me there?"

"I already interviewed the man who found the body, and his foreman. They were in here yesterday. I'll give Worley a copy of their statements," Borski said. "As for the crime scene, that's what you got this man for." Borski stabbed his thumb in my direction. "All the information and directions to the crime scene locations are in the file. Once you leave here you're on your own. And, if you ever come back here again, you better damn well show a little respect or you might not leave without getting a firsthand look at our basement bed and breakfast."

I might be dumb, but I'm not dumber, I knew it was time to go. I said thanks to the chief and to Harvey. Then, extending a handshake to both men, I turned to Kerrigan, "Do you have any more questions, Mark?"

Kerrigan looked at me with a bit of a surprised look on his face.

"I told you to call me Lieutenant."

"I would, except that would be a sign of respect."

Kerrigan sneered and turned to Borski. Scowling, he said, "I'm ready to go."

I followed Kerrigan as he followed Chief Borski toward the elevator on our way back to the main lobby. Borski stopped by his office and handed me the statements of the two men who had found the latest body.

As we emerged through the electronic door, the chief turned to Kerrigan, "Before you leave with that evidence bag, you need to see the desk sergeant and sign for it."

Turning to me, Borski said, "Lou, I don't envy you one bit, but if you need anything let me know. Good luck with this one, and I sure don't mean the murder case." With that, Chief Ivan Borski disappeared behind the electronic door.

Kerrigan was solemn as we made our way to the van. I didn't have much to say either. I figured I had said enough to ruffle already ruffled feathers. I unlocked the van and clicked the button that released the passenger side door. Kerrigan leaned against the side of the van while finishing a cigarette.

"You know what I'm trying to figure out about you, Worley?"

I didn't really care, but decided to humor him. "What's that?"

"Why someone with your wealth and prestige would get involved with a case like this in the first place? What's in it for you anyway? Those dead girls were just so much trash. Probably had it coming; maybe even brought it on themselves. What do you care who killed them, or why? Why don't you just go home to your wife and your big fancy house?"

I started the car and Kerrigan flipped his cigarette away and climbed in.

"Wealth and prestige doesn't make a man. I'm the same guy I was when I was hauling logs for wages back in Darrington, Washington, before I ever came to Alaska. Your problem is you don't know who *you* are, that's why you feel like you need to be in control of everything." I expected a rebuttal, but didn't get one, so I poured it on a little thicker. "Furthermore, it doesn't matter who those victims are, or what the circumstances were under which they met their demise. They were still part of the human family and certainly did not deserve to have their lives snatched away from them by some crazy lunatic on a power trip. So keep that in mind because the whole motivation for murder in the first place is the exercise of power by one human being over another. I'm surprised you haven't figured that out by now, seeing as how you've been a homicide detective for the last twenty-five years and know so much about it."

"Eighteen years."

"What?"

"I've been a homicide detective eighteen years. Before that I was in vice."

"Whatever!"

Kerrigan looked at me sideways, half out of the corner of his eye, and half out of consternation.

"So, are you saying I'm on a power trip?"

"No, you're saying it, by virtue of the fact you go way out of your way to show off your authority over everyone involved in this case, who, by the way, are only trying to help you."

Kerrigan stared straight ahead without further comment. For that matter, neither of us said much the rest of the way to the school.

I pointed out a few things to Lieutenant Kerrigan around the campus grounds that I thought he might find useful, like the location of the flight school and runway, the cafeteria, and my personal apartment where I would be staying. Then I took him to his room on the first floor of the men's dormitory.

"This facility is intended as the living quarters for the dean of men, but we haven't hired another one yet since the first dean retired. You can stay here for now, and if we find someone to fill the position before this case is solved, we can put him in my apartment in the interim."

"Where will you stay in that case?"

"Well, if you work real hard on your people skills, maybe I can bunk with you."

"I'm sure we'll have this case wrapped up before it comes to that."

I thought I had detected a little dry humor in Kerrigan's tone, but it could have been my overactive optimism.

"So, Lieutenant Kerrigan, what do you have in mind for tomorrow and how can I help you?"

"I want to talk to the guy who found the body of the most recent victim and visit the crime scene, then maybe talk to some of the people in that town, what did they call that place?"

"Kake. It's in the medical examiner's report. There's not much to it, just a fishing village with a population of about five-hundred. By the way, I'd like to read through those files too, if you don't mind?"

"That's what I plan on doing right after I've had dinner."

"Great, let's get you squared away here and take the files with us to the cafeteria."

"I'd rather find someplace in town. I'm sure your cafeteria doesn't serve alcohol, am I right?"

"You're right about that, Lieutenant. However, I know a place I think you'll like. It's called the Dockside Bar'n'Grill. My wife and I go there occasionally, she loves the fish and chips and they make the best coleslaw in the world."

"I'm looking for a good steak dinner?"

"They got that too."

"Is there a vehicle available I can use? I'd rather go by myself."

I was a little surprised at that remark, but after considering the source, my surprise was replaced with relief. I figured I would get a chance to look at the files sooner or later, and to tell you the truth, I had had about enough of Lieutenant Mark Kerrigan for one day.

"Sure, you can use the van. I'll draw you a map to the Dockside, then you can drop me off—"

"I can find my own way, thanks anyway."

"That's no problem, I can make a phone call and have another vehicle brought over to me."

I tossed Kerrigan the keys to the van, which he quickly stuffed into his pocket, as if he were afraid I might change my mind and take them back.

Without looking at me, Kerrigan remarked, "I'm going to grab a shower and take the evening off. I'll see you in the morning. Be here at seven AM."

I was on my way out the door when I stopped short and turned to face the lieutenant. "You got it wrong pal. I plan on jumping in the air at six AM, so if you're going with me, you'll need to be at the airport ready to go by oh-five-thirty-hours."

"Why so early?"

"Because, you're not retired yet and we're not here on vacation. We're here to stop a killer…before he kills again. And in southeast Alaska, this time of year, daylight is the most valuable commodity there is."

CHAPTER 5

I left Lieutenant Kerrigan to his own recognizance, which left me without transportation, so I called the superintendent of the flight school operations, Genneta Williams. Her husband, Jeffery, flies for our family mining corporation. It was Genneta's father, Arthur Bold, who sold me his home and property way back when I first came to Alaska in the spring of '95'. Also, it was Arthur's younger brother, Jayson, who was responsible for saving the lives of sixteen mixed race orphans out of China during WWII. In fact, a book has been written about that whole story, entitled *The Fruit of Atrocity* by D.L. Waterhouse.

Genneta picked me up at Kerrigan's apartment in one of the three courtesy cars the school FBO keeps online for transit pilots. She handed me the keys and I dropped her back at her office. The next morning, I arrived at the school's maintenance building at the Mausoleum, I mean, the Sitka airport, at precisely 0500.

I parked in front and went to the pilot lounge located in the hangar to check on the weather. Then I rolled out the Kodiak and did a preflight inspection. The sky was a solid milky gray overcast with ceilings of 2,500 feet or less. The weather forecast predicted existing conditions to gradually deteriorate throughout the day, eventually becoming low IFR by late afternoon.

At 0545, I called Lieutenant Kerrigan on his cell phone. There was no answer. I sent him a text and left him a voice mail. The text read,

"Yur late prtnr. Btr hrry. Wx going dn pm."

At 0600, I called again, still no answer. No one shows up to work at the maintenance shop until 0700, so I jumped in the courtesy car and headed back to the school. As I pulled up in front of the dean's quarters

I noticed immediately that the van I had loaned to Kerrigan was not there. None-the-less, I went to his apartment and rang the doorbell. There was no answer. I wanted to go in but didn't have another key to the apartment. Probably passed him on the way over here. I turned around and hurried back to the airport.

As I parked next to the Kodiak I saw Gary opening the huge hydraulically operated doors on the hangar. I waved to him and inquired, "Gary, have you seen my passenger this morning?"

"No, sir, Mr. Worley. Would that be the same fellow that was with you yesterday?"

"Yes. It seems I've misplaced him."

"Haven't seen him, Mr. Worley. I see you moved your plane out of the hangar, are you taking off right away?"

"If I can find my passenger, I am. Do you need me to move it?"

"No, sir, if I need to, I can move it with the Tug."

"Okay, listen. If Detective Kerrigan shows up while I'm gone, would you give me a call?"

"Yes, sir, no problem."

I locked the doors of the airplane, pulled out my cell phone, and called the Sitka Police Department. Maxi answered the phone.

"Sitka Police, is this an emergency?"

"Not unless you want to call a misplaced homicide detective an emergency," I said, unable to camouflage my growing irritation.

"Good morning, Mr. Worley, do you mean you lost your detective?"

I brought Sergeant Unger up to speed on the events that had taken place since we left the precinct the day before.

"The last time I saw him was when I gave him the van because he wanted to go to dinner by himself. Evidently he didn't want to be seen eating with me. Then we agreed to meet at the hangar this morning at 05:30, but he didn't show up. I'm going to look around town for a while. Could you have your people give me a call if they spot the school van anywhere?"

"Sure thing, Mr. Worley. Is this a good number for you?"

"Yes. One more thing, Maxi, if your people do happen to see him, have them watch him for a while. I'd like to know what he's up to."

"You got it, Mr. Worley, I'll pass the word right away."

It occurred to me the previous evening that Kerrigan seemed a little disinterested in knowing where the Dockside-Bar 'n' Grill was located. At the time I just assumed he was about as anxious to get rid of me as I was of him. But now, after the fact, it made me wonder if he had any intention of going there in the first place. I decided I needed to get into his apartment and have a look.

I drove back to the administration building, got another key, and soon was un-locking the door to Kerrigan's apartment. One look in all the rooms substantiated my theory. Kerrigan had not even spent the night and none of the luggage he had brought with him from Anchorage was in his room.

I headed back to town where I paid a visit to the Dockside. There, I found a short, stocky young fellow with a name tag on his shirt that read MANAGER. I said to him, "Excuse me, I'm trying to find a man who I believe may have had dinner here last evening. Could you tell me who was on duty, say, from five pm to ten PM?"

The young man looked at me suspiciously, but thoughtfully. "I did work the late shift yesterday, what did he look like?"

"Big fella, six-foot-four, looks like Bret Maverick in the movies."

"I would have remembered someone like that. Sorry. If you want I can ask some of the others, but I don't usually miss anybody coming through that door."

"Okay, well, I'd appreciate it if you checked around. If you do find someone who remembers him, here's my card. Give me a call if you think of anything."

"You're Lou Worley?"

"Yes."

"The same Lou Worley that found that diamond smuggler's airplane that went down in 1953 up at Glacial Lake?"

"That's right, except I'm working on a homicide investigation this time."

"I sure will, Mr. Worley. Wow, I've heard a lot about you. You're really famous."

I slipped the manager a twenty along with my state police business card and returned to my car.

For a long while, I sat staring out at the marina reflecting on another adventure long ago involving a big fish. A chill spread over me and I shivered. What I remembered most about that trip was spending the night in the cold rain, flat on my back in a landslide of huge rocks with six broken ribs, a broken arm, and a leg shattered in two places, waiting to die. I shook my head to bring myself back to the present case at hand.

Kerrigan certainly surprised me with this move. I not only didn't see it coming but wouldn't have expected for a moment that he would react the way he did just because he didn't want to work with me.

Then again, maybe I offended him when I told him he demonstrated the same kind of power trip behavior that is the driving force behind every other criminal mind all over the world, be it murder, fraud, thievery, or whatever. It all comes down to the manifestation of the ego. Either way, I had to find my detective and try to get to the bottom of the homicide case Captain Daily had handed us. Captain Daily, hmmm, maybe I should call him. Maybe Kerrigan has been in touch with his boss, or his partner, Sergeant Foster. Naw, I better wait, he's probably just mad at me and has gone off to work this case by himself.

The Kodiak turbo was running at full power when I signaled for Gary to remove the chocks from in front of the amphibious wheels. I released the brakes and began a slow taxi to the active runway.

The controller cleared me for take-off and soon I was level at one-thousand feet above the water on my way to the fishing village of Kake, Alaska.

I had no idea if Kerrigan had even left Sitka, or if he had, by what means he would have left. But something told me he wanted to stay out in front of me in this investigation and I had no doubt he was capable of doing just that.

Half-way to Kake I remembered Kerrigan had said he wanted to see the crime scene where the latest victim had been found. I decided to swing by the south end of Hamilton Island.

The clouds were about fifteen-hundred feet and getting lower by the minute. I had an eerie feeling that the weather was about to go sideways on me, but knew that if it did, I could always climb up into the soup and get a clearance from Juneau Center for the LDA approach back into Sitka.

I maneuvered my way through the maze of islands until Hamilton Island came into view. The water was flat and smooth in the inlet and I set the Kodiak up for a glassy water approach. Moments later the floats settled into the water only a few hundred feet from the shore. Slowly I let the craft drift towards the shoreline. Twisting in just enough prop to scoot the pontoons firmly onto the shore, I feathered the prop, and left the turbo running while I lashed the pontoons to a drift log laying nearby.

The first thing I noticed as I stepped onto the beach was the fresh boot tracks in the sand leading up to the tree-line. I immediately went back to the aircraft and retrieved my trusty 10-gauge. The next thing I noticed was that the yellow crime scene tape that had once marked the boundaries of the crime scene had been removed and now lay strewn about in the brush.

Since the only thing I had to go on was my memory of what Harvey Stiffler had shared with us in the morgue, I carefully approached the crime scene as if I was the first investigator on the scene.

I could see old evidence of human activity in the vicinity, but most of it had been rained on. The only fresh sign was the boot tracks leading from the water's edge up to where the vegetation began.

I carefully inspected the area to determine where exactly those boots went after leaving the sand. One by one, I was able to identify the impressions they left in the undergrowth. Soon I was looking at another impression that lay on the far side of an ancient deadfall, appearing to be about four and a half foot in length and a foot or so in width. It was obvious to me that I had happened on the place where they had found the body.

Old evidence of the vegetation that had been trampled during the initial discovery and crime scene investigation was still detectable. But compared with the recent evidence left by the person who wore the boots, it was clear to me that someone had been back to the crime scene as recently as within the last twelve hours. I returned to the Kodiak to fetch my camera.

I'm not sure why, but for some reason I seemed inclined to suspect that it could have been Kerrigan who had come to visit the crime scene. After all, he had said: the first thing he wanted to do was look at the crime scene, but how would he have gotten here? I decided to eliminate that as an option, which left only three other options that I could think of off-hand. One, Borski. Two, the surveyor. And three, the killer.

I was confident that Borski had been thorough enough in his documenting the scene, and I wasn't trying to upstage him or anything, it's just that since he had been there, it appeared that the boot man had also been there, and I wanted to see if he had left anything behind that might give away his identity or purpose for coming. For that matter, maybe the boot man and the killer were one and the same. They say that most criminals return to the scene of the crime. Which raises another question. What if the victim was killed somewhere else and the killer deposited the body on Hamilton Island because the real crime scene was too close to the killer's home turf?

I began to circle the immediate area of the largest impression in the grass, obviously where the girl's body had been discovered. Carefully, I searched around every shrub, bush, and blade of grass. After several times around the circumference of the sight, I saw something shiny. Parting the blades of grass and twigs surrounding it, I picked up a tabby from either a pop can or a beer can. It seemed just unusual enough that I felt it might hold some significance, so I placed it in my shirt pocket.

Tabs on pop cans or beer cans usually stay connected, eventually getting tossed away with the can. For some reason this tab had been twisted off. I don't remember ever seeing anyone do that before and certainly couldn't think of a reason why anyone would need to. I continued searching for a can with a missing tabby that might possibly have a fingerprint on it, but didn't find one.

The overcast had deteriorated to five hundred feet. The floatplane lifted off the water and in no time at all I was scraping the bottom of the clouds with the antennas. Visibilities were already down to less than a mile and were it not for GPS navigation I might still be looking for the fishing village of Kake.

I approached the village on the south end and as the shoreline came into view, I turned north to follow it to the marina. There is a dock there that most of the time is reserved for floatplanes, unless some rich guy in his own private yacht decides to take over the whole dock, usually because the smell of fish is so strong at the marina in town. In which case there is nothing to do but beach the plane and tie-off to any one of a million dead logs lying a hundred-yards onshore.

The dock was un-occupied by yachts, but a dark forest green, rather ominous-looking de Havilland Beaver on floats, with the initials G-A-S painted on the tail, sat in the harbor lashed to the north side of the dock, facing the open sea. I maneuvered the Kodiak in a clockwise circle and slid into the sloop directly behind the green monster.

I had no idea where I wanted to start, or what I was looking for. Maybe I would walk around town and watch for anyone drinking pop to see if they twisted their tabs off. Short of that, at least I could look for Kerrigan. I actually felt there was a very good chance he might be in Kake. I'm sure all he had to do was hire a charter plane out of Sitka. I decided to call Maxi.

The phone rang several times before Sergeant Max Unger answered, "Sitka Police Department, is this an emergency?"

"Yeah, same one, have you found the van yet?"

"Sure have, Mr. Worley. It was down at the marina parked behind Ken-Air Charters. We think he may have chartered a floatplane to somewhere."

"Thanks, Maxi. Has Borski been back over to Hamilton Island since yesterday?"

"No. Why?"

"No reason, if Kerrigan calls or comes back, tell him I'm in Kake, spending my valuable time looking for him, instead of the killer, would you?"

"Sure will, Lou, good luck. Now you know why the chief said he didn't envy you."

"Yeah, I got it. Hey, thanks, Sergeant, I appreciate it. One more thing."

"What is it, Mr. Worley?"

"Do you have a number for Ken-Air?"

"Sure."

I called Ken-Air. A lady logger answered the phone. At least she sounded like a logger.

"Ken-Air dispatch. Caron speaking. You got the doe, we take ya where you wanna go. Can I book you a flight today?"

"Good morning, my name is Lou Worley, I'm looking for a Lieutenant Mark Kerrigan, Alaska State Police homicide detective. He may have booked a flight with you last evening. If he did, I'd like to know where you dropped him."

"Sorry, Mr. Worley, no Lieutenant Kerrigan has booked a flight with us either yesterday or today."

"Really! That's odd. One more question, have you ever seen a dark green, de Havilland Beaver on floats bearing the initials G-A-S, come or go from Sitka before?"

"There is a private charter that flies out of Juneau, occasionally, called Green Air Service. However, I don't see them that often. Can you excuse me? I have phone lines blinking at me, will that be all?"

"Thanks, Caron, that'll be all."

I was getting nowhere fast. Well, at least the police managed to locate the van. I called Genneta Williams and asked her to make arrangements to have the van picked up and delivered to the big hangar at the city airport.

The walk from the floatplane dock to the village was less than a quarter mile and on the way I tried to figure out what Kerrigan was trying to prove. Was he so mad that he would put at risk his retirement pension? Maybe I should call Daily and see if he has heard from him. I scrolled up the captain's name on my call list and mashed on the green button.

"Homicide, Daily speaking."

"Captain Daily, this is Lou Worley. Have you heard from Kerrigan?"

"No. Why, is something wrong?"

"I don't know, still trying to figure that out. Evidently he's decided not to cooperate with me in this investigation and has gone off on his own and I can't find him."

"What does your gut feeling tell you is going on?"

"I think he got his back up because neither Borski nor I would bow down to him and worship the ground he walks on. At least that's my impression. He didn't stay in the apartment I provided for him and none of his belongings are there. I gave him a van to drive and the Sitka Police found it behind Ken-Air Charters. No sign of him or his personal belongings."

"Where are you now, Lou?"

"I'm in Kake at the moment, looking for him. I'll let you know if I come up with anything. If you happen to hear from him, will you let me know? I can't be his bodyguard if he's not going to cooperate."

"I see. So do you want to bow out and let him fend for his self or what?"

"What do you suggest, Captain?"

"Why don't you give it a little more time and see if he shows up? I'll let you know if I hear from him. In the meantime, just conduct the investigation without him and see what turns up."

"That's what I intend to do, but Kerrigan took the police files with him and I didn't get a chance to read through them before he took off. So I don't have a lot to go on other than what the ME told us the day we arrived."

"See if the medical examiner has copies and I'll send you what I have from here. Where do you want it sent to?"

"Send it to the flight school care of Genneta Williams."

"Okay Lou, sorry about Kerrigan, he can be a real piece of work sometimes. I've been working around his giant ego for the entire five years since I took over this office."

"Thanks, Captain. I'll give Genneta a heads up and she'll let me know when the files arrive."

I took my time walking through Kake. If you don't, you might miss it entirely. It's just a fishing village. There is a cannery that employs about a hundred people during the busy part of the fishing season. However, apart from the cannery personnel, there are only about five-hundred people that live in Kake year around. The problem is, the majority of the seasonal workers are transits that come from all over the world, which is not good news if you're looking for a killer who could be here one day and gone tomorrow. For that very reason, there are many murders in southeast Alaska that go unsolved.

As far as my three victims were concerned, I had no reason to believe that they were average random murders. The evidence suggested the bodies were placed by the killer, murdered in one location and deposited in another, and my gut told me that Kake held the key to all three cases, and was the first place I should start looking.

Most of the outlying villages and far-away communities in Alaska, with little or no law-enforcement availability, have what is called VPOs (village police officers). These officers receive very limited training and are not much more than eyes and ears for state law enforcement agencies, to call them in the event that a crime has been committed.

While keeping one eye peeled for anyone I might recognize, for instance a six-foot-four homicide detective, I kept the other eye looking for the domicile of the local VPO.

Across the only street in town and facing the marina was the local watering hole, more commonly referred to as a Tavern. I don't usually go into bars. The only thing going on in there is diametrically opposed to my whole way of life. But on this day it seemed the only place available where I might get some help. A bell above the door jingled as I pushed my way through the maladjusted door.

The air in the place was filled with smoke and reeked of the smell of stale ale, not to mention bad personal hygiene. No one paid much attention to me until I ordered, then the whole place went quiet. The large husky woman tending bar leaned forward and smiled as she looked into my eyes. She asked, "What's your pleasure, mister." An obvious seductiveness accompanied her manner.

I tried not to notice the lack of clothing over her oversized bust and while attempting to divert my gaze to something more appropriate for a happily married man to stare at, I said, "Information."

She straightened up and stepped back from the bar, "We don't sell information here, mister. Do you want anything to drink?"

"Water will do. Where can I find the town VPO?"

"He's over there in the corner, passed out. When he wakes up I'll tell him you stopped by."

"And just who will you say, is looking for him?"

"Oh, don't worry. I know who you are. You're that guy that built them learning centers, which have nearly run me out of business."

I couldn't help but grin a little over that one. I said to her, "Why don't you find another line of work?"

"Like what?"

"Like teaching school or something."

She stared at me un-expectantly, like I had just told her fortune. A forlorn look of past dreams and aspirations gone by the wayside spread across her plump face. "How did you know I was a school teacher?"

Actually, I didn't, but I thought why not play along and see where this goes?

"I know who you are too." By then the whole joint was as quiet as a mouse. She handed me a glass of water with a rather sheepish look on her face, like she had a lot to hide and wasn't real sure how much I actually did know about her, or how I happened to know it.

"So the VPO is passed out in the corner, is he? Let me see if I can wake him up."

I moved to the back corner booth where an obviously intoxicated, southeast Alaskan 'Tlingit' native gentleman lay curled up on the bench seat of a four place booth. He was alone, probably because it was apparent from the smell that he had had an accident. I turned to one of the patrons sitting at the table nearest to me and requested his help. He looked at his watch, got up, and headed towards the door. The fellow sitting next to him looked away when I looked at him, but this time I didn't bother with a request. Pointing my finger at him I said in a stern voice, "You, front and center, buddy, help me get this man to the restroom." Without a word he jumped to his feet and began lending me a hand.

"Can anyone tell me this man's name?" Over half the patrons that a second before could not utter a sound suddenly found their voice and in harmonic unison they sang out, "Leroy."

"Thank-you, now would someone get him a change of clothes and we'll need several towels and wash rags."

The first one to arrive with the towels and wash rag was the barkeep. She even helped with getting Leroy into the men's room and disrobing him.

It's amazing what people can accomplish when they have the motivation. Inside of thirty-minutes, we had Leroy washed, redressed, and sitting at the bar, chugging down a full thermos of hot coffee.

I sat next to him to make sure he remained right side up and the barkeep, who finally confessed that her name was Elizabeth, kept his thermos filled and even brought him some food. I slid a C-note across the bar and winked at her.

"You're a good soul, Elizabeth, thanks for your help."

"I appreciate it, Mr. Worley, but you didn't need to do that." I knew she was talking about the C-note, but I also noticed she wasted no time in getting it tucked away in her brazier, that safe spot where women know respectable men don't dare to go, if they know what's good for them.

"Elizabeth, as soon as Leroy comes around I need to talk to him. In the meantime, do you mind if I ask you a few questions?"

The bar-tender paused briefly from wiping her beer mugs and looked at me quizzically.

"What do you want to know?"

"I wonder if you've seen a man around here either last evening, or today, about six-foot-four, maybe two-hundred-twenty, or thirty pounds. Kind of looks like the TV cowboy, Bret Maverick."

Everybody in the bar started chuckling and even Elizabeth grinned a little.

"Looks like Mike. What do you want him for?" Elizabeth said.

"Actually, his name is Mark. He and I are working together on a project and I sort of misplaced him. By the way, what is Mike's last name?"

"You work with him and you don't know his last name?"

"He's a little hard to get close to, that's why I'm asking."

"I don't think he's ever said, what's the name of the guy you're looking for?"

"Kerrigan. Mark Kerrigan. Do you think it might be the same guy?" I turned on my bar stool to face the patrons, half of which were already headed for the door. "Does anyone know him?" No one answered and in a few moments the bar had emptied out with the exception of Leroy, Elizabeth, and me.

Elizabeth seemed suddenly agitated, "You just ran off all my customers." Her face turned the color of beet juice spilled on a white table cloth. "You better come up with a few more of these, or get the hell out of here." She wagged the C-note in my face.

"I'll do you one better than that, Elizabeth. What if I buy you out and pay for your re-training in whatever field you want."

"You mean go to that school you got over there in Sitka?"

"That's right, and when you're finished, I'll set you up in any business you want, other than this kind."

"I already got a business, at least I did until you came along."

"Think about it anyway. Here's my card. And give me a call if you're interested in changing your life."

"What! Are you some kind of Santa-Clause or something? Why would you do something like that for a perfect stranger?"

"You're not a stranger to me, Elizabeth. I told you already, I know you. You're a heap of untapped success waiting to be educated and turned loose on society, as are a thousand other people just like you. All you need is a little confidence and a kick-start." I turned to Leroy who was showing signs of recovery.

"Leroy, do you think you can show me where you live?" Leroy muttered something about being homeless and pointed in six different directions at once. I asked Elizabeth, "Do you know where he lives?"

"Yeah, I'll take you there if you can wait until I lock up."

I kept Leroy right side up while I waited for Elizabeth. Then, with her on one side and me on the other, we began shuffling Leroy down the wooden sidewalk to the north end of town.

"Elizabeth, would you do something for me?"

"Like what?"

"I'll give you another C-note if after we get Leroy home you make sure he's still there in the morning when I get back?"

"Sure, I might as well, I'm sure I ain't got no bar business no more. What is it you want from Leroy?"

"I need to hire him to do a job for me."

"What kind of job?"

"The kind that pays good money, like the kind of money you've been making since we met today."

"Do you need any more help other than Leroy?"

"I sure do, are you interested?"

"I am interested, and I think I'm interested in that other offer you made too."

"Excellent, consider it done. As soon as my job here is finished I'll get you registered in the learning center over at Sitka."

"So what is it you want me to do?"

"I need you to tell me more about the big fella you call Mike, and let me know immediately, if and when, you see him. I want any information on him I can get. And, I need you to babysit Leroy. Don't let him out of your sight. Agreed?"

"I can watch Leroy. But as far as Mike is concerned, I see him only occasionally, he flies in here from somewhere, I don't know where—"

"Wait a minute, I'm sorry to interrupt, did you say he flies?"

"Yes, sir."

"Does he have his own plane?"

"I think so."

"Do you know what it looks like?"

"No, I've never seen it. I've just overheard him talking about planes in the bar before, so I assumed he had one."

"Maybe we're not talking about the same guy. The guy I'm looking for doesn't fly. At least if he does I sure didn't know about it. What does he do over here when he comes around?"

"I don't know that either, but I sometimes hear him talking about, the cult on the hill."

"What kind of a cult? What hill?"

"There's a religious cult two miles from here up the old Swan Lake Mill Road. Follow this road in front of my place out of town, right after you pass the old mill on the left, take the next right. Follow that gravel road for a mile or so, you'll come to a locked gate. The compound is encircled by a chain link fence and the gate is guarded day and night. However, if the guards don't know you, you aren't getting in unless you know someone inside that can vouch for you."

"Who's the leader of the outfit?"

Elizabeth looked uneasy, shifting from one foot to the other as she looked around. Then in a low tone she said, "A man named Joseph Morning. His followers believe he's a prophet."

"Do you know anyone inside?"

"I once did, but she's not here anymore."

"What happened to her?"

"I don't know. I was told she went back home to the lower forty-eight."

"How long ago was that?"

"One year ago this month."

"What was her name?

"Camilla. Camilla Diaz."

"Do you know what state she was from?"

"She talked a lot about Yuma, Arizona, but I don't know for sure if that's where she came from originally."

"Was she Latino?"

"Yes." Immediately, it occurred to me. I'll bet that's our second victim.

"So, how would you describe your relationship with her?"

"Good friends, that's all. She would come to the bar sometimes for a burger and soda. Their religion didn't allow them to eat meat or drink pop."

"Her religion, or the cult religion?"

"The cult religion."

"How old was she?"

"Twelve."

"You let a twelve-year-old kid come into your bar?"

"It was the only safe place where she could get away from those people. Besides, she stayed in the back away from the clientele."

"So what was the problem? Was she not completely sold on what they were teaching up there, is that why she left?"

"You could say that, I suppose. She did seem awfully confused."

"How did she become involved in it in the first place, and where are her parents?"

"Like a lot of the other children, she was a runaway, looking for redemption for their past lives, I guess."

"Past lives? How much redemption could a twelve-year-old girl need?"

Elizabeth continued, "Most of the young girls that run away and wind up in cults were abused sexually and most cult religions teach that they are responsible. That somehow the victim brought it on themselves."

"Is that what this…Joseph, what's his name, teaches?"

"Morning, Joseph Morning. "Yes, he does. Don't get me wrong. I understand how people can make mistakes and wind up dealing with the consequences of their own actions. After all, I'm a perfect example of that and I even admit it, but I don't see how that makes it their fault when they are violated, or that it somehow gives someone the right to violate them, especially a child. That just seems so sick to me."

I decided to wait until a more opportune time to discuss this very important topic any further, so I kept my answer brief. "Neither do I. Do you really think children are being violated up on that hill?"

"Absolutely, I do! Then after he has made it their fault, he promises them redemption if they submit to his rule and accept him as their prophet, and savior, or whatever else."

"Did Camilla tell you she was being molested?"

"I could never get Camilla to come right out and say so. I think she was afraid to. But I could never get her to say she wasn't either."

"Have you ever been up there?"

"Yes, I went with Camilla to a few of their meetings when they had open house day."

"What was that like?"

"I don't know, just preaching. They're real nice for the most part, but Camilla said it was all a front."

"How do you mean? A front for what?"

"A front to make people think they're just an innocent Christian group who want to be left alone."

"So you don't think that's what they really are?"

"No, not by a long shot."

"What are they then?"

"It's not *they*, it's *him*. The prophet and his understudies."

"What do you mean by understudies?"

"He has elders and deacons that hang on every word that comes out of his mouth. They also guard the place and carry out his wishes, whatever they are."

"Are they armed guards?"

"Oh yes, and according to Camilla they have a whole arsenal up there."

"Did you ever go back to the compound after she disappeared?"

"I went up there a couple of times and was told that she had left and gone home. They all claimed that they are free to go anytime they want, but I don't believe it. Then one day I saw Shirley in town."

"Shirley! Who is Shirley?"

"Shirley was one of the mothers Camilla stayed with sometimes. Most of the orphans, older girls or boys, live with a guardian when they're not living in the dorm."

"Where's the dormitory?"

"Camilla said the dorm was next to where the prophet lives."

"I'd like to speak with Shirley. How can I reach her?"

"I'm not sure. You would have to get into the compound and ask around. I've only met her once, so I can't help you with that."

"One more question, what do you think the connection is between your friend Mike and the cult?"

"I didn't say he was my friend. He just comes around once in a while."

"Okay, so what—"

"I don't know. But it could have something to do with the adoption agency."

"What adoption agency?"

"There's an adoption agency in Fairbanks that sends their overflow of kids down here that they can't find homes for anywhere else."

"Really, do you think it's a front for a human trafficking operation?"

"I don't know, but it sure smells fishy to me."

"What do you think this Mike has to do with all of it?"

"I think he's the one who brings them down here."

"How do you know this?"

"As far as I can tell, he's the only one who ever goes up there on any consistent basis."

"How consistent?"

"I see him around here at least two or three times a month."

"Well, Elizabeth, you certainly have helped me a great deal. You have a lot of insight and I can tell you care a lot about kids. How would you like to close that saloon and open a half-way house?"

"A halfway house for what?"

"For kids."

"You mean the kids from the compound?"

"Any kids that might need a place to stay. I would be glad to finance the project and we could remodel your bar into a multi-dwelling apartment. I'll pay you ten times what you make now, plus all the expenses, and provide any help you need. Wha-da-ya-say?"

"I'm not sure what to say. This is all so sudden. I'm not even sure this isn't a dream that I'm going to wake up from any minute."

"The dream was that life you were living before I walked into your bar, only it wasn't a dream, it was more of a nightmare. Don't you agree?"

"It certainly hasn't been my idea of paradise."

"Did you actually have an idea of paradise at one time?"

"When I finished college, I did."

"When was that?"

"Ten years ago, in Seattle. I had earned a master's degree in childhood education from the University of Washington and was planning on pursuing a doctorate, when I heard there was a lot of money to be made up here in the canneries. So I figured I would put everything on hold until I made enough money to live on while I went back to school. Except…"

"Except what, Elizabeth?"

"Except, when I arrived, I found that the fishing was the poorest it had been in years and the work in the canneries had all but dried up. I had a little money saved and this tavern came up for sale, so I bought it and have been a barmaid ever since. I thought I would be stuck here." Elizabeth's lips began to quiver and she looked away. I waited a moment for her to regain control. "And then you walked into my bar."

"Well, Elizabeth, I might walk out of your bar. But, as long as you want my help, I'll never walk out of your life. Tell me one more thing. You said you are from Seattle. Is that where you were born and raised?"

She was quiet for a long moment as if she were not so sure she should trust me with too much of her personal information.

"I was born in Haiti, Missouri. My father was in the military when he met my mother and after a short courtship they married. Within a month he was on his way to Iraq. Eight months after he left I was born."

"Did your dad make it back from Iraq?"

"Yes. But when he got back he went to live in Memphis."

"Didn't he come to see you?"

"He says he did."

"Don't you believe him?"

"I suppose so."

"What did your mother tell you about it?"

"After my dad went to Memphis she met someone else and asked my dad for a divorce so she could marry again."

"Are they still together?"

"No. They were together off and on for about two years, until he killed her."

"Good Lord, Elizabeth, I'm so sorry! So, what became of you?"

"Actually, he murdered my grandma at the same time, shot both of them to death right in front of me. My grandmother died instantly. I held my mother in my lap while she died in my arms."

As I listened to Elizabeth tell her story, I found myself so shocked at what had happened to her as a little girl I was completely at a loss for words. It took me a long minute to gather myself.

"How old were you when all this happened."

"About seven."

"What did you do? Did your dad ever come and get you?"

"I ran to the neighbors. I didn't know where my dad was at the time. I didn't find out until many years later that he had moved away from Memphis, Tennessee, about four years before my mother got killed. I never heard any more from him."

"Then who raised you?"

"My mother's older sister."

"So how did you end up in Seattle?"

"It was twenty-three years later. I had found a box among my mother's things that had some old letters in it from my dad's mother. I read them and discovered that she lived in Portland, Oregon. When I called information I was given the phone number of my dad's older brother. That was how I got his phone number."

"Have you ever tried to contact him?"

"No."

"Do you want to?"

Elizabeth pointed to a rundown shanty of a dwelling that looked more like a wood shed than it did a home. "This is Leroy's place."

I could see that Elizabeth had entered a dark place filled with the horrible memories of her past. I knew the rest of the story would have to wait until another more appropriate time. Elizabeth pushed open the door to Leroy's dwelling.

Together we managed to get Leroy into his home where Elizabeth agreed to keep him sober until I returned and had a chance to talk to him.

"I'll be back, Elizabeth. By the way, have you ever known anyone that was in the habit of twisting the tabs off their beer cans?"

Elizabeth jerked her head around and looked at me, a startled expression on her face.

"Mike does that."

I wasn't sure if Elizabeth's Mike and my mystery-man were in fact the same fellow or not. But I knew one thing for sure, I wanted to find both of them. Something told me, when I found one, I would find the other.

I walked the three blocks back to the marina to see if I could find a vehicle for sale, all the while keeping an eye peeled for Kerrigan.

I finally felt like I had a list of suspects. A list that now included the cult leader and his understudies. I also was now not only baffled at Kerrigans bizarre behavior but at the fact that he either had a twin or was leading two lives that were diametrically apposed to each other. Maybe, I needed to add the detective to my list as well.

I decided to go back to the plane where I could check the crime scene photos I had taken. If the beer-can tab showed up in one of my pictures and not in one of the photos that the ME had taken it would mean that the one who deposited the body and the boot man who visited the crime scene after the fact may not be the same person after all—unless, of course, the killer returned to the crime scene for some other reason.

The weather had deteriorated to below flying minimums and a cold stiff breeze had picked up coming in from the sea. I decided to head back to Sitka before it got any worse. On the way to the dock, I rehearsed the information I had gotten from Elizabeth.

What if her Mike and my Mark were in fact the same person? And what if Elizabeth's Mike and my Mark was also the pilot of that green float plane tied to the dock in front of my Kodiak? What if Kerrigan was not only the pilot, but also the killer? Forget it. Kerrigan might be a narcissistic, arrogant pinhead, but I can't imagine him as a killer.

I looked at the sky and realized that flying conditions would not last much longer. Then, something caught my eye. A trail sign, with an arrow pointing in the direction of the hill Elizabeth had pointed out to me. The sign read: SWAN LAKE 3 MILES. Maybe that trail goes by the cult compound. I better get my jacket and have a look.

CHAPTER 6

Rebecca Holt had been crying; not just from the dread of what ramifications awaited her if she were caught, but the fear of what additional evil she may suffer at the hands of the leadership if she remained any longer in her present situation. She straightened herself, wiped the tears from her eyes and mustered the courage to move forward with her only remaining option.

At fourteen years old, she was small for her age, but strong willed and had decided the time had come for her to make her escape from the prison camp where she had been forced to live for over a year. Rebecca opened the note pad that lay on the kitchen table, picked up a pen and began to write.

>Dear Frances,
>
>Thank you and your family so much for opening your home to me this last year. I am so sorry, but I can no longer stay here. I can no longer tolerate the things the leaders do to me. Nor do I believe in what they teach, or their methods of disciplining those who they say have sinned. If what they do is God's way, I do not want God's way. Please forgive me.
>
>I am eternally grateful to you all for letting me travel with you and your family from Seattle two years ago. After getting sent here from that terrible orphanage in Fairbanks, I was both glad and grieved when I found you. I believe the people who run that place are as evil as the devil himself, and it is a horrible crime what they and the religious people in this compound are doing to all the children my age. Please! You must get your family away to someplace safe as quickly as you can.

> I hope you don't tell anyone, but my friend Tracy left barely more than a week ago and I am running away tonight to meet up with her. Good-bye. I love you all.
> Rebecca.

Rebecca's friend, Tracy, was eleven at the time she made her escape from the religious compound. They had known each other since Rebecca's arrival at the orphanage in Fairbanks and one year later, they both had been sent to the compound in Kake.

Rebecca had tried to talk Tracy out of leaving without her, but she had just spent a week locked in a storage room with only dry bread and water to live on. It was her punishment for talking to a boy.

The leader of the fanatical religious group, Joseph Morning, who claimed to be a prophet of God, forbade all girls under the age of eighteen to talk to any boys over the age of eleven.

Rebecca and Tracy had talked about running away together, but Rebecca had not entirely made up her mind and Tracy was eager to leave before she lost her nerve. It truly was a fearful decision. Tracy said she would wait for two weeks at her friend's place, a lady she knew in town named Elizabeth, who owned a tavern and had volunteered to help them.

Two years ago, Rebecca had traveled on a boat from Seattle with Frances and her family on her way to Anchorage. Frances and her children had disembarked at Sitka on their way to join up with the religious group living in Kake, Alaska. For some reason, Frances thought their leader, Joseph Morning, was a prophet, and that he was especially chosen of God to lead them to their spiritual paradise. To Rebecca, he was not a prophet at all but a satanic cult leader and child abuser.

Rebecca had not joined Frances initially, but had continued on to Anchorage where she tried in vain to survive, alone on the streets. It wasn't long until she became a ward of the state. Eventually, she was transferred to a private orphanage in Fairbanks, Alaska, owned and operated by a religious organization, one she later realized was affiliated with the cult.

The more Rebecca thought about Tracy, the more concerned she became for her. It was then she resolved to make her escape and try to find her friend.

Rebecca placed the note on the table, confident that her friends would not betray her.

Rebecca had no coat to put over the lavender sweater that her mother had given her before she left Seattle. She had run away then too, fleeing the steady reign of sexual abuse she endured from her stepfather. Now, two years later, nothing had changed but the geography and the faces of the predators.

With less than an hour of daylight remaining, Rebecca slipped out of the camper trailer and disappeared into the encroaching darkness of the evening.

Silently she navigated her way through the underbrush from tree to tree pausing behind each one knowing that if detected, she would find herself again before the cult's public tribunal where she would be condemned to the fires of hell for her unbelief and treachery, a punishment she was much more willing to tolerate than the *hell* that would come after--the *hell* that always awaited her, in the prophet's upper room.

In the dark timber, a cold breeze drifted down from the mountains above. Rebecca shivered from the chill and pulled the sweater tighter around her shoulders. She glanced this way and that, fearing that at any moment she might be discovered.

Over and over she reiterated her plan in her mind. Then it occurred to her. *What if Tracy is already gone? Where will I go if I can't find her? Or, what if someone recognizes me and reports me to the cult leaders?* Rebecca had heard that there were people in town who received payment for such things, and without knowing who to trust she would have to be very careful indeed.

She could now see the two guards at the gate, sitting in their warm car. She could even hear their muffled voices as they laughed at their own filthy jokes. Rebecca recognized the oldest one. His name was Maurice, and once, when she had approached the gate, he had tried to coax her into the woods. She had been out walking the fence line and decided to see if they would let her leave by herself. Maurice had insinuated that he would, but on one condition. Rebecca knew what that condition was, and flatly refused. She had once thought, maybe it would be worth it just to get outside the gate and finally get away, but she knew that even if she did give in to him, and Maurice were to let her go, he would immediately report her and she would undoubtedly be caught. No. It would be much better this way. Besides, she knew that if she had to suffer even one more day, the kind of perverted abuse that had already nearly destroyed her will to live, she would gladly die at her own hand.

The brush was much thicker at the boundary of the compound and it tore at her flesh as she fought her way through.

Rebecca wasn't sure which way Tracy had gone when she made her escape, but in the days prior to this night, Rebecca had discretely marked a way to the property line where she had used a large spoon to dig an impression in the ground under the cyclone fence. Climbing over it was out of the question due to the coils of barbed wire fastened on the top.

Carefully, she removed the brush and leaves she had placed over the impression to conceal her escape route, then, sliding her slender body under the wire, she committed herself to her escape. She paused for a moment to free herself, as her sweater snagged on the jagged wire halfway under. Suddenly, she was on the outside.

I made it. Now if I can just get to the village.

The farther away from the compound she got, the faster she moved. Finally, she made it to the hiking trail that would take her to the fishing village, a mere two miles away.

As it grew darker, it became more difficult to make out the trail, and her pace slowed. Frantic thoughts raced through her mind. *I wonder if Tracy came this way. I hope none of the guards from the compound are still searching for her.*

Rebecca stopped to listen. Was it just her imagination, or had she heard something? She looked around, then began to move faster. *I don't care if I do die.* Her thoughts were almost audible. *It would be better than life; at least the only kind of life I've ever known.* She wondered if all girls her age had to grow up as a sex doll for grownups. Or was it just her? Was it because she was pretty and valuable, or because she was ugly and worthless? Rebecca wasn't sure, nor did she any longer care.

She had tried to talk to Frances about what they did to her, but Frances was not listening. Frances was a disciple of the prophet, and her eyes were blind to reality. She carried a Bible everywhere she went, but Rebecca had never seen her read it for herself. Her understanding of scripture consisted of what the prophet told her, and *his* was the voice of God to all the members of the cult.

Suddenly, Rebecca sensed movement coming from the dark shadows. Then, from her left side a large dark figure loomed above, lunging at her from behind a tree. Her heart exploded with terror while her body froze motionless. Her paralyzed legs turned to rubber as a strong, heavy hand firmly grasped her left arm. She opened her mouth to scream, "NO, DON'T HURT ME PL—" A large, cold, rough, metallic glove covered her mouth and nostrils. She frantically clawed at it with her fingers.

Far away she thought she heard someone yell, "Helllooo…" Then, her terrified thoughts within her own mind were suddenly all that was left. One last time she cried out, *PLEASE, DON'T HURT ME. MOMMY,* MOM—

Rebecca felt a sharp pain in her head. Then, the darkness of unconsciousness gently released her from her terror.

The first thing I noticed as I approached the dock was that the dark green floatplane was still tied up in front of my Kodiak.

I slipped on my jacket, strapped on my .45 caliber Glock seventeen sidearm and grabbed a flashlight. Stepping from the pontoons onto the floating dock I headed back to the Swan Lake trail-head that Elizabeth had told me would lead to the religious cult's compound.

Darkness was less than an hour away so I knew I would have to hurry if I was going to get back before dark. I didn't plan to go very far, just far enough to maybe find the entrance to the compound.

At first the trail appeared to be hardly distinguishable, but the farther I went into the heavy timber the more distinguishable the path became.

I was careful to keep an eye out for any sign of either wildlife or human that would indicate how recently the trail had been used. There was very little of either. I concluded that if Swan Lake was three miles away, then the cult compound must be at least two, judging from the way Elizabeth had described it.

The trail started off fairly level, then gradually got steeper as it switch-backed up the side of the mountain. I'm not as young as I used to be and found myself pausing frequently to catch my breath. What do you think you're doing, Worley? It's almost dark, I should wait to do this tomorrow when its daylight. Just a little farther, then I'll turn around.

About a mile into the hike, I thought I heard a sound. I stopped to listen. There it was again, a faint whimper, or muffled cry, like someone was hurt or injured.

I called out, "Hellooo, is anybody there?" I listened for a response, but no one answered. Then, not far ahead, I heard something, or someone, crashing through the brushy undergrowth. I began to run up the steep hill, stopping only briefly to gasp for air and listen, trying desperately to hear above my heavy breathing. Suddenly, I saw a form in the trail. At first, in the dim light, it appeared to be an animal. As I approached, I drew my weapon and switched on the maglight attached to the sidearm. There, in the path before me, her legs folded under her crumpled and motionless body, lay a young girl, either dead or un-conscious, her face and head covered in blood that had seeped from a gash in her scalp, matting her jet black hair.

I looked around for any sign of an assailant, but didn't see anyone, and could no longer hear the crashing in the brush. *Whoever did this is probably watching me from a distance. Oh well, I'll worry about that later, right now this girl needs my help.*

Carefully, I lifted the girl to a sitting position and leaned her toward me, cradling her head against my chest and shoulder. I checked her pulse and found she was just barely alive. Holding her with my right arm I opened her eyelid with my left hand while pointing the maglight at her pupils, they were seriously dilated. I suspected instantly she might have a concussion, which made her need for medical attention even more urgent.

Retrieving my cell phone from my coat pocket I checked for signal strength. There was none.

"You hang in there, sweetheart, I'm going to have to carry you for a while," I said, half to her and half to myself.

The closest hospital was in Sitka, except they didn't have a trauma center. However, the learning center did, so as carefully as possible I hurried down the hill I had just hiked up.

Suddenly, moments before we emerged from the dark timber, I heard the familiar sound of a radial engine, burping and backfiring at first and then, with hardly a minute of warm-up time, the engine RPM increased to a water taxi level and soon the roar of a huge radial engine reverberated against the mountainside.

My arms ached and were fast losing strength as I stepped from the forest into the semi darkness of the evening. Somehow I staggered to the Kodiak, and as I suspected, the green de Havilland Beaver was gone. Something told me he was probably the same guy that had attacked the girl. Carefully, I laid his latest victim on the dock next to the pontoons. *If that was him, how did he get here so fast?*

My arms quivered from the exertion and at seventy-one-years-of-age, I felt like cursing the aging process that had crept up on me, stealing away my youthful strength and stamina. My hands shook as I fumbled to unlock the door of the airplane. Moments later, I had my passenger lashed to a stretcher that I interned, lashed to the floor of the aircraft.

By now the weather had not just deteriorated, it had completely crashed, with no more than a hundred-feet of forward visibility in light rain and fog. I shoved the float plane away from the dock, jumped onto the pontoon, and climbed into the pilot's seat. As I switched on the turbo and quickly went through the startup procedures, I silently prayed, *God, don't let there be any boats on the water in front of me, or airplanes flying around in this fog. And enable me to get this girl some help, in time,* "Please, God," I said aloud. Once again, I remembered the green monster. Somewhere out in that fog was another floatplane doing exactly the same thing I was about to do.

The Kodiak came quickly up onto the step and a moment later, we were airborne. The instant the pontoons left the water the outside world disappeared. I pitched the prop to a high performance climb and leveled off at an altitude that would guarantee terrain clearance in all directions as well as radio reception with Juneau Center. The controller granted my request for a pop-up IFR clearance and soon handed me off to Juneau Approach who cleared me for the LDA approach into Sitka. Soon I was talking to the boys in the tower.

Sitka tower reported field conditions: ceilings of fifty feet (MSL), with a visual range (RVR) of less than one-hundred feet. I got the impression they were trying to convince me I should go somewhere else, so I said to them, "Eight-six delta, final approach-fix inbound, passenger emergency on-board; request AMR team back up, on the ramp for the Learning Center, Trauma Unit."

"Roger that, eight-six delta, you are cleared to land one-one-right, decision height, pilot discretion. Be careful, Mr. Worley."

Conditions were below minimums and the airport was officially closed, so I figured there would be a pile of paperwork and maybe even a letter in the mail from the FAA. But, what-the-hey, I had a little girl in the back about the age of my granddaughter who was fighting for her life. What did it matter if I bent a few FAA rules?

The amphibious wheels came into touch with the tarmac and I exited the runway at the nearest taxi-way. The American Medical Response team was already doing sixty miles an hour headed in my direction, lights and sirens blaring. Once on the ramp, I stopped, set the brake and feathered the prop. By the time they reached the Kodiak I had the side door opened, the stretcher unlashed, and was frantically waving at them from the ground beside the door. Moments later the injured girl was on her way to one of the finest trauma centers in Alaska.

I returned to the cockpit to finish my taxi to the maintenance facility. For a moment I sat at the controls rubbing my forehead and temples until my hands and knees quit shaking.

With the aircraft put away for the night I called the tower to thank the fellows on duty, and to explain to them the circumstances that compelled me to break every FAA rule in the book concerning weather minimums while landing at a controlled airport in IFR conditions. For some reason they didn't seem to know what I was talking about—never did get a letter.

It was well past supper-time when I arrived at the university's trauma center. I checked on the patient the AMR team had just brought in and was told she was in critical condition and the doctor wanted to speak with me.

I took a seat in the waiting room and minutes later a lady doctor, wearing a surgery gown and a sterile mask hanging loosely around her neck, emerged through the swinging doors that led to the urgent care facility. She looked around the waiting room and called out, "Mr. Lou Worley?"

"Right here," I said.

She carried a clipboard in her left hand and approached me with her right hand extended toward me in greeting. "I am Doctor Mellissa

Brady, the neurosurgeon on duty. I have heard a great deal about you, Mr. Worley, even seen your picture hanging on the wall in the main lobby. It's so nice to finally meet you."

"Nice to meet you too, Dr. Brady."

"I understand you're the one who brought the girl in with the head injury, is that right?"

"Yes, ma'am."

"Can you tell me what happened to her?"

"She was attacked by someone. I think he may have been trying to kill her. How is she, will she survive?"

"How awful. Well, we're going to do everything we can, Mr. Worley. She has suffered severe head trauma and it is very fortunate that you were able to get her here when you did. But, I need to know more about her. Can you tell me her name?"

"I have no idea, but I intend to find out. When I do, I'll be sure and let you know."

"Can't you tell me anymore than that, for instance, family history, or any medical history?"

"No, ma'am, except she probably lives with that cult group up on the hill above, Kake."

"A cult? I've never heard of a cult around here."

"I didn't know it was there either until I recently talked to an individual who lives nearby. I was actually on my way up there to check it out when I walked up on this girl, evidently in the middle of her attack. Fortunately, I scared the attacker off before he finished the job."

"That is fortunate. Do you think someone from the cult is responsible for her injuries?"

"Possibly. I intend to find that out, and whatever else that might be going on."

"I have every confidence that you will do just that, Mr. Worley. I think that's about all I need for now. If you learn any other information please contact me."

"I will, Dr. Brady. By the way, here's my number." I handed Dr. Brady my business card. "As soon as she's able to talk I would appreciate it if you would let me know. Send me a text or an e-mail. It's very important that I talk to her as soon as possible."

"That may be awhile, Mr. Worley. We have her in an induced coma right now to try to control the swelling in her brain."

That wasn't what I wanted to hear because I knew that little girl had information that could save me a lot of leg work. But, more important was the fact that she was still alive. I said to the doctor, "I understand. There is one more thing Dr. Brady. I need you to keep her sequestered. I don't want anyone to see her. I'll make arrangements for someone to guard her room."

"Thank-you Mr. Worley, you can be sure I will do whatever I can to keep her safe and alive."

On my way back to the airport, I called my oldest son-in-law, Rusty German. He's married to my first born daughter, Keera, who is the chief of staff for all of the medical facilities financed by the Shearer/Worley Foundation.

Before Rusty and my other two sons-in-law joined me in the mining business, Rusty was a very successful private detective. Before that, he spent six years in the army as an Army Ranger defending our country in places he still is not allowed to talk about. He's also a darn good lawyer.

I brought Rusty up to speed on my latest adventure and persuaded him to join me in the investigation.

"When do you think you can be here, Son?"

"I can come down tomorrow morning, Dad. Will that be soon enough?"

"That'll be fine. I have to go see Borski first thing in the morning. After that I plan to go back to the latest crime scene. I want to look around. So if you get here in time you can go with me."

"Okay, Dad. I'll bring someone to watch the hospital room and if you're gone when I get there I'll meet you at the dirt strip over at Kake. Can you land your float plane in there?"

"Yeah, I should be able to. I think it's in fairly good shape. If I'm not there, you can try to call me, but the phone service isn't that reliable. If that doesn't work, look for me at the tavern in town."

"The tavern?"

"Yeah, don't worry, it's not what you think. The gal that owns the place is helping me with this case."

"Okay, Pop. I'll see you there."

The next morning, I went by the dean's quarters again to see if Kerrigan had miraculously appeared. He hadn't, so I went to the cafeteria, had some breakfast, and headed downtown to the police station. Sergeant Max Unger looked up as I came through the door.

"Good morning, Maxi. Is the chief in yet?"

"Go on in, Mr. Worley, he's expecting you."

Maxi buzzed me through the electronic door.

Borski was on the phone when I entered his office. I took a seat and pretended I couldn't hear him yelling at his teenage kid for getting caught with pot at school. Borski slammed the phone down and said to me, "Lou, let's get the hell out of here and go fishing."

"I wish I could, Ivan, but I'm over my head in this case and need some help."

Borski opened his desk drawer and appeared to be looking for something. "What kind of help? You know I'm understaffed as it is."

"I don't mean that kind of help, I mean, I need copies of those files Kerrigan took with him that I didn't get a chance to read before he disappeared."

"That's no problem. Harvey keeps everything on a secure hard drive. I'll have him make copies for you."

"What about pictures? I need to see the pictures that were taken of the crime scenes."

"I'm sure he's got that too. So, other than that, how's the investigation going?"

"Not so good. Did you know there's a religious cult compound on a hill above Kake?"

"Yeah, I'm aware of that. Why, do you think they have something to do with the murders?"

"I don't know. Maybe that's where the girls come from. I know at least one of them did."

Borski stopped fidgeting with the odds and ends in his desk drawer and look up. "How do you know that?"

"I met someone in town that knew the second girl. Name was Camilla. Camilla Diaz, said she was Latino, only twelve years old. Came from Arizona."

"You'll need to get a statement from that source and enter that information into the police file."

"What all do you know about them?" I asked.

Borski was searching through the bottom drawer of his desk. "About who?" he asked absent-mindedly.

"The religious cult. What are you looking for anyway?"

"A lure. I bought a new lure and can't remember where I put it. Not a whole lot. As far as I know they've never given anyone any trouble. Besides, they're out of my jurisdiction so I don't worry about them."

"Okay, I'll go see Harvey. Thanks for the help."

Borski had gotten on his knees and was piling the contents of another desk drawer all over the floor. "Don't mention it, Lou, good luck with that."

"One more thing, Chief. Maxi said you were expecting me. How did you know I was coming in?"

"There! the darn thing is right in front of me. Huh? Oh. Daily called, said you lost the files."

"I didn't lose them. Kerrigan disappeared with them, remember?"

"Doesn't surprise me, Lou. You're better off without him anyway. Good luck, and get that case wrapped up so we can go fishing."

"I'm on it, Ivan, seeya."

Just as Borski said, Harvey had entered all the case file data, including digital pictures, onto a hard drive which he burned to a disk. I'm not the type of person that usually carries a lap-top around with me everywhere I go, but I had brought one with me on this trip so I could keep in touch with my family as well as see to other business matters.

The disk I had in my pocket had a lot of information on it that I needed to see as soon as possible, so from the police station I headed back to my apartment where I spent the next two-hours reading police reports and staring at crime scene photos.

The pictures from the third crime scene intrigued me the most. They were the pictures Borski and one of his deputies had taken of the deceased African American girl on Hamilton Island. I was looking for something in particular. All of the pictures but one focused on the immediate vicinity: position and placement of the body comparisons, measurements, etc. But there was one picture that depicted a broader view including the area where I had found the beer can tab.

I focused in on that specific area, clicked on the approximate spot, and enlarged it. There it was. I could only see about half of it, but it was the same tab I had found at the crime scene, and still kept in my shirt pocket. I took it out and held it up next to the picture. There was no doubt. It was a perfect match.

My heart rate increased a few beats a minute over the new excitement I felt for finally finding something significant in regard to this case. After all, here I was sitting in front of a lap-top, looking at a piece of evidence that represented a huge step forward in my murder investigation and feeling the same exhilaration over a twisted-off beer tab that I felt during every gun fight I had ever been in. I couldn't help but feel that there might be something addicting to being a homicide detective, and maybe that is why Kerrigan didn't want to share the moment with a rookie like me.

Now I knew. Whoever visited the crime scene after Borski had recovered the body had not left the beer can tab. Moreover, it was also possible that whoever deposited the body in the first place also dropped the beer can tab, then later went back to look for it. That meant that when I found the person who twisted off his tabs, I would have my first viable suspect.

The weather had improved considerably since my harrowing experience the night before. Landing in practically zero visibility can make an old man out of you in a hurry. Most likely a dead man, especially if a person made a habit of it. I'm not a reckless kind of pilot, but sometimes, desperate circumstances require desperate action. Someone, or maybe even a lot of someone's, had made the statement to that little girl that she was of no value to them, or anyone else. I could never let a decision of mine make the same statement. Every person has value, and for that moment, and under those circumstances, her life was more important to me than my own. That doesn't mean I'm a hero. I mean that strictly as a principle. The most important thing in anyone's life should be the lives of others. The problem is: the perpetrator doesn't live by that rule. Therefore, he has made himself an enemy of society, like a rabid dog that must be destroyed to maintain the peace and safety of the community. For some reason, beyond my understanding, the responsibility always seems to fall on me to find the rabid dogs and put an end to their savagery. I was no stranger to it. I had done it before, and God willing, I would do it again.

On the way over to Kake, I climbed to an altitude that would ensure cell phone reception and called the hospital.

"Trauma Center, this is Barbara, how can I direct your call?"

"Good morning, Barbara, this is Lou Worley. I brought in a young girl yesterday evening with a severe head injury. Can you tell me how she's doing?"

"One moment, Mr. Worley, I'll connect you."

"Intensive care, this is Carman, may I help you?"

"Yes, this is Lou Worley, I brought—"

"One moment please."

"Mr. Worley, this is Doctor Brady."

"Good morning, Doctor, I'm calling to find out—"

"Mr. Worley, I'm afraid I have bad news. I'm terribly sorry, but, unfortunately, we lost the girl during the night."

I couldn't believe what I was hearing, or didn't want to believe it. At first I went numb all over, then my vision blurred, which is not good when you are the single pilot of an airplane flying through a maze of islands within a quarter mile of either side of the aircraft.

Tears pooled in my eyes until they began streaming down my cheeks. I tried to wipe them away so I could see where I was going before I slammed into a mountain, but they just kept coming. My stomach convulsed, and my chest heaved repeatedly as I wept un-controllably.

"Mr. Worley, are you still there?"

I could hear Mellissa, but couldn't reply.

"Mr. Worley, are you all right?"

Finally, I managed a response. "Yes, Doctor, I'm here."

"Oh, there you are. I thought I lost you, are you all right?"

I reached in my flight bag for a tissue and dried my eyes. Got to get myself under control. Redirecting the nose of the airplane away from the mountain that had suddenly appeared in the windscreen I re- established my route of flight in the direction of Kake.

"Doctor Brady?"

"Yes, Mr. Worley, I'm still here. You sound a bit emotional. I hope you're not driving a car."

"No, I'm not driving a car."

"That's a relief, Mr. Worley. I should have checked before I gave you the bad news."

"Doctor Brady, I'll have someone from the coroner's office retrieve the body. Could you prepare your report and provide it to him when he comes?"

"That won't be necessary, Mr. Worley. I will take care of all that. We have a temporary morgue facility right here. However, I would appreciate it if you would pick the body up personally and come to see me before you do."

I was a little surprised by Dr. Brady's request; however, because I was still a bit undone by the news of the girl's passing it didn't occur to me to ask any other questions.

"I can't right now, Dr. Brady. I'm on my way over to Kake. Can you keep the body there until I get back?"

"Of course, Mr. Worley. My god, I hope you're not flying."

"Don't worry, Dr. Brady, I'll be fine."

I did a low pass over the dirt runway at Kake, located a quarter mile east of the town, and northeast of the floatplane dock. It sits on a side hill, 172-feet above sea-level. The runway is plenty long, at four-thousand feet, but can get a little dusty during the hot and dry time of the year when a lot of airplanes are coming and going from the airstrip. During the spring thaw it can be rough when frozen and sloppy when wet.

The problem with landing an amphibious plane on a dirt strip is that it is more like landing a car instead of an airplane. You have to set the back two wheels on the ground first while making sure the longitudinal direction of the aircraft is perfectly in line with the runway before you let the front two wheels come in contact with the ground. If you screw it up too badly, which is entirely possible when landing on an un-even surface or in a side-wind, it can result in serious damage to the undercarriage, maybe even destroy the whole airplane.

I called Rusty after talking to Dr. Brady, and left him a voice mail to let him know we would no longer need a guard for the hospital room. However, I was sure it was too late and Rusty would be showing up with the additional manpower. If we didn't need him, I could always book him passage on a flight out of Juneau. Then again, maybe it wouldn't hurt to keep him around.

Rusty's Cessna 206 Stationair was nowhere in sight, so I taxied to the tie-down area and shut down. I was still feeling extremely sad over the loss of the little girl. Not just because I had temporarily saved her from her attacker but because I had held her in my arms and kept her alive long enough to get her to the hospital. It really tore me up to think that she had come so close to beating the odds. I didn't know anything about her, but suspected that she had not had many breaks in her life and sure could have used a good one there at the end. The thought of it made me emotional all over again. I felt something else happening inside too. Suddenly, this serial killer had made it personal, and I could feel the anger seething within me. Buddy, you better run, because if you stick around here very long I'm going to find you, and when I do...

Not far away I could hear an airplane, coming hard. The sound was familiar. I had heard it hundreds of times, and hundreds of times it had come with the same pilot and the same stone-cold intention. Yeah, buddy, you hear that? That's the cavalry. So, buddy, if you're going to run you better get started, cause that sound you hear is the sound of *justice*--coming for YOU!

CHAPTER 7

Watching my son-in-law land his big Cessna on the dirt runway at Kake reminded me of the time when he and I flew into the little nine-hundred-foot gravel airstrip at the old Alfred Creek gold mine back in '95'. My family and I were living in Darrington, Washington, at the time. I had taken a month-long vacation from my job to fly my straight-tail Cessna 172 to Alaska in search of a place I had read about in a book. It sounded like a crazy idea at the time, but I needed a break from hauling logs and it seemed to me like just the adventure I was looking for.

Quite fortuitously, and inadvertently, I discovered a stash of gold someone had hid in the bottom of an old pit toilet many years prior, which I excavated and relocated up to the airstrip and re-buried under the tie-downs. Because the runway was so short, and my airplane so under powered, I could only take a small portion of the gold with me and still be sure I could out climb the big hill looming off the end of the runway.

After flying back to Anchorage, I called Rusty who flew his Cessna 206 up from Spanaway, Washington, to Merrill Field. The next day we flew back into Alfred Creek and retrieved the remainder of the gold. Rusty did an investigation into who had originally stashed the gold and found it had belonged to an old prospector who had been found dead in his cook shack where he had laid for over a year before his body was discovered. I filed new claim papers and to this day, the old claim is still in my name. A world-renowned author volunteered to tell my story in a book he wrote entitled: *Alfred Creek* by D.L. Waterhouse.

A lot of years have come and gone since then, along with a few more adventures. And now, here we were in the middle of another one. I was beginning to think my adventure days were over, until last week when Captain Daily called me requesting my help in this triple homicide investigation, which, apparently, as of today, has become a quadruple homicide.

I walked over to Rusty, shook his hand, and gave my son-in-law a huge hug. He took one look at me and realized something was wrong.

"Dad, are you okay?"

"Yeah, I'm fine. Who do you have with you?"

"Dad, this is Rudy Crawford. He's one of the security people working with us at the Pistol Creek mine."

I extended my hand, reluctant to look Rudy in the eyes for fear he too would detect, as Rusty had, my most recent emotional distress. No matter how hard we try to protect our pride, men still have emotions inside them that cannot always remain buried beneath their egos.

After hearing Elizabeth's story, not all of my distress had to do with the fate of the poor girl that I had brought down off the mountain. Getting up close and personal with the notoriously evil nature of man can at times leave a person wondering if there really is a God. Despite anyone else's convictions regarding that, I for one believe that there is. Unfortunately, certainly within the last twenty-four hours, I had been provided a dramatic realization of the incredible depths mankind can descend to, apart from his divine influence.

"So, Dad, will we still need Rudy, now that, you know, the girl is—?"

"I've already considered that, I think we should keep him as an ace-in-the-hole for the time being. We'll go about this investigation as though we don't know him and he can do the same with us. We can communicate by cell phone."

I brought Rudy and Rusty up to speed on all the details I hadn't yet covered with them, especially the information contained in the police reports. Including the twisted beer can tab I found at the crime scene. They both agreed it was inconclusive, but the most feasible possibility was that it had been left there by the killer. Yet another remote possibility was that one of the surveyors had dropped it. I have trouble imagining that they were likely to be drinking on the job.

"Do you have a list of people you want to talk to?" Rusty asked.

"Yes, a few. We can start by having a talk with Leroy."

"Who's Leroy?"

"He's the VPO here in Kake. I'll also introduce you to Elizabeth, who up until yesterday owned the tavern in town, and is a material witness in this case."

"Witness! I didn't know you had a witness."

"I said, material witness. That means that she is privy to certain information relevant to the case. I thought you were a lawyer?"

"Not anymore, I'm a miner now. Or did you forget?"

I chuckled at Rusty's inference that it was me who was responsible for his leaving his private investigation practice to join me and my other two sons-in-law, Jeffery and Mitchell, in the mining business.

"You're not complaining, are you? It seems to me the mining business has worked out quite well for you."

"It has, Dad, I'm not complaining, just reminding you."

I turned to Rudy, who was beginning to look a little nervous.

"Rudy, I'd appreciate it if you would keep a record of who comes and goes from this airport and especially the floatplane dock. Watch for a dark green de Havilland Beaver on floats. I want to know who's flying it. When Rusty and I finish with Leroy we're going to pay a visit to that Cult compound." I handed Rudy my business card.

"Sure thing, Mr. Worley. I'll send you a text message if I see anyone suspicious."

Rudy entered my number into his speed dial and called my phone so I would have his. Then, retrieving his duffle from the Stationair, headed down the gravel drive leading to town. I watched him as he walked away.

Rudy was a small fellow, about five-foot-seven, maybe a hundred-seventy pounds. He appeared to be in good condition, but I wondered what chance he would have against our killer if he was a much larger man. I turned to Rusty.

"How long has he worked for us?"

"About two years. If you're wondering if he can handle himself, you don't need to worry. He was a light heavy-weight UFC champion before he came to work for us, defended his title for two years through six title fights until he lost it to a guy from Bulgaria."

"Why is he working security, why not in the mine?"

"He was an actor and stunt man before he got into the fight game and has shown an unusually high aptitude for undercover work. We use him in the field on assignments that require certain specific skills of that nature."

"Are you still having problems with people skimming gold ore?"

"Not nearly as much, since we hired Rudy."

"He looks a bit young, how old is he?"

"I know, but he's actually twenty-nine years old."

My wheels were turning, already inventing a plan, "In fact he looks young enough that he might be able to get into that cult compound. Does he have a family?"

"No. He's single. What do you want him to do in the compound, join up?"

"I don't know, maybe. My informant, Elizabeth, said they have visitor days. We'll ask her and see if she can figure out a way for him to get in."

"Is that where we're going now?"

"We can see her later. Right now I want to go back to the place where the girl was attacked last night."

I took Rusty to the sign that read SWAN LAKE 3 MILES. Rusty took the lead and together we made our way up the trail to the place where I had heard the girl cry out during the attack.

"Rusty, I think we're getting close to the spot. I wish I would have thought to mark the trail where I found her."

"Maybe there will be some evidence of the struggle."

"There should be blood on the ground. If only I could have gotten here one-minute sooner." I felt the lump in my throat return and choked off my words.

"So that's what it is, I knew something was wrong the minute I saw you, Dad. You're all tore-up over that girl dying, aren't you?"

"It did hit me pretty hard. I can't understand what goes on in the mind of someone who would do something like that. But I can tell you this, I'm going to put a stop to it, that's for sure."

"These tracks, leading up the trail. Are they yours?"

"I'm sure they are. Wait, no, those are not my tracks. Someone else has been on this trail."

I bent down to get a closer look at the boot tracks.

"They are leading uphill too. And I've seen this tread pattern before."

Rusty stopped and looked closer at the boot tracks.

"Where have you seen them, Dad?"

I reached into my pocket and pulled out my camera-phone. A moment later I was holding the picture of the boot man's tracks from Hamilton Island, alongside the tracks in the trail.

"Do those tread patterns look the same to you?"

"Looks the same to me, Dad. Where did you take those pictures?"

"About five miles from here at the south end of Hamilton Island, where they found the third victim last week. I paid a visit to the crime scene yesterday and realized that someone had been there since Borski and his people retrieved the body."

"Do you think it was the killer returned to the scene of the crime?"

"Could be. Of course, that's a popular boot pattern. But it still seems more than just coincidental."

A short way up the trail Rusty stopped in front of me and pointed to the ground.

"It looks like all the tracks terminate right here, Dad. Look. Is that blood on the bushes?"

"It could be. This looks like the spot where I found the girl. And you can see where someone has crashed through the brush going that direction." I pointed to the south.

Rusty examined the trampled vegetation. "I want to see where this goes," he said.

"That's the direction the killer ran when I interrupted him. Be careful not to trample on anything that might be evidence until I can get pictures."

Rusty continued searching the area for clues and I used my cell phone to take pictures of the crime scene and boot tracks left on the trail.

"Hey, Dad, check this out."

I fought my way through the brush to where Rusty was standing. He was pointing to the ground.

"Get a picture of this, Dad. It looks like our killer chews tobacco."

"See if you can salvage that. We'll take some of it with us and use it for DNA evidence."

"Did you find any of this at the last crime scene?"

"No! But of course it had rained several days by the time I got to it. But there wasn't anything in the police report about it."

Rusty took his cell phone out of its case and, using a piece of bark, began retrieving a sample of the tobacco juice left by the killer.

"Maybe that's where that beer tabby came from," Rusty commented.

"How do you mean?" I asked

"Don't most tobacco chewers carry something with them to spit into? Maybe the killer uses a beer can, and that's why he twists off the tabby so he can spit into the can easier."

"Can't they spit into a can that still has the tabby on it?" I asked.

"I suppose they could, except…"

"Except what?" I asked curiously.

"What if he has a mustache or beard and the tabby snags his fur. Wouldn't that be reason enough to remove it?"

"Actually, Rusty, that's a pretty good theory. Except he obviously didn't have a spit can with him yesterday or he wouldn't have been spitting all over the ground, so why would he have one with him when he took the body to Hamilton Island?"

"He had to get over to the island somehow. Maybe he had a six-pack of beer with him in his boat, or airplane."

"That means if we find the airplane, we'll find the can. Maybe even evidence of the dead body that was in it. "Do you think the girl we found on Hamilton Island was killed here too?"

"We'll have to assume that she was, until we find some evidence that suggests otherwise. After all, you're now the only living witness to the fact that he kills his victims in one place and stashes the bodies somewhere else. If you hadn't happened upon him when you did, he might have taken the body of this last girl and placed her on another island, and we still wouldn't have a clue where the actual crimes take place. As it is, we not only have a fresh crime scene, but a very worried killer who might either make a mistake or try to come after you."

"I wish he would come for me. It would certainly be his last and fatal mistake. We could bury him right here and get back home to our families."

"Dad, be careful. Don't let your emotions get in the way of justice."

"Didn't I tell you? Captain Daily is operating on a tight budget. The only justice we're interested in is putting an end to this killer, by whatever means necessary. "Which reminds me, are we done here? We still need to talk to Elizabeth and Leroy today."

"Not yet, Dad. Tell me again what happened last night."

I paused briefly, not anxious to relive it again in my memory. It's not that I haven't been around death before. I was around plenty of it during my two tours of duty in Vietnam. It's the kids, you know? They're so vulnerable and defenseless. I guess you could say I have an above average soft spot in my heart for them, especially kids that are misused or abused by the very adults who are supposed to be their protectors and guardians, the very ones, kids that age are supposed to be able to trust. I get downright mad when I see it, and if that anger serves as motivation to hunt the perpetrators down, then so be it. I don't know how far they're willing to go, but I'm willing to do whatever it takes to either put them away or take them out, budget or no budget. However, for the present, I was well aware that the feelings of guilt and remorse I was carrying for that little girl would have to be put on hold, at least until we finished making a reckoning on behalf of not only her, but the other victims as well.

"Dad, did you hear me?"

"Yeah, I heard. Well, I was coming up the trail on my way to the cult compound when I first heard the girl cry out. It was muffled at first, but I started running as fast as I could, which wasn't very fast cause this hill is so steep. Then I saw the silhouette of a large person take off in this direction." I pointed to the spot where Rusty and I stood.

"I wanted to go after him, but when I checked the girl and realized she was still alive she became my first priority. And by then the killer was long gone."

"I don't think he was that long gone."

"Why? Do you think this tobacco juice was left here after the attack?"

Rusty paused, contemplating his response. "I think so."

"If that's true, why didn't he come after me while I was carrying the girl down the hill? By the time I reached the bottom I was so wiped out, he could have easily overpowered me."

"I thought we were looking for a killer, not a man. Maybe it isn't a man at all."

"Okay, even if it's a woman, she would have to be a large woman and as tired as I was she could have still taken me down. I'm not as young as I used to be."

"I know, Pop, don't forget, I'm the one who's always reminding you of that fact. But to answer your question, he probably saw that you were wearing a gun."

"He would have had to see me before I put my jacket on."

"When did you do that?"

"On the dock by the plane, just before I started up the hill."

"Maybe our killer saw you in town before you ever went for your hike. At any rate, I'm ready to go whenever you are. How much farther up this trail is the cult camp?"

"About another mile or so, I think."

"Shall we go on up and have a look around?"

"We don't want to spook anybody. I think we should talk to Elizabeth first about getting Rudy into the compound as a visitor."

"Whoever the killer is, he's already spooked. You spooked him last night. What I don't understand is, why are there tracks going up the hill and not down the hill?"

"I'll tell you something else that's strange."

"What's that, Dad?"

"The green monster."

"What's a green monster?"

"It's a de Havilland Beaver on floats with the initials G-A-S. painted on the side, stands for Green Air Service."

"What does the green monster have to do with it?"

"Well, the weather was down to the ground and no one in their right mind would be flying in it unless…"

"Unless what?"

"Unless they were running from something or…"

"Or what, Dad?"

"Or trying to get a critically injured person to the hospital before they died."

"I see, so what your telling me is that you flew in zero visibility conditions too, is that right?"

"Didn't have much choice. At least not one I could live with."

"Where was the green monster when you took off?"

"When I started up the hill it was still tied up at the dock in front of the Kodiak. However, just before I made it out of the woods with the girl in my arms, it took off in an awfully big hurry."

"What do you mean by *big hurry*? That's the only way there is to take off on the water."

"I mean the pilot didn't even take time to let the engine warm up, just untied it, started it, and slammed the power forward. Why would anyone need to be in that big of a hurry? Any aircraft owner would know that is the worst thing you can do to an engine."

"That does sound a little desperate. I can understand why *you* had to fly in those conditions, but I see your point. Why would *he* need to if he wasn't running from something?"

"The problem is that now, I'm not so sure it *was* the same guy that attacked the girl. If he waited here like you say he did, how could he have possibly gotten to his airplane ahead of me?"

"I see your point, Dad. Maybe there were two people involved. But if there were two people, where is the third set of tracks? Unless they split up," Rusty said, as he continued to look around for more evidence.

"Does this mean we're looking for two killers, or one killer and one body snatcher?" I asked, as I followed Rusty farther into the timber.

"Could be, Dad. Hey, look at this."

I stepped up beside my son-in-law to see what he was looking at.

"This looks like another trail. I'll bet the killer, and the pilot of that green monster, are wearing the same set of boots, and I'll bet while you were carrying the girl down that trail, he hoofed it down this alternate trail and got ahead of you."

I felt like Rusty had a valid point and looked for boot tracks that I could compare with the pictures I had taken, but the trail was not well used and was so covered in foliage that there were no tracks.

Rusty stood, placed the evidence bag into his coat pocket, and remarked, "I think that's what happened, Dad."

"I think you're right, Rusty. And now, we can assume the killer knows who we are and that we're on his trail."

"Correction, he knows who you are, Dad. As yet, he doesn't know anything about me or Rudy."

"Maybe we should start looking for that green monster. I could get hold of Borski and have him—"

"I think we should go on up the hill and check out that compound," Rusty interjected. "I'm sure the green monster will be back sooner or later and we need to figure out the connection between the killer and his victims, and I think it begins with the cult compound."

"All right then, you talked me into it. But we'll have to be as quiet as we can the rest of the way. Maybe we can find a way in without going through the gate."

Rusty fell in behind me and both of us stopped talking as we continued our trek up the trail. I studied the surroundings as we made our way through the forest, memorizing every twist, turn, and landmark along the way.

After about thirty minutes of hiking, I stopped to whisper to Rusty, "It seems to me that this forest would be a very scary place for a young girl that age to hike through, especially in the late evening. I wonder what made her so desperate that she would venture out into these woods alone the way she did, which is apparently what got the other girls killed too."

"So you think the first three girls were killed in these woods just like the last one?"

"I'm pretty sure they were. Elizabeth says she knew the second girl before she disappeared, and that she was also involved in this cult."

"Do you think the girls were fleeing some kind of abuse, or just running away from the cult religion?"

"I don't know. But it seems to me that regardless of the religion, as long as they had a safe place to live they would likely be satisfied to stay put. No, I think they were running from something they feared worse than these scary woods, which could also be somebody's motive for murder."

Rusty considered the idea. "Who do you think that somebody is?" He asked.

"Well, if the leadership in that cult is behind the abuse, then that leadership would be the ones with the motive." I paused to listen to the breeze filtering through the trees.

"So if we can figure out if in fact there is abuse going on and who is responsible, we can prove motive. But there still must be time and opportunity as well as capability? How do we prove all that?"

"That's what Rudy's job will be. If we can get him inside, and find some witness's that will testify, we can get to the person or persons who are not only responsible for the abuse, but who ordered the girls killed.

I just wonder how many kids over the years have tried to get away from this place and met their demise on this same path."

"I hate to think of it, Dad."

"And, one other thing. It's like someone seems to know when the next girl is going to run away, and is passing the word onto the killer, or killers. Otherwise, that guy would be sitting in the woods twenty-four hours a day, every day, waiting for his next victim."

"I see what you mean, Dad. There's obviously a web of conspiracy here. Once we find the informant, we'll have the whole network."

I let Rusty take the lead and we continued on up the hill. We had gone nearly a mile when Rusty stopped in front of me.

"Dad, do you hear that?"

"Yeah, sounds like a car coming."

"Coming or going, I'm not sure which."

We continued on until we came to a gravel road. I whispered to my son-in-law, "This must be the road that leads to the main gate from the old Swan Lake Mill. We should stay in the timber. If we walk up the road they'll see us. I think that car is coming out of the compound."

"Who do you expect will see us, Dad?"

"The guards at the gate."

"How many guards?"

"I don't know for sure. Elizabeth said at least two."

Rusty and I stayed low and crept back into the woods, away from the road.

"Listen, I hear voices coming from that way." Rusty pointed south in the direction of the compound. "That car sounds like it's coming toward us."

"Whoever it is will stop at the gate and talk to the guards on their way out. I think we're pretty close to the property line," I whispered.

Rusty nodded. "I think you're right."

A few steps farther, I stopped. "Look, there's a chain link fence. Maybe we can see inside the camp from there."

"Okay, Dad, go ahead, I'm right behind you."

We crouched low and moved very slowly to make sure the guards didn't hear us as we made our way along the fence line looking for an opening in the trees that would give us a view of the compound. Suddenly Rusty tugged on the back of my jacket.

"Dad, look." He pointed at something at the bottom of the cyclone fence. The earth had been removed from the bottom of the wire leaving an indentation in the ground just large enough for a very small person to crawl under. Then I saw it. It was a piece of fuzzy material stuck to one of the sharp protrusions of the wire. I removed it and held it up to the light.

"Rusty, this material matches the sweater the little girl was wearing last night. This is where she crawled under the fence when she made her escape. Do you think we could get a warrant with this?"

"Should be able to. Stick it back on the wire and take a picture of it. Then put it in an envelope and send it and the sweater to the lab along with that tobacco juice we found earlier."

"I'm on it, counselor." I placed the material back where I found it and took out my camera. "I hope those guards don't see this camera flash, it will blow our cover for sure. They're only about a hundred yards away."

"I'll watch your back, go ahead."

I snapped a close-up picture of just the sweater material stuck to the wire, then removed the cloth and placed it in my shirt pocket. Then I backed away and snapped a picture of the fence line itself. This time when the camera flashed, the guards started yelling.

"Hey, who goes there?"

"Let's get out of here, Dad. Don't even answer them."

Suddenly, two shots rang out.

"Run, Rusty! That was an AK-47."

We could hear the guards yelling and talking amongst themselves as they tried to investigate the source of the flash, but by the time they made it to the fence line, Rusty and I were long gone.

For an old man, with a hip replacement that was only about five years old, I made pretty good time getting back down the hill. I was feeling like we had accomplished a great deal by hiking up that mountain. Number one, we had found the tobacco juice left by the killer while he waited silently in the brush while I was making my getaway with his latest victim. Number two, we had determined that the pilot of the green monster, and the killer, were apt to be one and the same. And, number three, we had found where the little girl made her escape from the compound where she had been a prisoner for who knows how long. As a result, there certainly was ample evidence to suggest that the cult on the hill should now become the center of our investigation. I could hardly wait to tell Elizabeth.

Rusty and I had made it off the hill and were on our way to see Elizabeth and Leroy. As we walked past the airport headed into town, a sign read, KAKE 1/4 MILE, and an arrow pointed north. Rusty paused,

"Dad, we should make arrangements for some ground transportation. We're not going to get much done if we have to walk up and down that hill. I'm surprised you haven't had a vehicle brought over from Sitka by now. Isn't there a barge service available?"

"I'm sure there is, but it could take a week or more for that to happen. Keep your eyes open, maybe there's a vehicle for sale in town."

"Okay. What are you looking for, a four wheeler, a car, or a pick-up?"

"I don't care. Anything that runs decent, has a heater, and doesn't leak when it rains."

"So Dad, tell me again how Elizabeth fits in to all of this."

"Well, as ironic as it may sound, Elizabeth say's she knows someone named Mike that fits Kerrigan's description to a tee, who, as it turns out, also is in the habit of twisting off his beer can tabs."

"Actually, Dad, I've seen a lot of people do that. Most of them drop the tab inside the can while they're drinking the beer. However, its just as feasible that he tossed it on the ground. For that matter, it's also just as likely it was already there before the killer deposited the body."

"Maybe, except now we have compared the boot tracks on the hill to the pictures I took of the boot tracks from the crime scene. Which now leads me to suspect that it was the killer who did in fact return to the crime scene. I think he remembered he had tossed that tabby on the ground and went back to find it."

"I see your point. Sounds like this other guy, Mike, may be more than just a person of interest."

"Does he chew tobacco and fly green monsters, too?" Rusty asked.

"Who?"

"Mike. We're looking for a killer that chews and fly's green monsters, remember?"

"I'm still trying to figure that out"

As we walked down the gravel road towards town, we passed an old house setting back into the woods, a couple of hundred yards off the main road.

Rusty said to me, "Dad, look, there's an old Dodge pick-up truck with a for-sale sign on it."

I stopped, "Let's check it out," I said.

We followed the driveway to where the truck was parked, about three-quarters of the way down the drive to the house.

I walked around the vehicle checking for damage, "It's kind of old, although not too bad looking. Maybe early fifties vintage. We could ask the guy if it runs. If it does, it might even be worth restoring after we've finished using it. Let's see how much he wants for it."

As we got closer to the main house, I noticed more construction equipment in the back-yard. Equipment that was very old but apparently still useful. "I see a logging truck in the back. He must be a logger."

"You mean, he was. There's a for-sale sign on the logging truck too."

The old house was constructed out of rough-cut timber, probably still green at the time it was built. The windows had been covered from the inside with old newspaper, and the un-painted 1x6 vertical slats covering the exterior walls, over the years, had dried and were now separated by a shrink gap, through which one could see globs of shredded newspaper insulation on the inside of the walls.

It was a two-story home, apparently built by someone who was obviously a better truck driver than he was a carpenter. Behind the house stood a large shop surrounded by a variety of other old parts and equipment.

Rusty stepped aside and motioned for me to go first, then grabbed my arm, "Hold up, Dad. We need to back away."

I looked at him like he was crazy and started to object, "What's the probl—" Then I saw it.

"Grizzly bear, Dad. On the porch."

"Good Lord!"

Rusty and I slowly backed away as the big bear awoke from its nap and nonchalantly meandered down the steps of the front porch and around the side of the house to the backyard.

"You don't suppose that's his pet, do you?" I said.

"I doubt it, there's a lot of bears in this country and they have to sleep somewhere."

With the grizzly bear out of the way, we ascended the five steps to the top of the porch where I knocked on the door. There was no response at first, so I knocked again. Then we heard the distinct sound of a slide action charging a live round into the chamber of a shotgun.

"Do you suppose that's for the bear, or for us?" I said to Rusty.

"I expect it's for either-or," Rusty said as he tried to peer through the window.

I took a step back from the door and motioned for Rusty to do the same, while simultaneously unfastening the strap securing the Glock seventeen still in my holster.

With our right hands on our weapons, we waited and watched to see what would happen next. Soon I saw a finger pull back the corner of the paper curtain that covered the small window at the top of the door. A grizzled old pair of eyes peered out, looking first at me, then at Rusty.

A muffled and crotchety sounding voice from within the house yelled out, "Whatd-r-ya-want?"

"We'd like to look at your truck," I hollered back.

"Whichin?" he said, in what sounded to me like South Carolina modified English.

I looked at Rusty with a quizzical expression. He looked at me and silently mouthed the words, "Both of them."

"Both of them," I answered, emphatically.

We could hear a couple of lock bolts slide, and watched the door knob turn as it opened about an inch and a half.

"Whoeerya?"

"My name is Lou Worley and this is my son-in-law, Rusty German. I was also a log truck driver before I retired."

With only one eyeball looking at us through the gap in the door, we heard the man say, "What-der-ya-want-eh-nother-truck-fur, ifn-yas, re-tarred?"

"I think I might fix it up for my grandson, he seems to like trucks."

"Taint-nothin-rong-withit, thwayitiz."

"That's good. Will you show it to us anyway?"

The door eventually opened and a weathered old gentleman appearing to be in his early hundreds, stooped over from, probably, among other things, arthritis and rheumatism to every other degenerative affliction known to old people, slung his pump action 12 gauge shotgun over his shoulder and stepped out onto the porch.

I said to him, "Good morning to you, Sir. My name is Lou Worley, this is my—."

"Ya-said-that, ahridy. Trks-thataway," he interrupted, gesturing toward the old pickup. The old man waved his hand indicating that we should follow as he shuffled his way across the porch to the steps leading down to the ground. I figured it also meant, stay behind him.

"Do you carry that shotgun on account of the bears? We just saw a grizzly bear leave your front porch and head toward your back-yard." I pointed in that direction.

"Themthar bars ain't bothern-nothin."

"What did you say your name is?" I asked.

"Aintsed-yit."

I decided to leave it at that. I figured I would find out soon enough when I looked at the registration or the title of the vehicle.

The old man held tightly to the porch banister as one step at a time he descended the stair. When he reached the bottom he stopped and motioned for me to come closer.

"Git-uphair-sonnee, I-gotsta-hang-arn-ter-ya."

I moved closer to him and took hold of his arm. He shook my hand away and impatiently grabbed at my coat sleeve.

"Maybe if you left your shotgun in the house…" I didn't get to finish before he grabbed at my arm.

"Itsa-furpeice-out-thar-sonnee, whin-yers-oldaz-me."

I wondered if he was talking about his front yard, or South Carolina.

"How long have you had that old Dodge pick-up truck?" I asked.

"Boternuu-sonnee, bakn…fifteewon."

"When's the last time it ran?"

"Aint-shr, maybe-a-weekertu."

I was a little shocked. I could tell that Rusty was too.

"Do *you* still drive?"

"Not-nur-more, dauter-dus-tho, sheez-a-crazy-one-thatn."

"Whatrya…I mean, what are you selling it for if your daughter still drives it?" I could hear Rusty chuckling behind me.

"Jist-em, thar-she-iz-rightsh-yonder."

"What? The bear?"

"Tarnation-sonnee, you-gotsta-pay-some-tention—the-pikyup-truck!"

"Oh! I see."

Rusty and I stepped closer to the old Dodge and peered inside. There was a pile of trash in the floorboard and what appeared to be mud smears all over the seat, not all of which was dried, as if someone had driven it shortly after falling into a mud puddle. Other than that the old truck looked to be in darn good shape for its age.

"Does it run good?"

"Jizt-laka-top-sonnee, start-er-upn-see."

Rusty lifted the hood on the old girl.

"Hey, Dad, this truck was just run. The motor's still warm."

I said to the old man, "It looks like someone has been driving this truck today."

"Don't thinkso-sonnee. Aint-seen-th-yungn-fur-nigh-on-aweek-er-tu."

Rusty checked the water and oil and climbed in. At first he just sat there looking around.

"What are you looking for?" I asked.

"The key. there isn't even—"

I pointed at the floor board. "There is no key, see that switch on your left, that's the master switch. The starter is on the floor above the gas pedal," I said.

Rusty flipped the master switch on, pumped the gas several times and mashed on the floor-mounted starter. The old flathead-six turned over twice, started, coughed a couple of times, and in no time at all was purring like a basket full of Maine-Coons.

I turned to the old man, "Sounds like it runs good enough. How much are you asking?"

"Whatl-ya-gimmee-furit-sonnee?"

I was starting to become infatuated with the old man's way of getting right to the point, yet also thought maybe I should look into building a few learning centers in South Carolina.

"Well, Mister...what did you say your name is?"

"Grady."

"Well, Mr. Grady—"

"Perkins," he interrupted. "Namzs-Grady Perkins."

"Mr. Perkins, it appears to me that this is a one owner vehicle, which makes it worth a lot more to me. So how about I give you three-hundred dollars, cash money, right here and now?"

"Yur-wastn-muh-tym-sonnee."

Grady Perkins turned to go back to his house. I didn't figure he would get there right away, so I said to Rusty, "How much do you think I should offer him?"

"I'm not sure, but if we restored it to its original condition it could be worth upwards of fifty to a hundred grand.

I caught up with Grady and said to him, "How about a thousand dollars?"

Grady didn't even slow down. Of course he couldn't or he would have been going backward.

"Ten-thousand, I'll give you ten-thousand dollars for it."

"Ah-rekn-thtl-do," Grady said as he kept shuffling his way toward the house. "Duya-wontsta-see-the-log-n-trk-tu?" he asked, without looking back.

"Ah-rekn-thisnll-du-fur-now," I said facetiously. "You want cash or cashier's check?"

"Cash money."

I said to Rusty, "He certainly knows how to say *that* in plain English."

Rusty couldn't control himself any longer. On the other hand, I failed to see the humor in it. Between his uncontrolled fits of laughter, he said to me, "Dad, don't you realize what just happened?"

"Yeah, I bought us some transportation."

"Yes you did. But you also got *played*."

"What do you mean *played?*"

"As in swindled, by an old man from some Carolina holler, that can't even speak English."

"You're the one who said it would be worth a hundred-thousand dollars if we restored it."

Rusty eventually stopped laughing enough to get real, "Yes, I did, but first we'll need to find the right guy for the job."

"When we're done with it we can give it to the auto body shop at the learning center as a project. They'll restore it and use the profit for the school," I said

"Good idea. Dad. In that case, I think you made a great investment."

"I'm glad you think so. Therefore, you won't mind flying your plane back to Sitka and getting the money to pay Grady, while I go see Leroy."

"Not a problem, Dad, be glad to." Rusty headed toward the airstrip. I could still hear him chuckling even after he had disappeared around the corner.

CHAPTER 8

Over twenty-four hours had passed since I left Elizabeth at Leroy's little shanty on the north end of town. I had asked her to watch him while he continued to sober up so I could ask him a few questions. I wasn't sure if Leroy knew much of anything that would help me with the case but it was worth a try. Then again, maybe he knew too much, and that's the reason he stayed drunk.

I still wasn't completely sure Elizabeth would follow through with her deal with me, so as I walked by the tavern on the way through town, I knocked on the door to see if she was there. There was no answer and it didn't appear that anyone was around, so I continued on up the street to Leroy's dilapidated shanty…I mean, residence.

The door to the shack was ajar, which made me wonder if someone had broken in. I called out before I entered, "Leroy? Elizabeth? Anybody home?" There was no reply so I pushed the door opened and stepped inside.

The place was a mess. Clutter, clothes, magazines, and newspapers were strewn about in every room. Moldy food sat un-eaten on the table and evidence of mice lay scattered across the kitchen counter. Then I saw it. Sitting on the table was a relatively new package of chew, containing a half dozen individual containers. Instantly I began inspecting the beer cans. None of them were missing their tabs.

I looked into what appeared to be a bedroom. The only furniture there was a pre-historic television sitting on an apple box and a filthy smelling mattress lying on the floor; more dirty clothes, beer cans and trash cluttered the area.

"How can people live like this?" I muttered to myself. I was about to leave when I heard footsteps. Someone was approaching from the outside.

I drew my weapon and moved to the window, but did not get there before the door opened and in walked Elizabeth. She saw the gun and gasped, as she threw up her hands. "Don't shoot, Mr. Worley, it's only me."

"Elizabeth! I didn't expect you. Where is Leroy?"

"Isn't he here?"

"No, he isn't, unfortunately." I did not want to show my irritation at her for not watching Leroy like I had asked her to do, and for which I had paid her, handsomely. But I think she picked up on it anyway.

"I'm sorry, Mr. Worley. He was asleep when I left. I needed to go back to my place for a while. I thought I could—"

I held my hand out and said to her, "I'll take back that last C-note I gave you."

Elizabeth stared at me in bewilderment, "I, I don't have it."

"What did you do with it?"

"I…owed someone some money so I—"

"Don't lie to me, Elizabeth. I paid you in advance to do something for me and you didn't do it, plus you spent the money. What am I supposed to do, just walk away?"

Elizabeth's expression turned from deference to defiance. "Well, it isn't like you can't afford it. Everyone knows you're super rich."

"Yes, I am, but that has nothing to do with our agreement. I made you a proposition that would set you up for the rest of your life and you're not holding up your end of the bargain. So, I'll give you one last opportunity, give me the money back and tell me you won't ever let me down again, or the deal is off."

Elizabeth thought for a moment, then slowly reached in her brazier and handed me the crumpled one-hundred-dollar bill. I took it and said to her, "Do we still have a deal?"

"I guess so, but does this mean I'm your slave now or what?"

I laughed, "Of course not. It's slavery I'm trying to help you out of. It's when you're not in control of your own destiny that you're a slave, and the one who owns you is the one to whom you give your power. The first thing you need to understand is how to keep your agreements. Keeping agreements is your statement to the world of who you are. And know this, if you don't keep your agreements with me, I'm not going to invest my money in your future. If you don't like my proposition, you can walk away anytime, but don't make an agreement with me, take my money, and then not keep it. On the other hand, if you really want to take your life in a different direction, this is your chance. I'm giving you one more opportunity right here and now. Are you in or out?"

Tears were looming in the corners of Elizabeth's eyes. She wiped at them with her shirt sleeve as she nodded her head. "I'm sorry, Mr. Worley. Yes, I'm in. It's just that…"

"Just that what?"

"I've never known anyone to keep their word to me before, so when you didn't come back…"

"I can understand that, Elizabeth. But I'm here to change all of that. However, if you really want change you'll need to work with me and trust me implicitly. Can you do that?"

"I'll try."

"I don't want you to try. I want you to do it. It's not an option, it's a decision. Will you trust me or not?"

"I will, Mr. Worley. Honest, I will, I'm sorry."

"Apology accepted, but I also want your word you will never lie to me again."

"I won't, Mr. Worley, I promise."

"Okay then, let's get down to business. I stopped by your tavern a while ago. Did you hear me knock?"

"No, sir, I was in the back."

"Where do you think Leroy went?"

"He's probably looking for something to drink."

"Is there any more alcohol available in town other than your place?"

"Nothing legitimate, but we can go to his mother's place, she might know where he is."

"Where does she live?"

"A couple of blocks from here."

"All right, let's go. I'll follow you."

Elizabeth looked at my sidearm. "Do you always carry a gun?"

"I do around here. Yesterday, I walked up on a grizzly bear sleeping on a man's porch."

"Who's place was that?"

"A fellow named Grady Perkins, do you know him?"

Elizabeth was quiet for a moment, somewhat distant in her reply. "I know his daughter."

"What is her name?"

"Karen."

"How old is she?"

"Forty something, maybe early to mid-forties."

"Is there anything strange about her?"

"Why do you ask?" Elizabeth said, somewhat defensively.

"No reason, just wondered."

"She's quiet, keeps to herself a lot." Elizabeth pointed to an old run down building made of weathered plywood and rusted metal roofing, "This is Mildred's place."

"Who is Mildred?"

"Leroy's mother."

Mildred's home was not much different than Leroy's—another squalor. It was a small rectangular building with one door and a broken window in the front; boarded up to keep the rain and snow from blowing into the house. The door had been kicked open so many times it would no longer close all the way and was held shut by a chair set against it from the inside. I knocked twice, and announced myself.

"State police, may I come in?" Muffled voices from within told me someone was home, so I pushed open the door and stuck my head inside.

"Leroy, it's Lou Worley of the state police, I'm coming in."

I stepped into the doorway and was met by a petite elderly native woman who began crying and begging me not to take her son away.

"Ma'am, I'm not here to take your son, I just need to talk to Leroy. Is he here?"

I heard another voice and saw movement coming from a back room. Reaching for my sidearm, I called out, "Leroy, is that you?"

"Uh-huh."

Leroy was a full blood descendant of the Tlingit Indian tribe that had survived in Southeast Alaska for at least a millennium. He was of medium build, maybe a hundred-forty pounds and only an inch or two over five-feet tall. He appeared to be nervous and was either trying to put something in, or get something out of his back pocket.

"Leroy, I need to talk to you, and I need you to keep your hands where I can see them, please."

"WhadidIdo?"

"I'm not here because I think you did anything wrong. I need to talk to the VPO. You are the VPO aren't you?"

Leroy began to perk up a little.

"Yup. I gotta badge somewhere in my stuff." He continued to pull at his rear pants pocket until finally producing a Velcro stick-on patch that identified him as the village police officer. Leroy carelessly slapped the patch against his chest, but it fell to the floor.

"Do you have a jacket you wear with that badge?" I asked.

"Yup, somewhere."

"Let's see if we can find it."

I motioned for Elizabeth to help him look for his jacket. I felt that Leroy would be more apt to help me with the information I needed if he was not only reminded of his appointed position but appreciated for it as well.

"Is this your coat, Leroy?" Elizabeth said, holding up a wool-lined Carhart jacket.

"Yup." Leroy took the jacket and slid it on over his sleeveless arms and I pressed the VPO badge against the Velcro sewn over the breast pocket of his coat.

"There now, Leroy, you are officially on duty and I need to get some information from you about a murder that has taken place near here. Do you know anything about that?"

"Nope, ain't heard eh no murder."

"Have you ever seen anyone that chews tobacco and spits into a beer can or pop can?"

"Yup."

"Can you give me a name?"

"Nope."

"Why not?"

"Don't know everybody."

I turned to Elizabeth, "What does he mean by that?"

"He means almost everybody does that, and he doesn't know everybody."

"Oh! All right then, what about the cult up on the hill, do you know anyone from up there?"

For the first time Leroy looked into my eyes.

"Yup, there's a girl I once knew that went there until…"

"Until what?"

"Until she didn't come back no more."

"When was this?" I asked, leaning forward.

"Maybe two years ago, her name was Falling Feather. She lived with the prophet's people on the hill, but would sneak into town sometimes to eat sea-food. I would catch it for her."

"How old was Falling Feather?"

"Maybe thirteen or fourteen, she had a tattoo on the side of her ankle."

"A tattoo of what?" I asked.

"A tattoo of a bird sitting on a branch, a whippoorwill, I think, with a feather falling to the ground."

"Which ankle?"

Leroy paused to recollect.

"Her right ankle."

"Was Falling Feather Tlingit?"

"Nope, she was from Montana, belonged to the Rosebud Sioux from the Dakota country."

"What was your relationship with her?"

"Sometimes she would come here to stay with the Old One." Leroy indicated toward the other room, "But she would go to other places too."

I turned to Elizabeth. "What does he mean, Old One?"

"He means his grandmother."

"Where is she?" I asked. "I thought that lady in there was his mother." I pointed to the first room I had entered when I came in the house.

"She's Leroy's mother, and kind of a surrogate grandmother to most of the kids in the village."

I turned back to Leroy. "Did you have any kind of personal relationship with Falling Feather that was of a physical nature?"

"No, sir, Officer Worley. She was too young for that. She was like a little sister."

I watched Leroy closely as I questioned him, and it didn't appear to me that he was trying to hide anything, so I left that subject and moved on to the next.

"Leroy, have you ever been up to the cult compound, or do you know anyone up there?"

Leroy was quiet and began to fidget around as if he were at a loss for words.

"What is it, Leroy? Do you know someone up there or not?"

"Yup, my brother is one of the guards. We wanted to be policemen, but washed out of the academy. They made me the village policeman and my brother got a job working for the prophet on the hill."

"What's your brother's name?"

"Larry Mauktokta."

"Is Larry one of the prophet's understudies?"

"Nope, he hasn't been there long enough to be trusted in that way. He just works there as a gate guard. But, he doesn't work alone, there is always one of the other guards on duty with him."

"Thanks, Leroy. You've been a great help. One more thing, do you get paid as a VPO?"

"Nope."

"How would you like to work for me? I'll pay you, but you have to promise me something."

"Like what?"

"Promise me you won't drink any more. You won't be of any use to me if you are drunk, and I've hired Elizabeth to help you with that. Will you promise?"

"How much will you pay me?"

I pulled one of the last of the two one-hundred dollar bills I had left in my pocket, and handed it to Leroy.

"I'll give you this one-hundred-dollar bill now, and another one when the job is completed. Will that be enough?"

Leroy reached out and grabbed the money out of my hand as if I might change my mind before he could say, *yup*.

"Yup. What do I have to do?"

"I'll let you know when the time comes. Right now I just need you to stay sober and watch for anyone around town that looks like they might be from that compound up on the hill."

"Yes, sir, Officer Worley, you can count on me."

I wasn't at all sure what I expected from Leroy. I think I just wanted to help him. My hope was he would be another set of eyes and ears for me around town. If nothing else, at least maybe we could keep him off the booze long enough for him to start thinking straight and possibly talk him into going to school at the learning center. He was only about twenty-two or twenty-three years old and I felt that with some specified schooling and some good counseling, he might still have a shot at realizing his dream. After all, Leroy and his brother are the perfect examples of why I invested in the building of those schools in the first place.

It actually all started back in the mid-nineties when I got a call from SAR (search and rescue) to join in a search for a downed pilot up on the Yukon River.

My boys and I were in the middle of our second gold mining season at the Alfred Creek mine and were just beginning to get into some really rich ground, right on top the bedrock. I left my three son's-in-law to fend for themselves, jumped into my Cessna 180, Skywagon and joined in the search with two other pilots from Fairbanks, one of which was a friend of mine named, Jerod Aikin.

A Christian missionary from the village of Venetie, 160-miles north of Fairbanks, by the name of Bill Shearer had gone missing. Pastor Bill and his wife Sharon, of forty-five years, had lived and ministered among the native Alaskan Intuits'-for almost forty years.

As luck would have it, there had been a rash of aircraft emergencies throughout the state of Alaska at the time Bill decided to have his turn at it, which is why there was just the three of us looking for him.

After three days we were down to just Jerod and me. Around the middle of the next afternoon I was meandering along the mile-wide Yukon River about seventy-miles north of Fairbanks. The ceilings had me down to about two-hundred feet under a solid four-hundred-foot overcast. Suddenly, I saw smoke coming from an old dilapidated cabin.

I had just begun a counter-clockwise circle around the cabin when a man ran out waving an orange construction vest. He was pointing to the west. I leveled my wings in that direction and there at the south end of a short landing strip, alongside the river, I saw the mangled remains of a 1949 Piper Clipper.

Of course, it was the missionary Bill Shearer, and long story short, Bill and I became great friends. It was he who suggested to me that I should do something for the Alaska natives. The boys and I were doing well in the mining business and because of Bill's mighty persuasive powers of persuasion, I agreed with him that it was only right to re-invest into the economies of Alaska by sponsoring the education and training of the Alaskan natives. That is the story of how the William Shearer Centers for Learning were imagined and ultimately brought to fruition. Since then, hundreds and even thousands of out-of-work, alcoholic, drug-addicted Alaskan natives as well as many Native Americans, African Americans and Caucasians have not only recovered from their addictions but retrained or learned new skills altogether, on their way to becoming productive contributors to the economies of Alaskan towns and villages.

Sad to say, my good friend Bill Shearer was murdered by the drug lords, whose drug profits were significantly diminished by the many lost customers that had gone through our drug rehabilitation facilities, successfully kicking their debilitating habits.

This was what I had in mind for Leroy. Needless to say, I had to be certain Elizabeth was on the same page with me in regard to that matter.

I had given Elizabeth back the hundred-dollar bill I took from her and again left her with Leroy, with instructions to watch him and keep him sober while I got back to the business of catching a killer. I headed back to the airstrip and as I was passing Grady's place my phone rang. It was Rusty.

"Hey, Dad, I'll be on the ground in ten-minutes. I brought the ten-grand, plus an extra five-grand, just in case you might want to buy a boat or something."

"You're a barrel of laughs, but that's okay, we might need to hire a few other people."

"Hire other people for what?"

"To get them on our side so they're not so apt to shoot at us from the other side."

"Who are you talking about?"

"I'll tell you when you get here. Meet me at Grady's."

"Okay, Pop, watch out for that bear."

I was already at Grady's house by the time Rusty arrived. I paid the old man for the truck and a grin spread across his face so large it made him look thirty years younger. I began to wonder if maybe it was me who was the one getting old and losing it. After all, it isn't everyone that would pay ten-thousand dollars for a tired-out pick-up truck that hadn't been new in over sixty-years.

Rusty opened the driver's side door and began rummaging through the trash on the floorboard and behind the seat of the old truck.

"This thing is sure dirty inside. You'd think for that kind of money he could have at least cleaned it up."

"We'll clean it up later, right now I want to drive up to that cult compound and see if we can get past those guards and maybe speak to that self-proclaimed prophet."

"Hey, Dad, look at this." Rusty held up an empty cardboard container of Copenhagen, chewing tobacco.

"Where did you find that?"

"It was under the seat."

"Let's see what else is under the seat."

I put the empty container in my shirt pocket and joined Rusty in carefully examining every piece of trash in the truck.

"You might want to see this too, but don't touch it." Rusty was holding an empty beer can between his thumb and forefinger—a beer can that was missing it's pull tab.

"Is there tobacco juice in it?" I asked

"I don't know, I didn't taste it, but it's about half full of something."

"Check the rest of these cans. I have some plastic bags in the Kodiak we can use to protect this evidence. But don't touch anything else in the truck or even the truck itself."

"Do you think this truck is part of the case now?"

"It's very possible. Just in case, we need to get a forensic team out here to go through it and look for any DNA evidence that might connect the first three victims to this truck. And find that girl, Karen, as soon as possible."

"Who's Karen?"

"Karen is Grady's daughter."

"Is that the one the old man called a 'crazyone'?"

"Probably, unless he has more than one daughter. Rusty, if you don't mind, will you stay here with this vehicle? I need to run up to the Kodak. I'll be back shortly."

"Sure. Dad."

I checked my phone for a signal—which in Kake, Alaska, can be there one minute and gone the next, and sent Rudy a text message.

Need u @airpt asap.

I rummaged through the cupboards in the Kodiak until I found a dozen twelve-inch by twelve-inch plastic seal-tight food bags and stuffed all but one of them in my coat pocket. From my shirt pocket I retrieved the cloth sample of the most recent victim's sweater, along with the blood sample on the leaf we had found under the cyclone fence up on the hill and the tobacco juice Rusty had retrieved from the crime scene. The beer tab I kept in my pocket. I then took a black marker pen and identified the evidence samples along with the time and place each one was recovered. The empty snus carton I put in a smaller sandwich bag.

Placing each one in a cabinet in the airplane, I locked the door and retraced my steps back to where I had left Rusty, all the while expecting to meet up with Rudy at any moment.

When I arrived at Grady's, Rusty was nowhere to be seen and the old Dodge pickup was gone. I looked around for Rudy, but didn't see him either.

I checked my phone to see if he had responded to my text. There were no new messages. Suddenly, I heard footsteps coming up the road. I drew my weapon and concealed myself behind some bushes. A moment later Rudy walked by Grady's driveway on his way to the airstrip.

"Rudy," I called out in a whispered voice.

He turned around, surprised. "Mr. Worley, are you expecting trouble?"

I realized I was still holding my weapon in my hand so I secured it back into its holster.

"Did you see Rusty go by, driving an old Dodge pickup truck?"

Rudy looked at me quizzically.

"How old?"

"Real old. 1951, to be exact."

"I saw an old truck like that but didn't see Rusty, why?"

"I just bought it from the old guy that lives here, and it had some evidence in it that might be connected to the murders. Which way was the truck going?"

"North, out of town."

"Did you see who was driving it?"

"Some big guy and a lady."

"What did they look like?"

"You'll probably laugh at me, but as soon as I saw him I thought it was that movie star that used to play, what's his name?"

"Maverick?" I said, impatiently.

"Yeah, that's him."

"What about the girl? What did she look like?"

"Didn't see her too well. She was sitting on the other side of the truck. But she had long hair and kept her head down like she didn't want anyone to know who she was."

"Was there anything in the back of the truck?"

"I didn't notice."

"Well, let's look around here first and see if we can figure out what happened."

"Do you think they took Rusty too?"

"Either took him or did something to him. If we can't find him we'll jump in the air and see if we can spot that truck from up above. Check all around the yard, I'll see if the old man heard anything."

I left Rudy to search the front and back yards of Grady's place while I headed for the house. I was so focused on getting to the front door to talk to Grady, I didn't even notice what was on the porch.

Bam, Bam, Bam. I pounded on the door with my fist while standing on my tiptoes in an effort to see through the window. Suddenly I heard a groan and saw movement out of my right peripheral vision. I grabbed at my Glock and had it almost clear of the holster when I realized it was Rusty lying injured on the porch, attempting to get up.

"Rusty!" I yelled, running to him. "What happened?" I re-holstered my weapon and knelt beside him while doing a rapid examination to determine the extent of his injuries. Suddenly, the front door opened.

"Whathe-tarnation-hellsgoinon-har?"

I turned to see a 12-gauge shotgun pointed at my head. Frantically, I lunged forward over the top of Rusty and swung my left arm in a high arc, catching the underside of the gun barrel just enough to redirect it away from my face.

The blast went off within twelve inches of my head and nearly burst my eardrums. When I lunged toward the shotgun my momentum had carried me head first against the side of the house with half my body still on top of Rusty. I couldn't hear anything except the ringing in my ears, but I still had sense enough to keep my eye on Old Man Perkins, who was rapidly recovering from the blast that had knocked him backwards against the door, and who was presently in the process of jacking another live round into the still-smoking chamber of his 12-gauge.

I had landed on my right side, which is where my weapon was holstered, and had to maneuver my body in a position that would permit me to get to it. But Grady was way ahead of me, and by the time I had my hand on the Glock to pull it, he was already reloaded with his finger on the trigger and once again taking aim at my head.

Pop, pop, pop. The gunshots from Rudy's 9mm Berretta sounded like they were coming from the other end of a tunnel, a million miles away.

The shotgun slipped from the old man's hands as his body slumped face forward onto the porch—deader than a box of hammers.

"Mr. Worley, are you all right?" Rudy ascended the steps in two bounds.

"What's that you say?"

Rudy stepped closer and raised his voice, "I said, are you all right?"

I couldn't make out the audible words, but recognized them as his lips formed the words in slow motion.

"I think so, but Rusty is hurt bad," I yelled, barely able to hear my own voice.

Rudy ran to him and helped him sit up with his back against the front wall of the house. I sat down next to Rusty and took a deep breath. Slowly, my hearing began to return.

"Thanks, Rudy, you just saved my life."

"Don't mention it, Mr. Worley."

"How's Rusty? Has he been shot?"

"No, just hit in the head. He's starting to come around now."

"As soon as you can get him on his feet, we'll take him to urgent care at the learning center and have him checked out."

"I'm all right, Dad." Rusty was sitting up and rubbing his head."

"What happened to you, son?"

"I'm not sure. I was waiting for you one minute, and now here we are sitting on the porch. Maybe you could tell me."

"Let's go inside and sit on one of the old man's couches. It doesn't look like he'll be using them anymore." For the first time Rusty realized that the dead body of Old Man Perkins was lying next to him on the porch.

"My God! Is that Grady? What happened?"

"Rudy and I were looking for you. I had just knocked on the door to see if Grady knew anything about where you went when I saw you lying on the porch. When I went over to check on you, Grady come out the door with his shotgun and was about to blow my head off. Thank God, Rudy came around the corner when he did. If it wasn't for him, we'd *both* be dead by now."

"That's it, I remember now. I was watching the truck." Rusty stopped short and looked around. "By-the-way, where *is* the truck?"

"We don't know. Rudy saw someone that looked like Kerrigan driving the old Dodge through town. He had a passenger with him, a lady. We think it was Grady's daughter, Karen."

Rudy and I helped Rusty to his feet and we all went inside Grady's house to sit on something more comfortable.

There wasn't much in the way of furniture in the house, and what furniture there was, was covered with stacks of newspaper and cardboard boxes. I scraped the bundles of paper off a recliner nearby and helped Rusty into it. Then I cleared off the end of a sofa and also sat down.

I turned to the man who had just saved my life. "Rudy, will you have a look around? There should be ten-thousand dollars around here someplace that I gave to Grady earlier for that old truck." Rudy's eyes grew wide.

"You gave him ten-thousand dollars for that old thing?"

"Yeah, but since they took the truck I want the money back, if it's still here." Rudy began looking through the house.

"Rusty, let me know when you feel like walking up to the airstrip. We'll head back to Sitka."

"I'm okay, Dad, honest. We need to get that truck back."

"Not much point in it now. By the time we find it, they'll have cleaned it all out and chances are, we've lost our DNA evidence."

"So, you think that truck was used to move body's around?" Rusty asked.

"Not only that, but I'm sure those beer cans contained the DNA of the killer. Why else would they hit you over the head to get it back?"

"I don't know, maybe they thought we were stealing it. It seems to me that if they were the real killers and wanted me dead, I would be dead by now."

"Maybe whoever hit you over the head thought they were hitting you hard enough to kill you and left you for dead."

"Maybe, except how did I wind up on the porch?"

"You mean you didn't walk up here?"

"No, I would have remembered walking, I think."

"Whoever hit you might have thought you were dead and put you on the porch to hide you long enough for them to get away."

"Maybe, but I don't think the people who hit me and took the truck are the actual killers."

"Then why did Grady try to kill us both?"

"I don't know that either. Maybe he thought you were here to steal the money back. This *was* in fact his home. Maybe he was just defending his self and his property."

I thought about what Rusty was saying, but it all still seemed too bizarre to me, to be that simple.

"Mr. Worley…catch." I turned towards Rudy's voice, just in time to see a package sailing through the air in my direction.

"Good catch, Dad," Rusty said. "Is that the money?"

"Yeah, same money, different package. Looks like it's all here, though. Rusty, are you ready to go?"

"I guess so, if you insist."

"Rudy, do you see anything else around here that might be relevant to our case?"

"You mean like dead bodies?"

"That too, judging from the smell of this place. Remember, what we don't find now cannot be considered legal evidence until we get a search warrant."

"Why get a search warrant?" Rudy said.

"Cause that's the way the law works. We're cops, remember?"

"From listening to you two guy's I get the impression that the cops don't want anything to do with this case and that's why they sent you down here."

"What could we do that the state police couldn't do?" I asked.

"Find out what's going on around here, find the killers, and make it all go away."

"Are you suggesting we just kill them all and go back home?"

"Not me, but your Captain Daily might be suggesting that. Maybe you should talk to him again and see just how interested he is in bringing a forensic team down here now that you have not only a vehicle that may have been used in several crimes but also a dead body. He'll probably have to send half his department.

"Rudy's right, Dad, I'll bet you anything Captain Daily purposely put you with Kerrigan because he knew you would figure out what's going on around here and could make it all go away."

I thought about what Rudy and Rusty were suggesting, but not for very long. I said to them, "I think both of you guys have been smoking your breakfast. Let's go. We're going to take Rusty to the hospital."

I rose from the filthy chair I was sitting in and headed for the door. Suddenly we heard a muffled voice coming from under the house.

"Dad, did you hear that?"

"I heard something. Sounded like someone talking downstairs. Is there a basement in this place?"

"Maybe, let's find out."

Rudy was already ahead of us so I followed him, and Rusty followed me.

"I don't see a door, other than the back door to the backyard." Rudy said.

"What about a—"

"Here's something," Rudy said, as he peered into a walk-in pantry.

"There's another door in here, but it's got a padlock on it."

Rusty handed me a fireplace poker that had been leaning against the wall by the back door.

"Here, try this."

I handed it to Rudy.

"Be careful when you open that door. There could be another shooter waiting for us."

Rudy soon had the padlock ripped off and carefully opened the door.

"It's dark down there. Does anyone have a flashlight?"

"Rusty, see if you can find a flashlight."

"There's one right above your head, Pop, on that shelf."

I handed the flashlight to Rudy, who began making his way down the stairs to what appeared to be a root cellar.

I pulled my weapon and followed close behind him.

"Is anybody here? This is the Alaska State Police, Is anybo--?

A raspy voice called out from the dark, "It's about damn time you got here, Lou Worley. What the hell took you so long?"

"Kerrigan, is that you?"

"Who the hell else do you think it is, you beautiful son of a---."

"Kerrigan, if you would learn how to talk to people, maybe they wouldn't lock you up in basements to shut your vulgar mouth. How did you wind up in here, anyway?"

"I woke up in this cage, the night before last."

"Are you hurt?"

"Just my head. Some son-of-a—"

"Rudy, hold the flashlight on the lieutenant."

"Are you tied up or handcuffed?"

"Handcuffed, the old man took the key."

"Rudy, go see if the old man still has the key on him. I'll take the flashlight."

I held the light on the stairs for Rudy so we wouldn't wind up with another head injury and then shined it around the root cellar.

"This is pretty cramped quarters, Lieutenant. Have you had anything to eat or drink since they brought you here?"

"Some woman brought me a little water a couple of hours ago. But that's all."

"Well, we'll get you and Rusty both over to urgent care at the learning center. They'll check you out and get you re-hydrated. Looks like you need cleaned up too. "What happened to you, anyway? How did you wind up over here? You were supposed to meet me at the airport yesterday morning. What happened with that?"

"I went to that bar-n-grill you told me about. What was it?"

"The Dockside."

"That's it, the Dockside. Anyway, some guy seated me. I ordered a drink and went to the restroom. When I returned, my drink was on the table so I tossed it back and ordered another. While I was waiting I returned to the van to get the police files on the three victims."

"Where are those files now?" I asked.

"I'm getting to that, just hold your horses. I was on the way back to the bar when everything started going fuzzy."

"Are you saying someone spiked your drink?"

"I would if you'd quit interrupting me."

"Sorry."

"Anyway, I saw those two coming toward me. That was when the lights went out."

"What two?"

"Some really big guy. Hits like a mule. He was leaving the bar with that lady that brought me the water. Anyway, all of a sudden he took a swing at me. I don't remember anything after that."

"So they got the files, is that right?"

"Yeah, I guess."

"I thought you were the best homicide detective in the whole wide world."

"Did you really? Why didn't you tell me? I would have bought your dinner."

"If you'd have taken me with you when you went to dinner in the first place, this wouldn't have happened."

"How do you figure that?" Kerrigan pointed at Rusty. "He was with you, and look what happened to him." I looked at my son-in-law. He was rubbing his sore head.

The lieutenant had a point, so I let it go.

"So, you saw some guy, with Karen, then what?"

"Who's Karen?"

"Karen, she's Grady's daughter. She's the one who kidnapped you."

"Who's Grady?"

"He's the dead guy on the porch. This is his hotel you been staying in."

"Oh! You mean the old man is dead? I wondered what all the shooting was about."

"Yeah, we'll tell you about it later. Go ahead with your story." I said, a little impatiently.

"So anyway, the lights went out, and I woke up in this dungeon with blood all over my head and face and a big headache. I think it was the day before yesterday, I'm not sure."

"I thought you said he hit you with his fist?"

"I said he took a swing at me. I don't know what he hit me with. I might have been hit from behind."

"Here's the handcuff key, Mr. Worley," Rudy said as he descended the stairs holding another flashlight he had found.

"It sounds like there might have been three of them."

"Maybe, plus the one that spiked my drink," Kerrigan replied.

In a few minutes we were all sitting back in Grady's living room while Lieutenant Mark Kerrigan's eyes adjusted to the light of day.

"Here you go, Lieutenant. I made you a baloney sandwich," Rudy said. "Here's one for you too, Mr. Worley."

"Thanks, Rudy."

"Who are these guys?" Kerrigan asked.

"The big one is my son, Rusty."

"This is your son?" Kerrigan seemed surprised.

"My son-in-law. He's married to my oldest daughter."

"What are they doing here?"

"Well, you disappeared on me, so I called Rusty to come down and give me a hand."

"Who's this other guy that you have fetching flashlights for you?"

"He's our bodyguard, pretty good one too. Only been here a few hours and has already saved all three of our lives, plus made you a sandwich. So you should show him some appreciation."

"No big deal, I would have figured a way out of here sooner or later."

Rusty and Rudy both looked at me with their mouths opened.

"Mr. Worley, you want me to put him back in his cage?" Rudy asked.

"Naw, just ignore him. He doesn't know the meaning of the word *grateful*, but because he's a good detective, and we need him, we'll let him live for now."

"What-da-ya-mean, Worley? As soon as I realized it was you, I called you a 'beautiful-son—"

"I know what you called me."

"All right then, how much more grateful do you want me to get?"

"Eat your sandwich and let's go."

"So, which one of you killed the old man?" Kerrigan asked.

"I did," Rudy confessed.

"What did you kill him for?"

"He was about to shoot me and Rusty." I said.

"How do you know he was going to shoot? Maybe he was just trying to scare you."

"Well, he had already unloaded one double eagle at me, do you really think he was going to miss two times in a row?"

"How long have you guys been here?"

"I've been here two days. Rusty and Rudy got here this morning."

"Have you learned anything since you got here?"

"Yeah, we've learned that the killer chews tobacco and twist off the tabs from his beer cans."

"Really? I thought you were the world's best detective. To listen to you I would have expected you to have solved the case by now."

"I never said that!" Suddenly I realized I was getting defensive.

Rusty raised both his hands.

"Hey, you guys, you sound like a couple of seven-year-old kids. Get over it."

I had to admit, Kerrigan had really gotten under my skin, to the point that I was playing right along with him.

"Okay!" I said. "Here's the deal, Lieutenant. You either agree to work with us on this case, or you can go home. I'm not playing your game anymore."

"What do you mean work with you? This isn't your case, it's mine."

"Not anymore, you work for me now. If you don't like it, we'll put you back in your cage where you belong."

Kerrigan thought for a moment.

"What do you want from me?"

"We've decided we're going to handle this case our way."

"What do you mean by that?" Kerrigan squinted his eyes and looked sideways at me.

"Captain Daily sent me down here for a reason and I believe I've finally figured out what it is."

"Keep talking."

"Daily doesn't have the manpower or budget to spare to investigate this case, so we're going to make it go away for him."

"How are you going to do that?"

"We'll show you if you're willing to work with us."

"I'm listening."

"We think we know who we're looking for now, and have a pretty good idea what's going on around here. As soon as we have the physical proof we need, let's just say, it will never have to go to court where it will likely get thrown out anyway."

Kerrigan sat back against the couch. A sly grin crept across his face.

"Now you know why Daily put me on this case. And why I didn't want you following me around. That's been my intention all along."

Suddenly I got it. It finally made sense to me why Daily wanted me to work with Kerrigan.

"All right then, do we have a deal?"

"You got a deal, Worley, I'm in."

We all helped ourselves to the food Grady had left us in his refrigerator and stashed the old man's remains in his own jail cell in the basement. I tugged on Rudy's coat and motioned for him to step aside.

"Rudy, I think it would be a good idea if you stayed here for a while, at least while we're gone. Try to keep a low profile. Maybe clean up any evidence that we were here. If anyone comes around, hide somewhere and listen in. We might wind up with some valuable information. But don't get caught. They'll kill you if they find you."

"I get it, Mr. Worley. I'm on it."

"Also, search through the place as much as you can without disturbing too much."

"I don't think anyone would notice if I did disturb something. But what am I looking for exactly?"

"I don't know, pictures, drugs, evidence, you name it. You'll know it when you find it. Take pictures of everything you see that looks suspicious."

"Sure thing, Mr. Worley."

"And I'll get you my 10-gauge shotgun out of the Kodiak."
"That's okay, I'll use the old man's 12-gauge if I need it."
"All right, we'll see you when we get back. You be careful, ya hear?"
"I will, Mr. Worley, don't worry about me."
"Oh, and one more thing. Make sure there are no grizzly bears on the porch before you go in or out."
"Grizzly bears?"
"Yeah, just take my word for it."

CHAPTER 9

From Kerrigan's account of what happened to him, I was now inclined to believe it could be the same Mike Elizabeth told me about who I should make my primary suspect; along with Grady's daughter, Karen, who are either the killers or are otherwise involved with the murders. But how could they have possibly known that Kerrigan was the homicide detective assigned to the case? Unless someone on the inside told them. But, who? It would have to be someone who was privy to the information, someone from either the Anchorage cop shop or the Sitka Police department. Furthermore, if someone did inform them, why would they go after Kerrigan and not me? And why didn't they just kill him? It was obvious this was not going to be a cut and dried case.

In Vietnam you didn't have to concern yourself with evidence. They shot at us, and we shot back—cut and dried. In the late nineties when I went to war with the drug lords, the evidence was much more simplistic: airplanes full of white crystal meth and big suitcases full of money. We caught the bad guys and ask them real nice if they would please rat out their partners in crime, then we went after the rest of them until they were all either dead or in jail—cut and dried.

I knew that was exactly what needed to happen here, find Karen, then Mike the Marlboro Man, and induce them all to spill their guts. I mean…ask them real nice.

For the moment, however, the investigation would need to be put on hold while I got Rusty and Kerrigan to urgent care, during which time I fully intended to have a talk with the Maître' D' at the Dockside Bar 'n' Grill.

I slowly opened Grady's front door and checked the porch for sleeping pets before committing myself to stepping out of the house, a good idea in southeast Alaska.

As we walked back to the airport, Rusty said to me, "Dad, why isn't Rudy coming with us?"

"I asked him to stay at Grady's and search the place."

"Don't we need a warrant to do that?"

"*We* do, but *he* doesn't."

"What about the body we left in the basement and the bloodstains on the porch?"

"I have a feeling that after he finishes searching the house, there might be an accidental electrical fire."

"Sounds like a plan. Except for one thing."

"What's that?"

"Where would all the bears go to hibernate?"

"Never thought of that."

"Are you glad I brought Rudy along?"

"I don't think either one of us would still be breathing if you hadn't, or Kerrigan either for that matter."

"Dad, I think we should circle over that compound a couple of times on our way back to Sitka."

"We can do that later. Right now I need to get you and Kerrigan to a doctor."

My son-in-law can be very persuasive sometimes and I could tell he wanted to press the issue.

"It won't take that long to make a couple of turns around the place, and I'm sure Kerrigan won't mind."

"All right, as long as you feel up to it, maybe we'll see that old Dodge from up there. By-the-way, have you seen the inside of the Kodiak since I finished the interior modifications?"

"No! What all did you do to it?"

"Well, Kate and I are getting too old to be tent camping anymore, so I made it into a little apartment."

I approached the aircraft, unlocked the side door, and stepped aside. "Take a look."

Rusty climbed the ladder. "Wow! Dad, this is nice, but where's the bed?"

"Here, let me show you." I stepped past Rusty and un-fastened the hinged hideaway bed. "During the day, it's a table. At night, it's a single

114

bed with a sliding tray on the bottom that slides out into a double bed. The mattresses and bedding are in the luggage compartment.

"Very nice, Dad. What's in here?" Rusty opened a door that from the outside looked like a closet.

"That's my computer station. It slides in and out. There's an outside satellite antenna mounted on top of the airplane."

"Hey, Worley, you've got a pretty neat set-up in here."

I looked up to see Kerrigan coming through the door.

"Lieutenant, if you're tired, you're welcome to strap yourself into this bed and take a nap on the way over to Sitka."

"Thanks, I believe I will."

Rusty grabbed a mattress, and I laid out the bed for Kerrigan to lie on. After being handcuffed to a wall for two days in a dungeon, he welcomed the soft bed and was asleep before Rusty and I even made it to the cockpit.

I flipped on the power switch to the turbine and began going through the startup procedures.

Soon we were airborne and circling above the compound.

"It's not as big as I thought it would be," I said, straining my neck to take in the landscape below.

"Do you have enough battery left in your phone to take some more pictures?"

"I think so." I got out my phone and handed it to Rusty, who took about a dozen pictures of the encampment before the battery completely expired.

"It's like two sides of the tracks down there, a rich side and a ghetto side."

"I'll bet the ghetto side is where the rich side got all their money, whada-ya-think?" Rusty said.

"It wouldn't surprise me."

We circled the camp several more times. I said to Rusty, "We better get out of here before they get suspicious and start shooting at us. Let's head to Sitka and I'll have a closer look at these photos while you and Kerrigan are getting checked out."

The trauma center at the William Shearer Center for Learning has two aid cars. So on the way back to Sitka I called to make arrangements for one of them to pick up my two patients. I told them we would meet them at the school's airstrip. The operator patched me through to the charge nurse in urgent care and I related to her the sketchy details of Rusty's injury to his head and Kerrigan's case of dehydration mixed with another head injury.

Twenty minutes after departing the airstrip at Kake, we touched down at the learning center's private airstrip.

The aid car lit-up its lights and sirens and sped away with my son-in-law and new favorite homicide detective for the one-mile ride to the trauma center. Thoughtfully, I returned to the aircraft and sat down at my computer station.

After downloading the pictures from the cellphone to my laptop and saving them to the picture file, I closely examined the aerial photos of the compound and printed out the ones I thought were of special interest. After which, I drove to the police station and retrieved the DNA samples that as yet had not been sent to the crime lab in Fairbanks.

On the way I called Eric, the chief pilot for the Shearer Worley Foundation's flight operations, and asked him to fly my personal jet down to Sitka. I own a Cessna Citation CJ4 which I keep at my private airfield in Wasilla. Back when I first got it, it was the only business jet made that didn't require a two-man crew. It has great short field capabilities and can land and take-off at full gross weight on a 3,100-foot runway, or less if loaded lightly.

Two hours later I met Eric at the maintenance hangar and handed off the evidence samples to him, with instructions to deliver them personally to the State Police Crime Laboratory in Fairbanks.

"I'll call Captain Daily and asked him to send someone from the lab to meet you. After you drop this package off in Fairbanks I need you to come back here to Sitka and fuel up. Then land the jet over at Kake. It's a four-thousand-foot sod strip and in pretty good shape with good approaches, so you shouldn't have any trouble. I'll be there waiting for you."

"How am I supposed to get home?" Eric asked.

"Home will have to wait for now, Eric. I'm going to need you here for a while."

"Yes, sir, Mr. Worley. See you in about four hours."

I then went into the office and placed a call to Captain Daily. I felt it was only right to give him an update on the status of the investigation and let him know we had found our missing detective.

"Alaska State Patrol, how may I direct your call?"

"Good afternoon, Molly. This is Lou Worley. Is Captain Daily available?"

"I'll check, Mr. Worley. One moment, please."

"This is Daily."

"Captain Daily, Lou Worley here. Do you have a minute?"

"Sure, Lou, what's up? Has Kerrigan shown up yet?"

"We found him. He'd been kidnapped. We actually got into a gunfight with—"

"Wait a minute, Worley. Let me get back with you. Are you on your cell phone?"

"No, I'm—"

"Then hang up. I'll call you on your cell phone."

The familiar ding tone informed me that the captain had terminated the call. I put the office receiver down and checked my cell phone. It had only been on the charger for a short time, but there was already about a thirty percent charge available for talk time. As I was staring at the phone, it began to ring—it was Daily.

"Go ahead, Captain."

"Okay, Lou. Now, what were you saying?"

"I said we got into a gunfight with an old man named Grady over at Kake. He wound up dead and we found Kerrigan locked in a cage in the old guy's basement. We think his daughter might have had something to do with it."

"You mean with Kerrigan's kidnapping, or the murders?"

"Both. And I also think there might be a connection with the religious cult on the hill. By the way, I sent Eric to Fairbanks with the medical examiner's evidence bags. He should be there in about an hour and a half."

"Okay, I'll have a courier from the crime lab meet him at the airport. Anything else?"

"Is that all you have to say? Aren't you a little concerned that we might be in over our heads down here?"

"Not in the least, Worley. And don't call me on the office phone anymore, the less I know the better. Just make this thing go away. When it's done, you and Kerrigan can get together and write up a report. Leave out anything that I won't be able to explain."

"What about the lab work?"

"I'll see that it gets top priority and get the results to you ASAP. Is that all?"

"No, it isn't. I need some help and if you aren't going to provide it, then I'll hire the help I need. So don't be surprised if you get a few complaints, and maybe even a few extra bodies."

"I'd be surprised if I didn't. Are we done?"

"Not yet. It must be nice to have your own private broom to sweep all your dirt under the carpet. Now we're done." Click.

I felt a little bad about being so hard on Daily, but from where I was standing, he kind of brought it on himself. For instance, why didn't he let me know up front that this case needed to be handled under the table? Kerrigan and I certainly would have gotten off to a much better start and maybe could have started out with a much better plan, in which case Kerrigan might never have been kidnapped in the first place. On the other hand, we now have some very interesting persons of interest, persons that we might never have stumbled onto had they not kidnapped the lieutenant.

I checked my watch and decided to call the trauma center to check on my crew. Just as the front desk answered the phone, into the office walked both Rusty and Kerrigan.

"What are you guy's doing back already?" I said as I hung up the phone.

"They did a concussion check and released us, said we were fine, but that I should wear a helmet when I play football, and Kerrigan should drink more water when he goes hiking and watch out for low-hanging limbs."

I stared at the two of them with a blank look on my face until I realized that the fabricated stories they had told the nurses actually might ensure that our business would remain private. We certainly didn't need any reporters getting wind of our case. The last thing any of us needed was publicity. There would be no more *sweeping* going on after that.

"Dad, what have you been up to while we were goofing off?"

Kerrigan butted in, "Speak for yourself, Army brat. You weren't the one that just spent two days in a dungeon, locked up with neither food nor whisky."

"At least you weren't left unconscious on a porch to be eaten by a bear."

"All right, that's enough, you two. Are you guys ready to get something to eat? I want to pay that Dockside Grill a visit and see if we can get some info on the head waiter that spiked your drink."

"That works for me," Kerrigan said. "But first, I got to go in there." He jerked his thumb towards the men's room.

Suddenly I felt like a boy scout troop leader. I wasn't surprised that it would take more than a couple of nights in a dungeon to get Kerrigan to grow up, but I was surprised to see my son-in-law allow himself to get sucked into his little power struggle games. While Kerrigan was taking a bathroom break, I took Rusty outside to have a talk with him.

"Rusty, you need to understand that Kerrigan will drag you into a world you don't want to be in. Just ignore him. It's all just a game to him, one only he can win. So, be careful."

"I see what you mean Dad, but I think he just likes to play with people's minds and if you take him too seriously, he'll get to you, but if you play along you'll discover it's his way of making friends. You should try it. Maybe you guys could wind up bonding like you and Cal."

"What does Cal have to do with this?"

"Calvin Trent, the game warden, was your best friend and the two of you bantered back and forth all the time, right up to the minute he passed away."

"I know, but that was different."

"How so? You guys were friends and that was the way you showed it, and you had fun doing it, it was perfectly natural."

"Cal was not just a friend, he had my back. No matter what, I always knew he had my back."

"I know, and you had his. That's what made you guys so close. If you would give Kerrigan a chance you might find he has your back too."

"Kerrigan is out for Kerrigan and no one else."

"Maybe, maybe not. Maybe something happened when you rescued him out of that dungeon that might have changed the way he perceives you. Maybe he couldn't trust you to have his back at first, and maybe he does now. Give him the benefit of the doubt for a while and see what happens."

I thought back to the day when I first met Officer Calvin Trent. I had flown my 1957 Cessna 172 Straight-Tail into a terribly short airstrip located at the old Alfred Creek mine on the north side of Sheep Mountain, about seventy miles east of Anchorage. I hadn't realized it at the time, but under the green moss surface of the runway was about three inches of soft wet clay that bogged the airplane down as soon as I touched down. I had managed to get the craft taxied to the far end of the strip, but soon realized I was trapped with very little in the way of camping supplies and no shovel.

I did have a hunting knife and soon fashioned a plank left over from a dilapidated cook shack into some prehistoric resemblance of a wooden shovel.

After a full morning and half an afternoon of laboriously painful back breaking effort to clear the runway of the sticky substance, and in all that time having accomplished very little, I stopped to take a break, during which time I fell asleep. Before long I awakened to the whop, whop, whop of a state police game department helicopter coming up the Caribou Creek drainage toward me. That was the day I met Calvin Trent, and God bless him, he had a shovel.

Although it didn't happen in a single day, over time, Cal and I became good friends. We lost him to cancer about a year ago. I still miss the guy. Rusty was right, he really was a true friend.

I snapped back from my nostalgic moment in time to see the lieutenant emerge from the men's room door with the latest edition of the *Mt. Edgecombe Gazette*.

"I'm ready whenever you guys are," he said.

I said to them, "You and Rusty come over here. I have something to show you." I spread the pictures out across the horizontal stabilizer of a Cessna parked nearby. "Take a look at these photos we took earlier."

Rusty and Kerrigan moved in closer.

"Wow, Dad, that's a pretty nice home right there."

"I figure that must be the prophet's place. But look at all the campers and camper trailers over on the other side of the tracks. I figure they're the poor folks."

"Dad, what's that line right there? It looks like there's a fence or something dividing the property."

"I see that. I think the leadership lives on one side and the common folks live on the other, and the commoners are not allowed to come over without an invite. If you look close you can see the guarded gate on the road leading to the upper income side of the compound."

"He has a little miniature kingdom up there," Kerrigan said. "Which has me wondering what he teaches that makes those people so willing to stick around and be his subjects?"

"Well, if he's like every other religious cult leader, he holds the threat of hell and death over their heads and convinces them that his *special enlightenment* is their only hope of salvation. One day they're condemned to hell for their sins, and the next he offers them hope and salvation on the condition they acknowledge him as a prophet of God sent to save them all. Of course, I'm sure a little offering is involved as well."

Rusty shook his head. "It seems to me that for a scam like that to work they would have to have been awfully destitute, spiritually speaking, long before they ever made it this far, don't you think?"

"You're absolutely right, Rusty. And that's exactly the type of people those con-men prey upon."

"Hey, Dad!" Rusty pointed to one of the pictures. "What's that black spot in the shadows behind the prophet's place? Is that our pickup truck?"

"Could be."

"And what do you think that long building is next door?"

"I don't know, maybe a dormitory or a gymnasium."

Kerrigan leaned over for a closer view. "A dormitory for what?"

"A dormitory for the young kids they use and abuse…and then kill," I said. I tried to make it sound like I was speculating.

Kerrigan suddenly got serious. "What makes you think that?"

"My informant in town knew one of the victims, she told me about the dormitory, and my other informant told me he was once sweet on the first victim."

"Which one was the first victim?" Rusty said.

"Falling Feather, she was the Native American, from the Rosebud Sioux nation out in South Dakota."

Kerrigan straightened and put a hand on both Rusty's and my shoulder, "If this is true, then it's about time we put a stop to it."

I turned to look Kerrigan straight in the eye. "It's past time, brother. Long past time."

"Then why are we standing around? Let's get going," Kerrigan said.

We all climbed into the courtesy van that Rusty and Lieutenant Kerrigan had driven from the hospital and headed to the Dockside Bar 'and' grill where we had a hardy lunch. We looked around for anyone we might recognize and asked a few questions but didn't get any bites so we headed back to the school's airstrip where I had parked the Kodiak.

I felt like we had gotten a little behind the eight-ball by not pursuing the old pickup immediately after Rudy had seen Karen and the Maverick man driving through town. Legally speaking, it was still my truck and I had the title and the bill of sale, signed by Old Man Perkins to prove it. So we could actually get a warrant and go onto the property to retrieve it if we wanted. However, that warrant would not only take a lot of time to acquire, it would not allow us to search or interrogate any of the people on the compound. Furthermore, a warrant would have to include a lot of other legal systems that we would rather not have breathing down our necks, at least not yet. The way I figured it, the more people we involved in the case, the harder it would be to keep it from turning into a media circus. It was obvious to me that this case was turning out to be a lot bigger than anyone originally thought, and by the time we finished digging it could possibly get so big, a media storm might become inevitable. We needed to forestall that inevitability as long as possible.

"So what's the plan?" Rusty asked. "How are we going to go about this? Should we get a warrant and seize the truck? After all, it's now considered evidence in a murder investigation."

"No, I think that would be premature. I'm sure they've cleaned and polished it by now and will probably bring it back to us eventually. I'd rather wait and catch them after they've left the compound."

"Do you think the daughter, Karen, knows her dad sold the truck before he died?"

"I'm sure she does. When she was there, her dad was still alive and I'm sure he told her. That's probably why she took the truck in the first place, because she knew it was full of incriminating evidence. However, unless someone very close to us has been in touch with her, I don't see how she could know that her dad is now dead."

I parked the van in front of Genneta William's office and went inside to return the key.

"Mr. Worley, Doctor Brady sent this over for you." Genneta handed me an envelope with the hospital's logo on it.

"Thanks, Genneta. I parked the van outside. Thanks for letting us use it."

"Anytime, Mr. Worley."

I slid the envelope from Dr. Brady into the inside breast pocket of my leather flight jacket and returned to the Kodiak. Kerrigan and Rusty were waiting and shortly we were once again in the air on our way back to the fishing village of Kake.

Kerrigan said to me, "What is it you want with that old Dodge pickup?"

"I bought it from Old Man Perkins so we would have some transportation while we were trying to investigate these murder cases."

"I thought you got your money back before we left the house."

"I did, but I still have the bill of sale. And the title is signed over to me. Therefore, it's still my property."

"Then shouldn't that money go to his daughter?"

"It should. But it remains to be seen whether she will survive this investigation. If she doesn't, the money will go to whoever is her next of kin."

"Who would that be?"

"I don't know. You're supposed to be the greatest detective on earth, why don't you find out for me?"

"Don't worry, I will."

"Dad, I have an idea. Me and Rudy can lay in wait for the pickup, why don't you and the lieutenant go talk to Leroy about his brother?"

"Who's Leroy?" Kerrigan said.

"I want to talk to Elizabeth first, " I said.

"Who's Elizabeth?" Kerrigan asked again.

"And I think I'll fly over the harbor and see if the green monster is back."

"What's a green monster?" Kerrigan asked.

"You know, for a top-notch detective, you sure ask a lot of questions."

"That's my job. That's why I'm top-notch."

"Dad, don't you think you should fill Mark in on everything that's happened since he went on vacation?"

I looked over my shoulder at Kerrigan. While he was looking a little behind the eight ball, I was enjoying my feelings of detective superiority.

"Leroy Mauktokta is the VPO in Kake. He's an alcoholic that I'm trying to keep sober long enough for him to talk to his brother."

"Who is his brother and what does Leroy need to talk to him about?" Kerrigan asked.

"His brother's name is Larry Mauktokta. He's one of the guards at the compound. If Leroy can enlist his brothers help, we might be able to get Rudy onto the grounds as a visitor during visitor day. Then maybe get him to convert to whatever they're preaching up there these days."

"When is visitor day?"

"I don't know. Leroy will have to get that information from Larry."

"Why would Larry help us?" Rusty asked.

"Because I can pay him a lot more money to work for me than that prophet can pay him to work for them. He can give us information on the comings and goings of the leadership and who they are. Then maybe he can help us figure a way to get Rudy in there as a convert." Also, there's a lady that lives there named Shirley that I need to talk to."

"Who's she?"

"She's one of the house mothers. In fact, according to Elizabeth, our second victim stayed with her for a while before she went missing and it's possible that the other three might have stayed with her as well. If not, at least she may have known them well enough to give us the information we need."

"How do you know all this stuff? Kerrigan asked.

"Because once I got you out of my hair, I was able to do some real detective work. If I'd have had to follow you around, we'd still be arguing about who's in charge." A huge grin had spread across Kerrigan's face.

"We don't ever need to argue about that again, because everybody here already knows who's in charge. Me!"

"Whatever."

"So who is this Elizabeth you keep talking about and I thought we only had three victims?"

"She owns the tavern, but I'm going to buy it from her and turn it into a halfway house for all those kids, which reminds me I have to call Gerard."

"Who's Gerard?" Kerrigan asked.

"He's my architect. I need him to find a piece of property around there and design a building that will accommodate a lot of kids. Maybe it will eventually turn into an orphanage. And I think if we set it up right, we can educate the children right there and prepare them for adulthood without even putting them into other families, families that are oftentimes just as dysfunctional as the ones they come from."

Rusty spoke up, "Okay, Pop, let me see if I got this straight. First, we hire Larry Mauktokta, then get Elizabeth and Leroy Mauktokta to introduce Rudy, then he identifies the good guys from the bad guys and then we move in, is that right?"

"In a nutshell. But we'll have to wait and see if Larry is willing to go along with it first."

"What if he won't? What's to stop him from going to the prophet and blowing our cover."

"Money! Lots and lots of money."

Kerrigan began laughing. "I like you, Worley. You're all right. I guess if you don't know how to solve a crime any other way, you can always throw a few hundred grand at a couple of informers. Ha, ha, ha, must be nice. By the way, I bet you haven't even sent that bag of evidence to the lab yet?"

"You'd lose *that* bet and then I'd have all the more money to throw at informers. I did that while you were goofing off up at the nursery. I also had a talk with Daily."

Kerrigan looked up from his newspaper.

"What did he have to say?"

"It's like we thought. He wants this case to disappear under the rug. No questions asked, whatever it takes."

Kerrigan went back to his newspaper. "Told you so."

"There's only one problem."

"What's that?"

"This case isn't going to go away that easy. And we can't just kill everyone we think is a bad guy. That's nuts."

"So how do we do it then?" Kerrigan inquired. "Daily said they didn't have the budget to throw at this case even when it was small."

"We'll keep digging. It may be that this case winds up crossing a state line and if it does, we can turn it over to the Feds and go home."

"Haw, haw. That's hilarious," Kerrigan said. "In your dreams. That's exactly what Daily doesn't want. If the Feds get involved he'd be on the hotbox for involving a civilian in a murder case in the first place. Why, you're not even a licensed private investigator, much less a cop."

I thought Daily had already informed Kerrigan of my credentials, but I guess he must have forgotten. I reached into my pocket and flashed him my state police badge.

"Have a look at that, tough-guy."

Kerrigan examined it and tossed it back at me. "Where'd you get that, out of a cracker-jack box?"

"Read it and weep, Lieutenant. I'm just as official as you are. Now if you can get over yourself long enough for us to investigate this case together, I have a plan that just might put this killer right in our lap."

Kerrigan was sitting in the co-pilot's seat and Rusty sat directly behind him as I turned onto final approach for the Kake airstrip. I had not heard anyone announce themselves on the radio, so was surprised to see a twin-engine Cessna 421 already in the take-off roll for departure to the south.

"Hey, Dad, that airplane is taking off."

"I see that. I didn't hear him report on the radio, did you?"

"No, maybe he doesn't want anyone to know he's here."

"I'll throttle back until he's in the air, and we'll follow him."

"I don't think you'll have to do much throttling back. He's scooting out of there pretty good. Looks like he might be turbo powered. We'll never be able to keep up with that twin in this single engine Kodiak."

"I know. But we can at least see which direction he's going."

"Looks to me like he's headed back to Sitka. We could go there and see if he landed," Rusty said.

"Good idea."

"Hey, that's a pretty high-dollar airplane, who do you think it is?" Kerrigan asked.

"I don't know. Could be the prophet, or somebody that come to see him. We'll head back to Sitka. Maybe we'll get lucky."

"I wonder if anyone has made the connection between this yellow and black Kodiak and the camera flash up on the hill this morning." Rusty said.

"What camera flash?" Kerrigan asked.

"Rusty and I went for a walk early this morning up by the gate to see what we could see and almost got caught. We found the place where the last girl crawled through the fence and I took a couple of pictures. The guards saw the camera flash and started shooting at us."

"What last girl? Do you mean the victim from Hamilton Island?" Kerrigan's normal self-possession appeared to be coming unraveled.

"No! The one from yesterday."

"Do you mean there are now *four* murder victims?"

"That's right. Maybe if you hadn't taken so much time off we could have caught the guy before—"

"That is so much B,S. Worley. Get over it."

"I'm just sayin'..."

"So where were *you*, bigshot? Why weren't you able to stop him with all your billions of dollars?"

"I almost did. I happened up on the guy during the attack and he had to let her go and run away."

"Was she still alive?"

"Yes, I managed to get her down off the hill and to the trauma center but the doctor called me this morning and told me she died during the night."

Kerrigan squirmed in his seat. He clenched his jaw and staring at me said, "How do I know *you're* not the murderer? Maybe I should begin and end my investigation with *you*."

"Don't worry, I still have a few questions I'd like to ask you too."

The big twin had left us in the dust just like Rusty said it would. Minutes later we heard the pilot report his position and the tower cleared him to land. I quickly called the tower on my cell phone and asked for the supervisor.

"Sitka tower, Supervisor Franklin speaking."

"Supervisor Franklin, this is Lou Worley. I'm flying my Quest Kodiak and am coming in from the northeast not far behind that twin Cessna that was just cleared to land. I'm involved in a criminal investigation and the people in that twin are persons of interest. Can you give me a special designation so they don't recognize my aircraft number and become suspicious?"

"I can do better than that, Mr. Worley. Contact the tower on the published military frequency and use the designation Bumblebee. I'll pass it on to your controller."

"Thank-you, Mr. Franklin. I owe you one." "Rusty, have a look at the sectional and get me that published military channel for Sitka."

"The frequency is '243', Dad."

The controller issued a special clearance to military flight "'243/Bumblebee'" and a few minutes later we were touching down.

"Are we going to try to follow him if he takes off again?" Rusty asked. "I believe that '421' has gone through a turbo modification and he's now sporting a couple of seven-fifty Pratt & Whitney's. We'll need something a lot faster than this Kodiak to keep up with that."

"Take a look over at the maintenance hangar," I said. "Do you see anything familiar sitting over there?"

"Dad, is that your CJ4?"

"That's Eric. He just got back from Fairbanks. I sent him up there with the evidence samples right after you guys went to urgent care."

"Why did he come back here?" Rusty asked.

"I told him to come back and fuel up, then take the jet to Kake and wait for me. Now you can take Eric and go back over to Kake in this Kodiak."

"What are you going to do?"

"Kerrigan and I will follow that 421, if and when it takes off again. I don't think he'll be outrunning that Citation, do you?"

"How many freaking airplanes you got anyway, Worley?"

"Enough to do the job, How many you got? Just shut-up, sit back, and enjoy the ride. Things are about to get interesting."

I called the office at the maintenance facility and told them I would be taxiing directly into the hangar and that they were to shut the doors behind us and tell Eric to get his personal belongings out of the CJ4. Once inside the hangar I shut the Kodiak down and Kerrigan and I quickly made our transition to the small jet where I met up with Eric.

"The jet is fueled and ready to go, Mr. Worley. What do you want me to do now?"

"I need you to go with Rusty back over to Kake. Rusty's 206 is parked over there and I want you to keep your eye on the airplanes whenever Rusty is gone. He has another man working with him named Rudy. You can stay in the Kodiak. If you need more food have Rudy get it for you, but don't leave those airplanes unattended. Do you understand?"

"Yes, sir. What do I do if I need to defend the airplanes for some reason?"

"Talk to Rusty, he'll get you squared away with that."

Suddenly I heard Kerrigan holler. "Hey, Worley! That twin is on the move, we better roll."

"Let's get buckled in," I said.

As the two FJ44-44 turbo fans spooled up I grabbed my cell phone and called Supervisor Franklin in the tower.

"Supervisor Franklin speaking."

"Mr. Franklin, this is Lou Worley again. My suspects are beginning their taxi and I'm spooling up my Citation CJ4 over here at the maintenance hangar. Can you give me another military clearance and send me a copy of the twin Cessna's flight plan, clearance, and itinerary?"

"I sure can, Mr. Worley. Do you have fax capability on board your aircraft?"

"Yes, and I'll need the same clearance and any amended clearances they might make along the way. And could you inform Juneau Center of our special circumstances and ask them to keep us on this same channel for the duration of the flight?"

"Will do, Mr. Worley. Good luck and have a good flight."

I gave Mr. Franklin my fax number and received a duplicate clearance as the one the twin Cessna had filed. We listened on the general aviation tower frequency, and as the big twin Cessna was cleared for take-off, we were cleared to taxi on military channel '243'. Soon Kerrigan and I were airborne. I contacted Juneau Center and requested that they keep me advised of any fluctuation in the twin Cessna's airspeed.

The 421 had filed for non-stop to Fairbanks; however, I wasn't certain they would not decide to change their itinerary midflight. Someone who might suspect they are being tailed might be so inclined. So I stayed behind and throttled back to match their airspeed.

By the time Anchorage slid beneath us I had become reasonably sure that Fairbanks was in-fact their true destination. I contacted Anchorage Center, got a phone number for the supervisor, and gave him a call.

"Supervisor Carroll speaking, how can I help you?"

"Supervisor Carroll, this is Lou Worley. I'm a civilian aircraft flying a milit—"

"I know who you are. Juneau passed you off to us twenty minutes ago. How can I help?"

"I need to pass this guy and scoot on into Fairbanks ahead of him. Can you fax me an update on him if he should decide to divert or if he decides to cancel IFR to go VFR?"

"Sure, Mr. Worley. How dangerous is this guy, anyway? Are you sure you don't need help from the Marshals' office?"

"Oh no! Don't do that. It will spook him. I'm not even sure he's a bad guy yet. That's why we're following him to see where it takes us. But don't worry, if it's who I think it is he's too much of a coward to be dangerous to anyone accept defenseless little children."

"Okay, Mr. Worley, I'll keep you posted. But I'll have to log this in the shift record."

"Not a problem, Supervisor Carroll. Thanks for your help."

I asked for a higher altitude that would put us well above the twin Cessna 421 and shoved the power forward. In short order we were scooting along at 380 knots of true airspeed. I called the fixed base operator at Fairbanks municipal, Jerod Aiken, my friend from many years back and a man I have done business with on numerous occasions, answered the phone. I asked him if we could borrow a car. He said he would have one waiting for us at the general aviation ramp. Minutes later we were touching down at Fairbanks International.

I taxied to the general aviation ramp and shut down the Citation. Jerod was waiting by the charter office door.

"Howdy, Lou, how long will you need the car?"

"I don't know, maybe a couple of hours."

"Can you take me back to my office?" he asked.

"Sure, but we're waiting on someone, should be landing any minute. By the way, meet Lieutenant Kerrigan, Anchorage homicide. Kerrigan, this is Jerod Aiken, a good friend of mine."

"You have a friend?"

"Here they come, Mark. That's the twin on final approach. Let's step inside the FBO and listen to ground control until we see where they're going to park."

"Are you two guy's following someone?" Jerod asked.

"Don't worry about it. It's police business." Kerrigan said.

"Sorry, I was just curious." Jerod looked at me with a startled look.

"Don't worry about him, Jerod. He was born on the wrong side of the bed and raised in a crack house. He's never known anyone that wasn't guilty of something."

"What do you know about where I was raised, Worley?"

"I don't. Furthermore, I don't care."

"I have a handheld." Jerod pulled a handheld VHF radio from his belt and tuned it to the airport ground frequency.

"Looks like they're heading over here to general aviation. They probably have a car parked around here. Let's get ready to follow them. Are you staying here or coming with us?" I asked Jerod.

"He can't come with us!"

"Why not?"

"Because I said so."

"That's no reason."

Three men had disembarked from the big twin.

"Jerod," I said, "take a look at those guys and tell me if you've ever seen any of them."

"Yeah, that tall, ugly one in the dark suit. I'd know him anywhere."

"Who is he?" I said.

"Theodore Wallace, he runs an orphanage on the outskirts of town."

"An orphanage?"

"Yeah, and the one standing next to him is that cult leader…what's his name?"

"You mean, Joseph Morning? The guy that thinks he's a prophet?"

"Yeah, that's him. He rented airplanes from me when he first came here about ten years ago. Looks like he's done pretty well for himself since then. Those big twins don't come cheap, especially with two Pratt & Whitney seven-fifties perched on the wings."

"You think that twin belongs to the prophet?"

"I'm sure it does."

"Well, there they go. Which vehicle is yours, Jerod?"

"The Toyota Land Cruiser, here's the keys."

Jerod tossed me the keys and Kerrigan climbed into the passenger side.

"Jump in the back, Jerod, we're going for a ride."

The two men left their pilot with the aircraft and climbed into a Cadillac Escalade. I waited until they turned out onto the street and then began following from a reasonable distance.

"Kerrigan, where do you think all that money is coming from? Do you think there might be more to the picture than just an orphanage?"

Kerrigan kept quiet. I couldn't help but notice he seemed a little nervous.

I continued, "It seems like a lot of money is lining somebody's pockets to afford such pricey toys. But I'm not the type of person to judge someone for having a few extra dollars, if you know what I mean. I'm just saying. Jerod, what did you say that guy's name is?"

"Which one?"

"The tall, ugly one that runs the orphanage."

"Wallace, Theodore Wallace." I looked at Kerrigan. He was sweating.

"Lieutenant, do you know anything about Mr. Wallace and his orphanage?"

"Why would I know anything about it?"

"Because you've worked in Alaska law enforcement for twenty-five years. I thought maybe you might have heard of them."

"Don't know anything about it. For that matter, I still haven't figured out why we're here when we should be investigating four murders down in Sitka."

Suddenly, Jerod sat up in his seat, eyes as wide as moose antlers. "Four murders! You guys are investigating four murders?"

"Don't worry about it," Kerrigan said.

"He can worry about anything he wants to. If it wasn't for him we'd be walking," I said.

Kerrigan looked out the window and began fidgeting around with his seat belt. Then, looking in the mirror at Jerod, I said, "Jerod, where do you think these guys are going?"

"Probably to the orphanage."

"Where's that?"

"Out Gold Stream Road I think, not far from the old Sky-Flight airport."

"How come they don't fly into it?"

"I'm not sure. It's only nineteen-hundred feet long and sits at an elevation of eleven-hundred feet so maybe it's too short for that big twin."

"How far away is it?"

"About five miles out of town. I know how to get to the airport, but don't know where the orphanage is from there."

"How do you know it's up there?"

"I've heard talk that it is."

I looked at Kerrigan to see if our sketchy information was going to bring a response out of him—there was nothing. The lieutenant just sat staring straight ahead, sweating.

"So if I lose these guys how do I get to the airport?"

"Just keep going up University Avenue. It'll eventually turn into Farmers Loop Road. Stay on that until you see Ballaine Road branching off to the left. Follow that to Gold Stream Road. You'll see a sign directing you to the airport. The orphanage is off to the northwest somewhere, I believe."

I stayed back from the Escalade as far as I could while still keeping them in sight. However, by the time we reached Ballaine Road, the Escalade had disappeared.

"They must have turned off somewhere. Do you know if there's anyone at the airport that has an airplane? If one of us could get in the air, he could maybe spot the Escalade and direct us in."

"Old Man Larson has two or three airplanes. However, that doesn't mean they're all airworthy. We could go see," Jerod said.

Suddenly Kerrigan pointed ahead and said to me, "Take a left at the next dirt road."

"Do what? Did you say take a left?"

"That's what I said, take a left. Are you deaf too?"

"I thought you said you didn't know anything about the place."

"I don't. However, I didn't say I hadn't ever been to it."

By now I was sitting up in my seat. This was not only odd, it was downright exciting. What other secrets was Lieutenant Mark Kerrigan keeping in his brilliant little brain? I offered no objection and made a left at the next dirt road. In another mile or so, my new tour guide suggested I take a right and follow another dirt road onto a somewhat overgrown and un-maintained jeep trail.

"Keep going until you come to a ditch, then turn the car around and park facing outbound."

I wanted to ask a hundred questions, but didn't want to get Kerrigan upset so I decided to wait and watch. Soon we arrived at the ditch. I turned the car around and parked it behind some bushes, out of sight of the center of the jeep trail.

"Now what. Lieutenant?"

"Now you two stay put. I'll be back shortly. If I'm not back in twenty minutes leave without me."

"I'm coming with you"

"No, you're not."

"Oh, yes, I am. I'm your body-guard, remember? The last time I let you go by yourself, you got in trouble and almost got us all killed."

"Suit yourself, just don't get in my way."

"Jerod, do you have a sidearm?" I said.

"Yeah, there's one in the glove box. Do you want it?"

"No, but you might want to keep it handy. I need you to stay here and be ready to go in case we have to get out of here in a hurry."

Jerod's eyes got big as he suddenly realized we were leaving him alone and that there might be some risk involved.

"What if someone sees me?" Jerod asked.

"Tell them you're interested in buying some land and you're looking at property lines. Then send me a text."

The old jeep trail had at one time been a dog sled run providing access to the remote Alaska wilderness during the gold rush of 1849. In those days it had served as the highway to Poker Flats and beyond. Hundreds of gold camps peppered the landscape within a hundred miles of Fairbanks, and before reliable air service came along, every man, woman, and box of provisions moved across the very jeep trail we were walking on.

I couldn't help but reflect on the hardships the people must have endured during those times. Now, the portion accessible by four-wheel drive had ended and the original trail was all but obliterated by overgrowth. Only the occasional scrap of iron left along the trail by the unlucky majority, those who had failed in their enterprise, remained, serving as a testament of their attempted hopes and dreams, dreams upon which they had gambled not only everything they owned, but their very lives.

Kerrigan slowly picked his way through the thick overgrowth until he came to a large stream.

"This is Gold Stream," he said.

"Do you think there might still be some gold?"

"Shhh!! No talking," Kerrigan spait out.

I didn't want to get anything started between us so I kept my mouth shut. It was actually good to see Detective Mark Kerrigan participating in the investigation for the first time. Maybe, finally, we could start working together for a change.

I stayed about ten-feet back from the detective and only moved when he did, so as to minimize the sound of our moving through the thick trees. Suddenly he stopped. Through the limbs we could see the outline of a large building.

I felt a buzzing coming from my cell phone fastened to my belt. It was a text from Jerod.

"Vehicle apprchg. Stopd…now. Voices…don't thnk thay C me yet…I hope."

I quickly sent Jerod a return text.

"Keep me posted…is veh blkg retreat?"

A moment later, another text came through.

"2 men got out of the car. Am lookg 4 plc 2 hide."

I immediately sent Jerod another text.

"On my way."

I said to Kerrigan, "I have to go back to the car, Jerod needs…" I stopped short. Looking up I saw that Kerrigan was not there. "What the Sam Hill?"

Where did he go? Well, sorry, Captain Daily. Your boy will have to fend for himself for now. Now, I was sorry I had involved Jerod in our investigation at all. Should have just rented a car. Maybe if Kerrigan had been more forthcoming about the orphanage, I wouldn't have had to depend on Jerod to show us the way to the airport. There I go again, blaming someone else for my own stupidity. It wasn't anyone else's fault. I was the one that involved Jerod, not Kerrigan, regardless of the reasons why. So, it would have to be me that made sure he got out of this alive.

I first met Jerod when he ran a little hunting supply store in Toke, Alaska, back in the mid-nineties. I was passing through on my way to Alfred Creek, back when I first came to Alaska. I had stopped for a few supplies I thought I might need. That was when I learned he was a flyer like me. A couple years later he helped me look for a downed pilot, who we found up on the Yukon River. Jerod and I have been friends ever since. For years Jerod's family owned an FBO and flight school located on the metro airport in Fairbanks. Several years ago his father passed away and Jerod took over managing the business. We have continued to stay in touch over the years.

I had no intention of involving Jerod in anything dangerous. I expected we would need some transportation when we got on the ground and figured it would take too much time to go through the process of renting a car. Also, Jerod grew up in Fairbanks and so I thought he might have information about the orphanage, if in fact there was such a thing.

I really didn't give much thought to the fact that Kerrigan had disappeared on me, again. I had let myself become distracted with texting Jerod. I felt certain Kerrigan would be along sooner or later.

It's true, I was curious about the large cabin we had seen in the woods, but I was more concerned for Jerod so I carefully made my way back to where we had parked the Land Cruiser, stopping frequently to listen for movement or voices.

Finally, from only fifty yards away, I could make out little patches of the vehicle and the open area where I had turned the car around.

It didn't appear that Jerod was in the vehicle and there was no indication that anyone else was around. I wondered if maybe the men Jerod had seen were only a couple of hunters and I had left Kerrigan on his own for nothing.

I began to move slowly, hoping that Jerod had found a secure place and that I might find him before the other two men did. Assuming they were actually a threat.

Suddenly, I heard voices. Muffled at first, but coming closer and getting louder. My heart rate immediately increased. Even before I could see them, I instinctively knew they had Jerod. I unsnapped the strap securing my weapon and moved in as close as possible while remaining concealed.

Suddenly, out of the woods came Kerrigan, only he was wearing different clothing. He had hold of Jerod by one arm and another man with him was dragging Jerod by the other arm. "What the—?" I started to call out. But something stopped me. Something wasn't right with this picture. That is Kerrigan, isn't it? I moved in a little closer, very slowly, very carefully, to get a closer look. Now only fifty-feet away, I stared, totally baffled, at a man that by every feature was Kerrigan, but by every demeanor was not Kerrigan at all. Who in the world is that? Is that Lieutenant Kerrigan or not?

Jerod's hands appeared to be tied behind him and they were putting him into a strange vehicle.

The Maverick look-a-like said to him, "Get in the car and don't make a sound. If you so much as utter a peep, I'll kill you right here." Then he roughly shoved Jerod into the back seat of the Land Cruiser.

Maverick, that must be the maverick man I've been looking for! Suddenly, the Kerrigan look-a-like disappeared back into the woods. One of the two remaining men stayed with Jerod and the other climbed into the Land Cruiser. I knew I needed to make a move soon, before they made off with Jerod, and our only means of transportation. I moved along the tree line, closer to the car. Suddenly, a sharp pain associated with a bright, white light flashed across my brain.

The next time I opened my eyes, there was nothing but darkness. So dark in fact, I couldn't be sure they were really opened. I tried to reach my hand up to feel my face, but my arm would not move. I tried to wriggle my toes, but could only feel them moving inside my shoes, and when I tried to move my legs, they felt like logs. "I'm tied up," I said out loud. More as a reality check than anything else.

"What was your first clue?" The voice was not my own but sounded familiar.

My eyes had adjusted to the darkness somewhat and I now could see certain outlines of the room in which I was imprisoned. It was a good twenty-feet wide and at least thirty-feet in length. I could see the outline of various tools and garden equipment lined up in neat rows along the inside wall. There were no windows, but a very dim sliver of light could be seen coming from the top of a set of stairs in the vicinity of the voice I had heard, casting an eerie shadow in the room. Suddenly, reality gave way to horrible nightmares of the past; forgotten memories of events that had taken place long ago, in Vietnam.

I had tried to discard every dreadful memory of the place, forever. Yet, they were all still there, every detail of every battle, every scream of every dying soldier, still haunted me. And now, especially now, tied up like a sack of potatoes in a pitch black root cellar, it was all coming back. I began to shake and without realizing it let out a blood curdling scream.

"They're coming! They're all around us! Fall back! Fall back!

"Lou! Lou! Snap out of it, will ya?"

"Jerod's voice sounded a thousand miles away, but it was what I needed. I wanted out of the nightmare…out of the vivid memory of that ghastly place, and it took something from the real world. Jerod's voice had broken through. Jerod's voice had brought me back. Without it, without that tangible, present-tense thread of reality that re-connected my mind, I might never have returned from the utter darkness that attempted to swallow me.

"Lou! This isn't Vietnam! Do you hear me? This isn't Vietnam. I need you back here. Do you hear me?"

Suddenly I could see again. The basement, the wheelbarrow's, the shovel's and Jerod, helplessly tied to a post.

As reality slowly returned, my first thought was: I've got to get us out of here.

"Jerod, is that you?"

"Yeah, are you okay?"

"Who hit me? Where are we?"

"We're in the underground basement of a house a mile or so from where we parked. They blindfolded me when they brought me here, but I could tell it wasn't that far away. Then about ten-minutes later they brought you in and tied you to one of the support beams that hold up the house. I'm tied to another one. They must have brought you here in a different car."

"What time was that?" I asked, trying to reconnect the dots.

"I'm not sure, it was still light when they brought you in but that was seven or eight hours ago. I was getting concerned that you might not make it."

"I'm really sorry I got you into all this, Jerod. I should have never—"

"Don't worry about it, Lou. I've been in worse places than this before. What kind of a case are you and Kerrigan working on, anyway?"

"A series of murders down around Sitka."

"You're not going to believe this, but your investigator is a perfect twin to the guy that grabbed me."

"I saw that, just before the lights went out. God, my head hurts. Did you see who hit me?"

"No. But after they tied me up and stuffed me in the car someone called the big guy on his phone, the one that looks like the lieutenant. He left me and headed back into the woods where you and Kerrigan went. Then one of the other two men brought me here in my Land Cruiser."

"Who could have called him?" I asked, wondering if it was Kerrigan.

"I don't know, Lou. It might have been the guy that was watching me. He was on the phone when I saw him. Maybe he saw you."

"Did you see who dragged me out?"

"No. All that must have happened after they took me away. But I'm sure it was the big guy."

"You mean the Maverick man?"

"What?"

"Maverick, I call him Maverick."

"You're kidding!"

"I named him that because he looks like Bret Maverick from the telev—"

"I know who you mean. But how do you know the guy?"

"I don't. I just know that Kerrigan and him both look alike. I drew a deep breath and let it out in a long sigh of frustration.

"Maybe this Maverick guy is the same one Rudy spotted stealing my pickup truck down in Kake. If so, he might be the killer we're looking for. But we've got to get out of here somehow."

I tried to move my body enough to turn in that direction.

"Jerod, are you near a set of stairs?"

"Yeah, can you see me?"

"I think so, it's just so dark. I think there are some garden tools stacked around here, which means there might be an entrance to the outside. Did you see anything when they brought you down here?"

"There's a metal door but I'm sure it's locked from the outside."

"If I could get loose there might be something in here I could use for a weapon. Are you tied up or handcuffed?"

"Tied."

"I'm tied, too, all the way up to my elbows. Keep working your arms, maybe you can work the ropes loose enough to get your hands free. I'll do the same. Right now that's about all we can do."

It seemed like we were there for hours. My backside, my legs, and especially my feet were so numb I had to restrain myself from crying out. Furiously, I sawed at the ropes, up and down over the sharp corners of the square beam supporting the upper floor. Frantically, I jerked and yanked and tore at the ropes that kept me from my freedom.

Finally, I could feel the ropes loosening. Strands of hemp floated into the palms of my hands as the sharp edges of the post cut through the threads. The tightness had diminished. My arms grew weary, blood ran down my wrists, yet something drove me on. Some deep-seated anger, or hatred…or was it fear? Finally, the ropes gave way. I brought my arms around in front of me and rubbed my shoulder sockets feverishly to return circulation to my arms.

"Lou, did you get loose?" Jerod said in a whisper.

"Yeah, I'm loose. I'll be there in a minute." I placed my hands over my face and breathed a silent prayer to God. For I knew, and have always known, that it was God in heaven who had kept me alive in Vietnam, and it was no less He who had once again saved me from returning to that detestable place.

CHAPTER 10

Jerod crouched on the steps below me. From a prone position at the top of the stairs, I peered under the door. There was a sliver of light coming from somewhere that enabled me to see a portion of the surface of a hardwood floor in what appeared to be the kitchen.

During the hours we were tied up we had heard nothing coming from inside the house above the basement, but that did not mean it was altogether vacant. Our kidnappers could be sleeping.

"I don't think anyone is home," Jerod whispered. "If there is, they most certainly would have heard *you*."

"Did I make a lot of noise?"

"You scared the living daylight out of me. I thought for a minute you had gone over the edge. Has that ever happened to you before?"

I had other things to think about at the moment, so I made my response to Jerod's question as brief as possible.

"No!" I lied, emphatically.

Carefully, I tried the door. It was locked.

"See if you can find a sledgehammer," I whispered to Jerod. "There must be something down here we could use."

"What are you going to do?" he whispered back.

"We're going to have to bust this door open."

"Won't that make a lot of noise?"

"We'll have to take our chances. It's either that or stay here the rest of our lives, or until whoever put us here comes back to finish us off."

Jerod returned with a five-foot-long steel bar. It was heavy and had a sharp, thick wedge of steel on one end designed for breaking up hard-packed, rocky ground. It was too long to use to pry the door open, due to the confined space in the stairwell, so that left but one option. I hauled back and punched the door directly alongside the door knob. The momentum of the heavy steel broke through and the wooden door flew wide open, shattering the jamb into a mass of splintered wood. We waited breathlessly for anyone who may have heard the noise. There was nothing.

It was now apparent the light we had seen was coming from a refrigerator door that had been left open, a refrigerator that was empty. The sight of it reminded me that I hadn't eaten anything in over eight hours.

I held the steel bar in front of me like a spear as we carefully made our way through the other rooms of the house.

Satisfied that no one was home, I spoke freely, "I wonder who owns this place."

"We could find out easy enough, except I don't have a phone anymore," Jerod said.

"I lost mine too. That's okay, we'll find out later. Whoever they are, it doesn't necessarily mean they're involved in anything that's going on here. Obviously the people who winterized this place weren't planning on coming back for a while, that's why the fridge door was left open. The home-owners, more than likely shut the power off when they left and whoever it is that's using the place has turned the power back on."

"How long do you suppose that has been going on?" Jerod asked.

"Probably not long."

"How do you know?"

"Well, if it was much more than a month or two, the owners would have gotten an electrical bill. I'm sure they would be back up here in short order to see who has been pilfering their power."

"Why do you suppose they didn't kill us?" Jerod asked.

"Maybe they still plan to. In fact, I'm thinking they're coming back anytime to finish the job. Maybe they want to interrogate us first."

"Why do you suppose they didn't do that before they left?"

"Maybe they didn't want to wait for me to come around. Those guys may have just been the strong arms. It's entirely possible the brains of the operation could show up any minute."

"I wonder why they didn't leave someone here to watch us."

"I have no idea. Most strong arms are not that bright. Or maybe they had other fish to fry. Either way, it's our opportunity to be ready for them when they do show up."

"Shouldn't we be hightailing it out of here while we have the chance?" Jerod said, still whispering.

"I suppose if we had better sense we would. However, I'd like to know who they are. I just wish I had a gun."

"You may get your wish, Lou. If they do come back, I'm sure at least one of them *will* have a gun."

I looked at Jerod, "We better get out of here before that happens. I don't want to put you at any more risk than I already have."

"Don't worry about me. I can take care of myself." Jerod said, his confidence returning.

"Then how did you wind up in the basement?"

"They caught me by surprise, that won't happen again. I'll be ready for them next time."

"Well, it's up to you, but it could get dangerous."

"So is flying in a snow storm. Besides, I'm not the type of person who takes it lightly when someone kidnaps me, ties me up, steals my car, and leaves me to freeze to death in a dungeon."

"All right then, let's search every corner of this house--cupboards, closets, cabinets, everything. See what we can find. Maybe there's something somewhere we can use as a weapon."

Jerod started searching downstairs while I went upstairs. It was obvious that someone used the place from time to time, but for what, I wasn't sure. It didn't really look lived in, just used.

Suddenly Jerod come rushing up the stairs. "I hear someone walking up the driveway."

I had already looked in every closet and cupboard and the only thing I had found was an empty whisky bottle along with another one that was still half full. I decided it would have to do. I picked it up and along with my steel bar, headed down the stairs.

"I'll get him when he comes through the door." I said to Jerod, "You make sure and distract him, and try to get him to come all the way in so I can slam the door shut behind him."

The vacant cabin was set several hundred yards back into the forest from the main road and with no other lights on than the refrigerator, the interior of the cabin was mostly dark.

Jerod stood in the hall out of sight beside an open bathroom door, yet within sight of the front entrance. We waited. I could hear footsteps ascending the steps leading to the front porch and the main entrance. The doorknob turned slowly as someone tried the door. It was locked. Darn it. I was hoping he would have a key and walk right in.

The footsteps slowly retreated. His steps sounded heavy, I could tell he was a big man. Must be Kerrigan or the Maverick man, I concluded. Or, it could be one of the crew that had kidnapped Jerod and me. Either way, I was concerned that we might be letting a form of transportation get away from us, I called out, "Who is it?" The footsteps returned.

"Worley, is that you?"

"Who's asking?"

"It's Lieutenant Kerrigan, open the door."

"I will on one condition."

"What's that?"

"When I open the door, you stick your gun inside butt first, then I'll let you in."

"That ain't happening. Just open the door. What are you doing in there anyway?"

"You should know, you're the one who left us here, all trussed up like a couple of sacks of sawdust."

"What are you talking about, Worley? Have you gone completely loco? First you disappear on me right when we walked up on that other cabin in the woods, then you show up a mile away at this place. What did you want my gun for? What happened to yours?"

"Another cabin?" I asked, somewhat baffled. "Isn't this the same cabin we saw in the woods when…never mind, just a minute."

I stuffed the whisky bottle in my hip pocket and opened the door with one hand while concealing the steel bar behind me with the other. There, standing on the porch, was my missing detective.

I might not be as young as I used to be, and at least fifteen years older than Lieutenant Kerrigan, but combat training and tactics are two things that are not so prone to erode overtime, as are physical strength and conditioning. Facing the lieutenant, I opened the door. As Kerrigan stepped into the house, the detective looked first at me, then at Jerod.

I tried to evaluate the look on his face to determine if it was a look of surprise for us having gotten loose from our prison cell, or if it was a look of bewilderment that we were even alive. Maybe he was the one who had arranged for our capture and was returning, expecting to find our dead bodies. Or maybe he had in fact told the truth about not knowing we were here. I was about to find out, but not until I was the one holding the gun.

As Kerrigan stepped through the door, I tossed the whiskey bottle at his face.

"Here, catch, " I said. In the same instant, while he was ducking his head and raising both hands to catch the bottle, I swung the heavy end of the steel bar around in a circle that caught him on the side of his left leg just below the knee. Instantly, all six-foot-four, two-hundred-thirty pounds of the man went crashing face first to the floor.

"Uhh!" Thud. "Eh…Ohh…! Worley, what the hell?"

In one second I was on his back, smashing the steel bar across the back of his neck with my right hand. In another instant I had retrieved his service weapon with my left hand.

"My god, Worley, what the hell was that all about?"

"Just relax, Lieutenant." I sat straddled over the small of Kerrigan's back, the steel bar still across the back of his neck. "I'll ask the questions from now on. You can speak when you're spoken to. Now tell me, what's your involvement in these murders?"

"I'm the homicide detective, remember? And you're under arrest for assaulting a police officer."

"Good luck with that. You can file a complaint from death row; which is exactly where you're going if I find out you're involved in this. Why didn't you tell me you have a twin brother that's a serial killer?"

"Worley, you have completely lost it. Did somebody hit you over the head or something?"

"As a matter of fact, they did, just like this." WHAP! I slapped the back of Kerrigan's head with the side of his 9mm service weapon. "How does that feel? Would you like some more?"

"Ooohhh! My god, Worley, you got to believe me. I don't know what you're talking about."

"Consider yourself lucky. I should knock you out, like you did me, which is exactly what I will do if you don't start telling me something I can believe."

"You're sick, Worley. I didn't do anything to you. Get the—"

WHAP! "No swearing, Lieutenant. You need to concentrate on passing this test and so far, you're not doing too well." "Now, once again, what is your involvement in this murder case?"

"Okay, okay! I'll tell you what I know, just get the…I mean get off me."

"I don't want to shoot you, Kerrigan, so don't give me a reason, because I will if I have to."

I got off his back and Kerrigan slowly sat up, rubbing his leg with one hand and his head with the other. Scowling, he looked first at me and then at Jerod.

"Okay, have at it, and remember, if you try anything, I'll shoot you right here and Jerod will be my witness that you were a prime suspect in this case. Isn't that right, Jerod?"

"That's right, Lou. I got your back all the way on this one. I figured something wasn't right when he led us into the boonies on that jeep trail, and I'm real anxious to see how he talks his way out of this."

Kerrigan reached around and shut the door behind him, then scooted back against it. Suddenly, his shoulders slumped forward and he let out a sigh. I wasn't sure if it was a sigh of relief, or exasperation, but he seemed to be contemplating his next move—or story.

While Kerrigan contemplated and rubbed his sore leg, I backed away to sit beside Jerod against the far wall of the room.

"I'll have to go back a few years to give you the history," he said.

"That's okay, take your time. We're not going anywhere."

I suspected all along that there was more to Mark Kerrigan than met the eye. I also suspected that he was somehow personally connected to this case; far more personally than just as the investigation detective.

"Go ahead, Lieutenant, we're listening."

Kerrigan began, "Well, first off, you can rest assured that I have no connection to the murder case other than as a homicide detective. It's the orphanage that I have a history with. You see, a lifetime ago, I was an orphan at the same orphanage."

"I'm not interested in your sob story. I just want to know where the orphanage is and who's running it?" I said.

"I'm not sure now. Back then it was about a mile from here, that field where we left the car. But it's all gone now. Nothing left but a flat concrete slab that once was the floor of the building."

"How do you know that?" I asked.

"Because I went over there last night after you guys disappeared."

"Where were you when we disappeared? How come you weren't around to back us up?"

"I lost track of you. I thought you were behind me, then suddenly you were gone. I walked around that cabin to check it out and by the time I got back you guys had taken the car and left. So I walked over to the old site of the orphanage."

"Where did you spend the night?" I asked.

"In that cabin I found. There was a window that was unlocked so I spent the night in one of the bedrooms."

"Really, did you sleep on the floor?"

"No. I slept on the bed with a nice blanket pulled up over me."

"I'm happy for you. So what's all this about being an orphan?"

"I thought you didn't want to hear it."

"I changed my mind."

"Swell. Anyway, I was adopted out when I was three years old and lived with my adoptive parents in Palmer until I was eighteen."

"Are they still living?" I asked.

"Yes, but they're in San Francisco now."

"Were you aware growing up that you had been adopted as a child?"

"No. My parents didn't tell me until my wife and I started considering adoption as an alternative."

"An alternative to what?"

"Why don't you just shut-up and listen before I decide none of this is any of your business?"

I grinned a little, but decided to let Kerrigan go ahead and tell his story.

"I met and married my wife, Gloria, when we were in college at USC. Five years later we realized she couldn't have children. That was when my parents told me that I had been adopted and suggested we give the same orphanage a call."

"How long ago did all this take place?"

"It's been over thirty years ago. I had no idea it had been torn down since then."

"How did you know where it was located if you were only three years old when you lived there?"

"My parents came with us when we adopted our first child. The orphanage was still operating then. After we adopted, we decided to re-locate back to Alaska."

I was starting to become intrigued with Kerrigan's story. Hearing it kind-of made him seem more human, more flesh and blood like the rest of us. Instead of a cold-hearted—*always the* homicide detective man of steel. Unconsciously, my attitude toward him began to soften.

"Was that the only time you and your wife adopted a child?" I asked.

"No. We adopted three over the course of six years, all girls, all within two years of the same age, and all different ethnicity."

"Really!" I said.

"Yeah, really. You got a problem with that?"

"Not at all, I'm actually impressed. Didn't think you would be capable of so much ethnic-diversity. Where are your daughters now?"

"All but one live in Anchorage, the third one is in Seattle. Of course they're all grown now and have their own families."

"Who was running the orphanage then?"

"I'm not sure. I'd have to search through all that paper-work, which is probably in a box somewhere in the basement."

"What about your twin brother, the one I believe might be our serial killer?"

"I don't have a twin brother."

"Jerod, does this guy have a twin brother?"

"He either has a twin brother or they're one and the same and we should bury him in the back-yard."

I looked at Jerod. He appeared to be adapting very well to his new role as a detective's helper.

"We'll find out soon enough, as soon as we get the results back on the DNA samples. If they're not in fact one and the same, at least we'll be able to prove to our detective that, whether he knows it or not, he really does have a twin brother."

"Are you talking about the guy that kidnapped me?"

"Probably, you saw him, didn't you? Don't you think you two look alike?"

"All I saw was a blur. I couldn't tell you what the guy looked like. Furthermore, I think your imagination is on fast forward. And what

DNA samples are you referring to?" Kerrigan squirmed and rubbed his leg again.

"The evidence the killer left on the hill when he was waiting for his next victim, the same girl I took to the hospital the other day."

"Go on," Kerrigan said, his interest perking up.

"The killer chew's tobacco and was kind enough to leave a few splatters of spittle on the ground where he was waiting for the girl. I sent the samples to the lab. We should have the results in a few days."

"How do you know it's the same guy?"

"Rudy saw him driving through town when he and Grady's daughter were running off with the truck I had purchased from the old man; which, by the way, was loaded with all the evidence we would have ever needed to convict both of them. That's why, if we can find him, we have every justification to arrest him and take him with us. Rudy can tell us for sure if it's him or not. I'm also sure he's the same guy that stole Jerod's car."

Kerrigan considered what I had told him, but still was not totally convinced. "That still doesn't prove he's the murderer we're looking for, or that he's related to me."

"The DNA along with two eyewitnesses will be all the proof I need. Besides, Jerod and Rudy are not the only ones who saw him. I did too, just before you whacked me over the head."

"I told you, I didn't whack you in the head. If I'd have whacked you, you'd still be whacked."

"Hey!" Jerod interjected, "I just remembered. I took a picture of him with my cell phone."

"You took a picture of him?" I said, surprised. "When?"

"After I sent you that text. Just before I lost my phone."

"Where did you lose it?" I asked..

"After I took the picture I tossed it in the grass right before they grabbed me."

"Why would you toss your phone?" Kerrigan asked, agitated.

"Because I had taken a picture of your twin brother and if they saw it, they would have destroyed my phone or maybe even killed me."

"Well, let's go find it."

"Kerrigan moaned as he carefully staggered to his feet. "Okay, that still doesn't explain what you two are doing here, or what happened to the Land Cruiser?"

Jerod and I stood also. "You tell me. I'm still not sure it wasn't you and your accomplices who used it to bring me here, while one of the others brought Jerod in their car."

"I haven't seen the Land Cruiser since you and I left it with your buddy here. Nor did I have anything to do with your ending up in this place. So get over it."

"You mean you don't have a vehicle with you?" I asked, alarmed.

"Of course not." Kerrigan pointed to Jerod. "Maybe you should be looking a little harder at him. It looks to me like he's the only one of us who isn't bleeding."

I paused for a brief moment to reflect on that remote possibility.

"Why is that, Jerod? Come to think of it, why would a man who has already killed multiple times let you live, knowing that you could identify him?"

Jerod suddenly looked a little nervous.

Kerrigan looked surprised. "You mean both of you saw him and he didn't kill either one of you?" Kerrigan asked. "Doesn't sound like much of a killer."

Suddenly another thought occurred to me, "Yeah, but he couldn't have suspected me of anything other than trespassing. Unless..."

"Unless what?" Jerod asked, anxious to divert the suspicion away from him.

"Unless...there were four of you," I said.

"Four? What four?" Jerod asked again.

"You...the two guys who were dragging you...and the guy who actually hit me in the head, assuming for a moment that it wasn't Kerrigan."

"Hey, Lou, it's me, Jerod. I'm on your side. I didn't see anyone except the Maverick man and those two thugs. I didn't even see you until they brought you into the basement. I told you already. They brought you down ten-minutes after me, you were still out cold. If we can find the cell phone, you'll see, I really did take a picture. Why would I do that if I were one of them?"

"I see your point, Jerod. I'm just considering every angle. But that doesn't mean there wasn't a fourth person. Maybe even the girl. Maybe Karen is the one who hit me in the head," I said.

"Lou, I told you already. The lieutenants twin brother got a phone call, then went back into the woods right after that other guy called someone on his phone. I'm sure it was him that hit you in the head."

"Maybe Jerod's right, Lieutenant. Maybe it was your brother that whacked me."

Kerrigan thought for a minute, while he gently massaged the two sore spots on his head. "Too many maybe's, for me. However, it is possible that someone else knocked you out then called the *big guy* on the phone. If it was the girl that would explain why he went into the woods to drag you out. But as far as him being my twin brother, I won't buy that until I see the picture."

"Then let's get going. How far did you say it is?" I asked.

Kerrigan opened the door and peered outside. "A little over a mile, "he said.

The dirt and gravel driveway led us out to another gravel road that was only slightly more traveled than the private drive. Kerrigan approached the intersection cautiously as Jerod and I walked together behind the lieutenant.

"A half mile from here we'll come to another driveway that takes us to the cabin we saw in the woods. There's a little trail that goes from that cabin to the place where we parked the car when we first arrived."

"That's the one where you slept all night in a nice soft bed, is that right?" I asked, sarcastically.

"That's right, Worley. Hey, you're finally starting to get the hang of this detective business. Keep up the good work and someday maybe you'll be able to solve the crime of the century."

I ignored Kerrigan.

"How far down the driveway to the cabin?" I asked.

"About a quarter mile."

At the end of the drive, we all paused briefly looking both directions down the gravel road, almost as if we expected Jerod's white Toyota Land Cruiser to come by any moment to pick us up.

Short scrubby trees lined the narrow road on either side. Fifty yards away, a mother moose and her two calves appeared in the middle of the road, enjoying the respite from the dense forest of trees stacked so closely together a man could barely move through. They saw us and reluctantly melted back into the thicket.

It was already mid-morning and the sound of an airplane propeller clawing at the dense morning air as it departed a nearby airport droned past overhead.

"If you're waiting for a taxi you should have brought a lunch," Kerrigan said. It was a sarcastic statement, but I knew I had it coming. It was part of the game and I was now one of the players.

"I would have settled for breakfast," I said. "Why didn't you stop by McDonalds and pick-up takeout on your way over?"

Jerod chuckled. "You guys are a barrel of laughs. One minute you're hitting each other in the head and the next you're roasting each other, you'd think you were siblings."

"There's no way I could be Kerrigan's sibling, I'm not a serial killer." It was so easy, it had actually become fun. I thought of what Rusty had said: "Someday you and Kerrigan might become good friends."

"If you were, I'd have locked you up by now," Kerrigan retorted.

"If I were what, a sibling, or a serial killer?"

"Either one."

"Your twin is both, and you haven't locked him up yet."

Kerrigan didn't respond. I was almost sorry I had said that—*almost*, but not quite. No one said much the rest of the way to the trail.

Finally, we all emerged out of the dense foliage into the open area where we had initially parked the Land Cruiser. We followed Jerod to the place where he tossed his cell phone. I began looking around while Jerod searched through the tall grass.

"I found it!" he exclaimed.

"Good, let me see that picture," Kerrigan demanded.

"The battery is dead and it's been rained on. I'm not sure if it still works."

"Did you turn it off before you threw it away?" I asked.

"No, didn't have time."

"I have a charger in the car, but it won't do me any good until we find the car. We'll charge it up later.

"Brilliant deduction, Watson," Kerrigan said. "Jerod, you stay here. Worley, you come with me."

"Where are you going? Are you planning on hitting me in the head again?"

"You certainly have it coming." Kerrigan reached up and rubbed his two sore spots again. I grinned.

"I want you to show me exactly where you were standing when they hit you over the head."

I led Kerrigan back to the spot where it happened.

"I was standing right over there when I first saw the Maverick man and his two buddies. They had just apprehended Jerod and were dragging him toward the car."

"Good, don't go all the way in. I want to see if anybody left anything behind."

I returned to where we had left Jerod and waited with him while Kerrigan investigated the area. After twenty-minutes he returned.

"Did you lose anything in there?"

"Like what?"

"You tell me. Did you have anything on your person when you and I first went into the woods that you did not have when you woke up in the basement?"

I thought a minute.

"Yeah, as a matter of fact I did, my phone, and my weapon. I already told you that."

Kerrigan tossed something in my direction. It was my phone.

"You found it! Hey, you're pretty good."

He tossed me something else too. It was bigger and blacker. I dropped the phone as I caught my Glock-seventeen..

"You found my gun!"

"Yeah, it was a regular garbage dump back there. Can you think of anything else?"

I was beginning to feel like a bumbling idiot.

"No, not that I know of."

"What about this?"

Kerrigan pulled an envelope from his pocket. It was ripped open and the contents had been removed and roughly stuffed back in.

"I thought you said the girl was dead?"

"What girl?"

"The one on the hill that you said you took to the trauma center."

"She is dead! Dr. Brady told me the next morning."

"How long have you had this letter from the Doc?" Kerrigan shook the mangled envelope in my face.

Suddenly, I remembered the envelope Genneta Williams had given me back at the school's flight center.

"You should have read this before we left," Kerrigan said with a blend of exasperation and disgust in his voice.

I quickly grabbed the letter and began to read:

> "Dear Mr. Worley,
>
> I didn't feel right about lying to you. From what you had told me about the homicide detective, I thought it best to not let anyone know that the girl you brought in was still alive. At the time no one knew for sure if she would live or die and I wanted to do what I could to protect her.
>
> I hope I did the right thing. Please find who did this terrible thing before it happens to someone else. Thank-you.
>
> Signed: Doctor Melissa Brady, MD, Neurosurgery, William Shearer Trauma Center, Sitka Alaska.

I was stunned. Tears began to flood my eyes.

"She told me she was dead," I said, my voice cracking.

Kerrigan saw that I was visibly shaken and waited for me to get it together.

"We have a problem," he said. *His* voice was not shaking.

"I'm aware of that," I said. "Let's get going. I'll call Melissa as soon as I can get a charge on this phone."

"Call her now. You can use my phone," Kerrigan said as he tossed me his cell. "Tell them to get that kid somewhere safe, and call your people down there and let them know what the problem is and get someone over to that hospital right now."

I checked the lieutenant's phone.

"You have no signal. I'll do it when we get back to the airport."

"How long have you been carrying that envelope around with you?"

"Since yesterday morning before we left. Genneta Williams handed it to me when I dropped you and Rusty off to have your heads examined. I guess I got distracted with chasing that big twin and forgot to read it."

"Sounds like you're the one who should have had his head examined. We'll be damned lucky if they haven't gotten to her by now. And get someone to come and pick us up."

We walked until we reached the main road and hitched a ride from the first car that came by. I handed the driver a C-note to take us to the airport.

There was not much conversation between us on the way. I told Jerod to send me and Kerrigan the picture he had taken of the Maverick man as soon as he charged his phone, and promised to pay the expenses of another rental car until I could replace his car that had been stolen by our abductors. I also asked him not to report it just now.

Back aboard the CJ4, I quickly filed a flight plan to Sitka.

"Are you getting on board?" I asked Kerrigan.

"No. You go ahead. I have a few things to do on this end."

"Like what?"

"Like finding that orphanage and getting to know the people who run it."

"Okay, good idea. Here, take this card." I pulled a credit card from my wallet and handed it to Kerrigan. "You'll need this to get yourself some transportation. And keep your eyes open for Jerod's Land Cruiser. If you need air transportation, have Jerod fly you where you need to go. I'll make arrangements to get someone up here to watch your back while I'm gone."

"How do you know I won't abscond with this and go on an all-expenses paid vacation?"

"Because you're the best detective in the world, that's why. And I don't hold it against you just because your twin brother is a serial killer."

"What a guy! By-the-way, did you notice that the twin Cessna is gone?"

"Yeah, as soon as I get in the air I'll call my supervisor friend and see if I can find out where he went."

"Don't forget to call the Doc."

For the first time since I had met Kerrigan, I actually was starting to like the guy. The suspicions I had had of him were at last all gone. I was now sure that although he might possibly be related to the killer, he had no knowledge of it and certainly was not involved in whatever demented schemes his brother was involved in.

I left a message for Supervisor Franklin to call me. While I waited, I called the trauma center and asked to speak with Dr. Brady. Moments later a very excited and out of breath, Melissa answered the phone.

"Mr. Worley, I'm so glad you called. Where are you?"

"I'm in the air, Melissa. I'll be there in a couple of hours. What's the problem?"

"Mr. Worley, I thought when I gave you that letter you would get someone over here to watch the girl. Did you read the letter, Mr. Worley?"

"I didn't read it until an hour ago, Melissa. I'm sorry, someone should be there shortly. Is everything all right?"

"Mr. Worley, there's been a shooting in the hospital…oh…my! I'm so upset."

"Who got shot, Melissa?"

"First a man showed up who said he worked for you and was waiting in the girl's room when two other men showed up with guns…oh…my…I am so—"

"Take it easy, Melissa. Did the first man give you his name?"

"Yes. He said he was, uh, a German, I think."

"Rusty German is my son-in-law, Melissa. Tell me what happened after the shooting?"

"We called the police. Police Chief Borski is here. He wants to speak with you."

I was holding my breath, afraid of what Borski was going to say. At the same time the fires of revenge once again burned inside me.

"Lou, this is Borski. Where the hell are you?"

"I'm in the air, Ivan. I'll be there in a couple of hours. Can you tell me what happened?"

"Yeah, your son-in-law wasted a couple of goons in the hospital hallway. Now we got a big event down here. The news reporters have already started to show up. I don't know what you want me to tell them. I told you I didn't want this thing spilling over onto my turf, Worley. Didn't I tell you that? I need you to get down here and clean this up, get it back in the jar and put a lid on it. Do I make myself clear?"

Ivan didn't give me a chance to say one way or the other. He just punched the red button. I guess it was his way of making me and my mess go away.

I taxied into position to hold, as per the instructions from the tower, and moments later the Citation was climbing into the sky at a rate of twenty-five-hundred feet a minute. Once established on course and leveled at my assigned altitude, I called Rusty.

"Yeah, Dad."

"Hey, son. I was a little concerned about you for a minute."

"Why?"

"Melissa's account of what happened was a little sketchy. I wasn't sure at first who won the gunfight. I'm sure glad you're okay."

"Yeah, I'm fine, Dad. I'm still here at the hospital."

"I thought Borski had officers on the floor."

"He left one here but, I don't think he's fully aware of what we're up against and I'm not at all sure he's capable of providing the kind of protection she needs especially if they send more guys like those two they just carried out of here. So I'm staying until you get here."

"Where's Rudy? How come he's not there with you?"

"Rudy's in the compound."

"In the compound? Doing what?"

"Undercover work."

"How did he get in?"

"We gave Larry Mauktokta a wad of cash and he let him go in with Elizabeth."

"Is Elizabeth still in the compound?"

"No, she came out, Rudy stayed."

"Okay, that's good. Sounds like you've made a little headway. Maybe Rudy will dig up some useful information for us. Does he have his cell phone with him?"

"Yeah, he sends me an update text every few hours."

"Did the old man's house burn down yet?"

"No."

"Why not?"

"Rudy wants to talk to you first, but not on the phone."

"Okay, send him a text and tell him to find a place in the fence line where he can get me in and out. Not the one up by the guard shack, but one a little more secluded. Then have him mark the trail so I can find it."

"Dad, it would be a lot easier on you if I did all that. Why don't you stay here and watch the girl? I can inform Rudy that you want me to take care of everything."

"No, this whole thing has gotten too personal for me. I want to get this guy myself."

"Okay, Dad, but stick close to Rudy. I don't want either of you getting hurt."

"Don't worry, son, I'll be fine. One more thing, what's the name of the officer that Borski left on the floor?"

"Wait a minute, I'll ask."

Rusty put me on hold for what seemed like a lot longer than a minute, finally he returned.

"Parker, Ralph Parker. Do you know him?"

"Sounds familiar, but I don't think so. Must be that new recruit."

"He's leaving anyway. Borski sent him home."

"By-the-way, where's your Stationair?"

"It's at the school's airstrip. Eric has the Kodiak."

"Where is he?"

"I sent him to Anchorage to pick-up some extra people."

"What extra people?"

"I figured we were getting spread a little thin, so I asked Kevin to get us some help. Three more guys are on the way here to help us out."

"That's good, son. You read my mind. Anyone I know?"

"Yeah, they were involved in those undercover operations you and Cal put together when you guys took down that international poaching ring run by Dale Stanley."

"When will they arrive? I want to talk to them before they go to work."

"Eric left this morning to pick them up, so I imagine he'll be here by the time you get back."

"Good. I'll call him and have him meet me at the school's airstrip. As soon as I get these guys briefed, I'll get someone up there to relieve you."

I flew the LDA approach into Sitka and cancelled IFR immediately after emerging from the solid overcast. I gave the tower a heads up that

I would be diverting to the learning center's private airstrip. I had done this a hundred times since the learning center project had begun, so it was of no surprise to the controllers.

In another moment, I was on final to the school's private airport. The yellow and black Quest Kodiak-sitting in front of the flight center office told me that Eric and the three new recruits had already arrived. I parked the Citation CJ4 next to the Kodiak, and called Eric.

"We're at the school cafeteria, having lunch," he said. Once again, I was reminded that I had not eaten in what was now almost fourteen hours.

I walked into the cafeteria and headed straight to the chow line where I picked up a tray and silverware. I could see the three men sitting together in one of the booths and immediately recognized them but couldn't remember their names. It had been almost seven years since we had closed the case on Pasteli.

"Good afternoon, gentlemen. Hello, Eric," I said, stalling for time.

"How was your trip to Fairbanks, Mr. Worley?" Eric asked.

"It was complicated." I turned to the three ex-military personnel that had worked for me once before and apologized for not remembering their names. The biggest and huskiest of the three spoke first.

"That's all-right, Mr. Worley, we only met once anyway. I'm Scarf." He turned to the man next to him who was staring through me with one of those thousand-yard stares that I had seen so often in Vietnam; the look of a man who had seen about ten-months too much hard action.

"This is Morgue," he said. If I had a name like that, I'd stare too. In this business nobody gives last names, and first names are earned on the battlefield. Turning to the third man, he said, "This is Tripod, he's our designated hitter." That means sniper in war language. Scarf chuckled. Morgue stared.

"Glad to meet you gentlemen." I looked at Tripod who sat as though he hadn't heard a word anyone had said. "Well, thank-you for coming, gentlemen."

I finished the meeting by giving them a rundown of the case, and we arrived at an agreement concerning their compensation. Before I left I turned to Eric.

"Eric, I'm going to have Tripod and Scarf watch the girl's room and I'll take Rusty with me. I need you to take Morgue with you. You can fly Rusty's 206 over to Sitka, get the Citation and take Morgue on up to Fairbanks. I want him to take care of my detective up there. I'll brief him on that."

"Yes, sir, Mr. Worley. What do you want me to do then?"

"You can stay up there in case Kerrigan needs you to bring him back here, or maybe follow someone."

I gave Tripod and Morgue their personal instructions and we exchanged phone numbers.

"Do all of you men have your own personal weapons?"

All three men reached for the sidearms.

"Good," I said. "How about automatic weapons?"

"In the Kodiak," Scarf said. "A half dozen AR's five-thousand rounds of ammo, and a sack of grenades."

"Okay, men. Get your weapons and packs. You are officially on duty. Scarf, you're with me. Morgue, when you get to Fairbanks, I want you to stick close to Lieutenant Kerrigan. If he gives you any crap, just stare at him." Morgue stared at me without responding. "I'll send him a picture of you to let him know you're coming so he can pick you up.

"Tripod, you can come with me. I'll take you up to the hospital ward and you can relieve my son-in-law. You and Scarf can alternate shifts watching the girl. You can work that out between yourselves.

"Be aware, they have already tried to kill her twice, and I'm sure they're not going to give up until they finish the job or we find out who's paying them and can put a stop to it. That will be my job. Any questions?"

I studied the three men who made their living hiring themselves out as mercenaries to anyone who could afford their services, men who had all been in a lot worse conflicts then they would encounter working on our little murder case; men, whose particular skills and capabilities, were certainly what some might consider an 'overkill' on my part, no pun intended. But I had already given Daily a heads-up when I told him that I may need to bring on some contract help. Where did he think I was going to get them—from the local job source office?"

One thing is for sure. These guys Kevin had sent us do not mess around. You only have to catch Morgue staring at you one time with that 'thousand-yard-stare' to be fully persuaded of that.

While I waited at the flight school's FBO for Rusty to arrive, Superintendent Franklin returned my call. He said he would get the information I needed and send it to my fax machine in the Kodiak.

An hour later, Rusty arrived and I proceeded to brief him on the latest developments from my end. Rusty had managed to avoid the news media on his way out of the hospital, and we wasted no time in getting out of Dodge before they showed up at the FBO. Now that Scarf, Tripod, and Morgue had joined the team, I felt confident I wouldn't need to worry any longer over the welfare of the girl, which would leave me free to concentrate on following the chain of evidence that would lead us straight to the killer.

CHAPTER 11

Shirley Crowder finished her dinner and slid the plate to one side as she lingered over a copy of the week-old *Mt. Edgecombe Gazette*.

The headline read, "THREE BODIES IN TWO YEARS: WHEN IS ENOUGH, ENOUGH?" The main body of the article went on to say, "Is anything being done? When asked repeatedly, Police Chief Ivan Borski refuses comment. " The article further suggested " had the victims been Caucasian, would the killer be in custody by now?"

Shirley set the paper aside and burying her head in her hands whispered, "Those poor girls." Silently she prayed, "*Oh, God! I pray they were none of our girls. I pray for Camilla and for Falling Feather and Tracy. Wherever they are, oh Lord, protect them.*"

There had been several dozen girls that had been sent to Shirley's door over the last ten years since she had followed Prophet Joseph Morning to Kake, Alaska. Because of her devout faithfulness to her religion, Shirley had been selected by the leadership to provide parental instruction to many of the young girls, most of whom had come from the orphanage in Fairbanks. All under the guise of helping them adjust. In actuality, it was more of a last ditch effort to get them to learn submission to the authority of the church leadership.

Shirley Crowder was one of the faithful who had come alone from Salt Lake City, Utah, which had been her home since childhood. Growing up, Shirley and her parents attended a Seventh-day (Saturday) keeping Christian Church for as far back as she could remember, where obedience to God's law, particularly the Old-Testament Jewish Decalogue, was the standard of obedience and service expected of God and where anything short of perfect obedience would result in eternal damnation in the fires of hell.

Even as a little girl, Shirley never felt like she had ever completely satisfied the requirements of that law, written by God's own finger on tablets of stone and handed off to Moses for the children of Israel in the Sinai desert.

As Shirley grew into adulthood, her feelings of inadequacy grew deeper. The Ten-Commandments were so all inclusive in regard to every detail of her life she could never escape the constant condemnation of them.

There was the tenth commandment: "Thou shalt not covet" (Exodus 20:17). There were so many things she longed for: a simple ring, a pretty scarf, or a little makeup. Even to be loved; not just spiritually. She knew she was already loved in that way by her spiritual brothers and sisters, yet she desired more than that. Shirley desired the kind of love that a man has for a woman and a woman has for a man. She had seen it before between young couples and in movies and read of it in romance novels. She knew it was covetous thinking; her conscience tortured her continually and she shrank from the condemnation.

There was the first commandment: "Thou shalt have no other gods before me" (Exodus 20:3). In Shirley's personal possession's she had things she felt guilty for keeping. There was the necklace that had been her mother's, the pocket watch that had been her father's, and the letter that a young man had once written her long ago, declaring his love for her and begging her to marry him. Oh, how she regretted the day she had declined his proposal.

There is great power in revival preaching and Shirley had been swept away with it. It was early in her new religious awakening when Shirley's boyfriend, Lance, saw her tendency toward fanaticism and realized she was heading down a road where he did not want to go. He panicked and, in an effort to avoid losing her, asked her to marry him. Lance was not sure he was ready for that next step, but he felt if he didn't, the woman he had fallen head over heels in love with might be gone forever.

Then there was the seventh commandment: "Thou shalt not commit adultery" (Exodus 20:14). And in Matthew 5:27 and 28, Jesus had said, "Ye have heard that is was said by them of old time, Thou shalt not commit adultery: But I say unto you, That whosoever looketh on a woman to lust after her hath committed adultery with her already in his heart." There was no escaping it, the "law" extended to the very marrow of human nature, where it condemned even the most pious.

Shirley had never married, or even been with a man. She had been alone most of her life and even in the compound, at night, loneliness would torture her mind. No matter how much she prayed or fasted, or how hard she tried to control her thoughts during those moments, she still could not stop herself from thinking of a man. Because of it, feelings of condemnation tortured her every day of her life.

The church Shirley had been a member of her entire life kept the Seventh-day Sabbath---according to the fourth commandment in Exodus 20:8-11. It commanded that every secular activity, including every un-spiritual thought, be abandoned from the mind on the Sabbath day for the sake of absolute worship to God—on pain of death. The scriptures declared: "Sin is the transgression of the law; and the wages of sin is death," and Shirley could never remember a Sabbath that she had actually truly kept according to the letter of the law. Every morning and evening of her life was spent in prayer and repentance for the sins she had committed during the day and the thoughts she had entertained during the night. All the thoughts and feelings, the emotions and words that she had known, even at the time she spoke them against the letter of the law, required her repentance over and over again—yet nothing brought her peace.

Two years before Shirley had left Salt Lake City, Utah, an itinerant preacher came as a guest speaker to her home church. His name was Elder Joseph Morning. He preached of absolute victory over the flesh, absolute control of every thought and feeling, the achievement of the perfect character required to enter heaven's gate and to sit at the feet of Jesus as an absolute overcomer, completely, and finally victorious.

For almost two years, Shirley followed the man, who laid claim to being a prophet, from town to town and city to city. So compelling was his teaching that when he invited all who sought this life of holiness to follow him to Alaska, Shirley was among the first to volunteer. Generously she gave of her means. The only funds she kept for herself were for her own basic needs and expenses for the trip to Kake, Alaska. Yet she even felt guilty and selfish for that.

Shirley was not alone in the exodus of people fleeing the Laodicean Protestant churches. Over three-hundred came, people just like herself, looking for that ultimate spiritual experience of forgiveness and acceptance from God in return for their obedient service and offerings. To Kake, Alaska, they all journeyed. Some by boat, some by air, and some by whatever means they could manufacture or contrive. All with one aspiration: to sit at the feet of the self-proclaimed prophet, Joseph Morning.

A knock at the door of Shirley Crowder's thirty-four-foot travel trailer startled her. She was not expecting company.

"One moment please," she called out, not sure who it might be. Quickly, she put the newspaper out of sight in case it was the prophet or one of his understudies. Reading newspapers was frowned upon and considered worldly—it was time that could be better spent studying the bible or the teachings of the prophet, teachings that were considered the only writings superior to the scriptures themselves.

Shirley opened the door. The man before her appeared nervous, looking around as if he were afraid someone might see him. She did not recognize him as one of the company of believers and thought it strange that he was on the compound un-accompanied by a member of the church.

Rudy Crawford was about to knock for the second time when the door opened and a very attractive, slender woman in her early thirties greeted him, wearing a floor-length blue denim skirt with a white, cotton, long-sleeved sweater that extended a couple inches above her neckline where it neatly folded down into a collar. Her cheekbones stood out prominently on her remarkably sculptured face and drew attention to her dark blue eyes, along with her soft powdery skin and pouty lips. Her jaw line descended in perfect conformity to her beautifull features. Her hair was blond and splashed down her back like a lazy waterfall, all of which made for a very pleasant image to behold. Rudy stared at the lovely picture, speechless. He had not expected to see such remarkable beauty in a camp full of cult worshipers. Featured beneath her clothing was one more thing Rudy could not help but notice, a most exquisitely proportioned figure of a woman. He was instantly intrigued.

"Yes, may I help you?" She was very pleasant and her melodious alto voice was mesmerizing.

Rudy was a bit anxious and looked about to make sure he was not being watched.

"Good morning, ma'am. I'm looking for a lady by the name of Shirley. I don't know her last name. Would you happen to know where I could find her?"

Shirley took a step back, not sure what to say. Having never seen the man before she assumed that he must be an outsider. She knew that if he had not already met the approval of the guards at the gate, he wouldn't have been allowed onto the compound in the first place.

"I am Shirley Crowder. But I don't believe I know who you are, or why you would be looking for me."

"Yes, ma'am, I understand. My name is Rudy Crawford. I work for a private investigator by the name of Lou Worley. May I come in?"

Shirley was taken aback at his request. It would not be proper for a strange man to be in a camper trailer, alone, with a single woman, unchaperoned. What if someone saw them? Her reputation might be questioned.

Rudy took her hesitation as permission and entered her trailer, quickly drawing the door closed behind him.

"I'm sorry, ma'am, but I have to speak to you. I'm not trying to get you into any trouble, but it's very important that I ask you a few questions."

Shirley quickly closed the curtains so no one could see in.

"This is most improper, Mr. Crawford. I didn't intend for you to come into my home."

"I'm sorry, ma'am, but I couldn't take a chance on someone seeing me."

"How did you get onto the property? Are you a guest?"

"Yes, you could say that. I'm here because of certain information we've received from a lady in town named Elizabeth. Do you know her?"

"Yes, I do. How is Elizabeth? I haven't seen her for quite some time."

"She's fine, I guess. I've only met her once. I'm just following orders given me by the people I work for. They told me to locate you. They say I can trust you, is that true?"

"I don't know you. What is it you want?" Shirley asked, peeking cautiously through the curtains.

"I'm investigating the disappearance of a girl named Camilla Diaz. I've been told she lived with you at one time. Is that true?"

Shirley forgot about the curtains and looked at Rudy, her features taking on a concerned intrigue.

"Camilla? Why, yes, as a matter of fact she did stay with me for several months, but that has been more than a year ago."

Rudy now was the one leaning across the table looking through the slit in the curtains.

"Do you know what happened to her?"

"No! All I know is that she left. She had expressed, on a number of occasions, that she missed home."

"Where was home?"

"She was from Yuma, Arizona. At least that is what she told us."

"Has she made any contact with you or anyone else since she left?"

"Not that I'm aware of. Why do you ask?" Shirley returned to take her seat at the table. "You may sit if you like," she said, pointing to the vacant seat across from her.

"No thanks lady, I won't be here that long."

"Does this have anything to do with the deceased girls that I have read about in the paper?" Shirley asked. "Please tell me she is not one of them."

Rudy studied the woman for a moment, wondering if he told her the real truth would she be more likely to cooperate with the investigation. Taking a chance, he said to her, "Yes. We believe they all came from this compound. Was Camilla the only one you knew, or did you know the other two as well?"

Shirley hung her head. Tears formed at the corners of her eyes. She dabbed at them with her handkerchief.

"I'm hoping you can verify their names for me," Rudy said.

It was apparent to Rudy that this lady was learning for the first time of something she had suspected all along. Maybe even known, but could not admit to herself.

He said to her, "One was a Native American girl from either Montana or the Dakotas. We've been told her name may have been Falling Feather. Evidently she was a member of the Sioux Nation. We haven't learned the name of the third girl that was found only three weeks ago. I'm hoping to find someone who might have known her. Did you know her by chance?"

"Oh heavens, that must have been Tracy. Yes, they all stayed with me at different times before they left. Oh my, I hope it wasn't something I did that drove them away. They all were so worldly and would not submit to the teachings. I felt so bad for them. What about Rebecca, she has been gone for several days now? My friend Frances has been worried sick for her. Do you know anything about Rebecca? She and Tracy were close. We think she ran away to find her."

Rudy saw her emotional attachment to the missing girls and felt bad for having been the one to bring her the awful news of their demise. It was also obvious that Shirley was not aware of the last attack on the fourth victim, whose name he just learned. Rudy could not bring himself to add the additional grief to her already broken heart.

"Did you say there may be another girl named Rebecca?"

"Yes, she was staying with Frances, one of the other lady guardians. Rebecca left her a note."

"A note! Where can I find this note?"

"Frances has it."

"I'd like to see it. Can you get Frances to come over here and bring the note with her? I'd like to talk to her as well."

"I'll have to go over to her place and see if she's home. She lives about five minutes away. Would you like me to go get her now?"

"That would be great, but I need to tell you something. If you have any plans to inform the leaders that I'm nosing around about those missing girls, you need to understand that I'm prepared to shoot my way out of here." Rudy opened his jacket to reveal the 9mm Beretta sidearm that hung from a shoulder holster. "So if you don't want to see any of your friends get hurt, you better keep your mouth shut. Both of you! Is that clear?"

"It is quite clear, Mr. Crawford. Don't worry, I understand. Just one more thing, Mr. Crawford, forgive me for asking, but are you hungry? Would you like something to eat? I just made a fresh pot of lentil stew. It's very delicious, and full of vegetables. You're welcome to it, there is more than enough."

Rudy thought for a minute to the last time he had a hot meal. It had been over twenty-four hours. *I better not, don't want to be beholden to her.*

"No thanks, I'm not hungry," he said.

"Nonsense, you have been glancing at that pot of stew on the stove ever since you invited yourself into my home, so you might as well have some lunch while I go find Frances, and I won't take no for an answer."

Rudy blushed a little realizing he had been caught red-handed looking hungry.

"All right then, if you insist. I do appreciate it, that's right nice of you."

Shirley dished up a bowl of stew and fixed Rudy a cucumber sandwich, placing it in front of him with a nicely folded napkin. Rudy had never eaten vegetarian food before and looked at it as if he had never seen anything so disgusting in all his life. Shirley laughed and, smiling giddily, disappeared out the door.

Rudy waited until she had gone and looked into her refrigerator to see if there was any meat that she had forgotten to put into the stew. There was none, so he sat down at the table and slowly began to eat. Though half starved, he ate tentatively, expecting the lentil stew to taste horrible and the cucumber sandwich to ruin forever his taste for real food. However, his hunger took over his prejudice and soon he was wolfing it down like a pig in a slop trough, and helping him-self to more.

Suddenly there was a soft knock at the door, and before he could get up, it quickly opened. It was Shirley and behind her was another lady dressed very similar to Shirley but who wore her long brown hair in a bun rolled high up on the back of her head. Her clothing was the same, in-that it was simple and non-elaborate, yet clean.

"Mr. Crawford, this is Frances Archer. She is the lady who Rebecca stayed with before she ran away."

Rudy had stood and was still wiping lentil stew and homemade mayonnaise from the corners of his mouth.

"Nice to meet you, ma'am," he said with his mouth still full.

"Nice to meet you too, Mr. Crawford." Frances looked at Rudy and then at the table where he had been stuffing his face with lentil stew, then again at Shirley.

"I see Shirley has provided for your nutritional needs."

"Ahem, yes. It was actually quite good."

Frances looked back at Shirley. Shirley was looking at Rudy with the shyness of a little girl and Rudy was looking both shy and uncomfortable.

"Yes, Shirley is a good cook."

Suddenly Rudy remembered his purpose for being there.

"Come on in, Mrs. Archer, have a seat."

"It's Miss Archer."

"Yes, ahem, Miss Archer. I understand that a girl that was staying with you temporarily ran away recently, is that correct?"

"Yes. I've been so worried about her. Have you found her?"

Rudy was not ready to disclose any facts of the case, so he went straight to the issue.

"I understand she left a note. Do you have the note with you?"

"Yes, I do, I have it right here." Frances handed him the letter that Rebecca had written on the notepad paper before she left, and turned toward the door.

"Wait a minute," Rudy said. "I need to ask you a few more questions." Frances paused and slowly turned back around to face Rudy.

"I need to go, Mr. Crawford. I am expected in a Bible study that will be starting in a few minutes."

Rudy kept reading the note, ignoring Frances. As he finished, he looked up at Shirley.

"Did you know anything about the accusations this girl has made in this note?"

Shirley looked nervous and so did Frances. Shirley did not answer immediately and Rudy looked from her to Frances.

"How about you? Did you know about any sexual misconduct involving minors that has been going on around here?"

Frances appeared uneasy. She said to him, "There have been rumors from time to time about improprieties among the boy's but nothing to do with the leadership. They are all men of God with very high standards. None of them would ever do anything like this. I believe Rebecca just made these things up to justify her running away. She had a very good situation here. She had living conditions, room and board, scholastic opportunities, and certainly the opportunity to know and revere God, which in this day and age is a saving grace to a homeless girl her age." Frances leaned out of the door to see if anyone was nearby.

Rudy looked back at Shirley, who was looking somewhat disconcerted.

"What about you, Shirley?"

Shirley looked at Frances, who was still looking outside, then back at Rudy and silently mouthed the words, "I'll tell you later."

"Miss Archer, if you need to go, then go ahead. But if you don't mind, I'd like to keep this note." Frances stepped from the trailer and started to leave. Rudy stood and stepped to the door.

"One more thing you should know, I work for the Alaska State Police and we might need to talk to you again so don't leave this compound until we're satisfied that what you say is true. Do you understand?"

Frances paused momentarily, but did not look Rudy in the eye.

"As you wish, Mr. Crawford. But I've already told you everything I know," she said as she walked away.

Rudy watched Frances until she disappeared around the back of the trailer home, then turned back to face Shirley.

"Miss Crowder, I think she wouldn't believe it if the leadership admitted it to her face, do you?"

"Mr. Crawford, you may call me Shirley. And, no she wouldn't. However, I am not nearly as naïve as most of the people who live here."

"So are you saying you do believe the allegations by this girl?" He held up the note and shook it in front of her.

"I have suspected that something was not right for over a year."

"What did you mean just now when you said, 'I'll tell you later'?"

Shirley sighed and sat down at the table.

"I don't know."

"I think you do. At least you know something. If you're afraid of getting into trouble you don't need to worry. I'm not really a cop. I just work for one, and we're only after the people responsible for the deaths of those girls and any atrocities that led to their running away from this place. So if you can point me in the right direction, I'll make sure you have immunity from prosecution and protection from any ramifications as a result of your cooperation."

Shirley held her head in her hands and stared at the table-top.

"I have felt there was something wrong for a long while."

"What did you think was wrong?" Rudy asked softly.

"The young girls that come from the orphanage…"

"What orphanage?"

"The orphanage in Fairbanks, the children that have not been adopted out by the time they are eleven years old are sent down here to be made into believers to be raised within the teachings of the prophet's church.

"Anyway, they're sent to live in the dormitory on the hill above the rest of the camp. After that, the only time any of them are ever seen is when they appear, along with the prophet and his underlings, during the services on Sunday, or, on occasion, during the week. The rest of the time they are learning in special classrooms on the hill and not allowed to mingle with the rest of the members."

"What about these three girls that went missing? Weren't they sent down here from the orphanage?"

"Yes, but they were dismissed from the dormitory and classrooms as incorrigible and sent to live with foster mothers like myself."

"Why were they incorrigible? Was there something they were objecting to?" Rudy asked.

"I believe it was the teachings."

"What kind of teachings?"

"The prophet is a very strict disciplinarian. I'm sure the girls were objecting to that, more than anything else. It must have seemed to them that they would never be able to comply with the rules to the satisfaction of the leadership."

"Is that all? Are you sure it wasn't more than that?"

"It could have been. In fact, there have been times that I even suspected it."

"So, in other words, they're brainwashed before they're allowed to mingle, and the ones who don't buy into the program are handed over to ladies like you and Frances as a last resort, to try and fix them before they're exterminated. But before they're handed over, the leadership gets to use them for their own gratification. Is that about it?"

Shirley lifted her head and looked into his eyes. Her lips pursed and her jaw tightened. "Yes, I'm sure that is precisely the way it is."

"Why haven't you said something to someone by now?"

"To whom? I have no way off the mountain and anything I say to anyone would certainly get back to the prophet. So I have just tried to leave it to God to work out. And…"

"And what?"

"And I believe it is God who has brought you here for that very purpose."

"The only reason I'm here now is because there are three dead girls in the morgue. My question is, how many more girls would have had to die before you would have said something about it?"

Shirley cast her head to the table. Burying her face in her hands, she began to sob. "I'm so sorry. Please forgive me. Oh God, please forgive me."

Rudy knelt on the floor beside her. The smell of her hair filled his nostrils. Taking hold of her shoulders with both hands, he slowly pulled her to him. Shirley reached for him and wrapped her arms around his neck, burying her face between his neck and shoulder.

"I'll do anything to help." Shirley sobbed, her voice muffled. "Just tell me what to do, but please, please forgive me."

Rudy felt the warm curves of her body press against him. He combed her hair back with his fingers tossing it over her shoulders, his left hand firmly pressed against the small of her back. Strong feelings began to stir within him. Feelings that made him blush. His breathing became heavy and he could feel her own hot breath and the heat of her cheek against the side of his neck.

Rudy slowly took her arms and gently pushed her away. Not far, just enough to look into her eyes. They were closed, and soaked with tears. Her breathing too was heavy and came in gasps. He used the sleeve of his shirt and his forearm to dry her eyes. With his little finger, he brushed back the hair from her nose. He said to her, "Lady, are you married?"

Slowly she opened her eyes and released her hold of him. "No," she said in a whisper.

"Have you ever been married?"

"No. Never. But…"

"But what?"

"But…I think about it a lot." Suddenly it was as if she regained consciousness. Moving away from him she straightened her clothing, "I am so sorry, Mr. Crawford. Please forgive me. I didn't mean to…"

Rudy stood and pulled Shirley to her feet. Tenderly, he embraced her in his arms. Shirley rested her head against his strong, broad shoulders and stared blankly at the wall of her trailer, frozen, and powerless to resist.

His strong arms firmly wrapped around her slender waist. Suddenly, for the first time in her life, she felt safe. His powerful arms, those strong, hard hands; capable of crushing the very life from her, were now like a great wall, protecting her from all that she had ever feared.

"I've never been held by a man before, "she whispered.

Rudy didn't answer. He had expected her to resist, or to at least make some effort to be coy. But there was none of that. Her body surrendered to him, like a wounded animal suddenly rescued from a lifetime of torture. He held her tighter.

"You don't need to be forgiven, you haven't done anything wrong. And I'm sorry I inferred that you had." She buried her face deeper against him and he could hear her crying again. "Listen, I have an idea. Will you do something for me?" He could feel her nod her head. "I need you to pretend to be my wife for a while. I want you to tell everyone that I'm your long lost husband that you've never told anyone about. And I need to stay here with you while I nose around this place a while. Can you do that?"

Shirley stopped crying and stepped away from him while still holding tightly onto his arm.

"No one will ever believe it. They all know me too well. They will want proof. We will never get away with it."

"I don't care," Rudy said belligerently. "I'll let them think I've bought into their religion and become one of them."

Shirley shook her head. "If you are pretending, they will know."

"Then you can school me. Teach me what I need to know and how to act like I am an honest to goodness believer in whatever you are a believer in. By the time they can do anything about it, I will have the proof I need."

"And then what? Will you go and leave me here?" A fearful tone was in her voice.

"I'll take you with me…if you'll go," he said without hesitation. The words surprised even himself.

Shirley inhaled, and for a long moment held her breath. "I…will. Oh, yes, I will, I will, I will." She buried her face in her hands and again collapsed against him.

"Does that mean you'll teach me how to be a member of this cult?"

Shirley looked at him with a wry grin.

"Is that what you think we are, a cult?"

"Well, if it's not a cult, then what is it?"

"I guess I've never thought of it in that way. Maybe you are right. But regardless, yes, I'll teach you. But we'll have to really be married. I can't pretend *that*, and if *you* are intending to pretend it…I can't do it then either."

Rudy stared into the eyes of the beautiful woman standing before him. A million thoughts were screaming at him. *I have to have this woman. You can't get married. What the hell are you thinking? You don't even know her. Are you crazy, or what? I want this woman. She's everything I've ever imagined the perfect wife would look like, and be like. Not only that, she's a virgin. My God, I'm getting married, can you believe it?*

Suddenly she was speaking again. "It might take a while. In the meantime I can tell them you are taking Bible studies to become a believer. That would be far more believable. Of course you wouldn't be able to stay with me until we were actually—"

"Do you have a coat to wear?" Rudy interrupted.

"Yes."

"Get it. You're coming with me."

"Where are we going? I can't—"

"We're getting out of here."

Rudy hurriedly searched through her closet until he found her coat.

"Here put this on and change into some warm pants. Do you have pants?"

Shirley raised her skirt.

"I am wearing pants under my skirt."

"Good, follow me."

"Where are we going?"

"To Sitka, to get married."

"*Get married!* I don't even know you, and you haven't asked me yet."

Rudy was already out the door. Shirley, although she had not agreed to go, was right behind him. Rudy stopped and took hold of her shoulders.

"If I ask you, will you say yes?"

"I don't know. How do I know you will treat me nice and love me forever?"

"I promise I will love you forever and treat you like the queen you are."

"That was so sweet. In that case, I guess so."

"You *guess* so?"

"This is all so sudden. What if…"

"What if-- what?"

"What if you find out after we're married that you don't like me?"

"I'm running the same risk. What if you decide you don't like me?"

"Maybe we should wait until we know for sure."

"I already know for sure. How long will it take you? Besides, ask yourself the question, how often does love come around in a lifetime? Think about how long you've been waiting and how long I've been waiting."

Rudy was halfway from the trailer to the gate, clocking a fast pace, with Shirley right behind him half running to keep up. Several of the camp people had encountered them on the road and greeted Shirley and Rudy with looks of curiosity.

"How can you be so sure that you love me?"

"Lady, if you knew what a treasure you are, you would have been married a long time ago, and I'm not taking a chance on you finding out and winding up with some other guy."

Shirley's voice trailed off. "You say the sweetest things."

Suddenly, she ran to catch up. Grabbing him by the arm, she stopped Rudy in his tracks and pulled him to her.

"Kiss me, you…you *man*, you." Neither of them noticed the Mercedes Benz S550 that had just come through the gate.

Rudy heard it coming but was otherwise occupied and could care less who might be watching. The driver of the car slowed as it approached the two of them.

"Ahem, Ms. Crowder. Have you lost your senses? Or just given yourself over to the flesh for the devil to devour."

Shirley quickly pulled away from Rudy and spun around to face the car. The voice had come from the rear window and the man who had spoken to her was opening the door and stepping out of the car.

He was tall and intimidating, with a strong Scandinavian accent. Long, white hair flowed over his shoulders, covering his ears. A white, exquisitely trimmed goatee, the shape of a dagger, extended to his neckline, like an ascot covering his throat. His eyes were ominous, like cutting torches that bore straight through to your soul; capable of detecting every lie, or false impression.

"You seem to know this gentleman quite well, Ms. Crowder. Are you going to introduce me?"

Shirley brushed at her skirt and straightened her sweater.

"Yes, of course, Prophet. This is my fiancé, Mr. Rudy…" She leaned toward Rudy and whispered, "What is your last name?"

Rudy leaned toward her and replied, "Crawford."

Shirley looked back at the imposing figure standing before her,

"Crawford. This is Rudy Crawford. He is my—"

"Yes, your fiancé, how nice." Turning to Rudy, the prophet studied the young man for a moment and inquired, "Why haven't I seen you here before today, Mr. Rudy Crawford? Are you not a member of our community?"

"Not yet, sir. But I'm considering it. Shirley has been giving me Bible studies and I'm looking forward to learning as much as I can about everything you got going on around here." Rudy looked the prophet directly in the eyes, completely un-intimidated by his overbearing presence.

The prophet smiled faintly at him and turned toward the car. As he was about to get in he paused and said to Shirley, "When and where, is this wedding to take place, Ms. Crowder?"

Shirley was caught off guard for a moment and the prophet saw it.

"We are on our way to Sitka right now, sir, to be married."

"Isn't this all a little sudden?" the prophet asked.

"Well, it's just that…we are spending time together, having Bible studies and such, and I wouldn't want anything inappropriate to happen. So, we decided to—"

"I see," The prophet interrupted, "Well, Ms. Crowder and Mr. Crawford, I must insist that you allow me the privilege of counseling the two of you before you take this major life step. I'm sure you see the wisdom in that. Do you not?"

"Absolutely!" Rudy interjected. Shirley seemed surprised and a little relieved. The prophet noticed Rudy's somewhat over-the-top reaction and appeared curious.

"Well then, it's settled. Allow me to give you both a ride up the hill to my office where we can spend some quality time together and learn to know each other…much better."

"Fantastic!" Rudy said eagerly. The prophet looked at him even more curiously.

The car was occupied by two other men sitting in the front seat. From where Rudy stood, he could see the passenger had an automatic weapon between his knees, pointed to the floor, but could not see his face. The driver he did not recognize, but assumed he too was armed, probably with a sidearm. Rudy had already made a mental note of the situation and was rapidly coming up with a plan.

"Very well then, Mr. Crawford, would you be so kind as to sit in the front between my two associates? Ms. Crowder, you may sit in the back with me."

"Certainly," Rudy said. The right seat passenger, a big guy, opened his door and stood by the car. Instantly Rudy recognized him as the driver of the old Dodge pickup he had seen in town. And now, up close and personal, he could see his incredible likeness to Lieutenant Kerrigan.

The prophet stepped to the side to allow Shirley to climb into the back seat and Rudy went around the rear to the other side of the car where he proceeded to open the back door and slide in next to Shirley. The big guy grabbed the door and ordered him to get out and sit in the front.

Rudy smiled at him and said, "God bless you, brother." The prophet held up his hand and made a gesture toward the Kerrigan lookalike. Reluctantly, and obviously steamed, he climbed back into the front seat.

"Michael, I think Mr. Crawford does not want to be too far away from his bride-to-be."

The prophet and his driver chuckled. Big Mike settled down a bit, but Rudy could tell he was still peeved.

The Mercedes accelerated up the hill, through another gate, also guarded, to a huge building that appeared to be the prophet's home, built next to another longer building that looked more like a dormitory. A group of people, both adults, young adults, and small children, moved about freely, to and from the dormitory.

The driver of the car drove around behind the big house and down a driveway into an underground three-car garage with no doors.

Rudy heard a click and realized that his door had been automatically locked. He tried it to make sure. It would not open. Both the driver and the Kerrigan look-alike got out of the car and moved to the left side where the driver opened the door for the prophet, who stepped out and shut the door behind him. Rudy slid across the seat and reached past Shirley to try the other door. It too was locked.

Rudy looked into Shirley's eyes and instantly remembered that he had recently fallen in love. He kissed her on the lips and whispered into her ear, "I don't think counseling is exactly what he has in mind."

"What do you think is going to happen, Rudy?"

"I think we're about to find out."

The prophet talked briefly with the two men and turned to walk into an elevator that provided access to the main floor of the three-story home above.

The big guy moved around to the right side of the car and retrieved his automatic weapon from the hood of the car where he had left it. The driver stepped out of the car. Both men proceeded to unlock and open the two rear doors. Rudy again whispered to Shirley, "Don't ask any questions. Just do what I say. When I give the word, I want you to dive head first straight for the floorboard."

Shirley's eyes were big with apprehension. She had never felt excitement like this before.

"Rudy, are you sure?" she whispered.

"I'm sure. Wait for my signal."

"Get out. You're coming with us," the Kerrigan lookalike demanded. He held the rifle in his right hand, butt resting against his hip, muzzle pointed toward the sky.

On the left side of the car, the driver reached his hand toward Shirley to help her out of the vehicle. When he leaned forward Rudy could see the Glock .40 hanging from a shoulder holster under his armpit.

Shirley did not move.

"Come on, lady, get out of the car." Shirley stared straight ahead, frozen with fear.

Rudy slipped his nine millimeter from his own shoulder holster and flipped off the safety. Holding it concealed under his jacket he slowly began to slide toward the door on his right.

The big guy pointed his AR-15 at Rudy and said to him, "Keep your hands where I can see them, smart guy."

"If you don't mind, I'm holding my girlfriend's hand. She's coming out with me."

The big guy took his eyes off Rudy for one instant, while he looked across the hood of the car at his accomplice.

"Let her come out on this side with him, I got them cov—"

Rudy instantly reacted. "Get down!" he said to Shirley as he lunged toward the man smashing the barrel of the loaded nine against the big man's groin. He said to him, "Lay that weapon on the roof of the car, or you'll be singing soprano for the rest of your life. And, tell your buddy to do the same."

Both men swore. "Watch your language, there's a lady present," Rudy said, as he pushed the big guy out of the way and climbed out of the car. He turned to look at the driver. Both weapons lay on the roof of the car.

Rudy called to Shirley, "Sweetheart, you can get out now."

Shirley slowly crawled on her hands and knees across the seat and out of the car, her eyes wide with excitement.

"Shirley, can you drive a car?" Rudy asked.

"Yes."

"Good. Get in the driver's seat. You two goons, get in the back seat and if either of you try anything, I'll shoot you both dead. Is that clear?"

The Kerrigan look-alike muttered something that sounded like, "Whatever." The out-of-work driver didn't say anything.

"I don't have anything to tie you guys up with, so I'll be extra jumpy. If I were you, I'd sit real still."

Shirley started the car and began backing out of the driveway when she noticed the elevator door open.

"There's the prophet," she gasped.

"Keep driving, and just smash through that first gate. If anyone gets in the way, run over them."

"Rudy, I can't do that. I'm not like you."

"Don't worry, honey, you'll do fine."

Shirley sped back down the drive they had just come up only minutes before. As the car approached the first gate, she began to slow.

Taking his eyes off the two men in the back seat for only a moment,

Rudy glanced at Shirley, "Mash on it, Shirl!" Rudy yelled. Suddenly he saw a blur of movement coming from the back seat.

BAM, BAM. Two shots rang out inside the car. Blood splatter painted the left rear side window and interior of the car.

Rudy instantly trained the gun on the Kerrigan look-alike.

"I'll do you too, buddy, if you want to take the chance," Rudy said.

With his hands in the air, the Maverick man, sat back against his seat and stuttered, "I'm good, mister. Eh, Ima… I'm all good. This is your show…fff…for now."

Shirley saw the two men at the gate and smashed the pedal to the floor. The S550 blew through the closed gate and down the hill.

Rudy looked at his new fiancé with pride.

"Yahoo, from now on I'm calling you Bonnie, baby. Now, I want you to do the same thing when you get to that other gate and keep going until we get to town."

Shirley had never been so excited in her life. Suddenly she was free. Free from tyranny, free from oppression, and free from her life of gloom. She looked over at her fiancé. "I'm sure now, Rudy."

"Sure of what, darlin?"

"Sure, that I want to marry you."

CHAPTER 12

Lieutenant Mark Kerrigan had insisted on staying in Fairbanks to further investigate the orphanage and Mr. Theodore Wallace's current business activities. I expected he would be tied up with that long enough to keep him out of my hair while me and my crew chased down the actual murderer.

I was a little apprehensive about leaving the lieutenant alone, not sure what he might get tangled up in all by himself. So I sent him some help. I could only trust that Morgue, the mercenary, would watch over my interest in the detective. In other words, keep him out of trouble, and breathing.

Scarf and Tripod were now keeping an eye on the latest victim, who was still in the ICU. But with all the media hype surrounding the recent gunfight at the hospital between Rusty and the two guys who were sent to kill the girl, I was in a hurry to get as far away from Sitka as I could before any members of the press recognized me.

Rusty and I quick stepped it back to the school's airstrip, spooled up the Kodiak, and headed back to the fishing village of Kake.

"Dad, let's have another look at the compound before we land."

"Why?" I said. "We already have pictures."

"I know, but I'd like to have another look at the prophet's place."

"I guess it couldn't hurt. Maybe we can spot the pickup truck."

I leveled off at two-thousand feet and stayed a couple miles south of the town as I maneuvered the airplane into a position where we could get another look at the area. As we passed over the little city of campers, motor homes and shanties, something unusual caught my eye.

"That's weird," I said. I was circling counterclockwise, so from where Rusty was sitting, in the right seat, he could not see what I was looking at.

"What's weird, Dad?"

"A car just ran through the main gate at a rather high rate and is now speeding down the road toward town."

"Can you see the airport yet?"

"Yeah, and that big twin Cessna is still parked down there."

"That's probably the prophet heading back to the airport, maybe they're trying to get away. If we're going to have a talk with him, we'll have to get down there fast or they'll be gone."

"If you're right, something else had to have spooked them. I don't think they could have heard us coming in time to get going that fast. But if we can get down there in time, I can park this bush plane in front of that twin. They'll have to either talk to us, or find some other way out of town."

Abruptly, I pushed the nose over in a radically steep nose dive, straight to the ground. As airspeed rapidly climbed to redline, I reversed the props to prevent exceeding maximum airspeed. In only moments we were on short final.

"Whew, that was an exciting ride, Dad. Good job. You would make a good airobatic driver."

I set the Kodiak on the ground and fast taxied over to the big Cessna 421.

"Grab your weapon, Rusty, and let's hide behind the twin."

Suddenly the car I had seen from the air come speeding around the corner, heading straight toward the Kodiak.

"They're coming right at us, Rusty. I would have expected them to stop and make a run for it."

"Maybe they want to fight it out," Rusty said.

The glare of the filtered sunlight glancing off the windows of the Mercedes made it impossible to see who was inside the vehicle that had abruptly stopped next to my airplane. The driver turned off the motor.

Rusty and I cautiously approached the Mercedes S550, guns drawn. Suddenly the driver side door began to open and a woman's hand protruded upwards toward the sky. She called out, "Please, don't shoot me."

Then the passenger side door opened and Rudy Crawford emerged holding an AR-15 in his hand. Pointing it at the rear car door he opened it and spoke to the backseat occupant.

"Rudy, are you okay? Who's the woman?" I said as I stepped closer.

"Her name is Shirley Crowder. She's my fiancé. However, she's not the biggest surprise. Look what I got here."

A large man slowly emerged from the back seat of the Mercedes.

I caught my breath, "Is that Lieutenant Kerrigan? What's he doing down here? I just sent—"

"It's not Kerrigan, Mr. Worley. It's the guy I saw driving that old Dodge pickup the other day."

It took me a second, but I soon realized who I was looking at.

"He's also the guy that kidnapped me and Jerod up in Fairbanks two days ago," I said, "and I'm sure the one who hit me over the head."

"There's also a dead guy in the back seat on the other side of the car that used to be his buddy," Rudy added. "Do you think one of you could get a set of cuffs on this guy?"

"I'll take care of that, Dad."

"Bring my 10-gauge shotgun with you when you return."

I turned my attention back to Rudy and his prisoner.

"So where did you get the AR-15?"

"The dead guy in the back seat gave me his."

I stepped over to the car and opened the rear door to check out the corpse Rudy was referring to. I said to Rudy, "Most of his face is gone, but I believe he might have been the pilot of that twin Cessna sitting over there. What happened? Did he try to jump you?"

"Yes, sir, both of them did. But when this one saw what happened to his buddy, he backed off. I don't think he thought I had the guts to do it." "What do you want to do with the dead guy, Mr. Worley?"

"We'll take care of him later," I said as I searched through his blood-soaked pockets.

"What do you want me to do with this one, Dad?"

I looked up to see Rusty placing the cuffs on the prisoner.

"We can put him in that cage where we found the lieutenant. I'm sure he knows where that is. I'm pretty sure he's the one who put Kerrigan there in the first place. Then, when we get a chance, we can interrogate him and get to the bottom of what's going on around here."

The big guy laughed and wagged his head as if there was something ludicrous about my idea.

"He's sneering at us, Mr. Worley. I don't think he believes we're capable of that."

"He'll soon find out."

I took Kerrigan's *twin brother* by the arm and gave him a shove in the direction of the late Old Man Perkins' house.

"You lead the way, partner."

Maverick man remarked, "You guys don't have any idea who you're dealing with. If you had any sense you'd walk away from this whole deal before every one of you wind up dead."

"I seem to remember that you already had your chance to kill me up in Fairbanks the other day. If you were the actual killer we're looking for, I expect you would have done just that too. So don't try to sound like a tough guy. If you want to stay on my good side, I suggest you start spilling your guts, because this happens to be your lucky day, you actually caught me in a deal-making mood." Suddenly, Kerrigan's twin brother seemed a little less resistant.

I was walking directly behind the Maverick man as we approached Grady's driveway, holding tightly to his cuffed wrists. As we rounded the corner, suddenly Rusty and I both slid to a stop in the loose gravel. I held up my hand for Rudy and Shirley to do the same while yanking Mr. Maverick to an abrupt halt.

"You make one sound and you'll take a nap, is that clear?"

"What do you see?" Rudy asked.

"The pickup is back," Rusty said. "The girl must be home. That means she's found the old man's body and is probably laying for us. We better think this over before we go barging in."

Rudy stepped up beside me. "What did you say her name is?" he asked.

"Karen." She's Grady Perkins daughter. The same guy you killed on the porch," I said.

"You killed Old Man Perkins?" the Maverick man asked, astonished. Then, throwing his head back, he let out a hearty laugh. "Ha, ha. I wouldn't give ten-cents for your chances of living another hour around here. If Ral--...what I mean to say is...if her brother finds out you killed their old man, you'll be *carved,* I mean burnt toast."

I turned around to face the Kerrigan lookalike.

"You're the one who will be toast if you don't tell me his name. You started to say it. Rusty, what did that sound like to you?"

"I couldn't tell, Dad. It sounded like Ralph, or maybe Raphael. Do you want me to see if I can get it out of him?"

"It'll take someone a lot bigger than you to get me to talk, Jarhead. I've said all I'm going to say. You'll have to figure out the rest on your own."

"Well, Mister, you're talking now. Why don't you go ahead and tell us your name?"

"Ain't none of yur business."

"Okay, if that's the way you want it, we can take your picture and send it off to the FBI, I'm sure they have you on file somewhere." I pulled out my phone and brought up the camera feature.

"That's all right, you don't need to go to all that trouble. My name is Mike."

"Mike, what?"

"Just Mike. Everyone calls me Big Mike."

"Okay, Big Mike, tell me what your involvement is with that cult leader, Joseph Morning."

"I don't have any involvement. I just work for the guy."

"I want a detailed job description. Are you his bodyguard, hit man, muscle man, or all three?"

"Just a bodyguard. One of many. I'm not a hit man."

"You are a kidnapper though, aren't you?"

"I don't know what you're talking about."

"Your twin brother, Lieutenant Mark Kerrigan, Homicide Division, Alaska State Police. You remember? You and that girl, Karen, along with her brother, you all drugged and kidnapped the lieutenant and brought him here to Old Man Perkins place, then put him in that makeshift jail cell in the basement. Don't tell me that doesn't ring a bell. When you first saw the lieutenant, did that startle you? I'm sure it must have been like seeing yourself in the mirror. Or did you already know you had a twin brother?"

"You guys are crazy. I have no idea what you're talking about."

"Of course you don't. All right then, how about this? We're going to put you in that same cell and you're not getting out until you tell us what we want to know."

Big Mike was looking uneasy. I could tell I was hitting a nerve.

"If you don't talk, we're going to put a sign up on the door to the basement that says, 'I spilled my guts to Lou Worley and Lieutenant Kerrigan about the kidnapping, and everything I know about the murders,' Then we'll leave you there for Karen and her brother to find. I wonder which they'll believe, you or the sign."

Big Mike was not only looking uneasy, he was starting to sweat.

"Does Karen's brother chew tobacco?"

Big Mike looked at me. This time he wasn't smiling.

"Yeah," he said, looking toward the house as if he expected someone to overhear him.

"What does he spit into when he chews? Does he spit on the ground, a paper cup, what?"

Big Mike leaned forward, trying to see down the driveway. "He spits into a beer can most of the time. Why? What does that have to do with anything?"

"Is there anything he does to the can before he spits into it?"

"Like what?" Big Mike was getting really nervous.

"Does Karen's brother have any facial hair?" Rusty asked.

"Yeah. He's got a full beard that completely covers his throat, a regular Grizzly Adams."

I was fishing for something and I wanted Big Mike to tell me what I wanted to hear. I could just as easily asked him if Grizzly Adams twisted off his beer-can tabs, but it would be a lot more conclusive if I could get him to volunteer that particular bit of information.

I said to him, "I'm surprised that a guy with a large beard and mustache would use a beer can to spit into instead of a paper cup. I would think his whiskers would hang up in the beer tab. If it were me I would either find a paper cup, or maybe shave my beard. Better yet, quit chewing entirely."

"He twists them off." Big Mike said nonchalantly.

I was surprised at how matter-of-factly he acted, as if he had no idea that it was the very piece of evidence that tied Mr. Grizzly Adams to the last murder scene. I began to wonder if Big Mike actually knew how evil Karen's brother really is.

I asked Rudy to watch Big Mike while I took Rusty aside to talk to him in private.

"Rusty, I'm wondering if Big Mike even knows anything about the murders, or Karen and her brother's involvement in them."

"I noticed the same thing you did, Dad. If he doesn't, why did he help them kidnap Kerrigan?"

"Maybe he didn't. Maybe it was just Karen and her brother. After all, Kerrigan said he didn't get a look at the guy who tagged him, just said he was big."

I stepped back over to where Mike stood next to Rudy.

"Mike, have you ever heard of Green Air Service? Or have you ever seen a dark green de Havilland Beaver on floats anywhere around here?"

"Yeah, sometimes."

"Is that your plane?"

"Why would it be my plane? I don't even fly."

"Does Karen's brother fly? Would that be his airplane?"

"I don't know."

"I think you do, and sooner or later you're going to come clean. It would be to your advantage to do it sooner."

Rudy said to me, "Mr. Worley, why don't you ask him about the dead girls, and if he's involved with the prophet in the child abuse that's going on up on the hill?"

I looked at Rudy and again at Shirley. She was hanging her head as if she didn't particularly care for the new direction the conversation had taken.

"Is this information you got while you were up there before you ran into these two goons?" I asked.

"Yes, sir, just ask Shirley. One of her lady friends up there gave me a letter that the last victim wrote just before she ran away. According to the note, the girl was being sexually abused by the leadership, and I'll bet this guy was in on it."

"That's a lie," Big Mike said, taking a step toward Rudy. I immediately yanked him back by his handcuffs.

"Let me see the note," I said. Rudy reached in his pocket and produced an envelope which he handed to me. I read it, slowly and carefully.

"I think we need to go have a talk with the prophet and see what he has to say about all of this. Rusty, are you current in multi-engine?"

"Sure am, Dad. Why?"

"I want you to take Miss Crowder down to Juneau while Rudy and I take Big Mike over to Sitka. I'll have Borski lock him up in one of his jail cells."

"What do you want me to do with her after we get to Juneau?"

"Give Pastor Beltray Gibbons a call and fill him in on the situation. Ask him if some of the ladies in his church can put her up for a while until we can get this case wrapped up. If they can, hand her off to Pastor Gibbons. Get back here as soon as you can."

"Sounds like a great idea, but I'm sure they locked their airplane up and took the key."

I reached in my pocket. "Take this one, I took it off the dead guy in the car. See if it will work."

"That looks like it. So, what are you and Rudy going to do while I'm gone?"

"When Rudy and I get back, we're going to go pay the prophet a visit."

"Gee, Dad, I wish you would hold off on that until I can get back. I'd like to go up there with you."

I looked at Rudy. "What do you think, Rudy, should we wait for Rusty to get back before we raid the commune?"

"I'm game either way, Mr. Worley. Whatever you decide."

"Okay, Rusty, take Shirley and head to Juneau. We'll meet you here when you get back."

"Dad, while you're in Sitka, you might want to let the two new guy's know to keep an eye out for Karen's brother."

"Good idea, Rusty. I'll call them."

A mere twenty feet away, secluded in the bushes was the petite figure of an eavesdropper. While Worley and Rusty escorted their prisoner back to the car he had arrived in, she silently slinked back to her hideaway in the basement of the house where she had lived with her father for the last twenty-five years. From there she made a phone call, to Juneau, Alaska.

Rudy and I stood alongside the Mercedes watching the Cessna 421 as it roared up and away from the grass airstrip of Kake, Alaska. Inside the car, the Maverick man, aka Big Mike, sat handcuffed with one arm through the steering wheel and a gag in his mouth to keep him quiet. I'm not sure, but I think he might have even taken something to help him sleep.

"Rudy, I have a couple of shovels in the Kodiak. We better get a hole dug and cover that dead guy up before he starts drawing a crowd."

"We also better keep our weapons handy in case Karen and her brother show up. I'm sure they heard that twin take off out of here," Rudy said.

"I'm sure they did too. As soon as we're done, we'll go arrest them, and get my truck back."

"Arrest them on what charge?"

"Car theft."

With our graveyard chores completed, Rudy, armed with his semi-automatic rifle, and me with my 10-gauge shotgun and sidearm, returned to the house where we believed Karen and her brother, our new number-one murder suspects, were holed up.

"They sure have been in there a while," Rudy said as he peered through the bushes at the front of the house.

"Maybe they were up all night and are tired from moving bodies around," I said, trying to provide a bit of humor.

"I sure hope not. So, how do you want to go about this, boss?"

"I think you should try to make your way around back and when you're in a position where you can watch the back door, I'll go knock on the front door."

"Didn't you say that old Dodge pickup belongs to you?"

"It sure does, why?"

"Why don't I hide behind those bushes next to the front porch while you go start up your truck and take it up to the airstrip. Maybe that would bring them out of the house"

"I got a better idea, I'll hide in the bushes and you steal the truck."

"Why is your idea better than mine?"

"Because you got a long gun and I got a short gun. That's why."

"Good point, Mr. Worley."

"And, Rudy, I don't think you need to take it all the way up to the airstrip, just around the bend at the end of the driveway should do."

Carefully, I studied the house for any indication that someone might be watching through a hole in the torn newspaper covering the windows.

Satisfied to some degree, I made my move toward the front porch.

As soon as I was in position behind the bushes at the end of the porch, Rudy dashed for the truck and got in. The old flathead six fired on the second stroke and Rudy began backing away towards the driveway entrance.

I listened intently, but did not hear any noises, or voices, coming from the inside of the house.

Rudy shut the engine off and crept his way toward the far end of the porch opposite of where I waited. I checked my cell phone to see if I had a signal in case I needed to send Rudy a text message. There wasn't any. I waited and kept checking until finally a small dot appeared. Quickly, I sent him a text.

'go arnd 2 the bak dor'.

I knew it was a long shot. If Rudy didn't get the text message and wasn't in position at the back door when I made my move, our suspects might get away. Suddenly, my phone buzzed. I checked the message.

'already in position'

It was time to find out if anyone was home. Carefully I made my way around the porch and up the front steps.

Slowly I tried the door. It was locked. Then, I pounded on it with my fist, and yelled, State police! Open up! Alaska State Police, open the door! We have a warrant." There was no answer. I listened for any sound of someone moving about in the house, but there was nothing. Dang it, I hope they didn't get away while we were digging the grave.

I hollered, "Rudy, I'm going in!" I stepped back from the door and made a run at it, slamming my whole body weight against it. The door jamb splintered as it burst wide open, my momentum carrying me all the way to the floor where I landed on my left side. For a moment I thought I saw someone, but by the time I gathered myself and could get a look at the inside of the house, no one appeared to be there.

"Rudy, is that you?" I called out. There was no answer. He must not have heard me.

I held my shotgun at waist level, finger poised above the trigger, while I cautiously negotiated my way through the piles of junk in the living room. When I reached the kitchen, I paused to study the table in an attempt to determine if someone had prepared any food since the last time we had been there. Lying on the table were the recent remains of two Subway sandwiches and their wrappers. Someone is either here now, or has recently been here I concluded.

I felt certain that I wasn't dealing with just some possible witness or potential suspect in a crime. I was sure that these two were the killers themselves, and I was very close to an encounter with one or both of them. So close, in fact, the hairs on my neck were standing up. I was also keenly aware that I needed to locate Rudy before I attempted to search the remainder of the house, especially the basement.

Carefully, I made my way to the back door. Tearing away the newspaper that covered the window, I peered out at the backyard. Still no Rudy.

"Rudy!" I called out again, concern taking a very dangerous precedent over precaution—there was no answer.

I opened the door and stepped out onto the back porch. It was much smaller than the front porch with a set of narrow steps straight ahead leading down to the ground ten feet below the porch deck. Immediately to the right of the door was a set of exterior stairs that led to the upper story of the house, twelve feet above my head. I wondered why there was no access from the inside.

After scanning the back-yard area for bears, I carefully started up the stairs. The old stair treads creaked and groaned under my feet with each step. With my left hand on the banister for balance, I held the shotgun in my right hand, butt against my hip with the muzzle pointed straight toward the covered landing above me.

I had been in situations similar to this before and the two most important things you need to have in your favor going in is an escape route and someone you can trust watching your back. At this point, I had neither, and my gut was reminding me of that fact by tying itself into a square knot.

I wanted to call out again, but something told me to keep quiet. Maybe it was wisdom acquired from past experiences, I don't know.

Maybe it was because my throat was so dry my voice box wouldn't work. On the other hand, if I was prone to listening to the voice of wisdom, I would already be in my airplane, on my way home.

Half-way up I paused to listen. I could hear nothing but the soft whisper of the breeze flowing through the trees. I pressed close to the wall and tried to keep my weight toward the inside of the stair casing where there seemed to be less creaking. Suddenly, the door above me opened.

I halted and flipped off the safety.

"Alaska State Po--" I stopped midsentence as Rudy emerged from the door. Slowly he turned to look at me, his hollow eyes staring at something a thousand miles away. I immediately recognized it. I had seen it in Vietnam, many times. The thousand-yard stare; his face was an ashen gray.

"Rudy, didn't you hear me calling you?" I bounded up the remaining few steps to the top of the landing and looked inside.

"You don't want to go in there, boss."

I looked at Rudy more carefully and realized that whatever he had seen in that attic had left him traumatized.

"That's part of the job, Rudy. Sometimes we have to do things we don't necessarily want to do." I brushed past him and entered what appeared to be an attic bedroom.

It took several minutes to take it all in. The first and most obvious was the clear plastic sheets that covered the walls and floor, splattered with dried, caked blood. Various cutting tools such as meat cleavers and saws lay on the table, also painted in dried blood. Finally, in the back corner of the attic was a wrought iron cage. Like an old western movies jail cell. Except the bars were welded, both vertically and horizontally to form a rectangular web of rounded half-inch steel. In it lay the bodies of at least a half dozen young women of various ages and stages of decomposition.

I backed away, stunned at what I had witnessed. Slowly I retrieved my cell phone and began taking pictures.

I looked back at where I had left Rudy. He was leaning against the wall, staring out at the gray southeast sky.

"Are you all right?" I asked.

"Yeah, I think so. I just need a minute."

"Take all the time you need, Rudy. I'll look around."

There was no other exit to the attic that we could see. No windows or doors other than the one through which we had entered. But the fact that they had built an access to the attic from the outside bothered me. I decided to go back downstairs and have another look around.

As I stood in the middle of old-man Perkins' cluttered living room, studying the walls and ceiling, suddenly something occurred to me. The far living room wall appeared to be a couple of feet in from the actual outside wall. I had never noticed it before. I poked my head out the door and hollered for Rudy.

As he came through the door, I noticed that he was looking a little better and figured that this little quandary might help get his mind off of what he had just seen. Actually, Rudy's reaction didn't surprise me. In Vietnam, I had seen men lose their dinner over a lot less than what Rudy had stumbled across. Also in war, human beings not only die, but they die in the most grotesque manners you can imagine--bombs, grenades, mortars, machine gun bullets that leave men's bodies in so many pieces you can't tell which piece belongs to which body. But that's the nature of war. In war, it is to be expected. But this…this chamber of death we had discovered was not war, but a homemade slaughter-house invented by a homegrown-psychopath, and until we caught him, there would be no time to get sick or cry for the innocent. We would make time for that later.

"Rudy, take a look at that wall and tell me what you see."

Rudy studied it for a minute then reached over and grabbed the 10 gauge shotgun out of my hand.

"What are you going to do with that?" I asked.

Rudy didn't say, he just aimed it at the wall and fired two rounds into the sheetrock. From where we were standing, approximately eight feet away, the blasts opened up a hole about fourteen inches in diameter straight into a secret passageway that apparently connected the attic to the basement.

Instantly we heard noises coming from within the wall below the floor level, whispered voices that sounded like swearing, and the sound of scuffling.

"Check outside!" I hollered at Rudy. "I'll get the basement." I pulled my .45 Glock from its holster and ran for the basement door, only to find it padlocked. Shielding my eyes with my arm I blasted the lock with one .230grain, brass-jacketed-dangerous-game-solid-core that practically blew the door off its hinges. I yanked what was left of it open and dropped to the floor. Starting in low I slid down the first couple of steps head first, on my belly. A shot rang out from the darkness below. For one millisecond the muzzle flash lit the basement like a lightning bolt, and in that second I saw the small form of a woman crouched beside the cage where we had found Lieutenant Kerrigan. She was pointing a gun in my direction and her face wore the expression of a satanic demon.

"You have one second to drop that gun, lady, before I—" BAM, BAM. The wood splintered above my head as two more bullets smashed into the stairwell beside me. BAM, BAM, BAM.

I saw the muzzle flashes from my own gun more than I heard the gunshots. They were like bright orange spotlights briefly lighting up the darkness of the basement. The darkness returned blacker than ever, and I waited for my eyes to adjust before proceeding farther down the stairway.

I heard something above me at the top of the stairs and looked back to see Rudy, standing in the doorway with a flashlight in his hand.

"Shine that light into the corner, by the cage," I said. "I think I might have gotten her."

"I think you did, boss. That's her, all right, the same girl I saw in the truck with Big Mike."

"Come on past me and see if there's anyone else down there," I said, as I scrambled myself into a sitting position.

Rudy searched through the basement and I went to check on the girl.

"Are you certain this is the same girl?" I asked.

"I'm sure, boss. She's even got on the same clothes."

"Well, she's dead now so I guess we won't be getting any information from her."

"I don't think she was by herself in that staircase, boss. I thought I heard a man's voice too right after I blasted the hole in the wall."

"I did too, but I'd like to know how she got into the basement so fast?"

"That's what I'm looking for, Mr. Worley. I think somewhere down here, there might be an access to the outside."

"Well, keep looking. I'll go back upstairs and see if I can tear that wall open enough for me to crawl through."

"Okay, boss. But be careful. If that was her brother she was with, he might be a handful for you to deal with by yourself."

"I'm not worried about him. This .45 doesn't care how big he is. Just the same, what did you do with my shotgun?"

"It's right here."

Rudy handed the 10-gauge to me as I continued to search through the basement. Soon, I found a crowbar.

"Rudy, I'm going to tear open that hole a little and see what's behind that wall upstairs."

I returned to the living room where I proceeded to enlarge the hole in the wall. The secret stairwell was more like a glorified ladder than a stair; ascending from the basement all the way to the attic above where we had, only minutes before, made our gruesome discovery. Someone, either Karen and her brother, or some other accomplice, had been kidnapping people, imprisoning them in the basement, for who knows how long, then ultimately butchering them in that attic, and they had been doing it for a long time. Was it merely to dispose of the bodies, or was it far more sinister than that? I had no idea. Nor did I really care. My only objective was to put a stop to it—right here, and now. I reached into my pocket and replaced the two empty shotgun shells Rudy had spent.

The hidden stairwell was very narrow. Immediately I began to feel claustrophobic. My first thought was that if Karen's brother was as large as Big Mike had described him, there was no way he would be coming or going from the inside of this hidden passage. A chill went up my spine as I realized that in all probability I had already killed one of the most notorious murderers in the history of Alaska. And she had been a girl that didn't weigh more than a hundred and twenty pounds. My god, how do people get to a place like that in their minds?

At the top of the stairwell, I encountered a bolted door. I tried to smash my shoulder against it but could not get any leverage due to my inconvenient position on the ladder. I even tried to brace myself against the stairwell so I could blast the door open with my shotgun, but there was nothing to brace myself against. I knew if I fired the 10-gauge, without adequate footing, I could actually fall and injure myself. Suddenly, I began to smell smoke. I stopped to listen. At first I heard nothing. Then the crackling of flames coming from below me. I looked down the dark shaft that I was trapped in and could now see the orange glow of flames coming from the hole in the wall that I had crawled through only moments before. I started to descend the ladder, but the smoke was quickly filling the stairwell. For the first time in my life, I felt a panic like I had never felt before. I scrambled back to the top of the ladder and, placing the shotgun against the bottom door hinge, pulled the trigger.

The blast was deafening in the closed quarters of the stairwell. I fired again. This time at where I thought the top hinge might be located, but missed. Two more times the shotgun exploded. Suddenly the door blew open and I could see light. However, I needed more than just light, I needed air.

Coughing, choking, and gagging my guts in knots, I staggered through the splintered door and shredded, blood-stained sheets of plastic hanging on the walls of the human butcher shop. The room was rapidly filling with smoke and I could feel the heat of the fire on the boards of the attic floor. The killer has set the house on fire. For the first time, the thought actually produced a fear of him I had never before felt of any man. Frantically, I burst through the door to the outside. By now my eyes burned from the smoke, but through the haze I saw a man, a big man; wearing what appeared to be a uniform. At first I thought it was Rudy.

I called out to him, "Rudy, is that you?" But, even as I called, I knew that the man I had seen was much larger than Rudy. Rudy did not answer.

Stumbling and fumbling around for the banister, I grabbed hold of it and worked my way down the stairs to the bottom porch where the flames were already licking at the back door from the inside, turning the thin glass black. There was no way I would be able to get through to the basement.

I turned my attention to the man in the back yard, but he had disappeared.

"Rudy where are you?" I called. That couldn't have been Rudy. It must have been Karen's brother. I just saw the killer I've been looking for, and the one who started the fire. He's trying to kill us. Got to find

Rudy. Still coughing, I leapt from the porch and ran around to the front of the house.

"Rudy!" I yelled again. "Rudy!"

"I'm right here, boss." I turned to see Rudy crawling from under the front porch.

"My God, Rudy, I thought you were—"

"I'm fine, boss. How are you? There for a minute I thought I might have lost you too."

I wrapped my arms around the young man and embraced him.

"Did you see him?" I asked.

"See who, Mr. Worley?"

"The killer, Karen's brother. I saw him from the top of the stairs when I made it out of the attic. He's around here someplace. We've got to find him, but we need to stay together."

The fire was raging and by now had completely engulfed the interior of the house. The windows were popping like Ridenbaucher popcorn and flames were now shooting from every opening like thirsty orange tongues frantically lapping at the air.

"We have to get back, Rudy," I said as I grabbed him by the arm. "Let's go to the truck and get the airplane out of here before any burning material falls on it."

We ran to the truck, but before we could climb in I stopped.

"Rudy, listen. Do you hear that?"

"Do you mean the airplane taking off?"

"Yeah! I'll bet that's the green monster."

"You mean the float plane you were telling us about?"

"Yes. Let's watch for it. Maybe we can get a glimpse of it when it goes by, just to be sure."

The deafening sound of the three propeller blades mounted on the de Havilland Beaver float plane reverberated against the hills above Kake, Alaska, as it lifted from the surface of the water and into the air. For a brief moment it drowned out the sharp crackling roar of the flames that were rapidly devouring the house of horrors.

"There it is!" I said excitedly, as it momentarily passed through our field of vision. "There goes the green monster."

"Is that really our guy?"

"I'm sure of it. Let's go get the Kodiak and see if we can catch him."

There was nothing Rudy or I could do for the house, or for anyone in it. The bodies and the stench would be consumed along with any material evidence that might have contributed to our case against the perpetrators' so there was no sense sticking around trying to explain the cause of the fire to the curious onlookers already beginning to arrive; staring in amazement at the huge bonfire that had once been Grady Perkins's home.

Rudy and I hastened our way back to the airstrip to get the Kodiak and pursue the killer. As we approached the Mercedes, still parked where we had left it, I grabbed Rudy's arm and pulled him to a stop.

"What's wrong, Boss." He said.

"Rudy, did you leave the driver side door open on the car?"

"I don't think so."

"Well, it's open now."

We drew our guns and cautiously approached the S550. There, still handcuffed to the steering wheel, was Big Mike, his throat cut so deep, his head had been nearly severed.

Rudy gasped, "I guess our killer didn't want to leave any loose ends behind."

"We'll have to take care of this later, Rudy. Right now we've got to go after that guy. I don't think he'll be back so this might be our only chance."

The weather was half-way decent: about five-thousand and ten. That would be five-thousand-foot ceilings, and ten-mile visibility, in layman terms.

The Green Monster had only been visible for a few brief moments during its departure. But it was apparent that the pilot had intentionally remained low over the water in an effort to conceal himself behind the dozens of fishing boat mast's that cluttered the harbor. At the time we caught a glimpse of it, it was headed straight out along the shoreline, northwest toward Frederick Sound. By the time Rudy and I were airborne, there was no way of knowing for sure which way the green monster had gone after he was out of sight. The noise of the prop reverberating across the water completely distorted any directional perception. Our killer could have disappeared in at least a dozen different directions.

"Which way do you think he went, Rudy?" I asked.

"Your guess is as good as mine, boss. I'm not a criminal, but if it was me, I would want to get out of sight as fast as I could. Maybe even to someplace where I could get lost in the mountains."

"So do you think he turned north when he got to Frederick Sound?"

"Possibly. If I were flying something as slow as that Beaver, I'd head for Turn Mountain, then east down the shoreline toward St. Petersburg."

"Look in that door pocket and see if you can find a sectional map of this area. In the meantime, I'll take it up to about 4,500feet and head northeast. Maybe we'll get lucky and intercept him."

"I wouldn't get too high, Mr. Worley. That dark green paint scheme will be hard to spot if he stays low over the water."

I twisted the prop to maximum performance climb, pulled the nose up, and leveled off at three thousand feet on a heading of zero-five-zero degrees.

"As soon as we cross Turn Mountain and the east shoreline of Kupreanof Island, I'll turn north and let it back down to a few hundred feet over the water. From there we can slow it up and cruise along the shoreline. We'll need to check all the little inlets where he could possibly hide out."

"He might have already landed in one of those inlets somewhere, Mr. Worley."

"That's what I'm counting on. I'm sure he expected we would come after him, so I doubt he went very far. He knows what we're flying and that we can outrun him, so if we don't miss him we may catch us a killer today."

"Mr. Worley, it's also possible that he might go on the offensive."

"How would he do that?"

"I'm not sure. But if it was me, I would find a way."

Rudy and I sat quietly as we searched for the green monster. The air was abnormally smooth which made the flying experience extra special. However, under the circumstances, I was too preoccupied to fully enjoy it.

It almost seemed ironic that I had named the floatplane *the green monster* when it was really the pilot who was the actual monster, and he wasn't green at all. On the contrary, he was not only experienced, he was as professional a killer as I had ever encountered. I knew that our best chance of catching that monster lay in the fact that because he had been getting away with his crimes for so long, completely uncontested, there was the possibility, if we applied enough pressure, he might panic and make a rookie mistake—it was a long shot, but possible. Killers that go for years without getting caught are not as smart as they are emotionally *detached* from their victims. As soon as a killer becomes emotionally *attached*, he begins to overlook simple, obvious clues that can often lead to his capture. This was what I was counting on. The question was: had we made our killer mad enough that he was now ready to make his fatal mistake? And, was Rudy right? Would he actually go on the offensive? If so, how? When? And where?

"I got a question for you, Mr. Worley. It's about what we found back there in Grady's place."

"I'm sorry you had to see that, Rudy."

"That's okay, Mr. Worley. I can deal with it. It's just that it makes me wonder how people can become so evil that they're capable of such horrible things."

"Well, Rudy, I can only tell you what I believe. Apart from that you'll have to come to your own conclusions."

"I trust you, boss. I've always thought you and your family were the finest people I've ever come across. As a matter of fact, when I get married, which will be soon, I hope, I want to have a family just like yours."

"Well, thank-you, Rudy. I think that's the nicest thing anyone has ever said to me. So, how serious are you about marrying Miss Crowder?"

"Serious as a heart attack. I fell for her the moment I saw her."

"She is an attractive woman. I'll say that."

"It was more than her beauty that got to me, Mr. Worley. It was her innocence, her honesty and innocence. Somehow, all that enhanced her beauty and I couldn't help myself. Do you believe in fate, Mr. Worley?"

"In a sense, I do, Rudy. I believe that fortune, whether good or bad, comes as a result of one's faith and expectations in life. Some people expect good things to happen to them, and others expect the worst. I believe everyone's life is the sum total of their expectations."

"I think I feel the same way, Mr. Worley. I've always expected to win at everything I ever did."

"Well, Rudy, I think you've picked a good woman. Your girl seems like she's a real keeper. However, I think she's a little naive and mixed up concerning some doctrinal matters in regard to her salvation. At least from the perspective of what the Bible teaches; I'm hoping my pastor friend down in Juneau can help her with that."

"I don't know anything about any of that stuff either, Mr. Worley. So, it really doesn't matter to me one way or the other what she believes. I'd take her even if she was an atheist."

"Rudy, I need to ask you a question. Would you be willing to hold off on getting married long enough to finish this job we're working on?"

"Oh sure, Mr. Worley. I want to have a real nice church wedding anyway. Of course, all that may take a little time to prepare, and of course we'd love to have you and your whole family come. I've been saving a little and I'm sure I got enough to rent a church and pay a preacher. We'll probably have to do without all the fancy stuff, but who needs all that anyway."

I looked over at Rudy and could tell that he was serious.

"What do you mean by fancy stuff? Do you mean wedding cake and gowns and tuxedoes and photographer, things like that?"

"Yeah, we don't need all that."

"I'm not so sure Shirley would agree with you. Have you talked to her about it yet?"

"No. We were in too big a hurry getting off the hill."

"Rudy, I'll tell you what I'll do. You wait until we get this case wrapped up and take some time to talk to my friend, Pastor Gibbons, and I'll pay for the fanciest wedding Shirley could ever dream of—my treat. Will that work for you?"

"Mr. Worley, I don't know what to say. You don't have to—"

"Don't worry about it. You only get married once. That is, if you're lucky. So, if you let me help you, I'll make sure you get it right the first time. "Now, do you still want me to answer your question?"

"What question?"

"You wanted to know what causes people to do terrible things."

"Oh, yes, sir, go ahead."

"Well, first, you need to understand that I'm a Christian by faith. So I come strictly from the point of view of the teachings of the gospel."

I paused a moment to glance at Rudy to see what his reaction was to that.

"That's okay, Mr. Worley. I don't know that much about the Bible, but I do believe in Christmas."

"In Christmas? What about Christmas?"

"Well, that the Christmas baby was born in Bethlehem and all that."

At first I thought Rudy was being sarcastic, until I realized he was actually being totally honest with me.

"That's right, a bit simplistic, but still right. However, there's a lot more to it than that."

"Like what?"

"Like for instance, who the Christmas baby was, or more appropriately, *is*; why he came to this earth, what he did, and what he said, right up to the moment he died on the cross, was buried, and rose again the third day as was prophesied in the Old Testament, prophecies that long ago foretold his coming to this earth. After which, he ascended back to heaven, and to his Father from where he came, leaving his disciples with the promise that he would someday return."

I looked over at Rudy. He was watching out the window.

"Have you seen a green floatplane yet?" I asked.

"No, not yet, I don't guess I've ever considered any of those questions before. It all seems complicated to me. Does a guy have to understand all of that in order to be a Christian?"

"No. As a matter of fact, the only prerequisite to being saved is believing. The Bible says: 'For God so loved the world that He gave His only begotten Son, that whosoever *believeth* in Him, should not perish, but have everlasting life.' The problem is, if you don't understand the facts, there will be no basis to what you're believing. Do you get my point? The Bible says, 'Faith cometh by hearing and hearing by the word of God.' It also says, 'How then shall they call on him in whom they have not believed? and how shall they believe in him of whom they have not heard? and how shall they hear without a preacher?'"

"I guess I thought God…or Jesus, just came to this earth to teach the world how to live with one another, and the ones that did a good enough job of that got to go to heaven someday."

"How's that working out? Do you think the world has arrived? Or, do you think they ever will arrive?"

"It doesn't look like it. Hell—uh, sorry. I mean, shucks, it seems to me that everyone is worse off now than they were when He first came, whenever that was."

"That was actually about two-thousand years ago, Rudy. And you're right. The world is worse off than ever. So, there obviously had to be something far more important inherent in his first advent than just teaching us how to say please and thank-you to each other. Would you agree?"

"I guess so. What's an advent?"

"His first coming is referred to as Christ's first advent. I don't know if you realize this or not, but his second advent is right around the corner."

"You mean someday there's going to be two Christmas days?"

"No. The next time he come's, he won't come as a baby. He will come as King of heaven and earth, to retrieve his Church--that is: *his body of believers*, to be with him where he is."

"What's a body of believers?"

"That would be all the believers from the beginning of time, until the final 'day of the Lord' spoken of in Jeremiah. On that day Christ will take every believer, dead or alive; in the grave or on top of the ground, to be with him in glory, where every believer will spend the rest of eternity. Would you like to be a part of that, Rudy?"

"I don't know. I guess so. I just don't think I understand enough about it to make a decision right now."

"I can relate to that. There was a time when I didn't either. Still don't claim to be an authority on the subject, but as soon as we get this bad guy locked up we'll take a trip up to Juneau to see Pastor Beltray Gibbons. He can explain it better than I can. Anyway, to answer your original question about the evil of man's nature, let me say this. Apart from God and the Spirit of God dwelling in a man, there is absolutely no limit to the depths of evil the natural man can descend to. That human butcher shop we stumbled onto is certainly evidence enough of that. However, if you need more, you can read the history of Mussolini, Stalin, Hitler, or Radical Islam, along with the horrors of the dark ages and the horrific things that were done in the name of Christianity. History is rife with accounts of human history that reveal exactly what we all, as fallen human beings, are really capable of apart from the Spirit of God in our lives. And that is what the Lord Jesus Christ came to this earth to save us from. Only the ones who reject his Gospel, those who leave themselves un-guarded by the Spirit of God, will be susceptible to being overcome by the satanic forces that would produce such demonic behavior."

"I'll have to think about that for a while."

"That's all I could expect, Rudy. And I want you to know, I appreciate you hearing me out."

I figured that was about all the theology Rudy could handle for the time being. It was obvious that his understanding of spiritual matters was minimal, so I changed the subject.

"Well, Rudy, I'm not seeing a green floatplane out here anywhere. I'm wondering if he ducked into one of these inlets somewhere and we missed him."

"How much fuel do we have, boss? If you're right, we should keep looking until dark, or at least until we run short of fuel."

"Well, right now, fuel is not a problem, so we'll keep looking."

We crossed the eastern shoreline of Kupreanof Island, where I turned north and began a gradual descent to five-hundred feet above the water. As we passed through six-hundred feet, I noticed a shadow suddenly pass over the aircraft. I looked up through the Plexiglas overhead. There was nothing there, and the shadow had gone.

Suddenly, I heard a noise. Like the dull drone of an airplane engine, growing louder by the second. It immediately alarmed me because the inside of the Quest Kodiak is so nearly sound proof an aircraft would have to be practically on top—

WHAM! The aircraft lurched, and shuddered violently.

At first I couldn't comprehend what had just happened. The airplane suddenly went from a gradual, two-hundred-feet-per-minute descent to a nosedive straight toward the water. I knew I had to shake off the natural instinct to panic—that would certainly leave a pilot unable to respond efficiently to a critical situation—and focus on flying the airplane.

I looked out the windshield. The water was coming toward us at warp speed and I was just staring at it, transfixed.

I hollered, "Rudy, tighten your seatbelt. We're going down.

Midair collisions are a pilot's worst nightmare and I had just been involved in one. The reality of the situation soon replaced the initial shock that had left me practically paralyzed. Wind rushed into the cockpit from everywhere. Every loose article, pens, paper, hats, and coats floated weightlessly in space as the airplane fell freely to the ocean below. Reefing back on the control yoke with all my might, I glanced at the airspeed indicator. It had already reached redline and I was fully aware that at any moment, the aircrafts structure could begin to fail. It was imperative that the descent rate be corrected immediately, if not sooner. Silently, I sent up a prayer for divine help. Quickly, I reduced power and yelled to my passenger, "Rudy, help me pull the nose up!"

Rudy Crawford grabbed hold of the dual control yoke in front of him and added his strength to the effort.

"Mr. Worley, I can hardly see the windshield, there's so much debris in the way."

"I looked across at the passenger side of the cockpit and for the first time realized the roof had been penetrated. The upper console was completely destroyed. Above Rudy's head, through a jagged hole in the roof at least eighteen inches across, loose wires and shreds of plastic, insulation, and broken Plexiglas hung from the ceiling, while shards of mangled aluminum flapped violently in the wind, inches above our heads.

"Just pull, Rudy. If we can get this thing leveled off, I might still be able to land it on the water."

Rudy looked through the debris at the water below. The ocean filled the entire windscreen and was rushing toward us like a monster typhoon. The veins in Rudy's temples bulged as he pulled on the controls with every fiber of his strength.

Finally, the nose of the stricken aircraft began to rise. Slowly the descent rate decreased until the airspeed was once again back in the green arc.

"Whew!" I said as I took my first breath in what seemed like an eternity. Suddenly I realized: there was a terrible vibration coming from the engine. I attempted to feather the prop but the hydraulics controlling the variable speed were frozen. Quickly, I shut down the turbo-powered engine.

"Flaps!" I yelled, as if to remind myself of what should be done next. I reached for the hydraulic flap control and switched it to ten degrees.

Nothing happened. I recycled the control and reset it to twenty degrees. Still nothing. Lord, this isn't good. We need a miracle. Silently, I prayed again.

The prop spun freely, creating a dangerous amount of drag. It was then I realized the propeller blades had been severely damaged in the impact. The twisted, distorted shape of the four prop blades, as they turned in the wind, shadowed the contorted shape of the badly damaged propellers. A thought occurred to me: That green monster hit us purposely…and I'll bet his floats are toast.

For the first time I scanned the horizon for the green de Havilland Beaver. Straight ahead and one mile, was Turnabout Island.

With no power, a massive amount of excessive drag, and no flaps, I pointed the nose toward the small island in one last futile attempt to catch the killer of little girls.

CHAPTER 13

Lieutenant Mark Kerrigan leaned against the side of the rental car his arms folded, as he watched Lou Worley's Citation CJ4 disappear into the milky, grey sky. Deep down inside, he suddenly felt alone. There was something about Worley, he wasn't exactly sure what it was, or how to define it, but for some reason he found himself feeling a sort of…bond, maybe even a kinship for the man. But he would never admit it. Not to anyone, even himself. Kerrigan shook it off and turned to look for Jerod.

Jerod Aikens observed the detective as he stood watching Lou Worley's Cessna Citation disappear into the southern sky. As the detective turned toward him, he said, "What do you want to do now, Lieutenant?"

"I need a rental car. You can put it on Worley's tab. Can you do that?"

"I can, but what about my car that got stolen? When do we report that to the police?"

"I am the police. Consider it reported. Do you remember the license plate number?"

"Not off hand, but I can look it up." Jerod stepped into the office to find the paperwork on the Toyota Land Cruiser. A moment later, he returned.

"You can take that Jeep Waggoner over there." Jerod pointed to several rental cars in the parking lot. "Here's the key," he said, tossing it to Kerrigan. "The license number of my Land Cruiser is—"

"I'll get it from you later, when I get back," Kerrigan said as he headed to the parking area.

Lieutenant Kerrigan chuckled to himself as he retraced the route they had taken to the old orphanage. There were several things he had intentionally not shared with Worley before he left, one of which was the past history that he was more than aware of concerning his twin brother. Another, his longtime relationship with Theodore Wallace.

He had told Worley that he didn't remember the details regarding the adoptions of his three girls. He had also told him that he would have to search through boxes full of old records stacked in his basement. But that wasn't the whole truth. Although it was over thirty years ago, Kerrigan knew exactly who he had done business with. What he didn't know is where they all are now, or what they were involved in.

The lieutenant recalled standing next to Worley as they watched Theodore Wallace disembark the airplane they had followed to Fairbanks. However, he did not know the first thing about the man called Joseph Morning, who claimed to be a prophet. Finding Theodore, then Morning, would be high on his list of priorities.

Kerrigan scrolled up his wife's name on his speed dial and mashed on the green button.

"Mark, dear! It's about time you called. I have been worried sick."

"I love you too, muffin. Now, will you go down to the basement and see if you can locate the box where we stored all those adoption papers from years back?"

"Mark, sweetie, I threw that box out a long time ago."

"No way, Gloria. Why would you do such a thing? I need the—"

"Because I organized all that stuff and put it in a filing cabinet. What is it you're looking for?"

"You are awesome. I need information on Theodore Wallace, phone number, address, whatever you can find. Preferably something current."

"Are you going to come by and get it, or should I fax it to the office?" Gloria asked.

"No, don't fax it to the office. Take pictures of the primary documents with your Android and send them to my phone."

"When are you coming home, dear?"

"I don't know yet. I'm still up to my elbows in this case. But I should be able to get home for a visit in a few days. Why, do you miss me?"

"By then I might. If you're lucky. Do *you* miss *me*?"

"I'll let you know when I get home. If you're lucky."

"You better bring me something real nice, or you might be disappointed."

"I'm going to bring you *me*. That's real nice, isn't it?"

"Sure thing. Bye."

"Bye."

Kerrigan grinned as he placed the phone back into his coat pocket. They had been married forty-three years and the flame still burned. *Got to get this case wrapped up so I can get home.*

Kerrigan was just as mystified as Worley over the kidnappers who had left him and Jerod imprisoned in the basement of the vacation cabin where he had found them. He thought it mighty strange that they picked *that* particular home when there were a dozen others that were closer to the location of the old orphanage. He wondered too if maybe his twin brother, Mike, knew who the place belonged to.

He had not bothered to inform Worley how he managed to show up at that particular cabin. Primarily, because Worley never asked. At the time, Worley was too busy assuming that Kerrigan was somehow involved with the kidnappers; otherwise, how would he have known where to find them.

But there was a different reason the lieutenant went to that cabin when he did, a reason that had nothing to do with Theodore Wallace, the prophet, or the kidnappers, and it was the same reason Kerrigan was on his way back.

Kerrigan continued past the turnoff, where he had taken Worley and Jerod on their way to the site of the old orphanage, two miles beyond, to a neighboring development of vacation homes built on ten-acre parcels, to the place where he had discovered the two men hiding in the vacation home earlier in the day.

The lieutenant slowed the vehicle as he turned up the drive. He drove slowly, nostalgically, reminiscent of a day thirty-seven years past when he, along with his beautiful wife, Gloria, had stayed in that same cabin for over three months, waiting for their first adopted child to be brought to them.

Twenty-five years later, Mark and Gloria Kerrigan had finally saved enough money to buy not only the vacation home of their dreams, but the one that held so many special memories as well.

It had been a couple years since they had used the place. The lieutenant had been working long hours as a homicide detective for the Alaska State Police, headquartered in Anchorage. He had also taken a nighttime security job. All in an effort to pay off their dream cabin before the lieutenant retired.

Kerrigan walked around the twenty-five-hundred-square-foot, two story home, inspecting the exterior for any sign of breaking and entering. The only evidence of damage was a broken window, apparently caused by falling limbs from the nearby trees that often come down during stormy weather. Other than that, there was no sign of vandalism.

Kerrigan returned to the front of the house and carefully ascended the steps to the front door. Standing to one side he quietly unlocked the door and gave it a brisk shove.

Pausing momentarily to listen, in an effort to detect any sound coming from within the house, he proceeded to carefully peer around the door-jamb and into the room where Worley had attacked him from behind the door.

"That blasted Worley," he said under his breath. Before entering the lieutenant stepped over to the hinged side of the door to peer through the gap between the door and the door-jamb. Something was covering the half-inch opening. He couldn't tell what it was, but knew that nothing was supposed to be there. Kerrigan reached around behind his back and pulled his 9 mm Glock-nineteen from its holster.

Holding the weapon in his right hand, he pressed his left hand against the partially open door and pushed it hard towards the wall behind. The door swung freely until it came to an abrupt stop just before hitting the wall. Kerrigan again peered through the gap. This time he saw movement.

Kerrigan broke the silence, "You've got a nine millimeter aimed right at your back. I want you to drop to your knees and clasp your hands over your head. Do it now!

The lieutenant lunged through the door and yanked it away from the wall, his gun pointed at the space behind the door where he expected to see someone come bursting out at him swinging a baseball bat— or whiskey bottle. Instead, squatting before him, knees tucked against her chest, wearing a faded, patched pair of blue jeans and powder blue hoodie, was a wide-eyed, young girl approximately seven years old, with her hands clasped over her ears. She looked up at him with a terrified expression on her face. She had big green eyes and curly, auburn hair that cascaded down her back and splashed against the floor. Her lips quivered and tears streamed down her face as she whimpered for him not to hurt her.

"Who are you? And what are you doing here?" Kerrigan asked, in his usual caustic tone.

The girl had stopped looking at Kerrigan and seemed to be looking past him. He watched her eyes as they looked first at him, then beyond him to the kitchen.

Instantly, Kerrigan lunged forward to place his own body between the girl and any potential threat. Still holding the door with his left hand, he saw the form of a person, maybe a small man or large boy, dashing for the basement door—his right hand gripping a rifle.

A burst of flame erupted from the muzzle of the 9mm Glock and the explosion echoed off the walls of the empty cabin. Kerrigan saw splinters fly through the air as the bullet hit the wood trim beside the door leading down to the basement. One second sooner and the man who had been standing there would be dead on the floor. One second later, and it might have been Kerrigan.

He turned to the girl and grabbed her by the shoulder.

"Who was that?" He asked, looking straight into her eyes. She was shivering from fright, and a puddle began to form on the floor beneath her.

"Now look here, sweetheart." Kerrigan's voice took on a softer tone. The family man, fatherhood side of him, began to take precedence over the detective's tough guy exterior. "You don't have to be afraid of me. I'm a cop. Do you see this?" He held up his State Police, Detective Bureau badge. "I'm not going to let anything happen to you. Do you understand?"

Wiping at her eyes, the girl nodded her head. Her knuckles smeared the tears that had saturated her dirty face, turning them into rivulets of muddy water streaking down her cheeks.

"Can you talk to me?" She looked at him, sheepishly, still sniffling, and nodded her head. "Good," Kerrigan said. "I need you to tell me who that man is that just ran into the basement."

"Jayce," she said, almost in a whisper.

"Who? Did you say, Jayce?" Again, she nodded her head. "Is there anyone with him?"

The girl shook her head.

"You are alone with him here? Just the two of you?"

Again, the girl nodded her head.

"What's your name, sweetie?" Kerrigan's intrigue was growing. His years of dealing with hardened criminals had left him with only one opinion of human beings: they all were capable of every imaginable deviancy known to man, given the opportunity.

"Miley."

"I'm glad to meet you, Miley. My name is Mark. Detective Mark Kerrigan. Do you have a last name?"

Miley shook her head.

"That's strange. Most everyone has a last name. Why don't you have one?"

Suddenly, Kerrigan heard a commotion coming from the stairs to the basement. Picking up the girl he hurried across the room to the end of the hallway, where he stuffed the child into a broom closet. Whispering, he said to her, "You stay here. Don't move and don't make a sound. Do you understand?"

Miley nodded her head.

Dashing back to the basement door, expecting someone to come bursting through at any moment, he called out, "You in the basement, this is the Alaska State Police! Come out of there with your hands on your head, immediately."

No one answered. Kerrigan listened but the basement remained silent, and dark.

With no flashlight, and the light of the kitchen behind him, Kerrigan knew if he started down the stairs he would become a conspicuous target silhouetted against the backdrop of kitchen light through the open basement door.

"If I have to come down there and get you, you may get hurt." Kerrigan waited. Still, no one answered. Kerrigan slammed a fresh magazine into the Glock nineteen and started down the stairs. Suddenly a young boy, appearing to be in his early teens, stepped forward into the light.

"Don't shoot me, mister!"

"Show me both your hands," Kerrigan replied, training his nine millimeter directly at the boy's face.

The youngster complied and the detective put his gun away.

"What did you do with that rifle you had when you ran down here?"

"I dropped it when I was coming down the stairs in the dark. It's on the floor somewhere. It's only a bee-bee gun, anyway."

"Allright, keep your hands where I can see them and start backing up the stairs, slowly."

Lieutenant Kerrigan took hold of the boy as he reached the top of the staircase and led him into the living room area where he sat him on the floor, against the wall. He was young, but older than Miley by several years.

"You can come out now, Miley," Kerrigan called.

The door to the broom closet slowly opened and little Miley emerged, still looking frightened. When she saw the young man sitting on the floor, she hurried over and seated herself next to him. The boy put his arm around her and pulled her close to his side. Miley snuggled up under his arm and held tightly to his shirt.

"I take it you two know each other," Kerrigan began.

Miley sat quiet.

"That's a strange question, coming from you. You know exactly who we are. The question is, what are you going to do with us now?" The boy asked.

"If I knew who you are, I wouldn't be asking," Kerrigan said. "I think you have me confused with someone else."

"I don't have you confused with anyone. And why are you pretending to be a cop?"

Suddenly Kerrigan realized that they thought he was his twin brother.

"You must be referring to my twin brother, Mike. Is that right?"

The boy looked confused and sat up straight.

"Do you mean, you're not…him? Then, who are you?"

"My name is Detective Mark Kerrigan, Alaska State Police, Homicide, Special Victims Unit. What's your name, son?"

"I'm Jayce. This is my little sister, Miley."

"Do you have a last name?" Kerrigan asked.

"We've had several over the years. I don't know what our real name is, but the last one we were given was Roubideaux."

"So, are you kids orphans, or adopted out runaways?"

Miley eagerly began to speak, "We ran aw—."

Jayce poked his elbow into his little sister's shoulder. "Shut up," he said.

"Leave her alone. If she wants to speak you let her. Go ahead, Miley. What were you saying?"

Miley looked up at her brother, but refused to say any more.

"What was she trying to say, Jayce?"

The boy stared at the floor for a minute before relenting. Glancing first at his sister, he looked directly into Kerrigan's eyes.

"She doesn't know what she's talking about, 'cause she doesn't even understand what's going on."

Kerrigan looked around for something he could sit on. There was a step stool in the kitchen, so he went and got it.

"I'm with Miley on that deal, Jayce. I'm not sure I know what's going on either. So why don't you start from the beginning and tell me the whole story?"

Kerrigan listened for over an hour. Their story was not that different from a thousand other kids just like them; parents in prison for drug abuse and distribution, kids handed off to the juvenile court system, who in turn hands them off to any orphanage that can, dot all the i's and cross all the t's on the application forms. It might be legal, but its human trafficking any way you slice it, and Kerrigan was more than familiar with the routine.

By the time Jayce finished telling their story, the lieutenant was not only furious, but practically in tears. When it comes to kids Kerrigan had an above average soft spot. His normally cold, metallic, homicide detective exterior turned to jelly at the slightest mention of a child in need. But this was not the time to get emotional. Now was the time for action.

"So how did the two of you wind up here?"

"We were dropped off at the home of an elderly couple down the road. They were supposed to be our new foster parents. That was two days ago. Only I decided we would run away and live on our own. This place was the most secluded so I broke a window and we spent the night."

"I see. So you're the one who did that. Who dropped you off?"

"We just spent the last two years in five different foster homes. The last people we stayed with wanted to keep Miley, but not me, so I took

Miley and ran away. A week later we got caught trying to hitch a ride on a fishing boat down in Soldotna. I told them I would work to pay our way, but they took us for runaways and called the law. Mr. Wallace sent someone down to fetch us back to the orphanage. Gee, mister, please don't send us back there."

"Don't worry, kid, if you don't want to go back all you need to do is cooperate, then I'll see what I can do for you. Where's this Mr. Wallace now?"

"I don't know. But the old man will probably call him as soon as they realize we're gone."

"How old are you, kid?"

"Twelve."

"Why did you run away?"

"Because I knew that when they decided they didn't want us, which usually takes about three weeks, we would be handed over to the cult."

"What cult?"

"It's in southeast Alaska somewhere. I've heard that when the orphanage gets tired of trying to find a place for you, they send you down to the cult, and you're never seen again.

"What makes you think they're never seen again?"

"That's what I've heard."

"From whom?"

"The other kids. And, one time I even heard it from Mr. Wallace."

"Tell me exactly what you heard, and when you heard it."

"Well, Mr. Wallace was talking to you...I mean, to your brother, and he told him that if he couldn't find someone to take us in soon, they would have to hand us over to the church."

"The church? Is that what they think that is?" Kerrigan shook his head in contempt for the idea that anyone could possibly confuse Joseph Morning and his cult with a true church. "That's no more a church than I am a preacher. What else did you hear?"

"He said he had other kids coming in that he wouldn't have near as much trouble placing in homes, that my little sister and I were becoming too much trouble. But because we...that is, because we weren't—."

"Spit it out, son. What are you trying to say?"

"Because we're white, they would give it another year."

"Because you're white?"

"Yes, sir."

"Where do most of the kids come from?"

"I don't know, sir. But a lot of the kids I've known have come from back east in the lower forty-eight. Most of them are ghetto kids of color and Latino kids that have come across the border illegally from Mexico. They're the ones that wind up in the cult most of the time."

"Where do they go from there, if the cult doesn't want them?"

"Nowhere. As far as I know, no one ever hears from them again."

Kerrigan walked to the window and starred out. A black bear and her two cubs curiously sniffed around the enclosure where several garbage cans were stored. Thoughts of his childhood swirled in his head. Turning to the boy, he said, "You and your sister, wait here while I go make a phone call. I'll be right back."

Kerrigan walked out to the rental car and a few minutes later returned to the house. The two children waited for him in silent expectation.

"Jayce and Miley. I've just spoken to my wife and we have a proposition for the two of you."

"What kind of a proposition?" Jayce asked, skeptically.

"We would like the two of you to come stay with us for a while, down in Anchorage. Do you think you'd like that?"

"What do you want with two kids our age?" Jayce said.

"Well, all our kids are grown and have their own families now, and we're all alone. Besides that, I'll be retiring soon and will need a kid about your age to go with me on fishing trips, that is, when you're not in school. And believe me, both of you will go to school. As a matter of fact, if you think you can behave yourself, we might even think about adopting you. Do you think you might be interested? I'm sure you already know what the other options look like."

Miley was crying and scrambling up from the floor ran to Kerrigan, flinging herself against him. Jayce looked at Kerrigan skeptically.

"What happens if, after a while, you decide you don't like us?"

Kerrigan patted Miley on the head and took her by the hand.

"I'm more concerned about the other side of that coin. It will be entirely up to you two whether you want a real home life and a future or not. If you do, we can give it to you. However, if you want to be vagrants for the rest of your life, you can save us all a lot of trouble and tell me now. On the other-hand, it looks like Miley has already made up *her* mind. Isn't that right, Miley?" Kerrigan brushed her hair back from her tear-stained face and looked into her eyes. Still whimpering, she nodded her head. "It's all up to you now, son. Gloria and I have already decided."

Lieutenant Mark Kerrigan spent the next several hours getting to know the two new members of his family. Listening to their story, and watching Jayce and Miley settle into the idea of actually having a home to go to and parents that they could trust, made him feel young again, and excited at the prospect of retiring soon and spending some quality time with them. On the way back to the airport, the detective and his two passengers stopped at a McDonalds, and picked up take-out. Jayce and Miley scarfed it down like they had not eaten in a week.

The FBO main door was opened and as the lieutenant entered he noticed that Jerod was in his office, and with him were two other men. Kerrigan walked in with Jayce and Miley close behind. Jerod looked up, surprised that he was not alone.

"Looks like you've picked-up a couple of strays, Lieutenant."

"Yeah, and we need a ride down to Anchorage, do you think you—

"Lieutenant, these two gentlemen just came from Sitka and are looking for you."

"Kerrigan looked at the two men a little closer. The younger man he recognized as one of the pilots who worked for Worley. The older man, who looked like Scarface in the movie *Scarface*, starred at him as if he had some score to settle. Kerrigan decided he had never seen him before.

"What do you want with me?" Kerrigan said, as he turned to face the two men.

Eric gestured toward the man called Morgue, "Mr. Worley hired this man to be your body-guard and asked me to deliver him to you."

"I don't need a bodyguard," Kerrigan interrupted.

"Worley said you would say that. But you're stuck with him anyway."

Kerrigan looked back at the man who was still starring at him.

"What's wrong with him? Why can't he speak for himself? You got a name, mister?"

"Yeah, you can call me Morgue."

"You do look like some kind of a walking dead man. Is that where you live, in the morgue?"

Morgue refused to respond.

Kerrigan motioned for Eric to step out into the hall.

"Listen Eric, I want you to take these two kids to Anchorage. I'll call my wife and have her meet you at Merrill Field. She'll take them off your hands." He looked back at the man in the office who was still starring at him through the glass.

"What's up with that guy anyway? He keeps starring at me."

"Like I said, he's your body-guard and if you get on his bad side he may forget to guard your body," Eric said.

"Does he have a last name?"

"If he does, I don't know what it is. Just Morgue, I guess."

Kerrigan stepped back into the office. Morgue continued to stare at the detective. His face void of expression.

"Mr. Morgue, I want you to go with Eric back to Anchorage. Your job will be to deliver these two children to my wife who will meet you at the airport. After that, I won't be needing your services any longer." I'll make sure Worley pays you for your trouble."

"If I go to Anchorage, you go too. Otherwise I stay with you."

"The lieutenant was at a loss for words. He suspected from the man's demeanor that he was probably one of those ex-CIA types or maybe Secret Service, that were completely uncompromising. Not to mention a pain in the butt to have following you around all the time.

"Well, hell. Whatever. I'll go myself." Turning to Eric, he said, "I need to go home for a while anyway. But I'll need to come back to Fairbanks in a couple of days. Will you be able to bring me back?"

"Not a problem, Lieutenant. What's Morgue supposed to do while you're at home?"

"Hell, I don't care. He's not my problem. Worley's the one paying him. He can go back to wherever he came from for all I care. Worley should have asked before he sent him up here. Does he think this is my first rodeo or something?"

"I think he was just trying to look out for you because he can't get away from Kake right now."

"That's good. I don't want *him* following me around either."

"Did you hear what happened?" Eric said.

"What happened, where?"

"The girl in the hospital that Worley thought had died, well, turns out she's alive, but two men went to the hospital the other day and tried to kill her. Worley's son-in-law, Rusty, happened to be there and shot both of them dead. That's when he hired Morgue here, along with his two friends."

"Mr. Morgue has friends?"

"Yes, sir, two of them. They're alternating twelve-hour shifts watching the girl to make sure no one else gets to her. You should see those guys, they're—"

"Yeah, I can imagine. They look like zombies, right? Just like that one." Kerrigan poked his thumb toward Morgue.

"How did you know?"

"If you've seen one, you've seen them all. They're called *mercenaries*. Most of them have killed so often they're hardly human anymore, more like walking dead men."

"Well, they can't be all bad. At least they're working on the right side of the law."

"They'll work on any side of the law that pays the most money. All they are is a bunch of murderers that haven't been convicted of their crimes yet, and I don't need their help. So I'm going to spend a couple of days at home, and Mr. Morgue, or whatever his name is, can go back where he came from. Is that clear? Tell him Worley wants him back at Sitka or something."

"Worley won't like that, Lieutenant. That could cost me my job, especially if anything were to happen to you."

"All right, I tell you what, give me your phone number. I'll call you in a couple of days and you can bring me back up here to Fairbanks. If Morgue is still around, I'll deal with him then. How's that?"

"That sounds better, Lieutenant. I appreciate it."

Kerrigan was a specialist at diversion. He had pulled the stunt with Worley, and was now fabricating another diversionary scheme to rid himself of Mr. Morgue.

As the Citation II began to circle above the city of Anchorage Alaska, Kerrigan sent his wife a text.

"Honey, I'll be landing with the kids in about ten-minutes. I need you to call Aero Flight Service at Merrill Field and book me on their next flight back to Fairbanks. Don't say anything about it when you pick up the kids. We're coming in on a Cessna Citation II. It says, Shearer-WorleyFoundtion on the side of the aircraft. You can't miss it."

As the plane taxied to the ramp, Kerrigan leaned his head into the cockpit, "Eric, I'll call you in a couple of days."

"Okay, Lieutenant, I won't be far away."

Kerrigan motioned for Jayce and Miley to follow him and headed for the door. Morgue followed. As they entered the FBO, Kerrigan pulled the children off to the side and whispered to them, "My wife will be here in a few minutes. I want you both to go with her, okay? I'm going to ditch this Morgue guy."

"Yes, sir," Jayce said.

"Don't worry, you'll be safe here. I'll be back in a few days."

Kerrigan inconspicuously moved out of hearing range of Morgue as he glanced at the phone number on the FBO wall and dialed it into his phone.

"Aero Flight Service, Linda speaking. May I help you?"

"Yes, Linda. This is Lieutenant Kerrigan with the Anchorage Police Department. I'm presently standing in the waiting room. Can you see me over here?"

From behind the counter, Linda looked around the FBO waiting room and saw the person she was talking to on the phone. Kerrigan nodded at her while appearing to remain inconspicuous.

I believe my wife has booked me on a flight back to Fairbanks. Can you tell me when that flight will be leaving?"

"In about twenty-minutes, Lieutenant."

"Good. Now tell me, Linda, do you have a security detail working for you?"

"Yes, Lieutenant."

"Do you see that man over there at the newsstand that looks like Al Pacino? I need you to call your security and have him detained while my wife picks up our kids, and while I get on my flight to Fairbanks. Can you do that for me?"

"Of course, Lieutenant. Uh, Lieutenant, is that man dangerous? Should I be concerned for the other passengers?"

"No, Linda. He's harmless, unless someone pays him."

"Oh! Oh, my!"

Kerrigan put his phone away just as Gloria came through the door. She headed straight to her husband, "Hello, sweetheart, your fli—"

"Gloria," Kerrigan interrupted his wife. "I want you to meet someone." Quickly, the detective introduced the children to their new mother.

"In a few minutes there is going to be a small disturbance. When it happens, I want you to take the kids and go home. I'll call you in a couple of days."

"Okay," Gloria said, and handed him a manila envelope. "When you said you were coming down, I made copies of what you wanted."

"Good girl."

"Suddenly, four men in security guard uniforms entered the waiting room full of people waiting for flights to their various destinations in the outlands of Alaska.

Morgue saw them and gave a quick glance at Kerrigan. The lieutenant grinned and gave the mercenary a citizen's salute. Morgue made no effort to resist and followed the security guards to their vehicle.

Finally, Kerrigan was on his way back to Fairbanks. Opening the folder his wife had given him, he studied the information regarding the orphanage and the history of the adoption process that he and Gloria had gone through while adopting their own three children many years before. Most of the information was no longer current, but as he revisited in his mind the experiences repeated three different times over the course of three different adoptions, he was reminded of the roller coaster ride of emotions he and Gloria had gone through. Most of all, he was reminded of the children and how their lives had been impacted by the new lives they had found with him and Gloria.

It reminded him of something Worley had said about his Christian faith, "Before I found Christ, I was without hope, and without God, in the world, after I became a believer, my life took on new meaning and my hopes and expectations became spiritual instead of worldly."

Maybe Worley isn't that far wrong, after all, Kerrigan thought.

Kerrigan returned to Jerod Aikens' FBO and re-rented the rental car. He knew that the orphanage had been torn down but had no idea where the new one might be, or if there even was a new one, and the only address he had for Wallace probably wasn't current either, but it was all he had so he decided he would start there.

Theodore Wallace had started out as a parole officer in Fairbanks back in the early 1970s. Three years later he took a job in Social Services and eventually headed up the department.

During his tenure he had become quite familiar with the juvenile incarceration and detainment processes, resulting in the overwhelming demand upon the foster care system: delinquent children, orphaned children, children abandoned for any number of reasons, including incarceration of their parents, drug addicted parents, even parents killed on the streets in drug related acts of violence.

Theodore began his work with an optimistic approach to the problem. He really believed that through cooperation of the social service community, along with support from the public community at large, primarily through awareness programs, Theodore felt he could make a difference.

After only nine years on the job Theodore Wallace became restless. He was making only peanuts in terms of a salary, and his high, idealistic anticipations had long since been swallowed up in the system of bureaucracy. Theodore cleaned out his desk and retired from the Social Services department with political aspirations for an elected position.

About that time one of the major child orphanage programs—a non-profit organization affiliated with a church group in Fairbanks, Alaska—contacted Theodore, requesting he take over the job as Administrator of their orphanage program. The money they offered Theodore seemed too good to pass up, so Theodore accepted. Twenty-four hours later his first client walked through the door, a young couple named Mark and Gloria Kerrigan.

Lieutenant Kerrigan walked up the steps of the old building. Not much had changed except its age. He paused for a moment reflecting on the last time he had been there. Those were happy times in his life; times of hope and expectation that he and Gloria might find another child they could love and raise. It seemed so unfair that people who love the thought of having children and raising them, especially people who can afford to provide for them, are oftentimes the ones who are unable to conceive. Yet, to provide for a child who has been left an orphan for whatever reason seemed to Mark and Gloria to be an even higher privilege—maybe even a calling.

There was a sign above the door that read, NO CHILD LEFT BEHIND. The plaque on the door read ADMINISTRATION OFFICE. Kerrigan wondered where the new orphanage was now located, since it was now obvious that the old building had been demolished.

He tried the door, but it was locked. Peering through the narrow gap between the curtains over the window, he could see a portion of a waiting room. The doorbell was a metal hinged knocker attached to the door face. Kerrigan tapped several times. Clack, clack, clack. Soon he heard footsteps and someone was unlatching the door from the inside. He waited as the door opened about an inch and an elderly woman that he faintly recognized spoke to him through the opening.

"Michael, what are you doing here? You know you're not supposed to come here," she said in a shaky voice. Kerrigan held up his police badge.

"Good morning, ma'am. You may have me confused with someone else. My name is Lieutenant Mark Kerrigan, Alaska State Police, homicide division. I'm here to see Theodore Wallace."

The old woman paused briefly, as if not sure if she should slam the door and run, or let the police officer enter and pretend to be innocent. She chose the latter.

"Oh my," she said. "Wait here. I'll see if Mr. Wallace is available."

Kerrigan gently pushed on the door. "If you don't mind, ma'am, I'd rather wait inside." The old woman looked astounded and stepped back allowing the lieutenant access to the waiting room. "May I ask your name, please?" Kerrigan asked. The lady acted as though she had not heard him and shuffled her way down a hallway to a door where she paused and gently knocked. Kerrigan saw the door open and heard muffled voices coming from the hall, but was unable to make out what was being said. Soon, an elderly man, who Kerrigan recognized as Theodore Wallace, stepped into the hallway.

The lieutenant waited until Wallace entered the waiting room and, again, held up his identification wallet that contained his badge.

"Lieutenant Mark Kerrigan, Mr. Wallace. You may remember me. My wife and I—"

"I remember you, sir. It's been a long time."

"Yes, it has."

"I seem to remember that the last time I saw you, you were adopting your second, or was it your third, child?"

"Third, sir."

"Well, Mr. Kerrigan—"

"It's Lieutenant Kerrigan," Kerrigan corrected him.

"Excuse me, Lieutenant Kerrigan. Are you here to adopt again, or is this an official visit?"

"I'm afraid it's, official this time, Mr. Wallace."

"Then, how can I help you, Lieutenant?"

It did not go un-noticed to Kerrigan that Wallace was certainly a different personality now than the last time he had spoken with the man who had orchestrated the adoption of his three children.

"Do you think we could talk in your office?"

Wallace hesitated for a moment. His facial features unchanged from the moment he first saw the lieutenant.

"If you wish. Right this way."

The old lady stood half in and half out of the office door and Wallace said to her, "Dear, would you get Lieutenant Kerrigan a cup of coffee, please?" The old lady did not respond at first, then slowly made her way into another room where she shut the door behind her.

The office was plain and unassuming. There were no pictures of fishing trips or hunting trophies on the wall. No framed lifetime achievement awards or university degrees acknowledging a career of educational accomplishments. There were, however, pictures of girls, young girls—lots of them.

"Please have a seat, Lieutenant."

Kerrigan ignored the courtesy and continued to peruse the pictures.

"When your wife answered the door, she thought I was someone else, she called me, Michael. Do you know someone named Michael who looks like me?"

"I can assure you, Lieutenant, no one who works for me looks like you."

"Then who is this Michael that she spoke of?"

"I'm not sure, unless it was one of the gardeners who work under contract."

"I see." Kerrigan continued to study the pictures. "Is there something special about all these girls?" Kerrigan asked.

"They are all what we consider our success stories. They were girls who came from extremely dysfunctional environments and were placed into homes at a most unlikely age, in terms of opportunity, and yet successfully adapted to their new environments. We are very proud of them, and the adopting parents."

"Where are the pictures of the adopting parents?"

"Most parents choose to remain anonymous and we respect their right to anonymity."

"Why all girls? Where are the boys? Don't you have any success stories involving boys?"

"Very few. The boys who actually succeed in an adopted family scenario usually do so through the church, not directly through the adoption agency."

"The church?" Kerrigan turned around and looked directly at Theodore Wallace, who had seated himself at his desk. "What church?"

"We have affiliations with several of the churches in the Anchorage and Fairbanks area, and throughout southeast Alaska. They work with us in finding families conducive to certain particular personalities."

Kerrigan didn't take his eyes off the pictures, as if he were looking for a familiar face. "How about Kake, Alaska? Do you have any affiliations with that cult in Kake?" He looked back at Wallace to watch his expression. Wallace appeared uncertain.

"I'm not sure what you mean, Lieutenant."

"Do you know anybody down there?"

"Where is that exactly?" Wallace inquired.

"Southeast Alaska. About twenty-five miles east of Sitka. I'm sure you remember. I just saw you down there yesterday. We followed you up here to Fairbanks. You were flying in a twin-engine airplane and I personally watched you get off the plane with that guy from Kake that claims to be a prophet. What's his name…Morning?"

"Oh, yes, of course. I remember now. Brother Morning invited me down to inspect his facilities. He has submitted an application for providing homes for children. To be perfectly honest, Lieutenant, I was a little suspect. I'm not sure their environment would be in the best interest of our children."

"Really? Is that the only time you've ever met Mr. Morning?"

"Other than talking to him on the phone briefly, yes, that is the only time we have ever met." Kerrigan indicated toward the pictures on the wall.

"Well, Mr. Wallace, I'm more interested in the children that were not your success stories. What can you tell me about them?"

"What do you want to know, Lieutenant?"

"I want to know what happens to them."

"We only keep the children to a certain age and then turn them over to the state."

"What age is that?"

"About twelve or thirteen.

"Where do you get them in the first place?"

"Lieutenant, I'm afraid I am running out of time. I have several appointments that I must be to this afternoon. Do you suppose you could come back another time?"

"I don't think you understand, Mr. Wallace. Unless you cooperate with me today, the next time I come I'll not only have a warrant, but will bring a dozen men and a truck and confiscate every file box you have in here. Is that what you want?"

"Then I must insist that you go immediately, Lieutenant. I have no more to say without having an attorney present."

"What do you need an attorney for, if you've got nothing to hide?"

"Good day, Lieutenant. My wife will see you out." Wallace picked up an interoffice phone and pressed a button, "My dear, the lieutenant is ready to leave."

Kerrigan ignored Wallace, and proceeded to search the remaining pictures on the wall. Suddenly, he saw her. He reached up and took the picture down from the wall at the same time that Ms. Wallace came into the room. Turning to Theodore he said, "I want to see your records for this girl right here." Kerrigan thumped his forefinger on the glass covering the picture. Then two more pictures caught his eye. "And these," he said as he took them off their hooks and tossed them on Wallace's desk. "Are these girls an example of your success stories too?"

"Lieutenant, I must protest. It is most unconstitutional of you to not respect my privacy without a warrant."

"I've got a warrant, Wallace. Right here." Kerrigan pulled a folded paper partially out from the breast pocket of his blazer for a brief moment, and returned it without letting Wallace look at it. "I'm not going anywhere, and neither are you. Mrs. Wallace, you can have a seat over there by your husband."

Wallace reached for the phone and began to dial a number. "Who do you think you're calling?" Kerrigan demanded.

"I'm calling my attorney." Kerrigan grabbed the phone and ripped the cord out of the wall.

"I'll let you know when you can talk to an attorney. And when that time comes, one of my choosing will be provided for you. In the meantime, I want you to show me the files on every one of these girls."

Wallace walked over to a file cabinet and began searching through it. Kerrigan pulled out his phone to call Eric.

"Yes, Lieutenant, this is Eric. I just landed in Anchorage. What can I do for you?"

"Eric, I need you to—"

The lieutenant stopped in midsentence. Eric asked again, "Lieutenant Kerrigan, are you there?" He could hear what sounded like a scuffle, then two gun-shots rang out. A moment later, the phone went dead.

CHAPTER 14

Rusty German briefed Shirley Crowder on the basic passenger safety precautions involved in their short flight to Juneau, Alaska. After taking a few moments to familiarize himself with the twin Cessna 421, he fired up the two turbo-prop power plants and let them warm as he taxied into position for takeoff from the dirt runway at Kake, Alaska.

The combined thrust from the two 750 horsepower engines surprised him as he felt the extra G-forces pressing his body against the seat on departure. The available power felt good and he began to seriously consider trading his Cessna 206 Stationair for a new turbo-powered twin.

Shirley Crowder was wide eyed, but quiet, mesmerized by the experience of flying high above the beautiful land and seascape of southeast Alaska.

Rusty glanced back at the ground and waved at his father-in-law, who along with Rudy Crawford watched the twin Cessna as it roared past above their heads.

"The view is so beautiful from up here," Shirley said.

"Rusty German looked across at his passenger. "Is this your first time flying in an airplane?"

"Yes. It is so wonderful. Do you do this often?"

"Every day. You don't get very far in Alaska if you can't fly."

"You must see a lot of God's beautiful creation from up here. Do you ever get tired of it?"

"No, ma'am, never do."

"Are you married?" Shirley asked him, still starring out the window.

"Yes, ma'am. I married Mr. Worley's oldest daughter. Her name is Keera. We have twins, boy and girl."

"That is so wonderful. What are their names?"

"Manson and Michelle. They're eighteen now. How about you, do you have any children?"

"Oh no. But Rudy and I want to get married and then, maybe."

"I sure hope that works out for you two. Rudy works for me. He's a good man."

"I can't thank you and Mr. Worley enough for what you are doing for us, it is so generous of you."

"Just part of the job. Except my dad sometimes bites off more than he can chew, so this isn't the first time I've had to lend him a hand on one of his projects. If you don't mind my asking, how did you wind up with…well, you know, up there on that hill?"

"It's a long story that began all the way back in Utah when I first met the prophet."

"So, you really think that guy is a prophet?"

"Oh, I don't know amymore…I'm not even sure what a prophet is. He claims to be a prophet and he is so persuasive, I guess…I guess I'm just gullible."

"I can understand that. I'd like to hear more about it, but right now I need to contact Juneau Approach."

"Is that Juneau ahead?"

"Yes, ma'am. About twenty-miles. We'll be on the ground shortly."

The tires chirped their appreciation of once again being firmly on the ground. Rusty cleared the active runway and taxied to the fuel ramp.

"You can wait in the FBO if you want. I'll give Pastor Gibbons a call and make arrangements to have the airplane re-fueled."

Beltray Gibbons, pastor of the Juneau Bible Church and founder of the Juneau Gospel ministerial radio outreach program, was himself once upon a time also a drug addict and dealer. Back in the day when I was in the gold mining business, a small plane loaded with methamphetamine packaged and ready for distribution crash landed on our airstrip at the old Alfred Creek mine. The pilot was killed on impact and the plane completely destroyed in a fire, but his accomplice, Beltray Gibbons, had bailed from the airplane during landing. A couple of the boy's found the man badly damaged and unconscious lying in the ditch that run alongside the gravel airstrip. I got hold of Medivac, and they dispatched one of their helicopters to the scene.

Gibbons recovered from his injuries only to receive a five-year prison sentence in the Fairbanks Correctional Institution on charges of manufacturing, with intent to distribute, methamphetamine.

A few years later, during the time I was investigating the murder of my best friend, William Shearer, I again encountered Mr. Beltray Gibbons. This time, still bearing the scars of his near fatal landing at Alfred Creek, he was caught red-handed while involved in a drug bust at an old mining airstrip in northwest Alaska, twenty-five miles north of Norton Bay, where he nearly got his head blown off. Beltray once again escaped the grim reaper, primarily because I needed the inside information that Gibbons was, at the time, somewhat reluctant to share.

Between me and my boy's powers of persuasion, and my wife's fantastic home cooking, Gibbons finally came around. The deal was that if Beltray would turn state's evidence and tell all that he knew concerning the drug organization, I would guaranty immunity from prosecution and provide him free room and board, plus education in any field he chose at any one of the learning centers for as long as he wanted.

It was a long-shot and I knew it. Never in a million years did I expect Gibbons to make anything of himself. However, five years later, during which time I had completely forgotten about the boy, I managed to wreck my own airplane up at a place called Glacial Lake. At the-time I found myself all busted up and critically injured in a pile of rocks, about as near to death as one can get without actually being dead. Then, while contemplating my slim chances of survival, I remembered a piece of advice my friend Bill Shearer had given to me before he was killed. There in those rocks, starring my own grim reaper straight in the face, at a time when my self-sufficiency would normally never conceive of such a thing, I finally realized my need for divine intervention, and uttered a prayer to God for help.

The next morning dawned bright and warm. Surprised that I had actually made it through the night, I wondered what good being alive would actually do me, until I heard the airplane.

Well, long story short, the airplane not only found me but the pilot was none other than Beltray Gibbons. I didn't get the whole story from him until after my rescue and recovery, but the day finally came when

I had a chance to sit down with the ex-drug dealer long enough to hear his testimony.

It was a fascinating story of salvation, by grace, and grace alone. Beltray had met a young man who was studying to become a pastor. The things he shared with Beltray gave him a totally new perspective, not only of himself but, of God. After wasting a whole year doing practically nothing in terms of learning, Beltray suddenly decided he wanted to be just like his new friend. He engaged in a Bible study class where he became a believer in the gospel of Christ--that is, His life, death, burial, and resurrection, through which sinners might be saved, by grace, through faith alone.

Beltray then went on to become a pilot and eventually the pastor of a small Bible church in Juneau, where he soon began a radio ministry. As visiting pastor of twelve different churches throughout the Aleutian Chain, along with his radio ministry, when Gibbs isn't preaching, he's flying.

It was on one of those rare occasions that Pastor Beltray Gibbons received a call.

"Body of Christ Radio Ministries, Pastor Gibbons, May I help you?"

"Beltray, this is Rusty German."

"Praise the Lord, Rusty. Good to hear from you. What's on your mind?"

"Beltray, I'm working a murder case with my dad and we need a safe place for a lady that might be in danger. Do you have someplace she could stay?"

"I'm sure she could stay with one of the ladie's in the church. How long do you think?"

"Could be a week, maybe even a month, I'm not sure. We'll spring for the expenses."

"Not a problem. Are you bringing her here to the church?"

"I have her with me. We're at the Juneau airport. Could you send someone to pick us up?"

"I'll come get you myself. Are you at flight line services?"

"Yes. Oh, there's one other thing."

"What's that?"

"Pop wanted me to tell you, she's been a member of a cult in Kake for the last ten years, and may need a little, eh, you know, help, so to speak."

"I see. Well, we have plenty of that around here. So we'll do what we can. Is that all?"

"There is one other thing. It seems that one of the men that works for me rescued her off of the cult compound and the two of them have decided they want to get married."

"Really! Have they known each other long?"

"About two or three hours, I think," Rusty said, rolling his eyes.

"That's interesting. They must have really hit it off. Okay, I'll be there in about ten-minutes."

"Thanks, Gibbs."

Rusty slid his smartphone into his pocket and approached Shirley.

"He said he'd be here in ten-minutes. He'll make arrangements for you to stay with someone until we finish our case and then I'll get Rudy back over here where the two of you can go ahead with your plans to get married."

"Thank-you so much, Mr. German."

"Excuse me, sir." Rusty realized that someone had approached him from behind and turned to see who it was. Two men whom he had never met approached him. The first man was shorter than his accomplice, but stocky and more muscular.

"Yes, sir, can I help you?"

"My name is Dale Bowman. I'm with airport security. This is Clark Shatner. Would you mind showing us some identification, please?"

"Sure," Rusty said as he retrieved his wallet. "Here's my commercial pilot certificate, medical card, and picture ID."

"Did you just fly over here from Kake, in that twin Cessna parked outside?"

"Yes, sir."

"Is that your airplane?"

"Eh, actually, no."

Mr. Bowman carefully studied Rusty's demeanor.

"Whose is it?"

"Eh, actually, I forgot to check. We were in kind of a hurry to get away from—"

"In a hurry? To get away from what?"

"Well, it's kind of complicated."

"I'm sure it is, Mr. German. Would you like me to tell you who that plane belongs to?"

"That's okay, I'm sure it belongs to either that cult leader, Joseph Morning, or Theodore Wallace, the guy that runs the orphanage in Fairbanks."

"How is it that you're flying a plane that doesn't belong to you?"

"Because this plane is property that has been seized in a criminal investigation." Rusty handed Mr. Bowman his private investigator identification. "I'm sure you know of my dad, Lou Worley. He, and an Alaska State Police Homicide detective by the name of Lieutenant Mark Kerrigan, are working a murder case out of Sitka. I'm working the case with them. You can check with Captain Daily at the Anchorage State Police Homicide Division."

"I see, Mr. German. But I hope you won't mind if we ask you to stick around until we can verify what you say."

"Not at all. Take your time. Except I need to get going within the hour, if that's not too much to ask."

"We'll do the best we can, sir. But I'm afraid until we do, you'll need to come with us." Bowman took hold of Rusty's left arm and Clark the other.

"Sir, I don't think you understand. That twin Cessna may contain potential evidence related to the crimes we're investigating. If you detain me, or board that aircraft, you'll be impeding a criminal investigation."

Rusty heard the main door to the lobby open and recognized the voice of Beltray Gibbons.

"Mr. German, is everything all right? Why are those men putting handcuffs on you?"

"Hey there, Gibbs. Do me a favor and get hold of dad's jet pilot, Eric. Have him come down here and get me. And call Captain Daily in Anch—" Bowman inconspicuously slammed Rusty in the stomach with a clenched fist that felt like a Makita Jack-hammer.

"Sure thing, Rusty. But--"

"Just call Eric, will you?"

"Where's the lady I'm supposed to pick up?"

Another blow to his midsection caused Rusty to once again gasp for air as the two men dragged him out the door.

Gibbons watched as the two security officers escorted his friend out of the FBO. He wanted to chase after them and find out why they were arresting one of the most law-abiding citizens he had ever met, but he knew he must put first things first, and finding the lady he had been commissioned to protect was his first priority.

Gibbs looked around the room. Most everyone was talking amongst themselves about what they had just witnessed, but no one was paying any attention to Gibbons. *Maybe she went to the bathroom*, he thought to himself. After waiting for several minutes, Gibbs approached the desk and inquired about the lady who had arrived with the big man that had just been taken away in handcuffs. No one remembered seeing her.

Gibbs looked at his watch. It was getting late and he had services to hold in the evening. He searched through his call list for Eric's number, but it wasn't there, so he tried his friend, Lou Worley. The phone rang several times and then went to voice mail.

"Mr. Worley, this is Gibbs. Something just happened that I'm sure you'll want to know about. I'm at the Juneau airport and Rusty—" Suddenly, the phone lost its connection. Once again he searched through his call list. Scrolling up Captain Daily's name, he mashed on the green button.

"Homicide. This is Reagan." The voice sounded depressed, like it came from a man who had long ago given up any expectation of good news.

"Hello. May I speak with Captain Daily?"

"Daily's in a meeting, can I help you?"

"Maybe. On second thought, never mind. Do you know when he'll be available?"

"Probably tomorrow. Are you calling to report a crime?"

"No, but I would appreciate it if you would have Captain Daily call me. I'm in Juneau and it's regarding the case Lou Worley is working on."

"Okay. Do you have a number?" Gibbs gave the man his cell number and thanked him. The man never replied and hung-up. Then he remembered, *The foundation. I'll call the foundation, they'll have Eric's number.* Gibbs called information and got a number for The Shearer/

Worley Learning Center Foundation and placed the call, but before anyone could answer, he hung up. *That won't work, h*e thought. *If Mr. Worley's wife answers she'll ask questions and might get worried. I'll have to figure this out on my own.*

Gibbs stepped out the front door to the parking area and began walking toward his car. Suddenly, he saw them. The two men who had handcuffed Rusty German were just now leaving the parking lot in an unmarked car. Gibbs was unable to determine if anyone else was in the car with them, but he hurried to his own car and began to follow.

The pale grey Crown Victoria turned right onto the Access Road and made its way east to Yandukin Drive, to the far east end of the airport where it disappeared into a large hangar. Gibbs watched as the huge hangar doors slowly closed behind them.

"Something's wrong with this picture," Beltray muttered to himself. He flipped open the lid on his cell phone and pressed: 911.

"Nine-one-one. What is your emergency?"

"Yes, ma'am. I'm at the Juneau International Airport, and I believe I have just witnessed a kidnapping."

"Sir, tell me your name and phone number, in case we get disconnected, then tell me what makes you think someone has been kidnapped?"

"My name is Beltray Gibbons. I'm the pastor of the Juneau Bible Church and radio talk show host of—"

"Yes, sir, I know who you are."

"Well, anyway, I responded to a call from Mr. Rusty German, a well-respected friend of mine, to pick up a passenger at flight services. When I got there, two men, who had identified themselves as airport security, had handcuffed Mr. German and were taking him away and the lady I was supposed to pick up has also disappeared."

"Mr. Gibbons, I do not understand what the emergency is."

"Actually, I'm not sure there is one. It's just that…as I was leaving, I saw a grey Crown Victoria with the same two men in it enter a large warehouse or hangar at the far east end of the field. Wait a minute. Someone is coming out. I think it's the lady I'm looking for. It is. That's her. I'm sorry, ma'am, I have to go."

"Wait, Mr. Gibbons. Do not hang up! Pease stay on the—"

Gibbs snapped the lid shut and tossing the phone on the seat beside him sped toward the lady with the beautiful blonde hair that was suddenly running out of the hangar doors, only seconds before they slammed closed. In an instant he maneuvered the car alongside her as she ran toward the open field next to the huge hangar.

Rolling down the passenger side window, he hollered, "Get in, get in the car. Rusty German sent me."

Shirley Crowder looked confused. Her face wore the terrified expression of a deer, frantic to escape its predator. Regardless, the car beside her appeared to be her only option. She grabbed at the door handle and threw herself into the front seat.

Beltray held onto her with one hand and with the other swerved the car as he accelerated away from the warehouse and onto the Old Daily Road. A minute later, he turned onto the Float Plane Access Road and soon parked his car alongside the 185 float plane that had been donated to Beltray's ministry by the Shearer/Worley Foundation, nearly five- years before.

"Are you the lady Rusty called me about?" he asked, looking inquisitively at his traumatized passenger.

"I think so. That is, if you are the one Mr. German called when we were on our way over from Kake."

"That's me. Can you tell me what happened back there?"

"Oh, my! Those men, they have taken Mr. German. I don't know what they are going to do with him, but I was so afraid I tried to hide from them, but they found me and took me too."

"How did you manage to get away?"

"When they drove into the warehouse, they dragged me and Mr. German out of the car. One of the men ran to a nearby office and flipped a switch to close the big doors. About that time Mr. German kicked the other man and yelled to me to run. The huge doors were nearly close by the time I got to them but I managed to slip through just before they completely shut. It surprised me when you drove alongside. When I first…saw you…I thought you might be one of them."

Beltray knew instantly what she was referring to.

"Oh, you mean my scars? I apologize for that. I'm sure they're enough to frighten even a grizzly bear. But like the apostle Paul said,

"Most gladly…will I rather glory in my infirmities, that the power of Christ may rest upon me."

"Oh, praise the Lord. You are a Christian?"

"Yes. I'm the pastor of the Juneau Bible Church. Rusty asked me to find a place for you to stay, so I'm going to take you to my mother's home. She lives up on the north end of Auke Lake. We'll fly up in my float plane. There's a dock we can tie up to in front of her cabin. Nobody will know where you are so you'll be safe there."

"Oh, thank-you, Pastor. How did you…"

"How did I get these scars? Is that what you want to know?"

Shirley sheepishly nodded her head.

"They're the result of living outside of the laws of the land, and far removed from the grace of God; and yet it was that very grace that preserved my life for the day when I would come to know him as my Savior and the one and only true God of heaven and earth. How about you? Are you a Christian?"

"Yes, I think so."

Gibbs looked at the young woman wondering if she even knew what the definition of '"Christian"' actually was. He held up his arm and motioned for Shirley to stop. "Miss Crowder, would you wait here on the dock for a minute while I do a pre-flight check of the airplane?"

"Yes, of course, Pastor Gibbons."

Gibbs retrieved a hand pump from the cabin of the floatplane and began pumping water from the various compartments of the floats.

"Why aren't you sure?" he asked her.

"Sure of what?"

"You said you were not sure if you are truly a Christian. I wonder why?"

"I don't know. How can anyone be sure? Don't you ever sin, or make mistakes that you have to be forgiven for, and then wonder if you ever are truly forgiven?"

"Never!"

"*Never?*" Shirley appeared shocked. "Are you saying you never wonder, or never sin?"

Beltray paused to consider how to explain himself, "Let me say it this way, Miss Crowder. The Bible says, in 1 Peter 2:24, '"He himself bore our sins in his body on the tree, that we might die to sin and live to righteousness. By his wounds you have been healed.'" That means Jesus Christ took all my sin; past present and future; and by believing in Him, we are '"made the righteousness of God in Him."'Therefore, we have no need to continually confess and repent for every sin or mistake we may make during the rest of our lives as believers. We did all the confessing and repenting required of us the moment we first came to Christ. You must understand that the definition of the Greek word for repent is change of mind. At the moment we confessed that we are sinners in desperate need of a savior, the moment we repent or change our minds and turn from our evil way of unbelief to a new and living way of faith and belief in the gospel of grace and truth, we are saved—forever. From that moment forward there is nothing you can ever do to un-save yourself. '"For by grace are ye saved through faith, and that not of yourselves: it is the gift of God. Not of works, lest any man should boast."' "If your salvation cannot be earned by your good deeds, then, transversally, your bad deeds cannot take it away."

Shirley's heart leapt within her. "I don't think I have ever heard anyone explain it that way to me before," she said, "My life is so full of condemnation and guilt. Why, if I could believe that, I think I would be the happiest person in the world. But…I could never believe it…it just seems too good to be true."

"Yes, Miss Crowder. That's why it is called the *good news*."

Shirley watched Beltray as he moved about the airplane, inspecting the various flight controls for freedom of motion.

"I'm afraid if I were to believe that, I might be tempted to continue in sin because—"

"Because…'grace abounds'?" Beltray interrupted.

"Yes. I'm sure I would."

Pastor Gibbs continued: "In Romans 6:1, the apostle Paul, in anticipation of that very question, said this: 'What shall we say then? Shall we continue in sin, that grace may abound?' Paul's answer to them was in verse 2, "'God forbid. How shall we, that are dead to sin, live any longer therein?'"

"In Colossians 2:10, Paul tells us, 'And ye are complete in him.'" Don't you see, that is the whole purpose of Christ's coming to this earth,

God sent his Son into the world as a propitiation for man's sin. That is, as a *mercy Seat*, for you and for me. It is *his* righteousness that is provided in place of our, un-righteousness. It is *his* Holiness for our un-holiness, *his* resurrection and life for our death and damnation, *his* blood shed for the remission of *our* sins, all of which stands in substitution for any who will believe in him. It is only a question of faith. Faith is not an emotion. Faith is not a feeling. Faith is not based on some physical evidence or righteousness one sees in his/or her, own life. 'faith is the substance of things hoped for, the evidence of things not seen.'"Miss Crowder, faith is a decision. God has given to every man a measure of faith, and he has the right to declare it with his own mouth. Faith never doubts. Faith never relents. Faith never waivers or gives up, no matter what, at all times, in all places, and under all circumstance, no matter *what!* faith endures."

Shirley listened like a captivated audience. She had never heard the gospel preached in such a way. Suddenly it no longer seemed like a thing too good to be true, but like a thing that she wanted more than she had ever wanted anything in her whole life.

"I certainly wish I could believe it, Pastor Gibbons. I really do. Maybe if I heard more. I really would like to hear more."

"I'll see to it, Miss Crowder. I'll be glad to see to it."

Gibbs finished with the preflight inspection and helped Shirley board the aircraft.

As she climbed in he said to her, "Auke Lake is only about ten-minutes away, but you'll still need to fasten your seat-belt." Shirley did as instructed. Suddenly, it occurred to Beltray. As he un-lashed the ropes that secured the aircraft to the dock and gently pushed it away toward the open channel he realized that a lump the size of a walnut had formed in his throat. He tried to swallow it away but it grew even larger. Pastor Gibbons fired the big Continental, and moments later the aircraft broke free from the water and lifted into the air.

"Rusty tells me you have been living with a religious group over at Kake, is that true?"

"Yes. They are wonderful people. Such a loving family."

"What do they teach over there that has left you so un-sure of your salvation?"

"Well, I'm sure it's just me. The prophet—"

"The…who?" Beltray almost dropped his seatbelt.

"The prophet. Brother Joseph Morning," Shirley repeated. "Teaches us that we must live without sinning, and that if we sin we have never truly been converted."

"Really! I would like to meet this prophet."

"Oh, he would never meet with anyone who is not one of us. In fact, no one is ever permitted to talk to outsiders about what he teaches us."

"Why is that?"

"It is because probation has closed on the rest of the world and we are the chosen ones."

"Chosen for what?" Beltray could hardly believe what he was hearing.

"Chosen to be separate from the world and to prove our worthiness, so we may someday dwell with God in heaven."

"How are you supposed to prove your worthiness?" Beltray asked, all the more intrigued.

"By being perfect."

"So, has anyone over there ever achieved this ultimate perfection as yet? Or have you achieved it?"

"Oh no, not me. But some say they have. Yet, I see things."

"Things like what, Miss Crowder?"

"Things like, well…" She leaned closer to Beltray and whispered, "Things like sexual immorality."

"I see. In other words, none of them have ever reached this human perfection they seek either, have they?"

"No. I suppose not."

"That's because, the only thing that makes us worthy, is our own fallen sinful state. And, the only thing we are worthy of, is the Savior who went to the cross in our place, to redeem us. 'But God commendeth his love toward us, in that, while we were yet sinners, Christ died for us.' In other words, it is the confession of our own fallen, sinful condition that qualifies us to be saved, and our salvation is completely by the Grace of God, by the perfections in Christ Jesus, alone, on the ground of redemption, and by the blood of Christ."

Beltray paused. Through the windscreen he could see Auke Lake just before them. Beltray extended the landing flaps and set the floatplane onto the water. As the craft gently drifted to a stop against the dock, he scrambled down from the cockpit and secured the airplane.

"This is it, Miss Crowder. This is my mother's place." Beltray reached up to take Shirley's hand as she carefully stepped down onto the wood platform. Instantly, he felt it. It was like a warm glow that crept from his hand to the top of his head and all the way down to his toes. Because it was not a warm day, it startled him, and the lump in his throat grew even larger.

Shirley took his hand and as she did, a feeling of security crept over her. As she stepped onto the dock their eyes met.

"Thank-you," she said, softly. Beltray said nothing, but reluctantly released his grasp on her hand as he stepped back.

"I'll take you to meet my mother and then I must go."

"Where do you have to go?" Shirley inquired.

"I have a meeting tonight, and I need to go back and see if I can do anything to help Mr. German."

Beltray walked beside her on the way to the cabin that sat back against the tree line.

"What is your mother's name?" she asked.

"Lorrain." He said.

"You must be very close."

"Yes, we are. She actually gave me up for adoption when I was first born. We only found each other about five years ago."

"Oh my, what a beautiful story. How did you find each other?"

"Mr. Worley. It was Mr. Worley who saved me from going back to prison and who also found my mother. We've been together ever since."

"That is so beautiful. I can't wait to meet her."

They approached the front door and before Beltray could knock, the door swung wide open.

"My son, my beautiful son. Who is this you have brought with you?"

"Mother, this is—"

"Come in. Come in." Lorrain kissed her son as she took Shirley by the arm and drew her into the house. "What is your name?" she asked as she escorted Shirley to the nearest couch.

"Here, dear, you sit right there and tell me all about yourself." Lorrain was beaming from ear to ear. "How did you two meet?"

"Mother," Beltray stammered, "It's not like that." Beltray heard himself say it, but instantly realized he didn't want his words to be true.

"I brought her here to stay with you for a while because she's in danger. We're not…what I mean is…she's not…"

"Do you mean she's not your, girlfriend?" Suddenly, Lorrain looked as if someone had let all the air out of her tires.

"I'm so sorry," she said, giving Shirley a huge hug. "I've never seen my son with a…girl before, and I was so…excited. I thought…"

"That's okay, ma'am. It would be an honor to be your son's girlfriend. However, we've only just met, and I'm, well…"

"Miss Crowder is engaged, mother. She's getting married soon. In fact, I've been asked to perform the ceremony." Shirley was silent.

"Why are you in danger?"

"Mother, Mr. Worley and his son Rusty German are working on a criminal case in Kake, Alaska. This lady is a material witness and they have asked me to provide sanctuary for her until they can take her statement. Would it be all right if she stayed with you for a few days?"

"Of course it would. Miss Crowder, come with me and I'll show you to the spare room."

"I have to go," Beltray announced, 'I'll see you two later." Beltray kissed his mother good-bye and turned to Shirley. He could still feel the warm glow from the touch of her hand and it was preventing him from looking her in the eye.

"So long, Miss Crowder. I'll be in to check on you." With that he headed to the door.

Shirley followed after him.

"Pastor Gibbons," she said.

Beltray paused at the threshold and turned toward her.

"Yes."

"Thank-you, for helping me. I…I…" She thrust her hand toward him. He looked at it, suspended in space like a rose petal offering itself to the morning sun. Slowly, his hand reached out and slid into hers, as once again their eyes met.

CHAPTER 15

Airport security agent, Dale Bowman, shut the rear door of his unmarked, smoky grey, Crown Victoria. In the back seat, with his hands cuffed behind him, sat Rusty German. Riding shotgun, next to Bowman, was his partner Clark Shatner.

"Where are we taking him?" Shatner said in a low tone.

"We'll hold him in Building X for now while we find out what all he knows."

Shatner glanced over his shoulder briefly to look at their prisoner. Turning to Bowman, he remarked, "Have you noticed how big that guy is? If he decides to give us any trouble, we might need a little help."

"Don't worry," Bowman said, "I've got something that will take care of that." He patted his side-arm, and the high-powered Taser belted to his side. Suddenly, Bowman slowed the car and pointed at the rear view mirror.

"Look! There's that girl behind us. The one from the FBO office. Go get her!" Bowman stepped on the brake. Shatner threw open the passenger side door and ran toward Shirley Crowder who was still standing at the corner of the FBO building. She looked confused and offered no resistance as he took her by the arm and dragged her toward the waiting car.

"Lady, you need to come with us. We have a few questions to ask you," he said, pushing her into the front seat next to Bowman.

"What do you guys want with her? She doesn't have anything to do with me, or that airplane."

Bowman looked back at Rusty. "Don't worry about it. It's none of your business."

The car sped away toward the south end of the field to a large building where it disappeared into an old, empty WWII hangar. As the

244

car came to a stop, Shatner jumped out and ran to a corner office in the building where he pushed a button on the wall. Immediately, the huge doors began to close.

Bowman shut the car off, pulled Shirley out the driver side door, and ordered her to stay put. Opening the backseat door, he then ordered Rusty to get out. Rusty immediately complied, seeing a very brief window of opportunity that might provide Shirley a chance to escape.

Rusty watched the doors as they rolled toward each other and timed his reaction accordingly. As he emerged from the vehicle he stepped just close enough to Mr. Bowman where he could reach him with his leg, and as quick as a cat launched a side kick that knocked Bowman to the floor.

"Run, Miss Crowder! Run for the door before it closes."

Shatner saw her running toward the doors and sprinted to reach her before they closed completely, but he was too far away. As she rushed through, the huge doors slammed shut behind her. Shatner ran back to the electrical box and pounded on the green button. Slowly the doors began to reopen. Moments later, both men burst outside in search of the girl.

Bowman was furious. "Where the hell did she go?"

"I don't know," Shatner replied. "But, we'll find her. I'll check around the corner of the building. She couldn't have gone too far."

"Unless someone picked her up," Bowman added, following his partner through the doors.

"Who could have picked her up in that short amount of time?" Bowman thought a moment. "That guy. Do you remember that guy with the scars all over his face that asked us why we were handcuffing the big fella?"

"Yeah, who was he anyway?"

"I don't know, but I'm going to find out."

"Speaking of the big fella." The two men suddenly remembered they had left their most important passenger unattended.

Turning back toward the hanger, they abruptly stopped in their tracks. The huge electronic doors were once again closing, and both men were too far away to make it back to the hangar before they would be completely locked out.

Rusty German laughed out loud at his good fortune. *How stupid can you get?* he thought to himself. Quickly, he dashed for the office where the electronic button was located. Lunging at the shut door, he smashed it to pieces with his shoulder as he burst through, his momentum crashing him to the floor. Clumsily, with his hands still cuffed behind him, he staggered to his feet. Searching about for the electronic switch, he saw a green button on the wall and banged his forehead against it several times until he could hear the huge doors reverse and begin to close again. *Oh, God. Don't let those guys find her. And keep them distracted until those doors are closed.*

Immediately Rusty began to search for something that would break the cuffs loose from his hands. *If only they had cuffed my hands in front,* he thought. *No time to worry about that, got to find something, anything.*

Rusty searched through the equipment lining the back wall of the huge hangar. There in the corner, he spotted it. At the same moment he heard the two fake TSA agents hollering from the outside. They were running now toward the door. Rusty held his breath as the doors slammed shut only moments before they made it back into the building.

"Whew," he breathed a sigh of relief. *It probably won't take them that long to get someone to open those doors, so I better work fast.*

Rusty located the switch on the vertical band saw and turned it on. Instantly it burst to life and began to wind to full power. *Now, if only I can do this without butchering up my hands.* Fine flakes of white hot metal splattered against his flesh. The stench of metal mixed with melting skin reached his nostrils. Finally, he was free. Vigorously he rubbed his wrists as he ran for the car, breathing a prayer, *God, let those keys be in the ignition.* "Outstanding," he said aloud. "Thank-you, God." *What a couple of morons.* Rusty reached in and started the car, then ran to the office and, one last time, mashed on the green button.

As the doors began to open the two TSA agents pulled their sidearms and prepared to shoot to kill.

Rusty backed the car all the way to the rear of the hangar and made a mental calculation, timing the point when the doors would be open wide enough for the car to make it through. "NOW!" he yelled, and mashed the accelerator to the floor.

The tires screeched and the rank smell of burning rubber mixed with black smoke scorched Rusty's nostrils as the powerful V-8 sped toward the humungous doors. Rusty had let his adrenaline turn to impatience and his timing was somewhat off, and as the light grey Crown Victoria emerged through the doors, already doing over thirty miles per hour, both side mirrors exploded into smithereens as the car burst out into the daylight. In his peripheral vision Rusty saw Bowman and Shatner standing, one on each side of the car, guns drawn and pointed directly at him. Rusty prostrated his upper body against the seat. He did not hear the shots but felt the shards of glass hitting him in the face and arms. A moment later they were behind him and the bullets were coming from the rear, smashing through the front windshield as they passed by his head.

As Rusty sped away the firing finally ceased, but Yandukin Drive was coming up fast, and there was no other option but to make a hard left turn. Again, the tires screeched on the rough asphalt surface as Rusty accelerated into the left turn. "*Oh no!*" He sighed as he turned the wheel hard to the left. The heavy Crown Vic flew into the air and landed on the far side of a drainage ditch where it eventually bounced and lurched its way back across the same ditch onto the roadway. Breathing a sigh of relief, he whispered, "Thank-you, Jesus."

Rusty German needed to hide. Someplace out of sight, as soon as possible. Suddenly he spotted a carport only two blocks away. Seconds later, he backed the big Ford into the open but somewhat secluded garage.

Minutes passed as Rusty waited to see who might be looking for him. An hour later he emerged from the carport, on foot, and casually strolled to the end of the dirt drive. A floatplane had just entered the landing pattern for the water runway. "That looks like Gibbs," Rusty mumbled to himself. Seconds later the Crown Vic exploded out of the carport and headed for the floatplane access road. Rounding the corner and sliding to a stop along the water runway, he flung open the door, jumped from the car, and frantically waved his arms at the inbound airplane on final approach to the water runway.

Beltray Gibbons had just turned final when he saw the light grey Crown Victoria slide to a stop at the end of the floatplane access road. There was something familiar about the man who had jumped from the car and stood waving at him as he passed over his head. Gibbs had his own private ramp space at the far south end of the floatplane dock, but decided he should taxi back to investigate who the man was, on the off chance that it might be important. As the aircraft slid into the slip, he quickly realized it was Rusty German.

Gibbs killed the engine and Rusty stepped onto the floats and opened the passenger side door to the cabin of the Cessna Skywagon.

"Gibbs, do you have enough fuel to get to Sitka?"

"Sure, but I--"

Rusty was already pushing the floatplane out into the water runway. "Get this thing in the air before the tower realizes what's going on."

Gibbs fired the 300HP IO-520D Continental and began a water taxi back to the departure end of the waterway.

"When you contact the tower tell them we're VFR to Anchorage."

Gibbs looked at Rusty. "I thought you said we're going to Sitka. Don't ask me to lie to them. Surely you know better than that."

"We *are* going to Sitka. Except right now we're going to Anchorage."

Gibbs contacted the tower and reported ready for takeoff, VFR north. The tower came back, "Cessna N34276 Sierra, stand-by."

Rusty searched the sky for any aircraft inbound on the final approach path. There was none.

"Why are we holding short, there's no traffic on the inbound?"

"I'm not sure," Beltray admitted.

Rusty muttered, "I think they're on the phone to someone who's telling them a pack of lies. Put this thing in gear and let's get out of here."

"I can't do that, Mr. German. I'll lose my license."

"Let me have that microphone." Rusty grabbed the mic from Beltray and pressed the push-to-talk button.

"Juneau Tower, this is Rusty German. I'm working for the Anchorage State Police on a murder investigation in Sitka. I would like to know why we are being held up."

"Cessna 76 Sierra, one moment please."

Beltray looked over at Rusty. Serious concern telling in his expression.

"Don't forget, you're dealing with the feds, not just local authorities."

"Yeah, I know. By the way, the girl got away. I don't know where she went but at least she got away."

"She's safe," Beltray said. "I picked her up when she came through the doors of that big hangar. I took her to my mom's place on Auke Lake."

"*You* picked her up? Wow! Good job Gibbs. What a relief. Did you get a chance to talk to her?"

"I did, but only briefly." Beltray paused. "Mr. German, how sure are you that she's getting married?"

"Cessna 76 Sierra, the Marshals office is requesting that you taxi back to your slip and remain by your aircraft. They will be there shortly to talk to you."

Rusty leaned back in his seat and tossed the microphone back to Beltray.

"Well, here we go. The cats out of the bag." Beltray picked up the mic.

"Roger that, tower, 76 Sierra taxi, slip one-niner."

Rusty opened his phone and began scrolling through the contact list.

"Here they come," Beltray announced. Rusty looked up in time to see two black GMC SUV's coming around the north end of the water runway, red, blue and white strobe lights flashing—but no sirens.

"I'm surprised they don't have their sirens blaring so the whole town can know about it," Rusty said contemptuously as he tossed his phone onto the dashboard.

The doors of the first SUV opened, but instead of men piling out with guns drawn, one lone individual walked toward the floatplane where both Rusty and Beltray waited.

The float plane rocked lazily in the water, bumping gently against the row of rubber tires fastened to the creosote, wooden dock. Rusty opened the passenger side door and stepped out onto the right float as Beltray did the same and proceeded to tie off the aircraft.

As the man spoke, Rusty immediately recognized his voice.

"Captain Daily?" he said in elated surprise. "What are you doing here? I thought I was about to—"

"Rusty! I have some bad news for you," Daily said. Rusty now realized this was in regard to something far more serious than just stealing an airplane and a car.

"What is it, Captain?"

"It's…it's your…dad."

Rusty froze. "What about my dad?" Suddenly, it was like his heart had completely stopped, along with all breathing. Every thought and

249

every emotion went on hold as he waited for Daily's reply.

"I'm sorry to be the one to tell you this Rusty, but his plane has been reported down, and it appears he's missing."

Rusty was not the kind of person that lets emotions override his obligations. His years as an Army Ranger had provided many opportunities to practice putting his feelings on hold while he dealt with the necessary tasks at hand.

"How do you know this?" He said, as calm as a man would ask the time of day.

Daily answered, "I've been told they found the airplane floating in Frederick Sound, north of Turn Mountain."

"So is this report confirmed?"

"Not exactly, at least not yet."

"How long ago?" Rusty asked.

"About an hour, more or less."

Rusty seemed surprised. "You don't know?"

"I only arrived in Juneau three hours ago. I came down for a meeting with the state police big brass. Some fisherman found the craft floating in the sound. The aircraft was empty and there was no sign of anyone around."

"Empty? Floating? Does that mean he didn't crash?"

"We don't know what it means yet. Search and Rescue are on the way now."

Rusty looked around at the four men from the Marshal's office waiting by their cars.

"What's the Marshal Service doing here?"

"They're looking for two guys that impersonated a couple of TSA agents this morning and evidently kidnapped a pilot from the lobby over at flight-line services earlier. We were all in the same meeting. I got the call about your dad's plane at the same time they got the call about the kidnapping. The two men reportedly got away in a grey Crown Victoria and took off in a sea plane. I called the tower and asked them to hold all seaplane traffic until we could check them out. When we got here I was surprised to find you and was not sure if you had heard about your dad as yet."

"They didn't get away in a seaplane. And I'm the pilot they kidnapped and I'm also the one who stole their car." Rusty pointed to the grey

Crown Vic with the missing rear view mirrors parked beside the dock. "The last I saw of them they were emptying their guns into the side of the car, as I was getting away from them. It's pretty shot up. Gibbs here was about to fly me over to Sitka to get my own plane. That twin Cessna I flew over here from Kake a couple of hours ago is over at flight services, and needs to be seized as evidence in the murder investigation that dad and Kerrigan are working on."

"They shot at you?" Daily exclaimed.

"Yeah, but they weren't any better at shooting than they were at kidnapping."

"Sounds like someone hired some second hand help. Don't worry, Mr. German, I'll take care of that. If you guys want to go ahead I'll call the tower and get you released, and if you want to help look for your dad you can put this investigation on hold for now."

"Thanks Captain, but I'm sure what ever happened to my dad is directly connected to the investigation. By the way, have you heard anything from Lieutenant Kerrigan?"

"No, not a word. Do you know where he is?"

"The last I heard he was in Fairbanks, but I'll see what I can find out and keep you informed."

"All, right, then. Keep me posted." Captain Daily returned to his SUV. Rusty turned and motioned to Gibbs that he was ready to go.

"Do you still want me to tell them we're going to Anchorage?"

Rusty grinned, "Nah, we'll go straight to Kake. If you want, when we get there you can help with the search or come back to Juneau, it's entirely up to you."

"I'll help anyway I can," Beltray said. "I just have to make a phone call first."

Beltray Gibbons sat thoughtfully as he maneuvered the Cessna 185 through the assortment of islands and inlets from Juneau over to Kake, Alaska.

Rusty sat quietly beside him.

"Rusty, what do you want to do? Go get your airplane or go straight to the scene where they found the Kodiak."

"Actually, I've been thinking about that. My plane won't do me any good because it's a wheel plane, and as much as I hate to intrude on your plans, it would be great if I could talk you into flying me over to where they found the Kodiak. With this plane, we can land right beside it and check it out."

"I'll be more than happy to do that for you, Mr. German."

"Excellent, let's go direct to Kake and turn north toward Fredrick Sound. Daily said Search and Rescue are on the way; they may be there by now. If they are we'll have a quick look at the Kodiak, and then start looking for the green monster."

"What's a green monster?" Beltray asked.

"That's what Dad calls it. It's a dark green de Havilland Beaver with the letters G-A-S painted on the side. That will be the plane we're looking for. We'll have to get down low over the water and check out all the inlets, anywhere a float plane could hide. As a matter of fact, he might not be far from the Kodiak. Because I'm sure he had something to do with its going down."

"I've seen that plane before!" Beltray said.

"You have? Where?" Rusty said, curiously.

"He's based out of Juneau."

"That's strange. I go to Juneau quite often and I've never seen it there."

"He has a covered slip next to an old fuel dock that isn't used anymore. I ran into him one time when I was looking for a slip to rent for the one-eighty-five."

"So you've seen this guy before?"

"Yes."

"Can you describe him?" Rusty asked. He already had an idea and was hoping Beltray could verify that the pilot of the de Havilland Beaver and Karen's brother were one and the same.

"He's a huge man, I don't mean fat, I mean big, like a lumberjack or deckhand. Not the kind of guy you want to run up against in a dark alley, if you know what I mean."

"What else? Does he have any other identifying features or characteristics?"

"Oh, you mean the beard? Yeah, he's got a beard alright. Grows all the way down his throat and neck, like a grizzly bear. Except I'm not sure he's the guy who you're looking for."

"Why do you say that?"

"Because this guy is a cop or security guard. Every time I've seen him, he was wearing a police uniform."

"Did you get his name?"

"It seems to me his name was…Parker, or something like that."

Rusty German's mouth fell open. "Was it…Ralph Parker?"

"Yes, I believe that was it. Officer Ralph Parker, I believe he works for the Sitka police department."

"So that's how the two gunmen I shot got to the girl."

"What two gunmen?" Beltray inquired.

"Never mind. Okay, here's the plan. Do you have a parachute in this plane?"

"What do you want with a parachute?"

"After we find Dad's plane, we're going to keep looking until we find this guy's green de Havilland Beaver, wherever it is, and you're going to climb up high enough where I can jump out. If he's not around, he soon will be. I don't think he'll stay away from that airplane very long, and when he comes back to it, I'll be waiting for him."

"Mr. German, are you sure you want to tangle with this guy all alone?"

"I'm sure. Do you have a parachute or not?"

"Yes. There's one behind your seat."

"Okay, Mr. Gibbons, I may need to use it. But first, let's find my dad's Kodiak.

Beltray flew directly to Kake, Alaska, and circled the vicinity of the town several times.

"Rusty, it looks to me like there's been a fire. Some building burned to the ground recently."

"Recently, as in today," Rusty answered. "Looks like it was Grady's place and it's still smoking. I can even smell it from up here."

"Do you think it has anything to do with this case you're working on?"

"It absolutely does. I left my dad and Rudy here when I took Miss Crowder to find you. They were planning on arresting the occupants of that house, and then burn it to the ground."

"Well, they certainly managed to burn the house to the ground, that's for sure, but I wonder if they managed to make the arrests too."

"I'm inclined to believe that didn't happen," Rusty said thoughtfully. "If they had, they would have been on their way to Sitka, not Fredrick Sound, another reason why I believe they were in pursuit of that green monster."

"So, what do you want me to do?"

"Just keep going. Follow the western shoreline until it turns east toward Cape Bendel. Slow it up a bit and take us down to about three-hundred feet above the water, for now. That will put the shoreline on my side where I can check out the inlets along the way."

Beltray did as Rusty directed. Mile after mile they flew, weaving in and out of the hundreds of inlets that formed the shoreline.

Suddenly, Rusty's phone began to ring.

"Hello, Rusty German here."

"Mr. German, this is Eric. I'm on the ground in Anchorage. I hope I'm not interrupting anything but I'm concerned about Lieutenant Kerrigan."

"That's okay, Eric. What's the problem?"

"Well, he went back to Fairbanks on his own—"

"On his own? What happened to Morgue? I thought he was supposed to stay with him."

"He was but Kerrigan ditched him and took a charter flight back to Fairbanks. I don't know where Morgue is, but I just got a call from Kerrigan and he was about to tell me something when he got interrupted. It sounded like he may have been involved in a scuffle. Then I heard several shots in the back-ground and the phone went dead. I'm not sure what to do."

Beltray said to Rusty, "Mr. German, we're coming to the northeast corner of the island. The shoreline is going to turn back to the southeast in a couple of miles."

"I see that--wait, what's that over there by Turnabout Island?" Rusty pointed.

Beltray replied, "Looks like red lights flashing. Maybe that's Search and Rescue."

"Mr. German? Mr. German?" Eric repeated. "What do you want me to do?"

"Sorry about that, Eric. Just keep trying to get hold of Kerrigan. If you can't, call me back. In the meantime, I'll see if I can get hold of Morgue. I'm a little tied up right now, down here in Sitka."

"Yes, sir. All, right then, I'll keep trying."

Turnabout Island lay five miles north, smack dab in the middle of Fredrick Sound. Beltray's Cessna 185-floatplane made a sharp left turn and headed directly toward the flashing lights.

Moments later the Yellow and black Quest Kodiak appeared on the horizon. It was alarming to see it floating helplessly, abandoned, in the middle of the ocean. Arriving from the east, a Coast Guard patrol boat, still a mile away, sped toward the ghostly scene. In the air, an S&R helicopter hovered nearby the forsaken aircraft while two divers boarded an outboard-powered rubber craft they had let down from the MH-60 Sikorsky, and headed toward the Kodiak.

"There it is!" Rusty yelled. "There's Dad's plane. Set this thing on the water as close to it as you can get."

Beltray did as Rusty requested and set the Cessna 185 in the water about fifty-yards from the deserted Kodiak.

"How are you going to get over to it? We don't have a canoe with us."

"That's okay, I can swim."

"Are you sure? That water is awfully cold. I'd bet it's not much over forty-two degrees this time of year. A guy could get hypothermia in less than two minutes."

"Maybe I can get a ride in that rescue boat. I'll step out onto the float and see if they'll pick me up."

"Mr. German, I have an emergency raft in the rear baggage compartment. You can use that."

"That's okay, Gibbs. I got this."

Rusty stood on the pontoon and holding onto the strut with his left hand began waving and shouting at the two rescue divers in the rubber craft. They saw him, but made no move in the direction of the 185. He waved again and continued shouting. Finally, the rubber craft began to motor toward them. Several minutes later it pulled alongside the pontoon where Rusty stood.

Two men occupied the rubber craft. One controlled the outboard motor and the other tied off the craft to the floatplane's right pontoon.

"Hey thanks, guys. My name is Rusty German. That Quest Kodiak belongs to my dad, Lou Worley. I'm sure you've heard of him. I've been working on a murder case with my dad and Detective Mark Kerrigan from the Alaska State Police, Homicide Division. I believe my dad was in pursuit of a suspect that would have been flying a dark green de Havilland Beaver with the letters G A S painted on the sides. I need to get over there and check out my dad's airplane. I also believe there may have been a passenger with him as well, a fellow named, Rudy Crawford. So if that airplane is abandoned, we've got two missing persons to look for."

"Yes, Mr. German, we have heard of Mr. Worley. We got a call from some fishermen in the area a couple of hours ago. They reported seeing a midair collision involving two airplanes, the yellow one there and a green one. Probably the one you're looking for. We're just now arriving on the scene, but if you want you can ride with us."

"Thank-you, gentlemen. I appreciate it."

The two men introduced themselves as Rusty stepped into the boat designed to carry six people and belted himself into one of the fiberglass seats provided for passengers. A few minutes later the craft pulled alongside the deserted Quest Kodiak.

For the first time the significance of the situation hit home to Lou Worley's son-in-law. A lump the size of a golf ball filled Rusty's throat and, from somewhere, water began to blur his vision. Quickly, he shook it off. *No time for sentimentalism*-he told himself, and climbed aboard the abandoned vessel.

The first thing he noticed was the damage to the prop. It had hit something and was so bent and twisted that Rusty was amazed the engine had not come off in flight before the pilot had a chance to get the stricken plane back on the water. Rusty opened the pilot side door and looked in. The Plexiglas roof had suffered extensive damage. The smashed, upper interior left wires and oxygen equipment dangling uselessly from the ceiling.

"My god," he said out loud. "It looks like he got hit on top while in flight. Probably never even saw it coming. It definitely took some flying skill to get that thing down in one piece."

Rusty had not forgotten that the two men who had kidnapped him had also disarmed him and kept his sidearm. He climbed over the pilot seat into the aircraft and made his way to the rear of the airplane.

Rusty first checked the survival gear compartment. *The raft is gone* he contemplated. Opening the closet where his father-in-law kept his arsenal of firearms, Rusty helped himself to a Glock .45 and an AR-15 which he slung over his shoulder. Grabbing a military ammo box full of .223 Remington ammunition, along with several boxes of .45 auto, ammo, he headed toward the side door of the aircraft. Opening the door, Rusty addressed the divers.

"With the exception of the point of impact, the rest of the aircraft seems to be intact, "he said. "Of course, there's no one home. And it looks to me like whoever hit them did it intentionally, and I'll just bet you it's our murder suspect. From the looks of the prop, he got his pontoons mixed up in my dad's propeller and I'll bet he's either crashed by now, or looking for some shallow water where he can set it down. I don't know how much fuel he had on board but at some point he'll run out. My guess is he tried to kill my dad, and he'll keep trying until he finishes the job." Rusty gazed off into the distance, toward Turnabout Island. "He'll head for the same place my dad went."

The driver of the boat starred at Rusty with his mouth hanging opened.

"Sir, we can't let you on our craft with those weapons on your person."

"I understand," Rusty said. So if you'll move your rubber boat aside, I'll swim back to the same floatplane that brought me here."

"Are you sure you want to swim in that water?" the diver manning the outboard asked him.

"I'm sure."

"Is there a life raft on board you could use?"

"My dad and his passenger took their survival gear and a four-man raft. It's my bet they're already over on Turnabout Island, and the fact that they're *not* on the shore waving at us and jumping up and down with joy is because they're looking for that Beaver driver. That's why I need to get over there as soon as possible."

"What about the airplane?" the boat driver asked.

"You can have your guys in that helicopter call the NTSB. They'll take care of it. It's a crash scene now. Are you sure you can't give me a lift back to that floatplane?"

The two men looked at each other. The boat driver said, "We'll make an exception this time. But if anyone asks, we'll vehemently deny it."

Minutes later Rusty was back in the 185, fastening his seat belt as Beltray fired up the big Continental.

"So, what do we do now, Mr. German?"

"Let's get airborne and circle that island a couple of times. I want to see what's over there."

Gibbs maneuvered the 185 into the wind and pushed the throttle to full power. The floatplane bucked and rolled over the waves; saltwater hammered against the windscreen as the triple bladed fan tore through the wind, until the float plane eventually broke free from the grip of the water and lifted into the air.

Beltray banked to the north and headed straight toward the western end of the small island.

"Stay off shore and keep it down to about two-hundred feet for now, Beltray. Circle the island clockwise. Maybe Dad or Rudy will be out on the shoreline somewhere."

Gibbs did as Rusty asked until they had completed one entire circle of the island.

"We're almost back where we started from, Rusty. Do you want me to go around again?"

"Yeah, only get in closer and pull in a couple of notches of flap. That should slow it up a little. And this time, level off at a thousand feet AGL where I can look down into the trees."

Again, Beltray complied and soon Rusty was looking straight down into the dense forest of trees.

Turnabout Island was not very large. The trees, foliage, and downed timber from the vicious storms that beat at it year after year made it practically impossible to hike through, much less hide an airplane in, even a crashed one. Yet hide it did. As Beltray began to make his third turn around the northwest end of the island, Rusty shouted, "There it is! That's it, the green monster. It's down there." Rusty pointed frantically at the area directly below. "Do a hard three-sixty, and bring me back around."

"Are you sure it's the same one?" Beltray asked.

"I'm sure. It looks like the pilot pancaked into the timber. I think he purposely put it in a full stall and sunk it in under power."

"Why would he do that?" Gibbs asked.

"Well, from the looks of dad's prop on the Kodiak, I'm sure his floats were badly damaged to the point he knew he couldn't land on either water or land, so he really didn't have any other option. I'll say this, he's one heckuv-a good pilot, to have done that, that is, if he actually walked away."

"Do you want me to land off shore from the Beaver so we can have a look at it?"

"No, not yet. We need to keep on circling. We have to see if Dad and Rudy are on this island somewhere. If that green monster pilot did walk away, he'll be looking for them. We need to find them first. That is, if they're…still alive." Rusty paused. His voice began to crack. "Just keep circling, Beltray, maybe they'll signal us or something." Beltray glanced over at Rusty. He could tell from the emotion in his voice that he was extremely concerned for his dad's safety.

"I take it you're of the opinion that they swam to the island from the Kodiak, is that right?"

"Actually, I believe they took the raft. Dad has a four-man self-inflatable. I'm sure they took that."

"Why wouldn't they have stayed with the airplane? I'm sure their ELT would have gone off at the moment of impact. All they had to do was wait in the airplane for help to arrive."

"Naw. That's not my dad, or Rudy either. They probably saw the green Beaver go into the trees and knew that it was their chance to get the guy once and for all. So, I'm sure they're on this island."

"What about Mr. Worley's health? Are you sure he is strong enough to go through all this excitement? How old is he now…sixty- something, or is it seventy something?"

Rusty stared out the window without answering. Finally, turning to Beltray, he said, "You're right, Gibbs. There is a lot that he probably should have done. But Dad has always been like that. He probably shouldn't have gone looking for that old Russian bi-plane, either. Or retrieved that Cessna 180 that he sunk up at Glacial Lake. Or went after those poachers to rescue the game warden, Calvin Trent. But he's never been one to play it safe. He's just not the least bit timid when it comes to things like that. Yes, he is older. We've all tried to tell him to slow down, be more careful, don't go where angels fear to tread. But in the end the only thing that will slow him down is when his body won't function any-more, or the government takes away his badge and guns. Until then, I can just about guarantee you, he made it to this island, and if he's still alive, the one who's in more danger than anyone else is that green monster driver."

Beltray finished his last turn around the crashed de Havilland Beaver that lay ripped and torn, bashed and battered in a maze of broken trees and timber. Leveling his wings, he again headed east. Rusty stared intently out of the window, searching every opening between the trees.

"Gibbs, do you see that inlet on the north side of the island?"

"Yes. We've passed over it several times already but haven't seen anything."

"I know. Let's check it really good for snags or logs. If it's clean we can set down in there. Get us in as close to the shore as you can, before you set it on the water."

"Okay, boss. Whatever you say."

"I'm sorry to take you away from your work, Pastor Gibbs, but I was sort of out of people options, if you know what I mean."

"That's okay, Mr. German. Like I said before, I want to do anything I can to help. After what Mr. Worley did for me, there's nothing I wouldn't do for him."

"We are all still amazed at what's become of you, Beltray. It certainly is a miracle. "Let me ask you something, Gibbs. If my dad had told you to straighten up and fly right, so to speak, and had threatened you with prison, death, and taxes if you didn't. Would that have induced you to give up your life of crime for your Lord and Savior Jesus Christ and become a pastor?"

Beltray chuckled. "I know where you're going with this, Rusty. No, you're right, I would not. As a matter of fact, the change that took place in me was not a change that I could have manufactured by my own human effort anyway. Regardless of what anyone threatened me with. It was only when I realized that God had given his only begotten son, and that he had given him for *me*, that I fell in love with Jesus Christ. It is love, Rusty. I love the Lord, because He first loved me. By the same token, I would do anything for Mr. Worley, because he did so much for me. A changed life only happens in response to love, brother. Never in response to the threat of law and punishment."

Rusty paused thoughtfully as Beltray circled the inlet.

"Gibbs, will you do something for me?"

"Sure, Rusty. What is it?"

"As soon as we're on the ground, I wish you would pray that we find my dad. Okay?"

"I'd be delighted to do that, my friend. In fact, I've already been praying for that very thing."

Beltray slid the floatplane onto the calm water of the inlet, located on the north shoreline toward the eastern portion of the island.

"It looks like there's a place to beach the plane right through there." Rusty said, pointing straight ahead to the end of the inlet. "As a matter of fact, I'll bet we're not the first ones to do this. It looks to me like someone has built a makeshift dock to tie up to."

Gibbs said to him, "That dock doesn't look that safe to me. I think I'd rather slide it up onto the beach. Mr. German, as soon as I cut the engine, would you jump on shore and hang on to the rope until I can get there? I'll be right behind you to help turn it around."

"Are you sure you want to do that, Gibbs? If the tide goes out, the plane will be stranded until it comes back in."

"I thought of that, Mr. German. But if a storm comes up, the plane will get dashed to pieces against that rickety old dock. We can always wait for the tide to return."

"Good thinking, Gibbs." Rusty climbed out onto the right float and waited for Beltray to cut the engine. Shortly after the propeller stopped and the pontoons gently scraped the sandy shore, Rusty proceeded out onto the end of the float and jumped into the shallow water. Moments later Beltray joined him, turning the aircraft toward the north, facing the open sea. They slid it back a few feet onto the shore and tied it off to a downed tree.

"That should do it," Rusty said, as he immediately climbed into the aircraft and retrieved the weapons he had secured from the abandoned Quest Kodiak.

"By the way, Gibbs. Do you have a weapon on board?"

Gibbs paused and looked at Rusty.

"Yes, but it's part of my survival gear."

"Can you get it, please? That's exactly what you're going to need it for—survival."

"It's only a .22 long rifle," Gibbs said.

"A .22? Well, I guess that's better than nothing."

Beltray climbed back into the airplane.

"Grab an extra box of shells too," Rusty hollered.

Soon Beltray was back and handed Rusty the rifle.

"Well, at least it's got a scope on it," Rusty said. "And the shells are magnum hollow points. That's a good thing."

"Are you going to use it to…?" Beltray stammered.

"Not me. You. You're going to keep it. And, you can take my handgun too. I'm going to have a look around while you sit somewhere and keep watch over the airplane. And, while you're at it, you can pray that I find this guy before he finds us or Dad and Rudy."

"But, I…Mr. German, I can't. You keep your pistol. I don't need it."

"Beltray, if that guy see's you, he'll kill you without even blinking. And if he gets away with your airplane we'll be stranded here with no cell phone service, or haven't you noticed that there is no signal available out here?"

The color had drained from Beltray's face.

"I…never thought I would ever again be in situation where I would have to…"

"I understand, Beltray. Then just pray that I find the killer first."

"So, what do we do now?" Beltray asked.

"First, we find you a place to wait."

"Wait for what?"

"Well, if the green monster driver is alive and well, he surely heard us come in and will be wanting to abscond with our airplane. So in that case I expect that at some point in time, he'll show up here. On the other hand, if perhaps he did not survive his crash, then it's possible Rudy and my dad might show up. In either case we're going to find you a secluded place to hide where you can wait nice and quiet, and out of sight."

CHAPTER 16

Kerrigan stood beside the desk where Theodore Wallace had been sitting moments before the lieutenant ripped his telephone line out of the wall. Wallace had tried to call his attorney and certainly was within his rights to do so, except Kerrigan knew that was not all he was attempting to do. A call to his-so-called attorney would also result in reinforcements arriving. At Kerrigan's request, Wallace had stepped over to a nearby file cabinet to retrieve the files Kerrigan had asked him for, the files of the victims whose deaths he was investigating.

The homicide detective reached into his pocket to retrieve his phone, scrolled up Eric's name, and mashed on the green button.

Wallace subtly inched his way back to his desk and discretely picked up an ashtray from his desk drawer.

Eric answered, "Yes, Lieutenant, I just landed in Anchorage. What can I do for you?"

"Eric, I need you to—"

Suddenly, Wallace threw the ashtray at the lieutenant, hitting him square in the head. At the same moment the old woman opened the door, pointed a Walther PPK at Kerrigan, and fired three shots, each of which hit Kerrigan in the torso. It wasn't a large caliber, only a .380, but, at close range, three well-placed shots could easily kill a man, even a large man like Kerrigan. The lieutenant fell backward to the floor.

Wallace ran to pick up Kerrigan's phone. For a moment he held it to his ear, then snapped the lid shut and put it in his pocket. The old woman stepped from the doorway into the room. "Make sure he's dead, and see if you can get Michael up here to dispose of the body, and clean up this mess."

"Yes, Ma'am, " Wallace said. He reached into his desk drawer, retrieved a cell phone, and began searching through his call list. The old woman slowly closed the door and shuffled her way down the hall.

Suddenly, Kerrigan groaned. Wallace looked at him, startled. He turned toward the shut door where the old woman had stood only a moment before. Quickly he rushed back to his desk and began searching through the drawer for a gun he kept there, but it was too late. Kerrigan already had his nine millimeter aimed and ready to fire. In a whispered voice, he said to him, "Pull it, buddy. Go ahead and pull it. I hope you do, and if you try to warn that old lady, I'll waste you right where you stand."

Wallace raised his hands and backed away from the desk next to the wall.

Kerrigan painfully staggered to his feet. Opening his coat, he examined the three brass jacketed hollow-point slugs still buried in his Kevlar vest. He looked back at Wallace, gasping for air as he spoke, "Never take a knife to a gunfight, I always say. And never go to a gunfight without a-Kevlar." He smiled. Wallace looked away and swore.

"Turn around and put your hands behind your back, you're under arrest." Kerrigan placed the man in handcuffs and began rifling through his pockets. He paused as he found his own phone. Flipping open the lid he tried to call Eric again, but there was no answer. The call went to voice mail so Kerrigan left a message, "Eric, sorry we got cut off. I need you to head back up to Fairbanks as soon as possible. I'm going to need a ride. Call me when you land. Thanks."

Kerrigan returned to Wallace's desk where he retrieved the Colt Mustang .380 Wallace had been looking for. "Nice little ankle gun," he said as he put it in his pocket. In the bottom drawer he found a roll of duct tape. He searched through Theodore's pockets and found a handkerchief. Stuffing it into Wallace mouth, Kerrigan taped the gag to keep it from falling out. Moments later Theodore was ready for transport.

Kerrigan looked around for a place he could stash his prisoner while he went in search of the person who had shot him. On the far wall was a door that appeared to be a walk-in closet. Dragging the unwilling Wallace along with him, Kerrigan opened the closet door. The lieutenant yanked on a light string hanging from the ceiling directly in front of him and the small room lit up. Hanging onto Wallace with one hand he investigated the closet further. Several stacks of boxes all but obscured a plywood door at the far end of the small room. With one hand he pushed Wallace to the floor while he cleared away the boxes to pry open the door.

"What's at the bottom of these stairs, Theodore?" Wallace looked at him, his eyes wide with fear. He began shaking his head and moaning as if he were trying to say something.

"Is that a fact? Well, let's go have a look, shall we?" Kerrigan said.

Slowly the lieutenant reached out and flipped on a light switch as he led his prisoner down the flight of stairs. At the bottom he stopped and looked around.

Moving to the far side of the wall, dragging his unwilling associate with him, he switched on another light.

"What…the hell?" He stammered. "What is this, some kind of a torture chamber, or a…" He looked back at Wallace. "Aren't you and that old woman a little too old to be involved in sex games? You people are sick! Do you know that? You are absolutely sick! I'm ashamed to admit that I ever did business with you, you sick son-of-a-b—"

BAM. Another bullet slammed into Kerrigan's Kevlar. This time right in the middle of his back. He cried out, but didn't go down. Spinning he drew his gun and returned fire. BAM, BAM, BAM. The old woman's body fell face forward from the halfway point on the stairs above to the basement floor below, face down.

Kerrigan went over to her and nudged her with his foot, then reached down to retrieve the Walther .380 she still clutched in her hand.

"She might have been dumb, but she was a damn good shot, I'll give her that. She got me with four direct hits." Kerrigan removed his Kevlar and shirt and repeatedly rubbed the four red and purple spots that burned his body like fire. "Some of these vests are better than others. This one will save your life but leave you wishing you were dead," he said. "But that's okay, 'cause the worse it hurts the madder I get." Kerrigan stepped over to Wallace who began backing toward the wall. Ripping off the tape he removed the handkerchief he had used to gag his prisoner.

"I guess we won't be needing this any longer. So, who was in charge around here, you or her? It sounded to me like she was the one giving the orders."

Theodore Wallace made no attempt to answer. Kerrigan looked around the room at the myriad of apparatuses spread out across the basement floor.

"I have no idea what you guys do down here, but I'll tell you what I see. I see a man who is going to tell me everything he knows by the time I get done experimenting with all this equipment, just for the fun of it. So, you can either talk now, or later, it's up to you."

Wallace looked around the room and then back at Kerrigan. His eyes expressed fear, but evidently not enough to start him talking. Kerrigan grabbed him and dragged him toward a chain that hung from the ceiling. It had two hooks on the end. The lieutenant placed the hooks under Theodore's armpits. An electric motor powered a winch connected to the chain. Kerrigan flipped the switch and Theodore Wallace slowly ascended to the ceiling.

"I'll see you in a little while, Theo. I'm going to exercise a search warrant that I have somewhere and have a look around the place. Seeya later."

Lieutenant Kerrigan returned to Theodore Wallace's office where he continued searching through his file drawers. All the incriminating evidence was there, in plain sight, including the address of the orphanage.

Kerrigan also searched the rest of Wallace's home. From the downstairs to the old woman's upstairs bedroom, where he soon discovered that the old lady whom he had thought was Theodore's wife was really his sister, and more than that, the master-mind behind the business of trafficking children. Among her personal belongings Kerrigan found several stacks of letters…intimate letters, dating back twenty years and more, from none other than the prophet himself.

A knock on the door startled the lieutenant. He set aside the evidence and drew his weapon. Silently he crept to the front door. Having already been shot four times in one day, Kerrigan very carefully threw open the door as he jumped to the side. To his pleasant surprise, before him stood the man with the thousand-yard stare.

The two men stared at each other for a long moment without speaking, guns drawn, and pointed—at each other.

"I thought I told you I didn't need your help." Kerrigan said, holstering his weapon.

The man called Morgue grunted, holstered his weapon, and said, "As long as I'm being paid to do this job you ain't got no say in the matter. Now, how can I help?"

Kerrigan considered for the first time that maybe he actually did need some help, and that if it hadn't of been for Lou Worley he might even be dead right now. And this man called Morgue, who was so insistent on protecting him, might be useful after all.

"Come on in, Mr. Morgue. I do have something you can do for me." Kerrigan led Morgue through the house to the closet stairs that led down to the basement. "There's a fellow down there hanging from the ceiling. He needs your help remembering some information that will come in handy if we're going to apprehend everyone involved in this human trafficking scam going on around here. I was thinking you might be just the man for the job." A big smile came across Morgue's face.

"That's no problem, Lieutenant." Morgue started down the stairs.

"Oh, and while you're here, maybe you could watch this place for a while for me. If anyone comes around that looks like they might be part of this ring of scumbags, put a bullet into their heads and stack their bodies in the basement. I have to go find me a prophet."

Morgue looked at Kerrigan, not sure if he was serious or trying to be funny.

"This won't take long. If you want to wait a few minutes, I'll go with you."

Kerrigan thought, *This might be worth sticking around for-*"All right, I'll be upstairs looking around." Kerrigan continued to pour through the stacks of boxes and files stored throughout the house. Finally, he stepped out onto the back porch and realized there was a garage in the back at the end of the driveway. He approached the garage door and looked in. There was the SUV that belonged to Jerod. Suddenly, Morgue stepped out onto the back porch.

"Are you ready to go, Lieutenant?"

"Yeah, sure. By the way, how did you know how to find me?"

"I asked a fella real nice."

"What fella?"

"A fella that works at the Department of Social and Health Services in Anchorage."

"You asked real nice?"

"Yes, sir. Real nice fella. Told me everything I needed to know, just like that nice fella in the basement. So I'm ready whenever you are."

"So how did you get here from the airport?"

"Another real nice fella gave me a ride."

"It must be nice to know so many nice fella's. I didn't know there were that many nice fella's in the whole world."

"Maybe you don't know them like I do. Deep down inside, everyone is itching to tell you everything they know, that is, if you know how to ask them."

"I see," Kerrigan said. "I can think of one more fella who might like to spill his guts too. Maybe he'll turn out to be just as nice, and maybe you're just the guy to talk to him."

"I'll be glad to talk to him." Morgue smiled again.

"Why don't you go get your friend down there in the basement and bring him along? I think he might enjoy the trip."

Moments later Kerrigan backed the Toyota Land Cruiser out of the garage. Morgue was waiting, with the nice fella from the basement.

Kerrigan rolled down his window, "Mr. Morgue, there's a rental car out front. I need you to drive it back to the FBO at Fairbanks where I rented it. We'll turn it in there and wait for Eric to come up here in his jet and take us back to Kake. Can you do that for me?"

Morgue looked at Kerrigan suspiciously, "Okay. But I'll take this nice fella with me just in case you plan on giving me the slip again."

"Whatever you want. Just don't get lost. I need both of you guys with me when I go see the prophet."

"We'll be there, Lieutenant. You go ahead. I'll follow you."

CHAPTER 17

"Rudy, you better get your life preserver on. And be sure you have your weapon with you. I'm going to have to dead stick this thing onto the ocean and it's possible we could find ourselves upside down in the water."

Rudy let go of the yoke and turned in his seat. He grabbed two life vests and a floatation emergency kit.

"Make sure we got extra ammo. We may need it. It looks like that green monster is going down on the same island we're headed for." I pointed out of the windscreen at the dark-green De Havilland Beaver rapidly descending into the trees at the far west end of Turnabout Island.

I made one last glance at the green monster as he pancaked into the dense forest of pine and disappeared from sight. In front of me I could see the line of the waves. Fortunately, they were moderate in size. I lined up as parallel as I could and waited until the floats were about to touch the top windward side of the front wave, and flared as hard as I could.

For a brief moment the aircraft paused, suspended in space like a high fly ball at the apex of its journey to the second-level bleachers. Then it hit. Instantly, the aircraft became a boat. Without power and very little rudder. I struggled to keep the nose high and the wings out of the water. Fortunately, we had touched down on the perfect side of the wave. By the time the aircraft rolled over the top and started down the leeward side, the forward speed had all but dissipated. I extended the water rudders and stuffed right rudder. As the airplane rolled off the wave and turned its back to the wind, the right wing dipped into the sea only to emerge again as the aircraft leveled itself. We had survived a catastrophic mid-air collision. But unlike any other midair, this one was attempted murder, and for the second time in one day, Rudy and I were the ones the green monster driver had attempted to kill.

"Rudy, there's a four-man raft in the back. Open that side door behind you and throw it out. Just be sure you attach a line to it before you do. I'll be there in a minute."

I reached in my pocket for my cell phone. It wasn't there. I looked around but didn't see it close by, so I unbuckled my seat-belt. Taking one last look at the damaged Kodiak, I clenched my jaw and prepared to abandon the aircraft.

The emergency raft exploded into a boat the moment Rudy pulled the ring. It was supposed to be designed to hold four people but between Rudy and myself, it already seemed overly inhabited. Maybe it was due to the fact that I had tossed a couple of additional emergency packs into the raft that included: water, sleeping bags, military rations, gas stove, cooking utensils, an assortment of dehydrated foods, thermal blankets, a six-man tent, and raingear, and of course, my 10-gauge shotgun and .44 Magnum Desert Eagle.

I couldn't help but recall a similar situation I had found myself in back in '95'. Since that incident I had become a fanatic about packing emergency provisions. Fortunately for us, we didn't have to dive to the bottom of Fredrick Sound to retrieve it.

Because the radios had become in-operable as a result of the impact, probably because the antennas had been broken off, I immediately dialed in the emergency code: 7777 on the aircraft transponder. I also activated the emergency locator transmitter (ELT). Therefore, I knew that sooner or later, someone would find my beloved Quest Kodiak. I knew too that they would contact Search and Rescue who would in turn contact the NTSB. Of course, my airplane would be towed to the nearest port—probably Kake, Alaska—and from there it would take a ride on a barge to Juneau where the investigators would thoroughly examine it to determine the cause of the accident.

I also fully expected that before too long a search would be conducted for the pilot of the aircraft and any potential passengers. Of course I could save them all a lot of time and trouble by staying with the aircraft until someone showed up, but we had bigger fish to fry—with special emphasis on *BIG*.

Rudy rowed. I scanned the shoreline with my binoculars. There was not much in the way of a beach and I expected that trying to fight our way through the dense timber would not only be exhausting but noisy.

"Rudy, let's work our way around the west end of the island to the north side. Maybe there's a place we can beach our boat."

Rudy rowed, hard. I scanned, not so hard, but persistently.

"Mr. Worley, the longer we stay out on the water, the more apt it is that he spots us and if he has a high-powered rifle we could be sitting ducks out here."

"I know, Rudy. I thought of the same thing. The last I saw of him he had pancaked his airplane into the trees on the far west end of the island. If he survived, he might be searching the south shoreline to see what became of us. If he spots that Kodiak sitting out there, disabled, he'll know that we survived. And I'm sure he's smart enough to figure out which way we're headed, at least that's what I'm hoping for. On the other hand, it's possible he may not have survived the crash. I wouldn't count on it though."

"How long has it been since we went down?" Rudy asked.

"A couple of hours, I think. Why? Are you getting tired?"

"A little. But I'm okay, for now."

"Let me know if you want me to give you a break."

"That's okay, Mr. Worley. I'll be all right. You know, it almost seems…miraculous that we survived that midair. Do you think it was God that saved us?"

"I always believe that. No matter what happens I always believe that the Lord is right in the middle of everything I'm involved in, watching over me."

"I have to tell you, I wish I could believe that too, Mr. Worley."

"All it involves is a simple decision on your part. Are you interested in making that decision right now?"

"Well, I'd like to, but I'm not sure I know how."

"Well, remember earlier we talked about how God sent his only begotten Son into the world as a savior and substitute for mankind, bearing our sins and our sinful nature? Well, he, that is, Christ Jesus the Son of God took our sin, past, present and future, as well as the fallen sinful nature we inherited from the first Adam, and to the one who has made the decision to believe in Him, it means that Jesus Christ has taken not only the believers' sins, but the penalty as well. In 1 Peter 2:24 it is said, "Who his own self bare our sins in his own body on the tree." Therefore, it's simply a matter of deciding to believe God, at all times, in all places, and under all circumstances, no matter what."

"Does that include the one we're in right now?"

"Yes, it certainly does."

"Then do you believe we'll find this guy before he finds us?"

I put down my binoculars and studied Rudy. "I believe the Lord is with us in every venture. Even if this murderer finds us first, in the end, it will ultimately be turned into our favor."

"Did Jesus Christ take his sins too?"

I clenched my jaw, not sure I wanted to acknowledge what I knew was the fact of the matter. "Yes, he did. The Son of God bore the sins of the whole world. This monster, and every other monster that has ever lived included. However, that does not mean that they will be taken to heaven when the Lord comes. It only means that at some point in their lives they get the same opportunity to acknowledge the light that is in them that you or I get."

"What light?"

"John 8:12 says: That Jesus Christ is the light of the world, and in John 1:9 it says that: "…that light was the true light that lighteth every man that cometh into the world."

"Then why is he doing these evil things?"

"Maybe because he has never heard of the light and he can't help himself. Some peoplel life styles have practically extinguished their light, until sin and evil have such complete control over them they no longer are able to know the difference between right and wrong, much less able to choose between the two. I'm sure that at some point in his life he so completely grieved the Spirit of God, so completely ignored the influence of the spirit through his conscience, that the Spirit of God no longer had any influence upon him. Maybe as a young child, maybe as a young man. I don't know. This is called the un-pardonable sin. It is when the individual no longer can hear the voice of God speaking to him; that voice that says to him, as in Isa 30:21, 'And thine ears shall hear a word behind thee, saying. This is the way, walk ye in it, when ye turn to the right hand, and when ye turn to the left.'"

Rudy thought for a long time before answering. Then remarked, "So, are you saying there is no hope for him? Does that mean he is completely beyond saving?"

"I can't judge that, Rudy. Only God can. But let me ask you this. Do you find it hard to believe that God has forgiven you of all your sins? Do you find it hard to believe that through Grace, by faith, your sins have been transferred to another, and the righteousness of Jesus Christ Himself has been transferred to you? That is the exchange that takes place the moment one believes. Do you find it difficult to believe? So difficult in fact that you still, even this vary minute, struggle with the idea of giving your whole heart to him in faith?" Rudy looked up and fastened his eyes on mine.

"Yes, I suppose that is true."

"Let me ask you this, Rudy, how many people have you murdered and raped in your lifetime?"

"None. I have only killed if I had no choice. Like when I had to take out Old Man Perkins before he blew your head off."

"Exactly. Don't you see, Rudy, the longer a man puts off making the decision, the harder it is to make. Suppose I was having this conversation with the green monster driver. How likely would it be that he would be considering the same thing you are considering this moment?"

"Not very likely, I'm sure."

"I'm sure too. That's why I have no qualms about taking him out the first chance I get, just like I know you would do if you get the chance. But the question is, what if he gets you first? Are you going to take a chance on facing this killer without having made a decision for Christ?"

"I see what you mean, Mr. Worley. I do want to make it. In fact, I want to make it right now. But I don't know what to say."

"Then repeat after me, Rudy. God in heaven…"

"God in heaven…"

"And Father of our Lord Jesus Christ…"

"Father of Christ…my Lord"

"I believe that you, oh God, who has given up your Son, for us all… will, with him, freely give us all things."

"I believe—"

WHUMP. The rifle shot sounded like two railroad cars slamming together, a mile away. Instantly, I dove for the bottom of the life raft.

"Where did that come from, Rudy?" I waited, but there was no answer.

"Rudy!" I raised my head enough to see Rudy's slender frame slumped over the side of the boat. I grasped his arm and pulled him back into the raft.

"Oh, my Lord!" I gasped. Blood and grey matter oozed from a large, circular, open wound in the side of Rudy's head where the bullet had exited. "Oh, my Lord, my God, have mercy on his soul."

Sheepishly, I peered above the side of the raft, only enough to search the shoreline for any sign of the shooter. I saw nothing, but I knew that the shooter was not done yet. Out of sight, hidden in the thick forest of trees, he was waiting for me to make my own fatal mistake.

I frantically searched through one of the emergency packs for something I could throw over the raft to conceal it. Finally, I found a grey rain fly. This is perfect, the same color as the water. Maybe this will make this raft disappear.

WHUMP. Again a deafening rifle-report echoed across the water.

I found the rain fly and began to spread it over the orange raft only to discover that the raft was deflating itself of air. He shot the raft. Oh well, only one of the air compartments will deflate. I continued to search for something, anything, that would conceal my face. I found a black-cold-weather, woolen pullover and pulled it on over my head. Slicing a hole in the rain fly, I poked my camouflaged head through to the open air. Staying a couple of hundred yards away from shore, I began to row—hard, toward the north side of the island.

The partially inflated raft rode barely above the surface of the water. The action of the waves left me concealed half the time and exposed the other half. In addition, the excess drag of the deflated compartment slowed my progress through the water, quickly sapping my strength.

As far as I could tell the shot had come from the west shoreline. Maybe even the southwest corner of the island. Maybe, just maybe, I could make it to the north shore before the shooter could thrash his way through the forest of dense trees and blowdowns.

I rowed. And I prayed, that I had become invisible. The waves on the north side of the island were larger and I fought against the current to keep from arriving at the shoreline too soon. Finally, I reached the point where I felt safe enough to bring the raft into shore. At last, the current was working in my favor.

I found a small but well-concealed inlet. Furiously I worked to stow the raft and the supplies that we had retrieved from the Kodiak. I looked at Rudy. Tears began to well up in my eyes. I picked up his lifeless body and, placing it behind a log, concealed it with leaves, boughs, and moss. With the Desert Eagle strapped to my waist, I picked up the 10-gauge shotgun and began a slow and deliberate course toward the killer's last known position. With my pockets full of extra ammo, I checked the firearms which now included Rudy's sidearm as well as my own, to ensure that they were loaded.

"Lord God in heaven," I prayed. "I have never felt so vulnerable going up against a criminal as I do this moment. I have killed a lot of men in my life. All in defense of either country, home, or family, but I have never felt this inadequate, until now. God help me. This man is so filled with evil no mere man could ever stop him. Oh God, I need the same divine strength you gave to David the day you delivered the giant, Goliath, into his hand."

Suddenly I stopped. From far away I could hear a helicopter. The familiar sound of an Sikorsky told me that Search and Rescue had arrive at the scene of my abandoned ship.

"Somebody must have found the Kodiak and called it in." I whispered to myself.

The forest was so thick I had no visual of anything but the cluster of scrub trees and deadfalls surrounding me. It was impossible to move through without making noise, noise that could give away my position to the most dangerous individual I had ever encountered in my life.

Ten minutes later, another aircraft, a fixed-wing, arrived from the southwest. Possibly the north shoreline of Kupreanof Island. It began to circle the same area. Must be a floatplane, I mused. Sounds like it's setting up to land on the water.

That could be Rusty. Sounds like a 185. But where would Rusty get a float plane? He took Shirley Crowder to Juneau in the Twin Cessna 421...

The floatplane landed on the water and the sound of the engine was no longer detectable.

"Beltray Gibbons," I whispered. I'll bet Rusty got Beltray to bring him up from Juneau. But why? How could he have heard about our mid-air so soon? Suddenly I realized I was letting the outside distractions distract me. Get your mind back in the game, Worley. Only one thing was important, kill the killer before the killer kills you.

I kept moving steadily toward the west end of the island from where the rifle shots had come.

It was slow going, due to the downed trees, and I had to work along as silently as I could to keep from being detected. Suddenly, within twenty minutes of hearing the floatplane land, I heard it takeoff again. I listened as it turned northwest toward Turnabout Island. It *is* Rusty. He has figured it out and is coming to get me.

The noise of the aircraft's engine grew louder the closer it came. I moved faster, hoping that the extra noise of the engine would cover the additional noise I was making as I thrashed my way through the woods.

The aircraft was above me now, circling a second time and then a third, as if the pilot knew exactly where I was. I had no phone and didn't expect that there would be a signal on this remote island even if I had.

Then I realized, they're circling over the downed green monster. It has to be Rusty. He saw the damaged roof and the props and figured the green monster had gotten his floats mixed up in the propeller, and figured out that the pilot's only chance of survival would be to pancake the plane into these trees. My son-in-law is one smart guy. Praise the Lord.

I searched through the tops of the trees to catch a glimpse of the airplane. Suddenly, there it was, a red and white Cessna 185 on floats. The same airplane I had purchased for William Shearer over fifteen- years before. Right after he had mangled his little Piper Clipper on the Yukon River north of Fairbanks in an attempt to dead stick into a gravel bar.

I was one of the pilots that joined the search for Bill Shearer and after finding the missing pilot I took him to Anchorage where I purchased that very same 185 and put it into his name. Bill signed over the Clipper to me and shortly after, I had it refurbished. Years later, after Bill Shearer was murdered and after Beltray Gibbons became a minister of the gospel, Pastor Bill's wife, Sharon, donated the big Skywagon to Beltray and his ministry. It's funny how things come around in life. All these many years later, that same Skywagon was now circling above my head, to rescue *me*.

I continued in the direction where the Skywagon had been circling. By the time I arrived at the crash site of the green monster, the Skywagon had already headed east along the north shoreline. The sound of the engine faded until I could no longer hear it and concluded that Rusty and Beltray may have headed back to Juneau, or Kake, for the night. I looked at my watch. It was getting late and I was not only wet but had made no shelter for the night. The tent I had brought along was back where I had stashed the raft. Then it occurred to me, I was already looking at shelter.

Carefully I examined the crashed de Havilland Beaver. The pilot had slowed the aircraft as slow as possible, barely above a stall, until mere feet above the trees, at which time he pulled the nose up abruptly, forcing the aircraft into a full stall; resulting in the aircraft descended straight down, settling into the tops of the mass of scrub trees. The pilot's skill resulted in dramatically reducing the forward momentum of the aircraft, leaving the floats to absorb the majority of the impact. Although the wings were ripped entirely off the airplane, they absorbed the remainder of the impact and were shredded like logs shoved through a debarker. The smell of fuel drenched the air although it was obvious at the last second the pilot had shut off the fuel selector valve and master switch in an effort to avoid fire, or the entire place would have already been devoured in flames.

Amazingly, the fuselage remained intact. A perfect shelter for the night. Only one question remained to consider: did the murdering killer of little girls who had also just killed my partner intend to come back? I decided to stay, just in case he did. Crawling into the mangled cabin of the Beaver, I worked my way to the extreme rear baggage compartment. I could barely remember the last time I had had anything to eat. It was right after Rudy had killed the old man to keep him from blowing my head off with his shotgun. While searching his house of horrors, we found Lieutenant Kerrigan locked in a makeshift jail cage in Old Man Perkins's basement. While we were upstairs, bringing Kerrigan up to speed on the latest developments, Rudy found a loaf of bread and some ham and cheese, and made us all sandwiches. That was two days ago.

The back of the fuselage was a filthy pig pen. I tried not to imagine what kind of creepy crawly things might be creeping and crawling on my person by morning. But somehow I felt that a man as large as my killer must be living on a steady diet of something, so I searched for anything I could find that might be edible.

Under a cowling blanket I discovered a cooler full of stale bread, dried ham, moldy cheese, and beer. Beside it was a recently opened case of Copenhagen chewing tobacco and a pair of steel fish fillet gloves. I paused to examine them. Sure enough, buried in the metal strands were the fractured remnants of someone's fingernails. "DNA evidence" I muttered to myself.

I searched through the garbage can that at one time resembled an airplane and found a plastic food container full of empty beer cans, all of which were missing their tabs. The bottom of the container flowed in tobacco juice, mixed with spittle.

I looked at the food first, then the contents of the plastic container. Saliva began to fill my mouth as the nausea welled from the pit of my stomach upward. I knew I had about one second before I would puke my guts all over my bedroom. Making a mad dash for the open side door, I thrust my head over the edge outside. Standing on the limb of a tree, directly below, was a large, bearded man clothed in a dirty torn uniform, a scoped, high-powered rifle slung over his shoulder only seconds away from climbing into the airplane. Startled, he looked up at me, his mouth wide opened in abject surprise. By now the nausea had reached critical mass and the contents of my stomach, which was mostly bile, erupted like a waterfall, directly into his gaping pie hole.

I was as surprised as he. I wiped my sleeve across my mouth and jumped to my feet. Pulling the .44 Magnum Desert Eagle from its side holster, I peered again through the door. The big man in the uniform had fallen off the limb onto the ground and was frantically attempting to shoulder the large-caliber rifle. Quickly, I squeezed off the first round. The wooden stock exploded in his hands and he dropped the shattered rifle. Rolling to his right side he drew a handgun and turned toward me, still spitting out the contents that had moments before been in my stomach. I squeezed off two more rounds as, simultaneously, three flashes of light blinked at me from his right hand.

I didn't recall the bullets hitting the fuselage next to me, but I do recall the one that hit me in the arm. My right arm dropped and the

Desert Eagle fell to the ground below. Immediately I lunged back into the fuselage to retrieve the 10-gauge shotgun lying behind me. Returning to the doorway I searched in every direction, but the killer of little girls had disappeared.

I knew now I was in real trouble. The killer had gained the advantage. He could be anywhere out there. I had destroyed his high-powered rifle, but he still had a handgun, maybe two of them. Maybe even another rifle. Far away I thought I heard someone holler, but it was distant and faint, and the wind in the tree-tops carried it away.

I leaned my head out the door to listen, and to see if I could spot the Desert Eagle. Maybe the killer had not seen it fall. I was certain the animal I was hunting would come back and I had no windows to watch through, so the option of spending the night in the fuselage was no longer an option. Besides, I was too close to the killer to stop now. But, to level the playing field, I had to get out of the aircraft.

Quickly I tore away the blood-soaked shirt sleeve from my arm and examined the wound. I was fortunate. The bullet had not hit the bone, but the flesh slightly above my right bicep was torn wide open and bleeding profusely. I bound the wound as tightly as I could and descended down the tree. On the ground next to a mangled portion of the left float assembly lay the .44 Magnum Desert Eagle. I breathed a sigh of relief and sent up a thank-you prayer to God, who had once again spared my life. A refreshed confidence came over me. Somehow, I knew today the killer of little girls was going to meet his timely end.

Beltray remained to guard the airplane while Rusty worked his way through the jungle of foliage south to the southern shoreline and then west toward the crash site. At first, the water's edge appeared to be the easiest progress until what little shore there was disappeared into extinction. Facing high vertical cliffs and shoreless inlets, Rusty was out of options.

Two hours had passed since he had begun his hike. Reluctantly Rusty abandoned the southern exposure and turned inland to the northwest where, though the terrain was steeper, there was less brush. However, blowdowns and deadfalls lay strewn about like spilled toothpicks, a testimony to the ferocious winds that continuously assault southeast Alaska during the winter months.

Rusty knew the north shoreline would be far friendlier for hiking. He knew this because he had studied both shorelines from the air. He also expected that the killer would be far more likely to search for him along the easiest route. His reasoning being whoever it was that was hunting him was in all likelihood greenhorns, city slicker cops who had no stomach for roughing it. Rusty knew this too. He knew it because he had learned it in combat, engaging an enemy that was born and raised in the mountains of Afghanistan, where, as an Army Ranger, he had been sent to hunt them down and kill them.

Suddenly, Rusty heard shots—three of them. Then three more in rapid succession, the first three had come from a large-caliber handgun. *That was my dad*, he thought. *I'll bet those shots came from his .44 Magnum.* Rusty began to move faster. Crashing through the downed trees like a mad bull. Completely disregarding the necessity for stealth he hollered, "Dad! Dad! Are you okay?"

I quickly cleaned and secured my weapon, and melted into the woods in the direction my instincts told me the killer had gone. Instincts based on evidence he had left deposited on the bushes as he continued to spit up the contents of my stomach. At least I wasn't hungry anymore.

Minutes later I heard it again. Only this time it was closer and I was sure I recognized it. I was so excited to hear his voice, I wanted to answer, to holler back as loud as I could, but I knew the killer would hear me. I kept moving. I can't take a chance on the killer hearing me. Rusty will have to find me on his own. I have to stay on this killer. He may be heading for the airplane. The thought was so loud in my mind I was not sure if I had thought it, or screamed it..

The sound of Rusty's voice came from the southeast. The killer was headed more to the east and northeast. If Rusty landed somewhere on the north side of the island, why was he approaching from the southeast?

Suddenly, something occurred to me. It had been right in front of my face and I had missed it. The uniform. The killer was wearing a uniform. Where have I seen that uniform before? "Sitka," I said out loud. "I remember him. He's one of Borski's men." I stopped, frozen in my tracks, searching my mind for a face recognition. Somewhere, I know I've seen that face. For a moment I forgot where I was and what I was doing as I struggled to recall the face of the killer of little girls. Suddenly it hit me, the hospital. He was the new recruit I saw at the station, and the one guarding the door to the girl's room, that poor girl I brought down off the hill.

The anger returned. I called out, "Parker! Patrolman Ralph Parker!" I yelled again, "Parker! Officer Ralph Parker. If you can hear me, I know who you are. If you give yourself up I can guarant—" Pop,pop,pop. Splinters exploded off the tree next to me. I instantly dove for cover.

The shots came from only a couple of dozen yards away. "I don't want to kill you, Parker. But I will if you don't give yourself up. Come out now, and you won't die today. If you don't give yourself up now, today will be your last day on earth."

Suddenly, I heard something crashing through the brush toward me. I raised the 10-gauge and switched off the safety. "Dad, is that you?" Rusty hollered.

"I'm over here, son." I said. "Stay down, he just shot at me again, so he's not far away."

A moment later Rusty appeared from behind me. He whispered, "Dad, you have no idea how glad I am to find you. Are you all-right? What happened to your arm? Where's Rudy?"

"I'm fine, except that guy we're after nicked me." I adjusted the rag I had tied around my upper right arm. "Rusty, I know who he is. Do you remember the patrolman at the hospital that Borski assigned to guard the girl?"

"Yeah, I heard you hollering at him. So, what makes you think that's him?"

"Because I got a good look at him, and he's wearing his Sitka police uniform, badge and all."

"Which way did he go?"

"Where's your airplane? I'm sure he heard you come in and is working his way toward it. Probably figures he can make off with it and leave us on this island without any transportation. By the way, where's Gibbs? Is he with you?"

"Yeah, I left him to guard his 185. There's only one problem, all he has is a little .22 rifle, and I'm not sure he would even use that."

"A… .22 rifle?"

"Yeah. We need to spread out and keep moving, Dad. We don't want this guy getting back to the airplane without us. Where did you say Rudy is?"

I knew that was coming. I tried to ignore it the first time he asked, but nothing gets by my son-in-law.

"Parker killed him, Rusty. Shot him in the side of the head with a high-powered rifle while we were rafting our way over here from the Kodiak."

Rusty didn't respond. I looked around for him but he was gone.

Beltray Gibbons pulled the small book of New Testament scriptures, from the inside pocket of his jacket. Turning to the fifteenth chapter of John, he began to read, pausing momentarily over verse 5, he whispered it aloud, "I am the vine, ye are the branches: He that abideth in me, and I in him, the same bringeth forth much fruit: for without me ye can do nothing."

Pastor Beltray Gibbons pondered the words, reflecting upon his own experience since he had received the Lord Jesus Christ into his life. At first it all seemed surreal. But now, his experience as a branch had become so dependent on the Vine of Christ, he could imagine no other way to live. He read further, on to the end of verse 7.

"If ye abide in me, and my words abide in you, ye shall ask what ye will, and it shall be done unto you."

Immediately another scripture came to his mind; verse 27 in the previous chapter, a verse that had kept him through so many difficulties and perplexities since his spiritual walk began over five years before. He turned to it. Pastor Beltray Gibbons, again whispered the last part of the verse, "Let not your heart be troubled, neither let it be afraid." Raising his hands toward heaven, he prayed, "God, my father. Father of our Lord Jesus Christ. You who have given him up for us all, how would you not with him, freely give us all things, Lord, I am saved only by your grace. I pray to you in Jesus name. The name before which every knee shall bow and every tongue shall confess, that he is Lord and Christ and King. It is your grace, oh God, it is only by your grace, to me, through your Son, Jesus. Like a river flowing into the ocean of humanity, his abundant Grace flows into me and through me. Deliver me oh my God, this day, from the evil one. Deliver those that are with me this day who seek to stop this man who has so consented with evil that it should reside within him to such a despicable measure. God, have mercy on his soul. Rebuke the devourer for Jesus sake. Deliver this poor soul, oh God, into my hands that he might have one last chance to choose life. Restore in him that, that the locusts have eaten, in Jesus name, Amen. Praise you, oh God. Let the name of the Lord be magnified though all the heavens and the earth, for all ages to come, for thy name sake. Amen, and Amen."

Beltray's eyes remained closed for several more moments as he reflected on the power of the Spirit of God flowing through him. Slowly he opened his eyes. Setting aside the rifle that lay across his lap, he rose to his feet. Suddenly, he heard a thump on the ground. Like something or someone had jumped and landed heavily on the earth nearby.

He looked up and there before him, barely twenty yards away, stood a man wearing the uniform of a police officer. The scent of tobacco juice pervaded the air. Dirty and disheveled, his uniform appeared tattered, torn, and wrinkled. Dark stains the color of dried blood stood out on his clothing. He was a huge man, intimidating. But Beltray knew him as the one he had seen several times at the floatplane dock in Juneau. He studied the man's eyes, looking deep into them for some indication that some remnant of a soul remained that might be saved. To every other human eye, both body and mind had been completely given over to the resident evil. Yet Beltray saw something in him. Something that reminded him of…himself, nearly twelve-years ago."

The killer of little girls looked into Beltray's eyes and stepped closer. Grinning, he pointed to the aircraft and said to him, "Are the keys in the ignition?"

Beltray stared back at the man. As he nodded his head he took several steps toward him. The big man's grin disappeared as he realized the little man before him was unafraid.

The big man snarled, "You're about to die, little man."

"Beltray stopped. Looking into the man's eyes he spoke; not to the murderer, not to the killer of little children, but to the 'new-creation-inner-man, the last vestige of his soul, once inherent in the giant flesh that threatened him, the *inner one*, whom the Lord Jesus Christ had come, shed His blood, and died to redeem. To him he addressed the words of Romans 4:7, "Blessed are they whose iniquities are forgiven, and whose sins are covered."

The killer of little girls grew ashen. His huge arms reached for the sky, like a giant gorilla grasping at a vine above him. The killer's face turned to rage. He shuddered and shrieked like a giant gorilla. The chilling scream resonated against the mountains, echoing for miles across the southeastern Alaska Sound.

Beltray stepped closer. Now, a mere four feet separated him from the murderer. Raising his hands to the heavens he addressed the evil spirit that had long ago taken possession of the man who had become the killer of little girls.

Beltray pointed his finger at the man's chest and spoke directly to the demon. "I know who you are," he said, with an authority that came not from mere, humanity. "In the name of Jesus Christ the Son of the Living God, I command you, leave him."

Instantly, the huge man fell backward to the ground. Thrashing and moaning, he clawed at the sand and gravel, beating himself with the rocks and chunks of driftwood that lay nearby.

Stepping closer, Beltray reached down and placed his hand on the man's head. The killer of little girls stopped thrashing and relaxed under his touch. "Peace I leave with you, my peace I give unto you: Let not your heart be troubled, neither let it be afraid."

I froze as I stepped from the forest into the opening of the marshy inlet. There, sitting on a log a mere fifty yards away, sat Beltray Gibbons with his arm around Officer Ralph Parker. Parker's head was buried in his hands while Beltray held him close with his right arm.

I placed the 10-gauge shotgun against my shoulder and aimed it at Ralph Parker's back while I slowly advanced. A moment later I saw Rusty standing in the shadows of the trees. He saw me too, and held his finger over his lips.

I stopped and looked again at Pastor Gibbons. He was praying, and he was praying for the man I had come to kill.

CHAPTER 18

Eric sat in the pilot's lounge of the school's maintenance facility in Sitka. For the thirteenth time he flipped the lid closed on his phone in a failed attempt to contact Mr. Lou Worley. Suddenly, his phone began to buzz. Eagerly he looked for the name on the display. Disappointment was temporarily relieved as he recognized Kerrigan's phone number.

"Lieutenant! I've been trying to call you."

"Sorry about that. We got cut off. Did you get my message?"

"Nothing yet. When did you send it?"

"Doesn't matter now. How long will it take you to get back up here to Fairbanks?"

"I'm not sure. The Citation is in maintenance at the moment. Can you wait until they finish?"

"When will that be?"

"Maybe three or four more hours, plus flying time from Sitka."

"Where's Worley?"

"I don't know. I've been trying to get hold of him all day, left several messages and called at least a dozen times, but haven't heard back. I'm beginning to get concerned."

"What about his son-in-law, what's his name?"

"Rusty German?"

"Yeah…where's he at?"

"The last I heard he was on his way to Juneau with some lady from the cult compound. Evidently she's a material witness. He was flying the twin Cessna 421 that belongs to the cult leader. Are you at the Metro FBO?"

"I will be by the time you get here. I got Mr. Morgue with me, along with another fellow. I guess you could say he's a material witness too. At any rate, we need a ride down to Kake. I need to see that cult leader guy that claims to be a prophet. Him and me need to have a talk."

"Mr. German's Cessna 206 is over at the school's airport. I can get a ride over there and come up to get you. It will take a little longer, but it's better than nothing."

"How long?"

"Probably five hours. Give or take."

"Go for it. We'll be at Jerod Aiken's FBO."

It was nearly midnight, well after dark, by the time Eric picked up his three passengers in Fairbanks and arrived back at the Sitka airport. Eric taxied to the maintenance facility and tied down on the ramp. A hundred yards away sat Worley's CJ4 Citation directly in front of the maintenance building.

"Eric, are you staying here tonight, or are you taking that Citation back to Anchorage?" Kerrigan asked.

"I'll stay here, but I'll sleep in the jet. What will you guys do?"

"Do you suppose that apartment Worley gave me is still available?"

"Do you still have the key?" Eric asked.

"No. I left it on the bed the last time I was there."

"I could call Mrs. Williams. I'm sure she would find you something. Or you could stay in the pilot lounge at the school FBO. They have some basic accommodations for transit pilot's. There are shower facilities and several couches to sleep on, along with vending machines full of snacks. If you want, you can use one of those courtesy vans sitting over there." Eric pointed to the three white crew van parallel parked next to the maintenance facility. "The ignition key should be under the mat."

"All right, we'll do that. Mr. Morgue and I can take turns watching our friend here. If you're still around in the morning, we'll need a ride over to the Kake airport. I guess we'll have to walk once we get there, but at least we'll be there."

"What time do you want me to meet you here?"

"What time does that school cafeteria open in the morning? We'll want to have breakfast before we leave."

"It gets light about four AM, so I'll fly the 206 over to the school around six and we can all go to breakfast together."

"That works for me. See you then," Kerrigan replied.

Darkness settled in on the north-shore of Turnabout Island. Rusty and I sat around a campfire, visiting with Pastor Beltray Gibbons. His new convert, Officer Ralph Parker, sat quietly on a log nearby.

As the day gave way to night, dark clouds began to surround the tiny island.

"Storm coming in," I said leisurely. Within minutes, strong winds, growing rapidly in intensity, threatened to tear every tree on the island from its roots. Yet, for some strange reason, the place where we sat around our campfire seemed eerily unaffected, like it existed in a capsule, completely insulated from the storm.

Unable to sleep, I watched the water level rise as the tide continued to creep in. Several times during the night, I got up to check on the aircraft. Beyond the inlet, the frantic winds churned the water into gigantic waves, smashing against the distant shoreline as if for some demonic reason they intended to demolish the entire island. Yet the inlet where we camped remained curiously calm.

Rusty and Beltray slept comfortably in the airplane while I watched my prisoner. Did I say *prisoner*? From every visible perspective, Parker no longer appeared to be a threat, to himself or anyone else. None-the-less, I watched him as he sat quietly starring into the fire. I had no idea what he was thinking. He had little to say. Occasionally he would wag his head and mumble, almost as if he were, praying.

Rusty and I had been witness to a remarkable event. A transformation of epic proportions had taken place in the killer of little girls, a transformation that, for the average person, might be a bit much to believe. However, I too am a Christian, and can remember clearly the experience that brought me to the place where I first became a believer. Although Ralph Parker's experience may have been somewhat more dramatic from a visual standpoint, it certainly was no more miraculous. Anytime a lost soul, be it a murdering despot or an apparently, descent law-abiding individual, is transformed by the Spirit of God, from unbeliever, in the salvation of God provided through His Son Jesus Christ, to believer, it is a miracle of the highest order.

I expected the time would eventually come when Ralph Parker could give his own testimony in regard to being delivered from the demons that possessed him, possibly even remembering the evil deeds he had committed while under that demonic power. However, in the interim, certainly it would be in the best interest of him, and society, if he gave his testimony within the confines of a facility where he could remain safe from public retaliation. Without confiding with anyone other than Rusty and Beltray, I decided I would provide him that place; and because the man who actually did commit those atrocities was now—from a spiritual standpoint—dead, why would the world ever need to know what really happened to Officer Ralph Parker on Turnabout Island? It suddenly occurred to me how appropriate that name was.

Black, broken clouds still covered the sky. Soon the remnants of the storm that had tortured the island during the night would slowly give way to lighter skies in the east, revealing the damage caused by the storm. Like a graveyard, hundreds of trees that the day before stood straight and tall, today lay like matchsticks from one end of the island to the other.

"Did you notice anything, Pop?" Rusty asked as he and Beltray approached me from behind.

"Yeah, the airplane is right side up, with both wings still attached."

"Looks like the devil got pretty mad," Beltray said.

"What makes you think that?" Rusty asked.

"Because God snatched a doomed soul out of his grasp."

"What if he's faking it?" I asked, "He's not incapable of that, you know."

Beltray barely considered my question before answering. "What happened here last evening cannot be faked. The Spirit of God recognizes the Spirit of God, and when the testimonies of those two witnesses agree, you can be sure it is real."

"Are you saying he can be trusted now?"

"You should realize that at this point, he is pondering over the experience he has had."

"Do you mean he doesn't know what happened to him?"

Again, Beltray considered the question. "It is like the years of his life that he was possessed of the devil have become a bad dream to him, almost like a movie he saw a long time ago. At this moment, he is trying to understand who he is now. He's not sure what to do or where to go. He will need tutors to help him understand, tutors who will teach him from the scriptures *who* he now is, and *what* he now is, in Christ."

I remarked, "So, in other words, we'll have to give him an entirely new identity. Is that right?"

"That's right, Mr. Worley. Along with his new identity by faith in Christ, he will need a new identity literally, and to do that we will need to sequester him from the public and provide a safe sanctuary among believers who care, and who will accept him without regard for what he once was."

"I've been thinking about that," I said. "If we do this right, no one will ever need to know what he once was. What about putting him up in a secure apartment at the school? We could provide escorts or guards that could stay with him 24/7, and specially selected tutors that could instruct him spiritually. What do you say?"

"Sounds like a plan to me, Dad. I can find plenty of escorts."

"I can provide the tutors," Beltray said.

"Okay then. I don't want anyone to know what's happened here. And I mean no one. Not Kerrigan, not Eric, not anyone. We're going to make him a whole new person."

"That's exactly what the Lord has already done," Beltray said. "After all, according to the scriptures, he is now to be considered a new creation in Christ Jesus."

"Perfect," I said, "What shall we name him?"

Pastor Gibbs held his hands up to the sky, "Let's name him Ray Claimed, for he has been *re-claimed* by God through Jesus Christ our redeemer."

I looked over at Rusty. He nodded. "Then, Claimed it is. Ray Claimed. Has a sort of ring to it, don't you think?"

Beltray looked up at the steams of light emanating through the broken overcast.

"The name Ray is also appropriate for the rays of light that celebrate his new-birth."

"Sounds good to me," I said. "Rusty, will you get your people to make up new IDs for Mr. Ray Claimed? In the meantime, we'll keep him on ice. This is just between the three of us, agreed?"

"Agreed," Beltray said.

"Me too," Rusty added.

"All right then, let's pack up and get going. We can land on the school's float pond and walk up to the FBO. Rusty, you'll need to get hold of your two guys that are guarding the girl and transfer them over to their new job as *escorts*. Don't tell them anymore than you absolutely have to. If they ask, tell them Mr. Ray Claimed is under the witness protection program or something. Everyone who ever knew him as a killer is either dead or soon will be, so he should be able to have a brand new start."

"I got it, Dad."

"Once we get him squared away in a secure apartment, we can have breakfast and pay the prophet a visit."

"Dad, what about his job as patrolman for the Sitka Police Department? Shouldn't we let Borski know what happened?"

"No. We'll show him evidence that he was our killer and our story will be that he died in the airplane crash and his body was never recovered."

"Okay, Pop. If that's the way you want it. That's the way it will go down."

"Beltray, I hate to impose on you any further, but will you go with us to talk to this Mr. Morning that claims to be a prophet? If our new brother Ray was possessed of a demon, then the prophet is possessed of a hundred of them, and that's who we're going after next."

"I'll be happy to, Mr. Worley."

Suddenly I paused and turned to Beltray. "I hope you aren't planning to cast the demons out of him too."

Beltray turned to me with a look of surprise on his face. "If the Lord put it in me to pray for him, I would. When I was sitting, guarding the airplane, the Lord put it in my heart to pray for this man." Beltray pointed to the new man, Ray Claimed. "It was God who rebuked the demon, not me!"

"I know, Beltray. I'm just saying, I don't see this guy Morning as being savable, that's all."

"That is not up to man to decide. It is entirely up to God. This day, the Lord hath shown forth his grace, mercy and power to save the soul of one who appeared to man as, the most un-savable on earth. If the Lord decides to do the same with the false prophet, who are we to stand in his way? We can only stand back and watch the salvation of God as he chooses whom he wills to be with him in his kingdom."

"I understand where you're coming from, Pastor Gibbons. But don't forget what it says in Revelation about the 'false prophet' getting cast into the everlasting fires of hell, along with the devil and the beast he rode in on. I don't think we want to interfere with that either."

On the way back to Sitka, I sat in the right seat as Beltray's co-pilot, while Rusty sat in the back with our new spiritual brother, Ray Claimed.

I have to admit I still had mixed emotions about the man behind me. I do not deny that what had transpired in him spiritually was a miraculous thing, but it still didn't erase the feelings that churned inside me over his past, and especially what he had done to that girl, not to mention the butcher shop Rudy and I had discovered. That had to be the most demonic thing I had ever witnessed. Then again, maybe all that was the work of his kid sister that I had killed in the basement of Old Man Perkins's house. Either way, I easily sent up a thousand prayers for grace by the time we finally got the new man, Mr. Claimed, squared away in his new apartment.

It was early but I called Genneta Williams anyway. Without complaining about waking her at such an obscene hour, she provided us the same apartment she had designated for Kerrigan when we first arrived on the case. I chuckled as I imagined the look on his face were he to learn that the killer he had been sent to find was residing right under his nose, in his own apartment.

It had been a while since Rusty, or I, had been near a shower. So we took turns watching our new brother in Christ while we got cleaned up.

"Beltray, I have a beard trimmer in my overnight kit. Can you get Ray shaved and cleaned up? I'm going to see if I can find him some new clothes to put on."

"Sure thing, Mr. Worley."

I called Genneta again.

"Good morning, Mr. Worley. How can I help you?"

"Genneta, I hope I didn't wake you again, but I have an urgent problem. I need clothes for a man who we're holding in protective custody. He's big, real big, about six-foot-seven, and probably three-hundred pounds. Do you know anyone at the goodwill store you could call?"

"I do, Mr. Worley. We have a lot of cases that involve people who need clothing. I'll come up with something right away. Where do you want to meet?"

"Thank-you, Genneta. Just have them delivered to my apartment. I'll make sure someone is there to receive the items."

"I'm very glad to help, Mr. Worley."

When we landed at the school's floatplane waterway, I couldn't help but notice one of the maintenance shop's courtesy vans parked in front of the learning center FBO. Our plans had gotten a bit more complicated and no longer included time for breakfast at the school cafeteria. I decided to give them a call and have breakfast delivered. A good friend of mine, Steve Smith, ran the cafeteria from four AM till noon during the week. I first met Steve back in the days when we were mining at Alfred Creek. We hired him as the chief cook for our mess hall at the mine and I was impressed with how good the food was. So I gave him a call.

"Steve here. How can I help you, brother?"

"Steve, this is Lou Worley. Can you put together some breakfast takeout for four?"

"Sure can, Mr. Worley. Pick-up or delivery?"

"Delivery." I gave Steve directions to my apartment on the bottom floor of the men's dormitory and he said he would have someone there in thirty minutes.

I still hadn't heard from Kerrigan, but when I saw the courtesy van at the FBO it made me wonder if he might be back from Fairbanks. I decided to have a look.

The cafeteria is in the basement of the men's dormitory. Most everyone living in the dorm uses the stairs. Those coming from the outside enter from an outside entrance at the end of the building. I decided to use the elevator.

I punched the button marked 'B' and in three seconds the doors opened into a hall adjacent to the main entrance. Another ten paces and I was peering through the two-foot-square windows on the batwing, hinged swinging doors leading into the cafeteria. Three seconds later, I saw them. Lieutenant Mark Kerrigan, Morgue, Eric, and none other than Mr. Theodore Wallace.

I grinned. Kerrigan is actually a darn good detective, after all. Pushing my way through the swinging doors I headed straight for the chow line. As I passed by their table I said, "I need to talk to you boys, so don't go anywhere until I get back. I haven't eaten in two and a half days."

While I made my way through the line I gave Rusty a call. He answered on the first ring.

"Yeah, Pop."

"Rusty, I'm at the cafeteria. I ordered takeout for you guys. Steve will be sending it over shortly. Has Scarf and Tripod shown up yet?"

"Yeah, Pop. They just got here."

"Tell them to keep Mr. Claimed safe, in sight, and a secret, at all times. The only persons that are allowed access to him are you, me, and Beltray. Kerrigan and Eric are here, and it looks like they have Theodore Wallace with them. Evidently, Kerrigan was actually accomplishing something while we were chasing…well, you know."

"Okay, Pop. Do you want Beltray and me to come over?"

"No. You can stay where you are and get Scarf and Tripod lined out. I'll come by and get you when I leave here. I think Kerrigan is planning on paying the prophet a visit too. So we can all go together."

I stopped by Kerrigan's table and brought them all up to speed on the latest events involving our midair collision with the killer of little girls, including his crash, and demise, on Turnabout Island.

"He probably jumped out of the airplane when he realized he was going down," I said. "Only he was in such a hurry he must have forgot to put on his 'Mae West'. The currents during that storm last night probably carried his body half-way to Japan by now."

Eric's eyes grew wide in awe. Kerrigan looked at me and chuckled, while Morgue, stared. I knew instantly he didn't buy it. I also knew he didn't care. And it was me who was paying him plenty for not caring.

"I'm ready whenever you are," I said to Kerrigan. "I have to pick up Rusty and another fellow first. He's got a floatplane on the water runway next to the airstrip. The NTSB has my plane so we're stuck with him." I turned to Eric. "What are you flying?"

"Rusty's 206. The CJ4 was in the shop for service yesterday, so I took the Stationair to Fairbanks to pick up these men. We didn't get back until almost midnight."

"Really, you were flying in that storm?"

"What storm?"

"The storm that blew through here last night. It knocked down every tree on the island where we were staying."

"You must have had an awfully good tie down if it blew that hard, or your floatplane would be in Japan too," Kerrigan chimed in, still chuckling. I could tell Morgue wasn't buying that one either.

"We'll meet you guys over at Kake," I said.

"What do you have over there that we can use for transportation?" Kerrigan inquired.

"There's an old 1951 Dodge pickup sitting in Old Man Perkins's driveway that belongs to me. You can use that if you can fit into it."

"Is that the one you purchased with the money you confiscated out of Perkins's house?"

"Yeah, same one."

"What are you going to do with the money now that you've killed all his living relatives?"

"Not that it's any of your business, but I'm going to give it to his favorite charity."

"What would that be?" Kerrigan sneered.

"Like I said, it's none of your business."

Morgue was still staring, and still not buying. Shouldn't have even come in here. I could tell it was time for me to leave.

CHAPTER 19

On January 11, 1940, in Grindsted, Denmark, Anton and Anneliese Bielke welcomed into their world an eight-pound baby boy they named Anker. Anton was a minister of one of the mainstream protestant denominations that had established its religious roots throughout the majority of the civilized world. Hitler had already annexed Austria and the expectation was that he soon would invade Poland and Denmark. Anton Bielke sent several letters to his denominational headquarters, requesting that he and his family be provided visa's to the United States. By June 9, 1940 as Hitler moved into Denmark, baby Anker was happily bouncing on his father's knee in Loma Linda, California.

Raised in a highly conservative, religious family, Anker Bielke attended public school through the eighth grade, after which he worked as a colporteur, or literature evangelist, selling religious books to pay his tuition through their denomination's parochial academy.

The roots of the Bielke's denominational beliefs traced back to the early 1800's at a time when Christians pouring into the new land of America were spreading their wings of religious freedom. By 1844, hundreds of similar denominations had established theological foundation in the new land, each with historical roots tracing back to the early reformers that initially handed down to them the foundation of their particular teachings. For the Calvinist's it was the reformer John Calvin; or the Methodists, John Wesley; the Lutherans, Martin Luther; and so forth.

Other denominations originated from congregational divisions resulting from theological disputations, until hundreds of sects were born out of a relative few, dating as far back as the sixteenth century.

The command of the Lord, Jesus Christ, in Matthew 28:19, 20 to go forth into all the world and make *disciples* of *all* men, teaching them to observe all the things that their Lord had commanded them, compelled the various religious groups and denominations to not only make their way to the new world but to make converts of the indigenous peoples when they arrived. Regrettably, they failed to understand precisely *what* it was the Lord had actually commanded.

From the day Martin Luther first jumped for joy at the revelation that he had been saved by grace, through faith as a gift of God merely by believing, the gospel message of salvation by grace alone, plus nothing, began to spread.

Unfortunately, there is no monetary profit to be made in preaching a message that absolves the people of their sins and places their guilt and punishment upon another—even if that *other* is Jesus Christ the Lamb of God. Religionist's promptly recognized this and immediately began to amend the revelations of the reformers. Like an insidious leaven inserted into new bread, they added to the faith man's works, service, and confessions as complimentary necessities for salvation. Consequently, an admixture of law and grace, an amalgamation of works and faith, quickly corrupted the purity of the theological teachings handed down by the reformers, and subsequently the hundreds of sects and denominations that emerged from the dark ages into the eighteenth century.

Jesus taught that a new cloth cannot be sown onto an old garment, that you cannot put new wine into an old wine skin. Even the apostle Paul vehemently objected to the unforgivable sin of amalgamating the teachings of law and grace, declaring a double curse upon all who would pervert the pure teachings of the gospel.

Over 150 years later, since organized religion began to take root in America, Anker Bielke, like most of the spiritual conservative leaders of the time, held to this misguided interpretation of the scriptures. Seeking salvation through his own efforts, he tended strongly toward fanaticism. This fatal flaw continued to grow in intensity until the day he completely gave himself over to the ultimate deception, envisioning his mortal self, as the immortal, divine God incarnate.

Anker Bielke is not the only man who has made this blasphemous mistake. It originates from the fanatical misinterpretations of the simple doctrine of salvation by Grace alone, through faith. Simply put, that "God so loved the world that he gave his only begotten Son, that whosoever believeth in him should not perish, but have everlasting life."

This gospel, taught first by Jesus and then the apostle Paul and the disciples, teaches that as a believer in the finished work of Christ on the cross man is saved by one means only, the virtues of the life, death, burial, and resurrection of our Lord and Savior, Jesus Christ. That through faith in him and his *substitutionary* work on the cross, man *is* saved, not by human works, it is a gift of God.

The New Testament letters written by the greatest of all the apostles teaches that man is reconciled by the finished work of Christ on the cross and that he is complete in him who has shed his blood and died in the stead, and as a propitiation (mercy seat) for the sinner, and at the moment he believes, the inner man is "…made the righteousness of God in Him." It is then the work of the Spirit, not the flesh, that is responsible for working out the righteousness God has imputed (worked-in) by His Spirit. From the moment the believer's faith lays hold upon this gospel truth, that individual's relation to God is as a *partaker* of the Divine Nature. Romans 7:1-5 uses the analogy of a marriage between the woman (inner man) and the man (last Adam) Christ Jesus, the one who is seeking her hand in marriage.

The branch (the believer, or Church) is not the vine. The vine is the Lord, Jesus Christ. Though the vine delivers the life flowing sap (the Spirit) to the branch, it is the Spirit of Christ that is responsible for bringing forth the fruit of faith. It is always the vine (Jesus Christ) that is the source of the righteousness in the life of the believer. And as long as the believer is on this earth, there is never a time, place, or circumstance when the believer ever ceases being anything other than a sinner saved by grace.

The scriptures tell us that Jesus Christ, in his pre-Bethlehem eternal position as the Son of God, had many names, one of which was the *Bright and Morning Star*. Before his fall, Lucifer's given name had been *Son of the Morning*. So similar were these two names that Lucifer, the created general of all the host of heaven, confused himself to the point he actually came to consider himself an equal with the Creator, the Son of God *The Bright and Morning Star*.

Oftentimes this same deception takes place in fallen men when he reaches a point where his works and service to God become so valuable in his own eyes that he considers them as his right to heaven and if he has a right to heaven by his own works, then surely he must be not only a *partaker of divinity* but inherently possesses within him the very *source of divinity* as well. Convoluted? Absolutely. Sick? Of course. Demonic? The absolute epitome of it.

Over time, this delusion evolved in the mind of Anker Bielke until it reached its full maturation the day he changed his name to Joseph Morning, giving over his soul to the powers of evil, that his own body and mind might become the habitation of Satan.

I returned from the cafeteria and met up with Rusty and Beltray at the apartment. As we walked the one mile to the float plane waterway, we could hear Rusty's 206 Stationair warming up on the ramp, and watched as the big Cessna lifted into the air, disappearing into the glare of the rising sun.

"Was that Eric driving my 206?" Rusty asked.

"Yeah, he's got Kerrigan, Morgue, and Theodore Wallace with him. They're headed over to Kake to confront the prophet," I replied.

"What are they planning to use for transportation when they get there?"

"I told them they could use the old pickup. I figure we can borrow that Mercedes Rudy and Shirley brought down off the hill."

"Do you have the key?" Rusty asked.

"Right here in my pocket," I said, patting the breast pocket of my Carhart jacket.

We arrived at the float plane dock and waited as Beltray conducted his preflight ritual. Suddenly, my phone began to buzz.

"Hello, this is Lou Worley."

"Mr. Worley, this is Scarf. This guy that we're guarding wants to talk to you."

"Ray?"

"Yeah, hang on, I'll get him."

"Is this Lou Worley?"

I could barely recognize the voice of the new-man, Ray Claimed.

"Yes, I'm Lou Worley. How can I help you?"

"I'm not sure. I have a lot of questions and I don't understand what's happening to me. Who are these men that are here with me? And, where am I? What am I doing here?"

"Do you mean you don't remember?"

"Remember what?"

"Yesterday! Last night! This morning! How did you know to call me if you don't remember?"

"The men that are with me. They told me I should talk to you."

"Okay, just stay put, I'll be there shortly."

I turned to Rusty and Beltray and announced to them that we had to go back.

"What's going on, Pop?"

"I don't know, but it seems that the new Mr. Claimed is having a lapse of memory."

"Why is that important? Can't that wait until we get back?"

"Well, sooner or later we're going to need him to tell us what he knows. If he's going to conveniently have a case of amnesia, then I'm going to seriously question his 'new' state of mind."

"Mr. Worley," Beltray interjected. "If that were the case, why would he have bothered to tell you about it in the first place?"

"Point taken, Gibbs. But I want to talk to him just the same."

"Mr. Worley, before you go, I could use your help with something. The battery on the 185 seems to be low. I need to charge it up."

"Do you have a charger with you?" I asked.

"Yes, sir. But I don't have a cord that will reach that electrical box over there." Beltray pointed to an electrical outlet provided at the end of the dock. "It looks like I'll need about two-hundred feet of cord.

"I'll run up to the FBO. I'm sure they'll have a fully charged battery we can borrow."

I left Rusty and Beltray at the dock and walked back up to the FBO. A few minutes later I returned, dragging a 24-volt charger, mounted on a wheeled dolly, and two-hundred feet of electrical cord.

"No spare battery available, but I got this," I said. A few minutes later the charger was at work.

"I'll see you guys later. I'm going to go see what Ray wants."

"I'll go with you, Dad."

"Me too," Beltray insisted.

"Don't you want to stay with the aircraft?" I asked.

"It will be fine. What could possibly go wrong?" Beltray said.

Fifteen minutes later, we arrived back at the apartment where we had left Ray Claimed and his two guardians. I tried the door. It was locked. I knocked on the door. There was no answer. We tried to look through the windows but the curtains were closed.

Suddenly I noticed that I was standing in something sticky. I looked down…the walkway was covered in blood, and bloody footprints led from the porch toward the floatplane dock.

"There's your answer, Beltray. He told us about it so we would come back and he would be able to get to the plane ahead of us. What do you want to bet those two body guards are dead?" At the same moment, we heard the Cessna 185 screaming at us from the water runway as it plowed a trench through the surface of the water on takeoff..

"What will we do now, Pop?"

I reached for my phone. "I'll call Genneta Williams. I'm sure she has another key."

"What if one of the victims is still alive and in need of emergency care?"

"Ralph Parker doesn't leave people alive. Blast it, anyway. I can't believe I was that stupid."

Beltray interjected, "His name is Ray Claimed."

"Don't beat yourself up, Dad," Rusty said, "He even had Beltray fooled. And, don't forget, he did leave one of those girls alive."

I looked at Beltray. He was looking toward the east in the direction his plane had departed.

"What do you think, Beltray? How could he have let that evil back in?"

Beltray continued to stare at the sky. "How do you know he did?"

"What do you mean?"

"I mean, you really don't know who did what. There's some blood on the stoop, and you heard an airplane take off. That's really all you know for sure. You have to accept the possibility that someone else may be responsible for this."

I paused for a moment considering Beltray's feasibility study. "All right then, let's get this door open, now. Rusty, can you get us inside?"

"I can try." Rusty took out his wallet and fished through it for one of those gadgets that private detectives always carry, just in case. As he inserted a piece of metal into the key hole and began twisting, suddenly the door slid open. I instantly drew my weapon as we all took a step back, staring in shock, for standing in the doorway, completely composed, was none other than our new-man Ray Claimed. Or, was it the old-killer of little girls. I was no longer sure.

Rusty had his hands full, and it wasn't his sidearm. As he stepped aside, Beltray raised his hands and began praising the Lord. I moved forward keeping my Glock seventeen trained on the man who was, once again, my primary suspect.

"Keep your hands where I can see them, Parker," I said. "Is there anyone else in here with you?"

"Yes, sir. But I think they're both dead."

"Okay then, I need you to turn around and put your hands behind your back."

Parker offered no resistance and a moment later he was in handcuffs. I moved him to the side and told him to remain by the door. Looking around I immediately realized where the blood on the stoop had come from. In the next room, on the near side of the bed lay the two mercenaries, Scarf and Tripod. Both men had their throats cut. I turned to Parker, "Did you do this?"

He stared back at me as if he didn't comprehend what was happening.

"Do you want me to call Borski?" Rusty asked.

Suddenly I wasn't sure. Suddenly nothing made any sense. Why would Parker still be here if he had committed this crime? Who took off in Beltray's floatplane? Is Parker really as simple as he is making himself out to be?

"Beltray, do you think Parker did this?"

"Why don't you ask him? And, as I said before, his name is Ray Claimed."

"What do you think he's going to say, *yes*?"

"Ask him and see," Betray repeated.

"Parker, did you do this?" I asked the killer of little girls.

Parker looked at me. Tears began streaming down his face.

"No, sir."

"Then, did you see who did?" His cheeks were trembling.

"Yes, sir. I have seen him. It is the one who...I thought was God's prophet. He promised me that I would be with him in paradise if I helped him do away with the evil people. But he is not God's prophet. He is an imposter." Ray Claimed raised his cuffed hands to the ceiling. "For I have seen the face of Jesus, and he is kind and good and merciful, full of *grace and truth* compassion and forgiveness of sin, showing mercy to all who come unto God, by Him. He is not like the false prophet at all. I know this because he revealed himself to me in the light. Praise him forever, all ye heavenly host. The Lord God, he is good."

I turned to Beltray, "I'll give Mr. Claimed the benefit of the doubt for now, but he stays handcuffed. I'll call Borski and have him get someone over here to clean this mess up. Ray can go with us. We'll use the van and go get the Citation."

I called Borski. He wasn't happy, but what else is new, he never is unless he's fishing. We drove the van to the Sitka airport and boarded the Citation jet. I ignited the turbines and requested a local VFR scenic. I pointed the nose toward Kake. After making a couple of 360s around the compound, I was unable to find the old Dodge pickup truck. Neither in town, or on the hill. However, the car that Rudy had driven, the same car where we found the body of Kerrigan's brother with his throat slashed, was now parked up on the hill, behind the prophet's house. Suddenly it occurred to me.

"Rusty, do you remember when we found Mike's body in that car?"

"Yeah. Why?"

"I'm wondering if the same guy that killed Mike also killed Scarf and Tripod."

"I thought our *new-man* killed the Maverick man."

I knew Rusty was referring to Ray who was sitting in the back next to Beltray.

"Maybe he did, maybe he didn't, " I said.

"Then who do you think that somebody is?" Rusty asked. "Are you thinking the prophet did it? If that's the case, why did he come back here? And why would he kill Scarf and Tripod but not Parker?"

"Parker was his hired killer. He probably figured out that we had him and came here to get him away from us. I'm sure he expected us to be there, and intended to kill us too. Maybe Ray started prophesying and the prophet figured he had lost his biscuit or something. Probably left him alive to take the rap for *him*."

"How would he have known we had Parker in the first place?" Rusty asked.

"Well, I might have said something about it to Kerrigan when we were all having breakfast together."

"You already told me that. Do you think Kerrigan, or someone at that table, told him?"

"I don't know how else he would have known, except…wait a minute! What about Wallace?"

Rusty shook his head. "No way, " he said, "Theodore Wallace? How could he have called anybody? Surely Kerrigan wouldn't have been that sloppy, would he?"

"I don't think so. But there isn't anyone else, eccept…"

"*Eric?* No way, Dad! That's absurd."

"You're right. It has to be the prophet. Think about it. Since we've arrived on this case, the prophet has lost Old Man Perkins, his daughter Karen, Mike, and his body-guard and driver. Then suddenly, Kerrigan kills the old woman that runs the orphanage and shows up here with Theodore Wallace—the one man whose testimony could put the prophet away forever."

"Wait a minute. Did you say Kerrigan killed some old woman?"

"Yeah, didn't I tell you? He said she was the one that run the place. Turns out, Wallace and her were siblings."

"So what are you saying, Dad?"

"Here's my question. Why hasn't the prophet run by now? With all the damage we've already done to his little kingdom, why hasn't he up and fled the country? He certainly has had plenty of opportunity."

Rusty thought for a minute. "Maybe he already has, " he said. "Maybe that was him that stole Beltray's floatplane, and he's long gone. I say we get down there and find out."

"We will, but even if he did run, he won't get far. We have so much on him, we'll find him no matter where he goes. And I believe he's aware of that as well as we are. No, he's heading back to his kingdom, to make a stand."

"You make a strong case, Dad. But that still doesn't explain who tipped him off. Or why Scarf and Tripod let him in the apartment so he could kill them."

Beltray had been listening. "I have a theory. What about the two dead mercenaries?"

"What about them?" Rusty asked.

"They worked for me," I said.

"Maybe they changed sides," Beltray suggested.

"I find that hard to believe." I heard myself say it but at the same time, it seemed like the only logical conclusion left.

"He has a point, Dad. You know as well as I they would work for whoever paid them the most."

I stared in disbelief. "Do you really think they sold us out to the prophet?"

"Dad, it's a whole lot more feasible than Eric."

"You're right, son. What on earth was I thinking? Well, if they did, they sure got what was coming to them. I suppose he killed them so I couldn't buy them back and use them against him in the final showdown."

"I expect that's exactly what happened, Dad."

Moments later we were on final approach to the Kake airstrip. I set the CJ4 on the sod strip and, reversing the thrust, managed to stop before we ran off the end of the runway. Rusty's 206 sat parked next to the trees.

"Looks like Kerrigan is already up there," I said. I slid the Citation up next to the Stationair and we all went in search of the old pickup.

"Well, Dad. I don't see the truck anywhere. Shall we hike up the trail?"

"I guess. It's either that or take the long way up the road."

Rusty led the way and Beltray followed. Mr. Ray Claimed fell in behind Gibbs, and I took up the rear. As we neared the floatplane docks, where the trail head began, I saw Beltray's floatplane tied up in one of the slips.

"Beltray! There's your plane. Hang on, Rusty. I'll be right back." I quickly made my way to the end of the pier, where Beltray's floatplane sat in the water. I tried the door. It was unlocked. Searching through the contents in the back luggage compartment, I found my 10-gauge shotgun that I had left concealed under a stack of blankets. Stuffing my pockets full of extra shells, I returned to the trail-head.

"Where does this trail go to?" Beltray asked.

"It will take us the back way up the hill to the cult compound."

I kept one eye on Ray as we neared the place in the trail where I had found his last victim. He hesitated momentarily, as if he had recognized something.

I wondered if he remembered what had happened here, the place where he had lain in wait for me to rescue the little girl that had miraculously survived his attack, or if he had conveniently forgotten that too. Familiar sensations revived in me as I thought of how close that child had come to ending up in the medical examiner's cooler.

"Ray, " I said. Everyone ahead of me stopped in the trail. "Have you ever been here before?"

"Dad, are you sure you want to do this to him?"

"What is this place?" Beltray asked with obvious concern.

"I'm talking to Ray." I looked into his eyes, but could see no recognition of the place, or any evidence that he knew what I was referring to.

At times I felt like we all might be victims of a ruse. Did Almighty God really cast out the evil demons that were responsible for Parker's atrocious behavior? Was this new man, Ray Claimed, no longer responsible for the heinous crimes he had committed? Suddenly a scripture came to my mind that I had read long ago. "Now if I do that I would not, it is no more I that do it, but sin that dwelleth in me."

"As long as he stays in Christ, I guess he'll be safe to be around," I muttered to myself.

Rusty continued on, leading the way, to where the trail intersected the road. From that point we followed the road straight to the main gate.

Two young men guarded the entrance to the compound. One of them was the man who had by now spent all, or some, of the money I had paid him to allow us unhindered access. An old, rusted 1955 Oldsmobile Super88 sat parked near the gate.

I approached Larry Mauktokta and discreetly slipped him another fifty bucks.

"Who's car is that?" I asked him. He pointed to the man who stood talking to Rusty.

"Is he going to give us any trouble?"

Mauktokta shrugged and replied, "Mauktokta think maybe Maurice call the boss after you leave."

"Will he call on his own phone or do you have a phone in the guard shack?"

"There is phone, but more money make Mauktokta not let Maurice call." I slipped him another twenty. He looked at it with disgust.

"Has anyone else come through the gate this morning?"

"Yes. Boss man drive in only half hour before."

"The prophet? Are you sure?"

"More money, make Mauktokta more sure," he said, still staring at the twenty.

"I've given you enough money for one day. Has anyone else come through?"

"Only four men, fifteen minutes behind, boss."

"Did you or Maurice call the boss to let him know he had company coming?"

Mauktokta nodded toward his partner, "Maurice maybe call boss. Not sure."

I motioned to Rusty, calling him aside.

"I think the prophet might have laid a trap for us. It appears he's drawing us in, like bear bait, for the kill. I think we better cut their phone line, and take that Oldsmobile for a spin."

I retrieved a small jackknife from my pocket and stepping over to the guard shack, cut the phone line.

I said to Rusty, "Check Maurice for a cell phone before you let him go." Rusty retrieved the man's cell phone. Mauktokta was hesitant to surrender his, but relented when I threw in an additional fifty bucks.

"I'll see that you get it back before we leave, Mauktokta. I promise."

"Mauktokta think maybe you won't live that long."

"Is that your car or your buddy's?" I pointed to the Super88.

"Olds, my car."

"We need to borrow it for a while. Do you mind?"

"More money—"

"Yeah, I know. More money make Mauktokta not mind so much, right?" I reached in my wallet and handed him another C-note. "Doesn't this job pay very well?"

"Job not pay Mauktokta so well." "But Mr. Wallace pays Mauktokta pretty good."

"Why would Mr. Wallace pay you?"

"Mr. Wallace pay Mauktokta not to call boss."

"Really? I would think he would pay you to call the boss before he would pay you not to call the boss."

"Mauktokta think maybe Mr. Wallace afraid."

"Afraid? Afraid of what?"

"If boss man know who is coming, boss man shoot mortar. Blow up car."

Rusty looked at me. "Dad, maybe we better walk."

"I have another idea. Let's leave Beltray and Ray here with Mauktokta, while you and I take the car. You drive."

Beltray interjected, "We're going with you."

"We should stay together, Dad."

"Okay then, one other thing. When Rudy and Shirley left here that day they escaped from the prophet, they destroyed that other gate. Mauktokta, do you know if the boss had that other gate fixed on the hill?"

"No one come to fix gate, so far."

"Okay, Rusty. Just get going as fast as you can and maybe we can get to him before he has a chance to launch any bombs at us."

"Okay, Dad."

"Be ready to shoot if we have to ditch the car."

CHAPTER 20

I looked for a seatbelt as I climbed into the old Olds88. Rusty slid in behind the huge steering wheel and started the old girl up.

"She seems to run pretty good." Rusty saw me looking for the seatbelt. "Don't worry about buckling up, Dad. We may need to bail out of this thing in a hurry anyway."

I had to admit, the throaty sound of the twin straight pipes coming directly from the manifold was nostalgic. For a moment they took me back to the time of my youth, in the early sixties, when I owned an old '49Ford V-8 and raced the other high-school kids on the old two-lane straightaways for ten-bucks a quarter-mile.

My driver mashed on the accelerator a couple of times. *Varoom, varoom.* The sound was not just hypnotic, but romantic. Rusty mashed on the accelerator and the tires squealed as we rounded the curve directly below the entry gate to the upper middle class half of the cult compound doing about fifty. I was hanging on for dear life. The 1955 Oldsmobile 88 belched and blew a cloud of blue smoke high enough to see all the way from Sitka, as Rusty floored the old Super 88 324 Rocket V-8.

I tried to recall the aerial photographs I had studied as we flew past the somewhat familiar layout. Beyond the curve, I recognized the large dormitory building and saw nestled into the trees several classroom-type structures that had not shown up in the photos. On the hill straight ahead and to the left of the dormitory loomed the prophet's large home.

"Head for the back of that big house," I said, pointing to the large structure. It was obvious the shocks had never been replaced on the old Olds-probably since it was brand new, and it floated like a fishing boat as we lurched over several speed bumps, one of which might have been someone's wheel barrow.

At the top of the driveway, an ominous twelve-foot-high concrete wall awaited our arrival.

"Rusty, you better slow down or we won't make that turn," Beltray Gibbons hollered from the back seat. I turned around to see Mr. Ray Claimed gazing off into the wild blue yonder, perfectly at peace as my wannabe stock car racer son-in-law yelled something about the gas pedal being stuck and spun the gigantic steering wheel to the right at least fifty times as the old boat started into the steep turn.

About halfway through the corner, the left rear tire blew and the world around us began to spin. I saw the prophet's house pass before my eyes at least three times before the car slammed against the concrete retaining wall. Rusty's head slapped the driver's side window and fell helplessly against his chest as the distorted silhouettes of four men emerged from an opened air garage.

I rubbed my hand across my blurry eyes and tried to focus on the first two men approaching us, armed with automatic weapons. Reaching for my 10-gauge with one hand and the door handle with the other, I pushed against the car door with my right foot. But it was too late. The first weapon was already pressed against my temple.

"Worley. Is that you?" Kerrigan said, stooping down to look into the old car.

"I think so. Are you Lieutenant Kerrigan, or another twin brother he forgot to tell me about?"

"It's the real Lieutenant Kerrigan, Mr. Worley." My eyes were still blurry from going around in circles but I recognized Eric's voice. I blinked a couple of times and slowly the images before me returned to focus.

The first person I saw was Morgue. Reaching up I carefully pushed the barrel of the AR-15 away from my head.

"It's okay, Morgue. It's me. If you don't mind, I would appreciate it if you pointed that thing somewhere else. I can't pay you if I'm dead." Looking back at Kerrigan, I said, "Good to see you too, Lieutenant." Rusty groaned and looked around. He was slowly waking up.

"You should be glad you can see anything after that entry. Where did you guys think you were going in such a hurry?" Kerrigan asked.

"Mr. German said the accelerator stuck to the floor," Beltray said in defense of Rusty.

I said to Kerrigan, "We thought you might need some help so we came to rescue you."

309

"I like the first scenario better."

"What scenario?" I said, still groggy.

"The one about needing help. I think I'd take that one any day, over the one about you rescuing us."

Beltray and Morgue helped Rusty out of the car.

"He should get that fixed," Kerrigan answered.

I turned to face the lieutenant.

"Get what fixed?"

"The accelerator."

"That car isn't worth fixing. Have you arrested the prophet yet?" I said.

"Not yet. We just got here. We didn't have a Super88 like you did."

"You mean you didn't drive that Mercedes?" I pointed to the black car parked in the driveway, which was about the only thing we didn't hit during our arrival.

"No, we walked up the hill. Quite uneventfully too."

"You should have borrowed this Olds 88 from Mauktokta, it's pretty fast."

"I can see that. Goes around in circles really good too," Kerrigan remarked. "I don't know what you guys are planning on doing here, but I have a child molester to catch."

"He's more than just a child molester now. He murdered two of my men this morning and stole Beltray's seaplane," I informed the detective.

Kerrigan's face turned to stone and he checked his weapon.

"How do you know it was the prophet? Maybe it was that killer you've been looking for."

"I doubt that," I said.

"Who's this?" Kerrigan indicated toward the "new-man."

"This is Ray Claimed. He may be able to help us convict the prophet."

"Who is he and how does he fit in to all of this?" the lieutenant asked.

"I'm not sure, but we think he might be able to tie the prophet to the killings. At least we hope he can."

"You didn't answer my question."

"His name is Ray Claimed. He's a witness."

"A witness to what?"

"He says he knew the killer."

"How did he know him?" I didn't answer. Kerrigan looked suspicious and I was relieved when he changed the subject. "Where's your other man, what's his name, Rudy?" Kerrigan asked.

"Dead."

"The guy who fixed us sandwiches is dead?"

"Yes. He's dead?"

"How did that happen?"

"After Rudy and I were forced to land on the water, about three hundred yards off shore from Turnabout Island, we were rafting our way around the west end of the island when the pilot of the green monster shot Rudy in the head with a high-powered rifle."

"What did you do with the body?"

"I stashed him over on the north shore of the island."

"You mean you didn't bury him?"

"Didn't have a shovel. As soon as we're done here, we'll go get the body and take him back home for a proper burial."

"So what happened to the killer?"

"I told you already," I said, hoping this conversation would end soon.

"I remember that. But your story had a few holes in it."

"What holes?"

"You left out the part about trying to find the guy who shot him?"

"I did find him. I ran into him over by his downed plane. When I saw him he still had the rifle with the scope on it. I managed to get off a few rounds as he was running away. One of them hit the rifle and demolished it. I think I may have hit him, but couldn't find a body, so we think he tried to swim over to the mainland. Like I told you already, no one could have survived in that freezing water for very long so I'm sure he's halfway to Japan by now."

Kerrigan seemed somewhat satisfied for the moment. "Well, as soon as we get this prophet locked up, we can go back there and search some more. So, where did you find your witness?"

"We found him while we were searching the area. His name is Ray Claimed, and evidently he was a stowaway on board the killer's aircraft."

"Is that what he told you? How do you know he's not the killer? Are you guys stupid or something?"

"Well, Lieutenant, it's kind of complicated."

"What's complicated about it? He rammed you. He crashes. You find this man on the same uninhabited island, no bigger than your thumb. Sounds like a no-brainer to me."

"Well, you're welcome to question him if you want."

"I will. But right now we need to find this prophet guy before he slips away. And how come this man is not in handcuffs?"

"I already told you. He's not the killer. And as far as the prophet is concerned, I don't think he's going anywhere. I believe he intends to make his last stand, from right here."

"Why do you say that?"

"Because he had plenty of opportunity to slip away this morning after he killed Scarf and Tripod, and then stole Beltray's floatplane. But instead, he came back here. Knowing that we would follow him. No, I'm sure he has a plan, and if we don't figure out what it is, we may walk right into a trap."

Morgue was listening from only a few feet away and looked up.

"Did you say this prophet guy killed Scarf and Tripod?"

"Yes, Morgue. I'm sorry. I know they were friends of yours. None of us would have thought for a moment that they were in any danger."

Morgue didn't show any feelings one way or the other.

"Why do you think he killed your mercenary friends?" Kerrigan asked.

"I guess the prophet offered them more money than I was paying and they decided to go with the highest bidder."

"That wouldn't surprise me, but why would he buy them away from you just to kill them?"

"Because he wanted information about what we were up to. As soon as he got that, he slit their throats."

Kerrigan thought about it for a moment and replied, "Serves them right."

I became concerned that Mr. Morgue might take offense to that comment, but noticed that he had disappeared.

"Where did Morgue go?" I asked.

Kerrigan looked around. "I have no idea. He was here a minute ago. Speaking of going, do you have any ideas about where this prophet is? I really don't think he's in the house."

"Why don't you ask your prisoner?"

"Oh, you mean Wallace? I doubt he'll tell the truth anyway. Didn't you guys have some kind of a plan before you crash landed that old car?"

"Do you have to work at being sarcastic, or does it come natural?"

"Comes natural. But you still haven't answered my question."

"Well, we did. But now I'm not so sure."

"Did what?"

"Had a plan."

"What was the plan?"

"When I realized the prophet had come back here, I figured, if he was going to make a stand, he would likely make it from his house. So we decided to storm the place before he had a chance to lob any mortars our way while we were coming up the driveway. But evidently that's not what he had planned."

Rusty interjected, "Hey, Dad, have you noticed that there aren't any people around here? Where's everybody at?"

I paused to look around. Suddenly I realized it too. "You're right, Rusty. The place looks like a ghost town."

"I don't care where anybody is, except that prophet guy. All I care about is finding him," Kerrigan said.

"Well, if we find the people we'll probably find him, but we can't find anyone while we're standing here," I said as I headed for the opened garage.

The large four-car garage was empty with the exception of the Mercedes parked outside. On the back wall of the garage was a set of steel elevator doors. I stepped over to them and pressed the up button. Nothing happened. I looked around and in the far corner I saw a metal box mounted on the wall similar to the type of code boxes used in home security alarm systems. I took a closer look and realized it was the code box for the elevator.

"Lieutenant Kerrigan. Would you bring your prisoner over here?"

Kerrigan took hold of Wallace coat sleeve and pulled him toward the corner of the garage.

"Mr. Wallace. Do you happen to know what the code is for this elevator?" Wallace looked at me as if he were trying to see how he could use that piece of information to his advantage. I decided to help him with that.

"I can read you like a book, Theodore. I know that you know the code. Here's what's in it for you. Punch in the code, and I won't punch you in the belly with the barrel of this 10-gauge shotgun, which could go off in the process."

Wallace stepped over to the box and moments later the elevator doors opened.

I turned to the men that were with me. "Going up?" I asked. Myself, Rusty, Beltray, Ray, Eric, Theodore Wallace, and Lieutenant Kerrigan all squeezed into the small elevator. On the control panel there were three buttons: B for basement, level 1, and level 2. I pressed the button for level 1 and the doors moved closed.

We were smashed together like sardines in a walnut shell. Directly in front of me stood Ray Claimed. So close I could still smell the residual odor of chewing tobacco left over from his malodorous habit. For the first time I realized that he had, among other things, miraculously quit *that* revolting addiction. I considered for a moment. Maybe, this miracle is real after all.

Seconds later the doors of the elevator slid opened and we were staring at the living quarters of the prophet Joseph Morning.

"Wow! Pretty upscale for a poor preacher," Kerrigan remarked.

"Prophets obviously make more money than preachers," Rusty said.

"Don't you mean *steal* more money?" I added.

"That is a far more likley scenario," Beltray suggested.

The room was at least forty by eighty feet in size. Well over three-thousand feet of floor space. Fine, knotty-pine, log furniture: plush couches, recliners, stools, tables, and love seats lined all the walls but one. At the far north end of the room, a twenty-foot long, oval-shaped table with twelve chairs on each side sat neatly displayed with silver cups, bowls, and candle-sticks. Positioned in the center of the table was a Jewish Menorah, a lamp stand of seven candlesticks. Six golden branches, each an individual lamp stand, sprouted from the center lamp stand made of pure gold. Apart from that, only one piece of furniture occupied the center of the room: a large bed with four corner posts made of knotty pine. Constructed above the bed was a metal frame that supported a cast of cables, pulleys, and padded clamps.

"Hey, Theodore, did you make this for the prophet?" Kerrigan asked.

"Why do you think he made it?" I said.

"Because he has a whole basement full of contraptions just like this."

"What are they for?" Eric asked.

Kerrigan began laughing. Theodore looked embarrassed. I changed the subject.

"I wonder where everybody is?" I said as I walked toward a glass sliding door concealed behind a set of curtains at the far end of the great room. I pulled on the draw string and the curtains opened. On the far side of the glass was a large cedar deck approximately thirty-feet by thirty-feet. Four-foot by six-foot obscure shower glass panels framed into six-foot-high exterior walls lined the perimeters of the open air deck. In the center, a cloud of steam arose from a fourteen-foot by fourteen-foot hot tub, bubbling with hot water.

"I wonder if this is Hef's Alaska vacation home?" Kerrigan said.

"Who is Hef?" I asked, naively.

"Don't ask, Dad." Rusty nudged me and whispered an explanation in my ear.

"Ohhh!" I said. "What would he want with a Menorah? No. It's not Hef. But I'm sure I know who it is, and I'm sure I know exactly what goes on around here, and believe me, it all stops today. "Mr. Wallace, have you ever sat in on one of these parties?" Theodore was looking even more embarrassed. I poked him in the stomach with the barrel of my shotgun. "I'm talking to you, Theodore. I asked you a question." I poked him again, this time harder. Theodore began backing toward the hot tub. "Is this the place where you guys bring the kids to—"

"Mr. Wallace has never been to one of the services." I stopped dead in my tracks and turned to face Ray Claimed. Or was it Ralph Parker?"

"What did you say?"

Ray repeated, "Mr. Wallace had—"

"I heard that part. What did you call it, a service?"

"Yes, sir. The services take place once a month. Here in this room." Mr. Claimed indicated toward the great room.

"What goes on in a service, Ray?"

Kerrigan interrupted, "I thought you said this guy didn't have anything to do with this."

"I didn't say that. I said he's not the killer."

"Then what is he?"

Ray turned to face the lieutenant, "I am he that was dead, but is alive," he said.

"What? Who does this guy think he is, Jesus Christ? Worley, you got some explaining to do and I suggest you get started."

"Mr. Claimed is a new-creation in Christ, Lieutenant." Beltray interjected.

"What does that mean?"

"It means he is no longer the old man that was a slave to sin and evil, but by the grace of God, through his Son, Jesus Christ, has been made a new-creature, wholly acceptable to God. It means that his sins have all been laid upon the Lamb of God who was nailed to the cross of Calvary, who bore the sins of the whole world that all men who believe in him might have eternal life."

"So, in other words, this guy is the killer we've been looking for and you guys are covering for him because he had a *Jesus* moment. Is that right?"

Beltray reiterated, "It is *Jesus* who has covered him, with his—"

"That's right, " I interrupted, "It is him. So what. He's obviously not the same man he was. I told you, you can question him for yourself. Just look at him, why, he wouldn't hurt a fly now. Why punish him for deeds he committed while he was controlled by an evil spirit, a spirit that has been cast out of him? In fact, I saw it with my own eyes. We all did." I gestured toward Rusty and Beltray. "It was the most extraordinary thing I've ever seen, and as soon as the evil was cast out of him, it gathered up the winds and mustered a storm like you can't even imagine. Huge trees ripped out of the ground by their roots, waves as tall as the Empire State Building, while we sat next to the floatplane in a perfectly calm bubble, completely protected from the entire thing. I tell you, it was enough to scare the daylights out of you if you didn't understand what was going on."

Kerrigan starred in amazement.

"Are you sure you guys weren't over there sucking on a water pipe?"

"I'm sure. I'll tell you what else I'm sure of. The real killer is not Ray Claimed. The real killer is the guy who created this outrageous house of villainy." I gestured toward the great room and hot-tub.

"We need to stop *this*!" I pointed to the hot-tub. "Not *him*! Mr. Ray Claimed is not the threat." I pointed at Ray. "The man who contrived this outrageous barbarity is the source of the evil I'm looking for, the very Devil-incarnate." I stepped over to Mr. Wallace and grabbed him by the throat, "And you sir, are going to tell me where I can find him, or I'm going to toss you in that hot-tub and blow your head off, because without that information, we don't have any use for you. Do you understand me?"

I gripped Theodore by the throat, stuck the barrel of the 10-gauge against his belly, and began pushing him backward toward the tub of steaming water.

"He might be in the dormitory," Theodore blurted out. "There's a meeting room there that is large enough to accommodate the entire congregation."

"Which building is that?" I demanded. Theodore pointed to the long building next door, across from the prophet's home, perpendicular to the driveway.

"If it's locked, how do we get in?" Rusty asked. Wallace hesitated. This time I placed the barrel of the 10-gauge under his chin and shoved him back, only inches from the bubbling water.

"The basement. You can get in through the basement."

"What's he doing over there? Is he expecting us?"

"Yes, he's expecting you, and if you don't see anyone around, they're probably all in the assembly hall. It's…it's-possible he might be planning a mass suicide."

"A mass suicide? You mean like what Jim Jones did down in Guyana?" I shouted.

"Yes. He's been planning it for about a year," Wallace admitted.

"How's he planning on killing everyone? Are they all going to drink poisoned Kool-Aid, like the people at Jonestown?"

"No, he has installed a delivery system to gas them through the ventilation works, and anyone else that is anywhere near the building will get it at the same time."

Lieutenant Kerrigan stepped next to me. "Worley, I'll bet you that's what he's waiting for. He figures we'll come over there to investigate him and when he flips the switch he'll take us with him."

"Then we have to find the switch. " I said as I looked back at Wallace. "Where's the switch, Theodore?"

"I don't know. Honest, I have no idea."

I whispered into his ear, "Then you're going to go with us and help us find it." I looked at the people standing behind me.

"I want everyone eccept Rusty and Beltray to stay here." Kerrigan objected like he does about everything, but his objections were much less convincing than normal. I figured he was having second thoughts about arresting the prophet today, so I ignored him.

I held onto Theodore Wallace by the back of his coat collar and with the 10-gauge pressed against the back of his neck followed him down the stairs from the hot-tub deck to a walkway that led down the gravel path to the lower level of the dormitory, a hundred yards away. Rusty followed with Beltray close behind. Suddenly, I realized that Ray Claimed had joined our band of volunteers, and behind him, running to catch up, was Kerrigan and Eric.

Theodore left the main walkway and led us around to the back of the building, then down a set of concrete steps leading to a basement door. Although it was shut, it was not locked, and it appeared the lock had been recently torn off. *You're walking into a death trap, Worley.* The thought made me shiver. But I had shivered before, in Vietnam, plenty of times. There are times when you have to make certain decisions, regardless of the risk, even if you know you may die in the process, because if you don't, you wouldn't be able to live with yourself anyway.

I breathed a silent prayer to God, in the name of his Son Jesus Christ.

"Where does this go?" I whispered to Theodore.

"It goes to a heating and air conditioning room. The next room after that is where the electrical boxes are mounted. If he's going to deliver the gas through the ventilation system, it will have to be wired through there."

Suddenly I heard someone talking. The muffled voice sounded like it was coming from the floor above us. "Is that the prophet?" I asked Theodore.

He nodded his head. I turned to the men behind me and whispered to them.

"You guys take Theodore and keep looking for anything that looks like a switch. I'm going to take Beltray and crash that party upstairs."

Kerrigan objected again. "While we're looking for a switch, he probably has an electronic device of some sort, maybe a cell phone or computer. If you alert him he might panic and decide to activate the delivery system from his device before we have a chance to find it?"

"Good point. Okay, I'll give you fifteen minutes," I said. "If we wait much longer he might get impatient and activate it anyway, and I want to give Beltray a chance to talk him out of it. After what I witnessed over on Turnagain Island, I'm convinced, if anyone can do it, Beltray can."

I heard a quiet voice behind me. "I'm going with you, Mr. Worley," Ray Claimed volunteered. The big man stepped forward and added, "I want the man who calls himself a prophet to see what the grace of God has done in me. Maybe he too, deep down inside, hates his sin as I did mine, and maybe the Lord Jesus Christ will deliver him as he has delivered me."

"Fair enough," I said. "Did you hear that, Kerrigan? He wants to give his testimony to the prophet, declaring the grace of God that has restored him, transforming him into a 'new-man in Christ Jesus.' If he was still a killer, why would he do that?"

"Yeah, I heard. Personally, I'd rather hear him tell his story from prison."

"He isn't going to prison, but if you come with us, you can hear it now," I said.

"Then who will look for the switch?" Kerrigan responded.

"I already found it." I recognized Morgue's voice, but it startled me anyway. I squinted through the darkness to see Morgue coming toward us from the far end of the dark basement.

"Where have you been?" I exclaimed.

"I've been doing some investigating and it looks like your prophet is planning a mass suicide."

"We've already come to that conclusion," Kerrigan expounded. "What else you got?"

"He has this place rigged to deliver GB through an electronically activated air-compressor into the heat exchange system."

"Wait a minute. What the hell is GB?" Kerrigan asked.

"Serin gas. It's a nerve agent invented by a group of Germen scientists back in 1938, the stuff is about five-hundred times more deadly than cyanide."

I gasped. "Where's the heat pump?"

"Right over here," Morgue said and turned to walk away. We all followed.

Morgue stopped at the far back end of the basement and pointed to a large air-duct in the ceiling, "The heat pump is installed outside, but the heating and air-conditioning duct work fans out from this main duct coming from the outside pump. Now look at this." Morgue shined a flashlight on a large cabinet fastened against the concrete basement wall. "This cabinet door was locked but I managed to pick it opened with a crowbar." Morgue carefully opened the cabinet door. A cylinder the size of an acetylene tank stood upright in the cabinet. A copper tube emerged from the side of the tank, through the side of the cabinet and directly to the main duct that delivered heat to the building above.

"So, is that valve opened or closed?" I said, pointing to the valve at the top of the cylinder.

"It's opened." Morgue said.

"Can't we just shut it off, right here?"

"No. The valve has been welded open. Whoever wired this deal wired it to be activated by an electronic signal, probably from a cell phone. It has also been designed with a series of sensor's that run along the copper tubing and duct work which can detect any change in the design. In other words, if you even touch it, it may activate the flow of Serin gas."

"Why didn't it activate when you picked the lock?"

"There are no sensors on the cabinet itself. If there were, it would have activated the last time they shut the door and locked it."

"What about shutting down the heat pump from the outside?"

"There are sensors all along the entire system that would set it off immediately."

"So, what do we do?" I asked. "How do we de-activate the system?"

"We can't. Not as long as those sensors have an electrical source, probably-battery power."

"So, where's the power source for the sensors?" Rusty asked.

Morgue looked around at the dark basement. "I haven't found it yet."

"So what are we looking for?" I asked.

"Well, this whole thing looks like it was designed by someone with a military background, maybe even military training in weapons of mass destruction. So, we may be looking for something military, like an ammunition box or something that might possibly have a battery concealed in it.

"If you guys are planning on talking this guy out of his intentions, you might want to get started. I'll keep looking around down here. The longer you can stall him the more time it will give me to find the power source."

Beltray asked, "Why wouldn't he just tap into the main power supply for the building?"

Morgue replied, "Because he would be expecting you to shut the power off as a first response. I believe whoever installed this system may be Albanian, maybe Kosovo, or Serbian. Probably fought in the 1998-99 war. A lot of this kind of warfare went on at that time, and this guy obviously knows all the tricks."

"I'll bet that guy Rudy shot in the car was the same guy that rigged this contraption. All right then, I'll take Beltray and Ray with me. Rusty, will you take Eric and Theodore with you? You guys help Morgue find that power source. If we don't shut this thing down a lot of innocent people are going to die here today."

"We'll find it, Dad. You and Beltray go ahead."

I turned to Ray. "Mr. Claimed. Can you show us the way upstairs to the assembly room?"

"Yes, sir." Ray wasn't much for words. Without hesitation he led us back out of the basement and around to the west side of the building, to the original walkway we had been on before we diverted to the basement.

At the far south end of the building Ray paused. "Mr. Worley, the prophet is not aware that I am no longer under his power. It may be to our advantage that you and Pastor Gibbons go in as my prisoners. Although he might be suspicious, he would be more inclined to let us get closer to him if you did not represent a threat." I looked into Ray's eyes. His plan certainly made sense, but was also a scary proposition. What if Ray Claimed was really…still Ralph Parker? Our goose would be cooked for sure. I breathed another prayer, that Ray was really Ray, and Parker was really--*dead.*

"If you think I'm going to let you handcuff me, that's not going to happen."

"Then just walk in front of me and put your hands in the air. I will pretend to have a gun pointed at your back."

"That should work. " I reached down and pulled up my pant leg. Retrieving a .380 Colt Mustang from an ankle holster, I unloaded it and handed it to Ray. Or was it Ralph?

"Here, use this." Ray looked quizzically at the small weapon as he turned it in his hands. It was apparent that his oversized finger would not even fit into the trigger guard.

"Don't worry, your prophet will believe it's a real gun."

Ray looked at me with a serious look of defiance. "He is not my prophet. The Lord is my God, and there is none like him."

Somehow, I knew those words of scripture would have never come from a man who was acting. I put my hand on his massive shoulder.

"I know, Ray. I know that. I apologize." At that moment I was finally convinced that Ray Claimed had indeed been re-claimed.

We stepped around the corner and came face to face with two armed guards who seemed to recognize Ray. I even got the sense that they feared him, as they quickly stepped aside to allow us entry. I also got the sense that they might have been expecting us.

Beltray walked in front of me and Ray held the Colt .380 Mustang pressed against my back as we passed through a large set of well-built, wooden barn doors.

The assembly room was huge, and filled to capacity with at least five-hundred people. I was sure that every man, woman, and child in the camp was there, and I would have wagered not all by their own choice.

Guards with automatic weapons had been posted at all four corners of the large room, and every one-hundred feet along each wall. At the far end, a tall, slim, elderly man with graying hair and mosaic features stood at a pulpit. He had been pontificating to the assembly of people, but stopped as we came through the doors.

Leaning forward, he spoke into a microphone.

"Welcome, my friends. We have been expecting you." Suddenly I heard a thud and realized that a beam had been dropped in place from the outside to secure the two barn doors. I leaned forward and whispered to Beltray,

"We're toast now. Did you hear that thud? They just locked every one of us in here. You better do some fast talking, and make it good."

The prophet towered above us as we approached the podium. He was an imposing figure and from his Scandinavian accent I concluded he might be a Nordic immigrant.

"Mr. Parker!" The prophet exclaimed. "I have been expecting you too. Are these men your prisoners?"

Ray paused a moment. I turned to look into his eyes and witnessed a change coming over him that I didn't like.

"Yeah, boss. Whatdaya wont I shud duwithum."

"Thank-you, Mr. Parker. You can leave them where they are and take a seat. I think the church would like to judge these enemies of the saints according to the laws of God."

"So, is this a trial?" Beltray blurted out. The prophet was taken back by Beltray's boldness.

"What is your name, sir?"

"My name is Beltray Gibbons. Who are you?"

"I am Joseph Morning. The prophet that God has raised to deliver his people in these last days. For He has prophesied: 'The Lord thy God will raise up unto thee a Prophet from the midst of thee, of thy brethren like unto me; unto him ye shall hearken.'"

"What does that prophecie have to do with you?"

"I am he that is sent to deliver my people."

"So you believe that the prophecies of scripture concerning the first advent of our Lord and Savior Jesus Christ are actually prophesies of you?"

"I did not have you brought here to answer your questions, Mr. Gibbons. You are here to answer for your own crimes."

"You appear to be of Scandinavian descent, is that correct?" Betray continued.

The prophet stared daggers through Pastor Gibbons. "I am an American citizen, born in California, chosen of the Lord for this great cause."

"But you speak with a Scandinavian accent. Which tells me that Joseph Morning might not be your given name. What is your given name, Mr. Prophet?"

"The father has given me a new name that I may shepherd these people to their paradise." Joseph Morning swept his hand toward the mass of people witnessing the conversation.

"Then you won't mind telling me your given name."

"The Lord brought me into this world as Anker Bielke, to reside in this temple of flesh until the appointed day that I would accomplish the Lord's mission."

Beltray turned to the mass of people. "Brothers and sisters, this man is an imposter. He is not a prophet of God, and certainly not sent by God to deliver you. You must understand that the prophecies he claims as his authority are prophecies that refer only to the Lord Jesus Christ who has already come two-thousand years ago as a substitute for you and I.

"This man wants to place you back in bondage to the mosaic law that the Lord Jesus Christ already satisfied by his perfect conformity to the law in behalf of all man-kind. None of us will ever be able to satisfy a law that is divine. Only the Divine Christ himself has ever truly satisfied the demands of the law of God, and he sits this very moment at the right hand of the Father, in intercession for you and I, pleading his perfect life, blood, and sacrifice in substitution for our fallen sinful deficiency. By following men, such as this imposter, Joseph Morning, you stand in defiance and rejection of all that the cross of Christ represents in regard to salvation. Furthermore, the deliverance this mortal man is offering is nothing more than a mass suicide attempt."

"Mr. Gibbons," the prophet said. "You are wasting your breath. These people are the elect ones. They have chosen their eternal destiny, and have already consented to their departure from this earth."

Beltray turned back to speak one more time to the evil that had inhabited the body of Anker Bielke. Raising his hand above his head, Pastor Gibbons lifted his face to the heavens. A bright light descended, and rested upon his countenance.

"Father God, in the name of your only son, Jesus Christ, I rebuke the devil." Looking directly at the false prophet he pointed at him, "In the name of Jesus Christ, leave him."

The false prophet's face took on a contorted, satanic appearance. From the depths of his throat the most horrible, guttural screams I had ever heard emerged. The face of the false prophet contorted into the most satanic expressions imaginable. With superhuman strength he tore the lectern from the podium and smashed it to the floor.

Beltray stepped up onto the podium and as he did the evil-being lashed out at him, but was unable to hurt him. The false prophet retreated as Beltray moved toward him. Finally, the evil spirit cast the body of Anker Bielke, alias Joseph Morning, to the ground, momentarily discarding it.

Beltray Gibbons bent over the unconscious man to search through his pockets. Suddenly, Bielke's hand reached up and grasped Beltray's wrist. The pastor looked into his face. A satanic grin smeared across Bielke's face as the evil presence re-entered his body. Lifting his head, he look at Beltray.

"Are you looking for this?" he said. In his other hand the false prophet held a cell phone. As Beltray grabbed for it, Bielke cackled in a most satanic laughter and pressed the call button. Beltray froze, stunned as he watched Bielke toss the cell phone across the podium.

Pastor Beltray Gibbons stood and rushed across the deck to retrieve the phone, but it was too late. As he picked up the phone he heard the last ring and then a click. Moments later the soft hum of the heating system could be heard, turning on. Immediately Beltray turned to the people. Lifting his hands to the heavens he began to pray, "Almighty God our Father, and Father of our Lord Jesus Christ whom thou hast sent. By thy grace poured out upon the Body of believers, I interceded on behalf of these, poor bewildered and deceived people; the promise of your favor on the ground of redemption, and by the blood of the Lamb of God. I claim the divine promises in Psalms 91, that no weapon formed against thee, shall prosper. 'Surely he shall deliver thee from the snare of the fowler, and from the noisome pestilence…A thousand shall fall at thy side, and ten-thousand at thy right hand; but it shall not come nigh thee. Only with thine eyes shall thou behold and see the reward of the wicked…For he shall give his angels—"

"Pastor Gibbons! Pastor Gibbons!"

Beltray stopped and opened his eyes. There before him stood Morgue and Rusty. Rusty was holding something in his hands.

"Gibbs! It's over." Beltray wasn't sure he understood.

"What is over?"

"We found the battery. It's all over."

Captain Daily was both sad and glad. Glad because we had completed the investigation and apprehension of all responsible for not only the murders, but the crimes that had been committed against the victims before they were killed. Sad, because the case did not disappear like he had hoped. It's pretty hard to keep five-hundred people quiet once they have been set free from bondage. The sun had not even set before the news media was all over the hill where Joseph Morning slash Anker Bielke had ruled over his flock for nearly a decade.

Beltray Gibbons flew Lieutenant Kerrigan and Morgue back to the learning center FBO. Rusty followed in his Cessna-206. Eric flew the Citation while I sat in the back with Mr. Ray Claimed.

Eric parked near the FBO as we waited for the others to arrive.

On our way to the cafeteria, Beltray asked, "Mr. Worley what will become of Ray now?"

I turned to Mr. Claimed and asked him, "Ray, what do you want to do, now that you are a free man and in your right mind?"

Ray thought for a minute before he spoke. "I don't know what to do."

I looked at Beltray. "Do you have anything he could do at your church?"

"We could make him a custodian. Ray, would you like a job as custodian at our church? We'll pay a wage that you could live on and you can work there as long as you like."

"Can I live free from condemnation every day in the Lord Jesus?" Ray asked.

"You certainly can. You can talk to him all you want and testify for him every day."

"Okay, then. I'll do that."

"Can you still fly an airplane?" I asked.

"Yes, sir, Mr. Worley. I can fly anything."

"There you go, Beltray. It looks like you have yourself a pilot, too."

"Alright, it's settled then. Ray will work for the church."

"What about Shirley?" I asked. "Do you want to tell her what happened to Rudy, or shall I?"

"I'll tell her. And, Mr. Worley, if you will show me where the body is…"

"I will show you, Beltray. We'll go get him together. Would you be willing to give him a funeral?"

"Yes, sir. I'll be glad to. And, Mr. Worley, don't worry, I'll take good care of Shirley, and if she'll have me, I'll make her my wife."

"Beltray, I have no doubt the two of you will be perfect for each other."

Kerrigan approached me. "Worley, did I hear you say that you have a lodge somewhere?"

"I sure do. As a matter of fact, we're getting together with some family and friends next week for an Independence Day party. Would you like to come?"

"Can I bring my family too?"

"Of course! But you'll have to leave your ego at home. We don't allow ego's, and yours would be too big to fit into the lodge anyway."

"You're a barrel of laughs, Worley. Do you know that? Which reminds me, did I ever tell you the one about the gas station attendant that married a movie star…?"

Two years later, with a little financial and architectural help from the Shearer Worley Foundation, Elizabeth, Leroy, and his brother Larry Mauktokta opened the doors to the brand new Kake City Home for Adolescents.

The Cult on the Hill was gone, and the true Church that took its place became a beacon of light on a mountain overlooking the sleepy little town of Kake, Alaska, where nothing ever happens.

CPSIA information can be obtained
at www.ICGtesting.com
Printed in the USA
BVHW041152020323
659554BV00001B/83